THESE TWISTED BONDS

THESE TWISTED BONDS

BY LEXI RYAN

CLARION BOOKS
AN IMPRINT OF HARPERCOLLINS*PUBLISHERS*

Clarion Books is an imprint of HarperCollins Publishers.

These Twisted Bonds

 For information address HarperCollins Children's Books, a division of HarperCollins Publishers, 195 Broadway, New York, NY 10007.
www.epicreads.com

ISBN 978-0-35-838658-2

The text was set in Warnock Pro.
Typography by Andrea Miller
22 23 24 25 26 LBC 6 5 4 3

First Edition

FOR AARON —
WHO DREW THE MAP AND
UNLOCKED THE SEQUEL

WILD FAE LANDS
GOLDEN PALACE
CEMETERY
SEELIE COURT
SERENITY PALACE

UNSEELIE
COURT
UNSEELIE
PALACE
FUGEE
AMPS

THESE TWISTED BONDS

CHAPTER ONE

BEYOND THE CASTLE GATES, THE sun rises and the birds sing, but the Golden Palace is draped in a veil of night. *My night. My darkness. My power.*

I throw out magic with abandon, trapping those who dare to chase me. Darkness trails behind me like the train on an elaborate wedding gown. But I'm not anyone's bride.

I won't let them fool me with their pretty lies and manipulations. Sebastian betrayed me. They *all* betrayed me, but his duplicity cuts the deepest. The male who was supposed to love me, supposed to protect me, used me to steal the Unseelie crown.

Rage floods my veins and feeds my power.

I run, even when the path beneath my bare feet turns rocky and sharp. I focus on the pain, welcome the sting of the gravel cutting into my soles. It's the only thing that blocks out this other feeling—this anguish and frustration that belongs to the one I love. The male I'm bonded to forever. The one who lied to me, who betrayed me.

I don't want to feel him. I don't want to know that my departure is like a fracture down the center of his heart or that losing me has brought him to his knees. I don't want to understand that he's been trapped by his own duty or to comprehend the depths of his regrets. But I do. Through this bond between our souls, I do.

Sebastian betrayed me for the crown, and now he has what he wanted, while I have become that which I despised for so long. *A faerie. An immortal.*

Reason claws at me as I run.

I'm barefoot. In a sleeping gown. I won't make it far like this, but I refuse to let them catch me.

I double back to the paddock, and when I push inside, the stable boy's eyes go wide, his gaze fixed on the cresting wave of darkness looming behind me, ready to strike.

He's young, with sandy blond hair, bright blue eyes, and pointed elven ears. I've seen him before, when getting a horse to ride around the palace grounds. Back when I thought I was safe here, when I believed Sebastian's love was pure.

"Give me your boots," I say, lifting my chin.

"My . . . my . . ." he stammers, his eyes darting toward the palace and the dark destruction I left in my path.

"Your boots! Now!"

He keeps his wide, worried eyes on me as he unlaces them and tosses them at my feet.

"Now a horse," I command, stepping into the boy's shoes. They're a little too big, but they'll do. I tighten the laces and secure them around my ankles.

His gaze darts back toward the palace again, and I throw out another burst of power, making the night beyond pulse with malice. His hands shake as he guides a white mare from her stable. "Wh-what's happening, m-m-milady?"

I ignore the question and nod to the dark belt of knives buckled at his waist. "Your baldrick too."

He unlatches it, letting it drop to the stable floor. Moving quickly, I snatch it by the buckle and wrap it around my waist, tightening the clasp before swinging up onto the horse.

"Thank you," I say, but the boy is cowering, as if he expects me to end him with his own knives. His fear leaves a sour taste in my mouth. Is this who I've become?

This is who Sebastian made me.

I can't think about it as I nudge my horse out of the stables, righting myself on the saddle before I feel a tug at the center of my chest. A sweet ache that begs me to turn back to the palace. *Back to Sebastian.*

Shouts carry across the lawn. With my new fae ears, I can make out the sounds of the chaos in the castle—the scrambling, the shouting, the pounding of feet running my way.

The shouts grow closer. My magic has slipped; my darkness has loosened its grip.

I drive my heels into the sides of the horse. She takes off, galloping at full speed while I hold on as tightly as I can.

Come back. I don't hear the words so much as feel them, feel the ache that burns my chest and settles into my bones. *I need you. Come back to me.*

The reminder of my connection with Sebastian makes me

ride harder. I don't know if I can escape it, if I can mute his misery and heartache with distance alone, but I plan to try.

"I need a room for the night," I tell the barmaid behind the counter at a run-down inn. My voice sounds like crushed glass, and every muscle in my body screams with exhaustion.

I don't know where I am or how far I've ridden. All I know is that I raced away from the palace as fast as I could. I rode hard, passing through villages and farmlands until I couldn't keep myself in the saddle any longer.

I haven't ridden much since I was a child, and I've never ridden for so many hours at once or through such mountainous terrain as I've encountered in the last few hours. By the time I handed my reins over to the inn's stable hand, my legs were screaming in protest.

The female behind the bar has sharply pointed ears and pursed lips. Her cool blue eyes glitter with the kind of iciness people get from living a hard life. She looks me up and down, and I can imagine the mess she sees. My white sleeping gown is now the color of a dusty dirt road, and I'm sure my face doesn't look much better. My jaw-length red hair is a dirty, tangled mess, and my lips are parched from thirst. "I don't do charity," she mutters, already turning away to serve a more promising customer.

I plop a bag of coins onto the counter. My old thieving ways are serving me well. This fae gold is courtesy of a drunken orc at a tavern an hour west from here, where I'd originally planned to stay for the night. The orc had spotted me heading to use the facilities and thought he'd catch me in there and put his hands on me. I may have been exhausted, but I wasn't too tired to wrap him in darkness so deep he'd cried like a baby while he begged me to release him.

The barmaid opens the bag and peers inside, and her jaded eyes light up for a beat. Her lips curve in triumph before she schools her expression. "That'll do," she says, sliding a key across the counter. "Second floor, last door on the left. I'll have the maid take up some wash water for you."

I know nothing about faerie money—what it's worth, what I can expect from one of their shining gold coins—but I've clearly handed over a significant amount, and she's trying to play me for a fool. I arch a brow. "I'll need dinner too."

She nods quickly. "Of course."

Too easy. "And some clothes. Pants and a shirt. No dresses."

Those wrinkled lips twist in consideration. "I'm not in the business of selling clothes, and the tailor's shop is closed for the night." At my hard look, she sighs. "But . . ." She looks me over. "You could likely fit into something of mine. I'll make it work."

I nod my thanks and slide onto a stool, unsure whether my shaking legs can take another moment. "I'll take my meal here."

She tucks the bag away, then barks at a small child to get my dinner. He scampers off, his head down. When she turns her cold eyes back to me, they grow calculating. "Where are you from?" she asks.

I laugh, but I'm so tired it sounds more like a grunt. "You wouldn't know the place."

She arches a brow. "I know most places. Even spent some time in the shadow court during the war."

I just shrug, figuring she wants those coins too much to insist on an answer. "Nowhere special."

She sniffs, and I wonder what she smells. Do I still smell like a human despite being turned fae? Can she smell the palace on me? Faeries have impeccable senses, but in my short hours in this transformed body, I've only found the heightened awareness of every sound, sight, and smell distracting. It's too overwhelming to do any good.

The child returns, noiselessly. The barmaid takes a bowl of stew and a plate of bread from him and slides it in front of me. "As long as you don't bring trouble to my door, I don't need to know nothing. Sometimes it's better that way." She ducks her head to catch my eyes. "You understand?"

I pause, the first spoonful of stew halfway to my lips. What does she think she knows about me? "Sure."

She gives a sharp nod, then moves down the bar to help another customer.

I can hardly hold myself on the stool as I shovel the stew into my mouth. I shouldn't be this tired, even considering the long day on horseback, but my body's wrecked. As tempting as it is to ignore my stomach and go to my room, to climb into bed and surrender to sleep, I know I need to fuel myself for whatever's next.

And what exactly is next?

I push away the question. I don't know where I'm going or what I'm going to do. I need to be away from the palace — away from Sebastian. I can't think about the rest right now. Not about how unprepared I am to be alone in this strange land, and definitely not about how these pointed ears and this newly granted immortality mean I can never go home.

Never return to Elora.

Never visit my sister.

A heavy orc saunters up to the bar, takes the spot next to me. He's over six feet tall with a flat nose, beady black eyes, and two big bottom teeth that curl onto each side of his upper lip. He's massive, and solid muscle, as all orcs are, and his mere proximity makes me feel small and fragile. I bow my head, hoping not to catch his notice. After my encounter with one of his kind an hour ago, I'm not interested in getting this one's attention.

"Ale?" the barmaid asks him, those pursed lips treating him to a smile.

"Aye. And a meal. Hell of a day."

She pulls a tap handle and pours his drink. "Yeah?"

"The unclean ones have their powers back."

Unclean ones?

The barmaid laughs. "Sure they do."

"Nah." He shakes his head. "It's true."

She shrugs. "If this means you can hurt them again, I'd think you'd be happy." Her tone implies that she thinks he's full of it.

"I'm not lyin'. Happened overnight at the children's camp. Little fuckers killed ten of my men before we knew what was going on. The last eighteen hours have been complete chaos while we waited for the injections to arrive."

The barmaid shudders. "I don't know how you pump that poison into anyone."

"Easy." He mimes pushing the plunger on a syringe.

She shakes her head. "Got some stuck in me back during the war. Feels like death itself."

When Jalek was prisoner in the golden palace, he was given injections that blocked his magic. Is that what they're talking about? Are they injecting the children with the same thing?

When the barmaid turns to me and arches a brow, I realize I'm staring. I bow my head again.

"Rather kill 'em," the orc says, "but we have our orders. She wants the little bastards alive."

Children. He's talking about the Unseelie children in her camps.

Rage simmers in my blood. I hate all of them. The fae are liars and manipulators. If it weren't for their cruelty and political scheming, I could be home with Jas right now instead of here. Alone and aimless. Broken and stuck in this new, immortal body I never asked for.

But the children? They may be fae, but they're innocent in all of this. Taken from their parents and locked away as part of an endless power struggle between two courts that already had too much power to begin with. It's disgusting.

Maybe I was never imprisoned, but I spent my childhood caged by an unfair, exploitative contract. I know what it's like to be an orphan, and I know what it's like to have your choices stolen from you by those who have so much power they can't see anything beyond their greed for more.

The barmaid slides a bowl in front of orc, shaking her head. "The curse is really broken, then?"

"Aye."

She sighs. "I'm sorry to hear about your sentinels. Will you be needing a room?"

He shovels a heaping spoonful into his mouth and doesn't bother to swallow before speaking again. "Yeah. Need a few hours of shut-eye before I go back."

She grabs a key from the board behind her and drops it in front of him. "Careful tonight, ya hear?"

The orc grunts in response and returns to shoveling stew into his mouth.

My stomach is sour at the thought of children being injected with anti-magic toxin, at the thought of them being imprisoned at all. *The unclean ones,* he called them. Is that a term used for prisoners or for Unseelie? I think I already know the answer, and it makes anger steam in my blood.

I force myself to finish my dinner, because I'll need the energy, but the bread feels like ash in my mouth and the stew sits heavy in my gut.

After the barmaid has cleared my dishes away, I nurse my water while the orc finishes his meal and gets seconds. Only when he's finishing those and making satisfied noises do I drain my glass.

"Mind refilling this and letting me take it up?" I ask, hoisting my empty glass in the air.

The barkeep nods and uses her pitcher to refill it.

With one last glance toward the guard, I head for the stairwell. I hide in the shadows, wrapping them around me so none of the patrons see me as they pass. I wait in silence, my lids heavy as the shadows stroke my frayed nerves, my body begging for rest. I wait and wait until, finally, the orc appears in the stairwell and heads up.

Keeping to the shadows is easy in the candlelight, and the guard's lumbering breaths mask any sound from my own steps. He stops on the second floor and heads to the door two down from mine. When he enters, the door swings into the hall and not into the room. *Perfect.*

Once he's inside, I go to my own room. It's small, dark, and musty, but there's a bed and, as promised, clothes and a bucket of warm water for washing. I drain my glass and refill it with soapy water before returning to the hallway. I position the glass directly in front of the orc's door so it will topple over when the door opens. I wish I could set a more elaborate trap with my magic, but I'm too unskilled and I don't trust anything to hold while I sleep.

I'm exhausted and impatient, my instincts at war. Half of me wants to sleep forever while the other half wants to set out to help the Unseelie children right now. But I don't have the first idea where to go or what I'd be walking into, and I need sleep desperately.

I return to my room, strip off my dirty gown, and scrub my skin until it tingles.

As I continue washing, I notice the emerald hanging between my breasts. Sebastian gave this to me for our bonding ceremony. It seemed like such a thoughtful gift — a piece of jewelry to match the dress my sister designed for me — but now it's a cold reminder of his betrayal. I'm tempted to tear it off and toss it into the trash, but I resist. I don't have any money, and I might need something I can sell down the road.

I swipe the washcloth over my breastbone, ignoring the rune inked into my skin, the sign of my life-bond with Sebastian, right above my heart.

It's been only a day since I last bathed, but it feels like a lifetime has passed since I prepared myself for Sebastian and our bonding ceremony. I was filled with such joy and anticipation; now all I feel is the burning ache of betrayal, the steady lapping of his emotions through the bond, like waves against a crumbling seawall, threatening to overwhelm me.

Love you. Need you. Forgive me.

But forgiveness feels as distant and impossible as a return to my life in the human realm. Sebastian stole the last of my ability to trust when he bonded with me. He made me believe he wanted the bond because he loved me. I tied my soul to his so he could protect me from those who would end my life to steal the crown. And he let me. He let me bond with him, coaxed me into it while feeding me carefully selected bites of the truth paired with tidy, alluring lies. He took my bond even though he *knew* the curse and his Unseelie blood would kill me, even though he knew I'd have to take the potion and become fae to survive.

And he did it all for power. For the very crown he condemned Finn and Mordeus for pursuing.

Sebastian's no better than the rest of them, and now I'm tied to him forever. For my entire immortal life. Now I can *feel* him, as if he's part of me.

I push it all away. His feelings. Mine.

It's too much. Too big. And yet too small all at the same time. There are whole camps of children being drugged and locked away for the queen's nefarious purposes. Innocent children who have no more power over their circumstances than I had when I signed the contract with Madame V so Jas and I wouldn't end up on the streets.

When I found out about the camps, I was sick. Finn told me that when the golden queen's guard caught shadow fae in her territory, she'd separate the children from their parents and put them in camps, where she'd brainwash them—teach them that the Seelie were better, more worthy, and that the Unseelie should serve them.

Every instinct in my heart warned that those camps were a sign that I shouldn't trust the golden fae, but I let Sebastian's promise that he "opposed" the camps placate me. I won't be a fool again. I won't stoop to Sebastian's level and obsess about my own problems when I'm capable of helping. I won't be like him and turn a blind eye to his mother's evil deeds. I will do whatever I can to help those children—if only because doing so will disrupt whatever Sebastian and his mother have planned.

I'm stuck here. I'm fae. But I am not powerless, and I will *never* be like them.

Exhaustion makes it easy to turn off my spiraling thoughts. I want to sleep like this, clean skin on clean sheets, but I make myself put the new clothes on. The moment that trap springs, I don't want to waste time dressing. I need to be ready to go.

When I crawl into bed, I barely make it under the covers before I fall asleep.

I dream of darkness. Of gazing up at a comforting blanket of sparkling stars. Of Finn's voice behind me.

Abriella, every star in that sky shines for you.

The flutter in my chest turns to flapping wings, and I'm flying, soaring through the dark night sky, a tiny hand squeezing mine. I'm not even surprised when I look over to see Lark's silver eyes, her wide smile. Finn's niece has come to me in my dreams before, usually to warn me about something or share some sort of cryptic prophecy. This is the first time, I realize, that doing so won't shave days off her life. The golden queen's curse was broken the moment her son took the Unseelie crown. Now the shadow fae can use their powers without sacrificing their immortality.

At least something good came of Sebastian's betrayal.

The silver webbing on Lark's forehead glows as we fly through the star-studded night sky, but then suddenly we swoop down and the peaceful night disappears. We're in some sort of infirmary. The walls are lined with rows of beds occupied by sleeping children.

"They look so peaceful," I whisper.

Lark twists her lips, considering. "There's a certain peace in death, but unrest will follow if you allow it."

I shake my head. "I don't understand what you're telling me." Lark's gift is seeing the future, but she's never shown me an image as precise as this.

“They’re looking for you,” she says, her eyes bright. “You need to come home. For the children. For the court.”

I shake my head. “I don’t have a home.” My sister is the only person who truly cares for me, and she’s in a realm I can no longer visit now that I’m fae. “Sebastian has the crown. I’m sorry.”

She presses a tiny finger to my lips and looks over her shoulder into the dark night. “Listen.” A shout echoes in the distance, from another world. “It’s time.”

CHAPTER TWO

I WAKE WITH A START to the sound of someone shouting beyond the bedroom door. My eyes are gritty, my muscles still lethargic with sleep. I reach for Sebastian, wanting his heat and needing his comfort for as long as I can have it. Soon enough I'll need to crawl out of this bed and—

I bolt upright.

Someone's shouting in the hall, calling for the maid and screaming about incompetence.

Moonlight shines in through a tiny window, drenching everything in a silvery glow. It calls to me, and if I closed my eyes, it would sing me back to sleep.

My mind spins, scrambles, then clicks. I'm not at the Golden Palace with the male I love; I'm in a run-down inn a day's ride east. I'm not sleeping next to Sebastian; I'm running from him.

I hop out of bed and grab my satchel, slinging it over my shoulder before quietly opening the door.

The orc is grumbling in the hall, fussing about his wet pants, and glaring at the toppled glass and puddle of water. My crude trap did its job.

With my head down to hide my smile, I turn toward the stairs and head to the stables. The night is dark and starless, and clouds slide across the moon. The air smells of rain. Did I sleep through a storm, or is there one coming?

My horse brays when she spots me. I stroke the mare's nose and coo in her ear. Keeping one eye on the door to the inn, I throw on her saddle and tinker with the straps.

The orc pushes into the night and lumbers toward the stables. I keep my head bowed, willing myself to go unnoticed as he claims his massive horse. He hoists himself onto his steed, kicks him in the sides, and gallops off into the night.

Discreetly noting his direction, I force myself to count to thirty before climbing onto my own horse and making my way toward the road. I wait until we're away from the stables before I wrap myself and my mare in shadows, hiding us from the sight of anyone we might pass.

My muscles cramp in protest, reminding me that I spent far too many hours on horseback yesterday. The few hours of sleep I managed at the inn weren't nearly enough to recover, but they'll have to do. Swiping at my gritty, tired eyes, I ignore the aches that travel from my thighs, up my spine, and all the way down my arms.

When the trail turns deeply wooded, the orc holds his lantern aloft to light the way. Staying back, I let the dense black night fall around me, cradle me, disguise me, and I make a plan.

Finn and I were able to use my magic to free Jalek from the windowless, doorless cell in the Golden Palace, and that was before I drank the Potion of Life. Now that I'm fae, my power feels endless, like a constantly refilling well. Before, I needed to focus to find it, but now it's at my fingertips, as natural as breathing. If I can sneak into the prison, I should be able to use my gift to guide the children out through the walls and into the safety of the night. I won't risk taking too many at once, but I will return as many times as necessary.

We ride for nearly half an hour before the path turns out of the forest and back into the moonlight. Unintelligible shouts ring out in the distance, and the smell of fire tickles my nose. A final steep incline reveals pure chaos ahead. Cursing loudly, the orc dismounts and pulls a sword from his hilt before running into the fray. Fires blaze at random intervals throughout the clearing, and fae of all sorts dart in every direction. Some, dressed in the yellow and gray of the queen's guard, wield rope and nets and chase after children. Others swing swords and knives, felling the uniformed guards.

My mare whinnies and backpedals.

"Shhh," I whisper, turning into a patch of trees out of sight of the melee. I jump to the ground and grab her reins, tying her loosely to a tree. "I'll be back soon."

Beyond the flames and the chaos looms a large structure with metal roof and bars for walls. *The prison is an iron cage. The queen has caged the children like animals.* I feel it in my bones, in my heart. I feel the loneliness and terror of the children inside as clearly as if they were sobbing on my shoulder, and my rage becomes a living thing inside me, clawing and scratching to get out.

What kind of monster would do that to children? And what kind of monster would stand by and let her?

I knew I hadn't trusted the queen. So why did I trust Sebastian?

Slipping through the darkness to get closer to the clearing, I assess. A long-haired elven boy around Jas's age screams and thrashes as one orc holds him down and another plunges a needle into his backside. The plunger depresses, and the boy's scream slices through the air, through the night, and through my very core. It's the sound of agony, of life and soul being severed. I know that sound because I made it myself after bonding with Sebastian. I made that sound when I was dying.

I let my rage grow, feed it like the beast I'm preparing to unleash on my enemies — for these innocent children, for every member of the courts whose lives were cut short because of the golden queen's curse, for every human who was tricked out of their life when they bonded with a shadow fae, for myself and my own broken heart.

Power builds inside me, swelling alongside my anger, and when I cast my magic out, the darkness that blankets the clearing is so thick and so deep that even the light from the crackling flames is swallowed into the night.

Cries of surprise and dismay rend the air, and I use their voices to target my power — using all my focus to home in on the Seelie guards through the blackness and lock them in cages of darkness, one by one.

They push back against my darkness, trying to break through it with their own power, but I'm stronger and I don't let them.

"Nice trick."

I jerk away, reaching for my sword as I take in the male

crouched beside me in the thicket. I was so focused on the guards, I didn't even hear him approach.

Russet eyes glowing like an owl's in the darkness, he holds up two hands. "I'm on your side." He points down the hill from the direction I came. Silver webbing pulses with light on his forehead like pieces of broken glass illuminated by the moon. Pretha and Lark both have those markings, perhaps this male is Wild Fae as well. "The queen's sending reinforcements," he says. "We need to get these children to the portal and out of here before they arrive. Most of them have been treated and won't be able to defend themselves."

"Where does the portal go?" I ask, realizing only now that I had no plan for what to do with the children once I freed them. I came to protect them and to punish those who would hurt them, but leading a group of Unseelie children around in Seelie territory is a recipe for disaster.

"We have refugee camps in the Wild Fae Lands."

Can I trust this stranger? How do I know the children will be safer there?

"Not camps like this," he says, as if reading my thoughts. "Houses, not cages. Settlements where they can reconnect with their families. A safe place where they'll be fed and protected until they can return home."

Then I see it in the woods, more eyes like his peeking out toward the camp.

I knew that Finn's people were helping to move Unseelie refugees from the queen's land to the Wild Fae Lands, and since this male's story matches up with what I learned from Finn's people, I take a chance and decide to believe him. "Okay," I say, nodding. "I'll take care of the guards, you get the children to the portal."

"Take care of them how?" he asks.

"Trust me." I turn back to the camp and focus. I've always been able to see at night when no one else could, but now my night vision is better than ever. Focusing on the sentries standing outside the cage, I cast out my power, directing it like a dozen synchronized arrows flying from their bows. I aim for the sentries in the yellow and gray uniforms. Darkness grabs them, wraps them up, and traps them. One by one, I wrap the queen's sentinels in night so vast it swallows them whole.

The male beside me chuckles. "I like you." Then he's gone, racing toward the prison as quick as a fox.

But the whole camp is swarming with Seelie guards, and when I trap more, my focus slips and I lose my grip on another.

One lunges toward my new friend, shouting a warning to someone else.

My ally dodges, and I wrap the guard in a blanket of shadow until he too has vanished. My friend throws me a delighted grin before the bars bend and spread. Shackled children flood into the clearing. Suddenly their chains break and their shackles fall to the ground.

A branch snaps behind me, and I swing around in time to see a figure step from the shadows. He has glowing red eyes and curled horns. I do a double take, thinking of Finn's friend Kane, but this isn't the male I know. This horned faerie has dark hair and doesn't tower as tall as Kane. I half expect the children to shrink from the terrifying figure, but when he waves them toward the forest, they obey, running into the thicket — toward the portal? — as if their lives depend on it. *They probably do.*

A shout of pain brings my attention back to the camp. My friend has a sword to his neck, and the sentry holding it snarls. I focus on the guard and thrust him into his worst nightmares. His sword drops to the ground, and my ally gives a little salute in my direction before rushing to the next section of the massive cage.

My magic feels endless, always there with more to give when I reach for it, yet exhaustion swamps me, threatening to pull me from consciousness. But I don't stop. As long as I have power to help and children to free, I'll continue.

Minutes tick by, and sweat beads on my brow as I struggle to maintain my focus. I stop guard after guard with my power as more and more children rush from the prison, but the guards escape my hold almost as quickly as I can trap them.

A big hand grabs me by the scruff of the neck and drags me up. "What do we have here?"

I'm turned too quickly, my neck whipping back as I meet the murky brown eyes of the orc from the inn. A sharp sting buzzes through my shoulder, and pain blazes through my veins — hot and heavy. I try to lash out with my magic, but instead of pulling from an endless well of power, I find myself trying to fill a glass from an empty jug. There's nothing there.

In the next moment, I collapse.

"I found her."

"You wouldn't have found her if Crally hadn't told you where the magic was coming from."

"Well, I stopped her. I get the first shot at her."

"You? She sent me to the bowels of hell. I want to watch her bleed."

"The bowels of hell? You're really that scared of the dark?"

"Shut your mouth. You don't know what it was like becoming nothing like that. Best part of that curse gettin' broken is gonna be how good it feels to sink my blade in her heart. Unseelie filth."

"Either of you touch her before the captain questions her in the morning, and you'll have to answer to him."

I'm on the ground, and my whole body burns and aches in equal measure. Metal shackles cut into my wrists, but I stay still and keep my eyes closed, listening to the men around me talk.

"You ever see an Unseelie bitch with hair like that?"

"She looks like the Hendishi from the shadow valley."

"I never saw a Hendishi shorter than me. Can't be."

"She's probably got horns hiding under there."

"I say we kill her now. He'll never know."

"You have another way to explain what happened back there?"

Someone grumbles under his breath.

I reach for my magic and find nothing. It's like trying to take a breath and finding there's no room for air in your lungs. I try again and again. *Nothing.*

Panic swamps me and has me pulling against my restraints.

"Oh, look. She's waking up."

They've done something to me. Something to steal my magic.

The injections.

I shift my legs, testing. No bindings. But my wrists—iron manacles shackle them, and everywhere the metal touches me, my skin burns.

I keep my eyes on the ground, scanning my surroundings as best I can. A lone owl hoots from its perch above us, and insects fill the air with their nighttime song. A campfire crackles three feet from me. Two orcs lounge around it, as if they've set up camp for the night. A third looms over me.

"She's awake." A boot to my gut makes me cry out. "Say hello to the filth, boys."

"Sit your ass down and leave her alone," one of his companions says. "Once Captain has a chance to talk to her, you can have at her, but until then, back off."

There's a scuff of gravel, and boots come into my line of sight. The male stoops until his face is inches from mine. His breath smells like rot and decay, and his two curving teeth glisten in the firelight. "You ready to meet our captain? I'm gonna do you a favor, girl. Tell him who you're working with, tell him who helped you, and he'll only make it hurt a little."

"Don't tell her that," one of the lounging orcs says. "I want to see the bitch scream."

Once the captain gets here, I'm toast. I can't be here when he arrives, but I can barely stay conscious now. And even if I weren't fighting for consciousness, what would I do without my power and with my hands shackled?

Sleep, Abriella.

No. I can't. But the voice in my head sounds like my mother's.

Sleep, and let the shadows play.

The call is too sweet to resist, my body too weak. I close my eyes and sleep.

It's time to run.

My eyes fly open. Last night's fire crackles in front of me, and the first rays of morning sun slant through the trees. There's a funny smell in the air. Sitting up, I rub my eyes with my shackled hands — and *freeze.*

My stomach heaves as I take in my captors. The orcs are still around the fire, but instead of snarling at me the way they were last night, they're . . . dead. Bloodied and gruesome, their guts spilling out onto the forest floor. And on the ground before me is my dagger — the one I keep wrapped in shadow on my thigh, but it's unsheathed and bloody.

I stumble to my feet and back away. There's blood everywhere, but none on me. I'm still shackled and weak, so who killed the guards? And why did they leave me alive?

The sound of horse hooves beat in the distance and grow closer. *They're coming. The captain is coming.*

I gulp in air, and reason comes with it. I turn and *run.*

My feet are bare — they must've taken my boots — and the gravel bites into my flesh. The wet heat of blood coats the bottoms, but I run. On bloody feet, with lungs so raw they feel like they might tear apart, I race away from the sound of those hoofbeats.

I'm breathless, my bloody feet raw and numb, but I keep running.

The gravel path eventually leads to a stretch of fields. The spring wheat lashes at my legs and face as I sprint through it, but I don't stop. I see stables ahead and use the dregs of my energy to push through the doors with my manacled hands. By the time I pull myself into a corner inside, the last of the night has all but left the sky and I have no energy left to cling to consciousness.

I collapse against the wall, let my eyes close, and sink into a deep sleep, where I run even in my dreams.

Images flash through my mind. Sebastian's sea-green eyes as he promised to make me a home, the rune inked on my skin right above my heart that represents our bond, the iron bars of the oversize cage where the queen locked away the Unseelie children.

In every dream, past every memory, I'm running. Heart racing, lungs seizing, legs aching, running.

This is my life now. Running. Nonstop running, with enemies in every direction.

The thought grips me as I drift in and out of sleep. I want to rewind time. To go back to Elora before Jas was sold, before I knew Sebastian was a faerie, was a *prince.* I want to go back to that lonely, tiring existence. I didn't have many people who cared about me, but at least no one was *pretending* to care. At least I got to believe that the little I had was real.

CHAPTER THREE

"*THIS* IS THE GREAT BEAUTY Oberon's sons have been fighting over?" a male voice asks.

"She doesn't need beauty. The Fire Girl is a great thief; she steals hearts as easily as jewels," replies a vaguely familiar voice.

Bakken? What is Bakken doing here?

A scoff. "Sure she does."

I try to open my eyes and fail. My lids feel like they've been glued shut and my mouth feels like it's full of sand.

"She looks as foul as these untended stalls. And smells worse," the male says.

I try to sit up straight, groaning as every muscle locks in protest.

"Wake up, Princess Abriella. Your salvation has arrived."

My disgust and annoyance are powerful enough that I finally manage to open my eyes. I'm greeted by the sight of shining boots laced over heavily muscled, leather-clad legs. I lift my head and see a very large, very *tall* olive-skinned fae male smirking down at me. Through his mop of thick, dark hair, the fractured lines across his forehead pulse a glowing silver.

"There she is," the male says, his uptilted russet eyes dancing with amusement. "Welcome back to the land of the living."

I know those eyes. "You were the one helping the children escape."

I'm treated to a wide smile. He looks familiar somehow. Not just from the moments when we crouched in the grass together outside the Unseelie prison, but more than that.

"You're Wild Fae," I say, my voice hoarse.

He snorts. "Why, yes. Thanks for noticing. Can we leave now? Before your prince finds me on his mother's lands and makes me pay with my head?"

My gaze slides to the goblin standing beside him. It's not Bakken at all, but another goblin I don't recognize. The creature's too-long teeth gleam with saliva as he stares at my hair.

"Go where?" I ask. Talking feels like gargling daggers. I thought that being fae meant feeling healthy and energetic — full of life — yet I've felt closer to death than life from the moment I woke up with these elven ears.

The strange male chuckles. "Well, you used a great deal of power before you even had time to recover from your metamorphosis. Of course you feel like hell."

I glare at him. Is he reading my mind, or are my thoughts that obvious?

"Both. At least your feet healed."

He's right. The pain's gone. The only evidence of last night are the shackles on my wrists and the dried blood covering my feet.

He waves haphazardly in my direction, and the iron on my

wrists falls away. He offers me his hand. "Come. Prince Ronan's sentries will arrive in moments."

"How would he know where I am?"

"The bond?" the male reminds me with an arched brow. "If he'd bothered to come after you himself rather than sending a unit from his guard, he'd have you already. But you keep running, so his men have had quite a time trying to find you."

There it is — the distant sound of hoofbeats. *I'm so tired of running.*

The male takes one of the goblin's hands, and the goblin extends his other for me.

"Why should I trust you?"

The male chuckles. "Oh, you shouldn't. In fact, you should stop trusting anyone. That's a dangerous habit around here, and you've made quite a mess."

"Excuse me?"

The hoofbeats are closer now. Someone shouts, "Just ahead!"

Standing, I brush the hay off my trousers. I turn and look out the stable doors, expecting to see a group of horses bearing down on us, but I see nothing. "Where are they?"

"Beyond the hill, about a mile away and closing fast," the male says.

I twist my face up in disbelief.

The male chuckles. "You're not used to your keen fae hearing yet, but you'll adjust. Now, shall we?"

I hesitate. On the one hand, I have nowhere else to go, and I know this male helped the children escape their prison at the queen's work camp. For that alone I trust him. On the other hand, he's right. I *can't* trust anyone.

"We don't have much time, Princess."

I ignore him and turn to his goblin. "Where are you taking me?"

"The Wild Fae Lands," the goblin says, his eyes darting around the stables as if the enemy were hiding in the dark corners.

"But I've bonded with Sebastian. I . . ." I swallow. I can't think about it too much or I'll fall apart. "I *feel* him," I say through gritted teeth. "He'll be able to find me."

The goblin doesn't reply, but his companion nods. "Yes, but he won't be able to reach you without starting a war—one he cannot afford right now."

I can't go home. Even if I knew how to get back to Elora, I would be hunted for being fae, either killed outright or beaten and mutilated just like Oberon was before my mother found him and nursed him to health. Sebastian lived there for two years, glamoured to appear human, but I don't know how to glamour myself—or whether my powers would even allow it.

I could go to Finn. He came to me in that dream the night I took the Potion of Life . . . or I went to him.

Are you happy?

Of all the things he could've said or asked, he wanted to know if I was happy. A lesser male would've gloated about the mistake I made when I trusted Sebastian.

I'm confident that Finn would give me a place to stay—he said as much in his brief visit to my dreams—but I don't understand why. I no longer have the crown. I don't have anything he needs, except maybe this power—but he should have his own now that the curse is broken. And even if he would take me in, am I ready to trust him? Sure, Sebastian's betrayal was worse, but both males used me, manipulated me and tried to trick me. All for what? Power? The crown? *They can have it.*

"We don't have all day, Princess." Those russet eyes shift to the road outside.

"I am not powerless. If you're tricking me, I will lock you in a darkness so deep and vast, you will pray for the refuge of your nightmares."

He flashes a grin to his goblin. "I really *like* her." He takes my hand and the goblin takes the other.

Then I'm falling.

Flying, reeling, going left and right and nowhere all at once until suddenly we're in a dimly lit bedroom. The windows look out to the first tendrils of dawn stretching across a tree-lined vista below. The sun is just rising here, where it was full daylight in the Seelie lands. That takes me by surprise for a moment until I remember that the Wild Fae Lands are situated far west of the queen's Golden Palace.

"Take care, Fire Girl," the goblin says, then bows his head and disappears.

I frown at the vacant spot the goblin occupied seconds before. "Why do they work for you?"

"Excuse me?"

"The goblins—it seems that every powerful faerie has at least one at their beck and call, but they have this power that you need. Why do they serve you?"

The russet-eyed male gives me a crooked grin, as if this question somehow makes me more interesting. "Goblins take alliances with different courts for their own purposes, but usually for access to information, as their collective knowledge is the source of their power."

"Collective knowledge?"

He lifts his chin. "Indeed. What one goblin knows, soon all goblins will know. Never be foolish enough to believe a goblin who does your bidding is serving you. They play a bigger role in the politics of this realm than most realize. They always have their own motives and rarely share them."

His explanation makes sense to me. Bakken may have lived in my aunt's house as her servant, but I never had the impression that she truly ruled over him.

Nodding, I take in the room — the large four-poster bed piled with layers of linens that looks so soft my tired body sways toward it, the windows that overlook a mountainous landscape as lovely as the gardens at the Golden Palace and the lush green valleys beyond.

This seemed like the best choice when faced with returning to the Golden Palace or trying to find Finn, but now that I'm alone with this strange male, I'm questioning my judgment.

"Where are we?" I ask.

The russet-eyed faerie folds his arms and cocks his head to the side. "We're in my home."

My gaze darts to the bed again. If he thinks —

"Settle down, Princess. I don't take unwilling females to my bed. And even if you were willing . . ." With a wrinkled nose and a repulsed little shudder, he gives me a once-over and shakes his head. "I don't care for bed partners who smell like the dung pile my father forced me to shovel as a child."

I gasp. *Rude.*

He chuckles. "I speak the truth. You have . . . *an odor,* likely from last night's sleeping arrangements, but nonetheless you look like you haven't bathed in a fortnight. Forgive me for not finding you tempting."

He's *maddening.* "I don't want to *tempt* you. I just want to . . ." What do I want? Nothing. I want nothing but to escape this nightmare. Right now, the only thing that appeals to me is sleep.

"Then sleep," he says, waving to the bed. "But perhaps a bath first? I'll call your handmaid." He turns to the door.

"Wait."

Pausing, he arches a brow.

"Who are you?"

His slow smile stretches across his face and makes his eyes light up. "I am Mishamon Nico Frendilla, but you may call me Misha." He bows at the waist. "Pleasure to officially meet you, Abriella."

Misha. Pretha's brother. That's why he is so familiar to me. He resembles his sister. "No." I fold my arms. "You'll have to take me somewhere else. I do not need to involve myself with another prince of another faerie court. *No.*"

His eyes go wide. "Prince? Milady, I am *king.* And with all due respect, where do you think you can go? You want some time to gather your thoughts and figure out how you feel without Prince Ronan trying to influence you. I'm offering you that time."

"Get out of my head," I growl. Not only do I not want to involve myself with more fae royalty, the last thing I need is to take shelter where even my thoughts aren't private.

Misha sighs. "Like I said, Ronan can't come here without my permission — not without starting an ugly conflict."

"You can go into the Court of the Sun, open portals, and steal away the queen's prisoners, but I'm to believe that Sebastian coming to retrieve *me* would be considered an act of war?"

"Trust me, the queen would *love* to seek retribution for all I've taken from her, but she can't. Not without exposing herself to the entire realm as the slave-keeping, child-stealing, power-hungry bitch that she is."

"But Sebastian —"

"Ronan's power is tenuous at best, in either court," Misha says. "He can't risk losing the precious followers he has by sending soldiers to this mountain to claim a girl."

"And Finn?"

He shrugs. "Finn doesn't know you're here."

"And how do I know you aren't in alliance with him in exchange for access to me?"

"And why does he need access to you? What do you have to offer?"

I flinch. *Too true.* Of course. Why would they risk anything for me? I no longer have what they want. "Perhaps you'll sell me to the golden queen? Or maybe you're looking for information. I doubt you're doing this because you make a habit of helping random humans."

He looks me over again. There's no interest in his perusal,

only curiosity. "I don't help random humans, but you, Abriella, are neither random nor human."

"You know what I—"

He holds up a hand. "As for my reasons for helping you, you are correct in assuming my motivations aren't selfless. I'm responsible for my kingdom and all that reside here, and whether I like it or not, the actions of the other courts affect my people. And whether you like it or not, you're caught up in the middle of all of it."

"So I'm a pawn?" *Again.*

His eyes heat, and he steps forward. "You don't get to play the poor little abused mortal girl with me," he says. "Oberon gave you his crown and his power, and in doing so, he tied your fate to the fate of his kingdom. You weren't given a choice. But neither was I when I was born to rule these lands. Neither was Prince Ronan or Prince Finnian. You are not the only one who's been dealt a difficult hand, and feeling sorry for yourself won't change the fact that your actions will have an impact on my family, my people, and this entire realm."

Gaping at the beautiful, sharp-tongued fae king, I grapple for a smart reply, but my brain is too fuzzy. "I don't have the crown anymore. I'm just a human who's been made fae. I'm no one."

He looks me over slowly, and I feel as if he can see past all the dirt, past my skin, and inside my very soul. "You're filthy and exhausted. You've never fully recovered from the potion, and you've expended an extraordinary amount of power in the last day. Even the sacred fire gem around your neck can't save you from burning out if you keep this up."

My hand goes to the emerald teardrop hanging between my breasts. "The sacred what?"

"Fire gem," he says, eyeing the stone in my hand. "Don't you know you're wearing a talisman? An incredibly rare, highly valued one at that?"

I look closer and realize it's not a stone at all—not like one I've ever seen, at least. "Why is it called a fire gem if it's green?"

"They come in all colors, but I imagine it's named after the way it looks when you hold it up to the light—like there are flames inside."

"What do they do?" I ask. *And why would Sebastian give one to me?*

"Probably to ensure you were strong enough to survive the transition. Not all humans who've taken the potion have lived to speak of it."

I swallow hard as a flurry of emotions twist my gut. Is this a sign of Sebastian's love for me or further damning evidence of just how premeditated his choices were? He *knew* I'd die when I bonded with him, and he kept the truth from me. He stole my human life so he could take the Unseelie throne.

"You're thinking too much," Misha says. "I'll explain everything soon, but you need rest." He pokes his head out the door and calls softly down the hall for someone.

A white-haired female wanders in. Bowing her head, she skirts me and steps into what appears to be a bathing room.

"Holly will draw you a bath and get you some clean clothes," Misha says. "If your mind won't allow you to rest, there's a sleeping tonic by the bed."

As if I'd take anything—

"It's not poisoned, Princess. It's an herbal mixture prepared by my healer for a more peaceful sleep, but whether you use it or not is entirely up to you."

I take a deep breath. He's right. I need a bath and some sleep. I'm exhausted and heartbroken and—

I scream and jerk back as pain slams into my body. I press my hand to my gut, fully expecting to see blood seeping between my fingers; then pain seizes my limbs so forcefully that I fall to the ground. "What . . ."

I lift my gaze to meet Misha's and see confusion flash there before understanding takes its place. "The bond," Misha says, his eyes wide. "You're feeling Prince Ronan."

I gasp at the burning ache in my gut, in my chest. I'm being torn apart. "Sebastian's hurt?"

"You tell me."

He's right. I know it as surely as I know my hand is my own. This pain is Sebastian's. "He's been . . . attacked."

"With magic? With a blade?" Misha asks. "Is it a death blow?"

I shake my head. "I . . . I don't know."

"Focus," he says, his voice as soft as silk.

I close my eyes to focus and am pummeled by sensations and emotions that aren't my own. The pain rolling over his body, his despair, his heartache. There's more. Frustration and worry. And . . . *jealousy?* Ripe, green jealousy that's so potent it feels like anger.

Misha chuckles. "He must be with Finn. Ronan's still jealous of the shadow prince even after getting your bond. What an insecure child."

I glare. "Stop that."

He shrugs. "Just trying to help."

Another wave of pain, this one less intense, but it leaves an ache. How badly is he hurt? Will he be okay? I stomp down those questions. *He betrayed me.* "How do I make—" I gasp. "Make it stop."

"The bond?" Misha shakes his head. "You can learn to mute what you're receiving from him, but it will still be there when you let your guard down."

I need you I need you I need you I need you.

I press my palms to the sides of my head. He's there—not in words, but in this echo of feeling.

"He knows you're tuned in to him," Misha says. "He feels it, and he's trying to communicate."

I love you I love you I love you I love you.

Despair is a blow to my chest, his mingling with mine, and I slump against it. I grip the wooden bedpost to pull myself off the floor. "How does this bond work?" I ask. I'm a fool for not asking more questions before I accepted it. A fool for trusting a faerie.

Misha arches a brow and studies me. "It's a connection," he says. "An awareness."

"Does he know my thoughts?" *I love you I love you I love you I love you. I need you I need you I need you I need you.*

"Not exactly." He tilts his head to the side and studies the ceiling thoughtfully. "It's more like an impression. A strong empathic connection between the two of you. So if what you're feeling translates strongly into a word or a phrase, he might get the impression of that word or phrase. But usually it's more of a feeling."

"How do we undo it?"

Misha chokes out a laugh. "It's a soul bond, girl. You can't take it back."

"Surely there must be some way."

"Perhaps, but it's costly and painful and requires the full cooperation of both parties. You each have to choose to release the other. There's a ritual that requires many of our sacred fire gems — the one around your neck wouldn't get you close — and I'm told it's as excruciating as the Potion of Life."

My muscles lock up at the memory of the Potion of Life and the agony it wrought on my body. I don't know if I could go through that again, but maybe there's another way. The bond isn't the same between a faerie and a human. If I could transform back into a human somehow . . .

"The only cure for immortality is death. There's no reverse Potion of Life. Not anymore. Though it might surprise you to learn that you're not the first to desire such a thing."

I glare at him and his intrusive mind reading. "Tell me how to mute this bond."

He tilts his head to the side. "For you, the problem goes deeper than the bond. It's much more than being aware of your lover boy's feelings."

"Don't call him that."

"My point," he says, ignoring my objection, "is that blocking him won't free you from him."

"Help me shut him out."

Misha shakes his head. "It takes practice, fortitude, and empathic strength. You're too weak for any of that at the moment."

"Can you help me or not?" I snap.

"There's no instant fix. Bathe, drink the tonic, and rest. The reprieve of sleep is the best I can offer in your current condition. I'll see you when you wake." He retreats to the hall, and I glare at his back until he closes the door behind him.

But slowly the pain fades. The echo of Sebastian in my head fades. He's still there — *always* there — but quieter now.

Holly helps me into the bath, then leaves me. The warm water smells like fresh lavender, and my sore muscles slowly uncoil as I wash off the sweat and dirt from my capture and escape. The morning birds call outside the window and the water grows cool as the sun climbs above the horizon. All the while, I ignore the way this bond makes it feel as if Sebastian's in the room watching me. Ignore the relief that washes over me when his pain subsides and his emotions settle.

He's okay. He'll survive.

Only once the last of the heat has seeped from the bathwater do I climb out of the tub and dry myself. A fresh sleeping gown waits on the foot of my bed, and I pull it over my head and crawl under the soft covers, curling onto my side.

I feel him in my mind, cradling me, holding me close. I want to shrug him off, but I don't know how. I can't deny that in this moment, while I weave in and out of sleep, my mind clinging to worry for the male I loved, there's a comfort to this bond.

I drift off, wondering if he knows where I am. Wondering why he would care at all now that he has the crown.

My dreams drag me through violent ocean waves, put me back on the horse with my mother, riding away from that woman who scares me, and then drop me into a summer night before I can get my bearings.

The air is hot and sticky, and I can't bring myself to go inside to Madame V's cellar, where the air gets stale. I'm too beaten down tonight to look my little sister in the eye and pretend that I made today's payment through hard work alone.

Stealing, even from the worst people, takes a toll on my heart and mind. I never intended to become a thief. Never thought I'd be sixteen and already so deep in debt that I understood why other girls my age ended up selling themselves to the fae.

I take a seat on the ground and look up at the stars. They're not very bright tonight, but the sight still soothes me. I love the night. The sound of the frogs singing, the owls calling in the distance. It reminds me of a simpler time. When I didn't know what it was like to have my sister depend on me, when I still wished on stars and had a mother to tell me fairy tales at bedtime.

Once upon a time, there was a little girl with blazing red hair who was destined to save a kingdom . . .

"How did I know I could find you out here?" Sebastian asks, stepping out from Mage Trifen's back door. He's so beautiful in the moonlight, his white-blond hair blowing softly in the breeze, and my heart tugs with longing for the mage's apprentice.

"Maybe because I have no life, and if I'm not working or

sleeping, this is where I *always* am?" I say, laughing. I didn't think I wanted any company tonight, but seeing him makes me feel lighter. "I'm quite predictable."

He crosses the courtyard and lowers himself to the ground beside me, leaning back on his elbows. "Only in the best ways."

I pull my gaze from the stars to flash him a smile and find him staring at me, his expression serious. "Bash?"

"This is the first time I wanted to kiss you," he says. "I wanted it so badly."

I frown at my secret crush, trying to make sense of this. "Wanted? What do you mean?"

Sebastian flickers in and out of my vision, like a reflection in a pond that disappears with a ripple only to reappear when the water settles. For a moment, a sparkling crown of stars sits atop his head, but I blink and it's gone.

"You remember this night, don't you? You were exhausted—you were *always* exhausted, but this night you stayed outside with me and told me about your mother. You confessed that you missed her and sometimes still dreamed about her coming home. Then you fell asleep right beside me."

I shake my head. He's not making sense. What night is he talking about? What he says is true, but I've never said it out loud.

He swallows hard. "I carried you to bed, and when you clung to me in your sleep, I knew I couldn't do it. I knew I'd rather watch my mother die than betray you. But I ran out of choices."

What is he talking about? I study his face—the sharp line of his jaw, his straight nose, his soft lips. Some unfamiliar boldness has me lifting my hand to his face. His skin is soft. Perfect. And I know exactly how it will feel to have that face buried in my neck, his body over mine . . .

He brings his hand to my face and cups my cheek, but my attention snags on a marking on the inside of his wrist. A rune tattoo I've never seen before — the match to mine.

I drop my hand and jerk back. I don't have a tattoo. And I've never been with Sebastian. I don't know where that thought came from. But Sebastian pulls me into his arms before I can get too far, and I let him.

Past and present, dream and reality all sort themselves and click into place.

He's warm and safe, and I never want to leave. I am so sick of being alone. So I lean into his embrace, into his warmth. I feel his heart beating against my cheek and I want to cry. I want to cry because this is only a dream. Because it's not real. I want to cry because I was once foolish enough to believe it was.

Everything's different. Now I know what it's like to take a life and to lose my own. I know what it's like to plunge a blade into the heart of a king and feel no remorse. I know what it's like to die and be brought back through the excruciating magic of a sacred faerie potion. I know what it's like to love so deeply and have that love used against me.

Tomorrow there will be more running. I will still be alone. Sebastian will still have betrayed me.

"I thought it was real," I whisper against his soft cotton shirt. "You made me believe you loved me."

"I *do* love you."

I shake my head because this is a dream, and dream Sebastian will always love me. Will always protect me. He would never betray me.

When he pulls back and tilts my face up to his, he looks into my eyes for a long time. "You have every right to be angry," he says. "I am so sorry. I am so sorry I didn't find another way."

I stiffen. I don't want to have this conversation. I want to pretend no apologies are needed and that none of this ever happened. But . . .

"I should've come for you myself, but I couldn't, and now . . ." He shakes his head. "What's your connection to the Wild Fae court? Who took you there?"

I can only stare at him. This *is* a dream, but not a typical dream.

"Come to me at the Unseelie palace. I promise I'll keep you safe. I don't know what my mother has planned, but I fear—"

"You're visiting my dreams."

His smile is slow and unsure. "I *am* half Unseelie."

"I don't want you here," I breathe.

There's devastation in his eyes. Heartache that I understand all too well. That I feel in my bones, humming right alongside my own. "Brie—"

"Get out." Then I shove. With my hands and my mind, I shove until he disappears and I'm alone again and swept into another dream.

Later in the night, Finn appears in a dream, but I shove him out before he can say a single word.

CHAPTER FOUR

I SLEEP FOR HOURS WITHOUT stirring, even without the tonic.

When I wake, light peeks through the gap in the curtains. I press my palms against my eyes and groan. I need to be entangled with another Faerie court like I need a hole in the head. Never mind that I doubt Misha is exactly a neutral party here. He and Amira were working with Finn to rescue Unseelie refugees from the queen's camps. While knowing this makes it easier to trust Misha, easier to respect him, it also means that he has ties to Finn and those who want Finn on the Throne of Shadows.

Meanwhile, Sebastian is visiting me in my dreams and asking me to come to him at the Unseelie palace. Did he take the throne? Now that he has the crown, I'm not sure what would stop him, not sure what he might be doing that he would've found himself in the kind of pain I felt yesterday.

Sitting up, I swing my feet around to the cool stone floor. The room spins, and I close my eyes for a beat. I am still painfully exhausted. Misha said it was because I had exerted myself too much after taking the potion and I needed to rest, but I still I feel as ragged as I did during my worst days as a human. Perhaps the energy and vitality associated with the fae doesn't come to those of us who drink the potion. Perhaps those gifts are reserved for the natural-born faeries.

I use the facilities, and when I return to the bedroom, a strange female waits by my bed, a cerulean gown with heavy skirts draped across her extended arms, like an offering.

"Who are you?" I ask.

"I'm Genny. I heard you rise and prepared your attire for an early dinner." She smiles as if my waking from a nap is the best thing that's happened to her all day. "May I help you dress?" she asks, stepping toward me.

I point to the gown. "Not that." I'll no longer allow anyone to weigh me down in heavy skirts and tie me up in breath-stealing corsets. I'm done with flimsy shoes and fine fabrics. I'm done being controlled.

"Would you prefer a different color? We have many choices for you to—"

"Pants." I attempt a smile to soften the sharp word. "Please."

"As the lady wishes." She tosses the dress on the bed before crossing to the wardrobe and flinging the doors open. It's bursting with lush fabrics in a rainbow of colors. I wish I could send them all home for Jas. A smile tugs at my lips as I imagine her cutting them up and using the material for her own creations, but then it falls away as I realize I may never again get to watch her light up at the prospect of a new project.

If only I could be human again. If only I could return to Elora and leave the nightmare of this realm behind.

"Whose clothes are those?" I ask.

Genny flashes me a questioning glance over her shoulder. "Excuse me?"

"That wardrobe is full. Whose clothes are those?"

"They're yours, milady."

I frown and study the dress on the bed. I don't recognize it, but then I had more dresses at the Golden Palace than I could've ever worn. I let Tess and Emma choose my clothes and never paid much attention. "From the Seelie Court?" I ask.

"No, milady. These are new clothes, purchased for your stay in our lands. His Majesty asked us to prepare them for you while you slept."

How so quickly? With magic? And how did I not hear them bringing all the clothes into my room? But I don't bother asking. It all feels like a trick. Everything in this realm is a trick.

"We'll make adjustments, of course," she says, "now that we know you prefer pants to dresses." Pulling open a drawer, she produces a pair of light brown leather riding pants and a white blouse and sets them on the bed next to the discarded gown. Next she opens a drawer and removes a set of undergarments.

"I can dress myself," I say as she pulls a pair of riding boots from the wardrobe.

"Of course, milady. As you wish. I will wait in the hall and escort you to the dining terrace when you're ready." She gives a slight bow of her head.

I shift awkwardly. Even after weeks of being pampered and catered to at the Golden Palace, I'm still not comfortable with having servants. I'm so used to *being* the servant, I don't think being on this side of the exchange will ever feel right. "Thank you."

She turns to the door and stops, her hand on the knob. "It is I who should be thanking you," she whispers.

"For what?"

"For breaking the curse." She keeps her gaze on the door. "I lost a dear friend from the golden court. He was attacked by a shadow fae in his own home. He . . ."

"He couldn't defend himself," I whisper, and then cringe at myself for stating the obvious. The queen's curse made the Unseelie mortal and limited their magic, forcing them to make human sacrifices to use their magic and extend their lives. But the cost of such a great curse was, in part, taking away the Seelie's ability to physically harm the Unseelie, making the Seelie defenseless against Unseelie attacks and deepening the divide between the courts. "I'm sorry to hear that."

She nods. "Not all in her court are like her," she says, then scurries out the door.

I take my time dressing. The leather pants are soft and fit perfectly around my waist and thighs. The blouse has a square neckline and laces up each arm in a fashion that places aesthetics over function—like so many clothes for females at home and here in Faerie—but it's stitched of the softest cotton and allows me to move freely, so I don't mind the unnecessary frills.

I know the boots will fit even before I slide my feet into them. They're a darker leather than the pants and hug my calves, tying just below the knee. I take my time tightening the laces, comforted in knowing that I'll be able to run if I need to. I don't dwell too long on how Misha's servants knew my size or why the king is being so generous. I'm sure he has his reasons for such generosity, just as I have reasons for accepting it.

Because you have nothing and no one. Because you have no choice.

Pushing away the dark thoughts, I finish dressing and turn to the mirror hanging over the bureau. I stop short at the sight of myself.

The female in the mirror looks like me, but isn't. Her hazel eyes are the same shade as mine, but they somehow shine brighter. Her face is the same, but her skin is luminous, and her ears . . .

Swallowing back the hot surge of emotion bubbling in my throat, I tuck back my jaw-length red curls and examine my elven ears. Delicately pointed, these ears are the surest evidence of my transformation. In every other way, I could almost pass for human, but these ears mean I can never go back to Elora to see Jas.

Is she okay? Has she found work? Without any debts, her skills as a seamstress will be more than enough to support her, and I wouldn't be surprised if she moved in permanently with my friend Nik and her daughter, Fawn. I could see that arrangement benefiting all three of them.

But knowing she's okay doesn't make up for the fact that I may never see her again. Of everything Sebastian stole from me, this hurts the worst. If Jas needs me, I won't be able to return to Elora to care for her. I can never live there again. I can never go home.

Home. A memory cuts through me, too new and too fresh. Before I bound myself to Sebastian, I told him that Fairscape wasn't my home, that I wasn't sure I had a home anymore. He'd kissed me, and his words tasted so sweet against my lips.

I'll make one for you . . . if you'll let me.

Flinching, I drop a blanket of darkness on the memory, smothering it like an errant flame. Was it all a lie? Every touch of his lips, every whispered promise? Was it all a ruse to steal the crown? Was none of it true?

I can't think about that right now. I won't.

When I leave the room, Genny is in the hall waiting for me, as promised, but the hall is . . . *outside*. There are doors on the wall opposite mine, but there's no ceiling save for the dome of treetops looming high above. Birds chitter and swoop this way and that, and a soft breeze toys with the ends of my hair.

Genny leads me through the brightly lit halls until they open to a set of grand, twisting alabaster stairs with a shining wooden banister. If everywhere I looked in the Golden Palace reminded me of the sparkle and shine of a cloudless day, Misha's home reminds me of the most beautiful parts of the forest, as if earth and stone and trees all came together to honor him.

The sound of trickling water draws my attention, and I peer over the railing to see a small creek flowing through the corridor below, cutting through a stone floor that looks as old as time and gives the impression that everything else here was built around it.

"What is this place?" I ask.

She smiles but keeps her gaze on the steps as we make our way to the landing. "This is His Majesty's home, known to most of the realm as Castle Craige, named for the way it was built around and within the mountain itself. Is it not the most beautiful of all the courts' palaces?"

"I believe it is." Not that I've seen much of the Unseelie

palace—I wasn't exactly offered a tour on my visits with Mordeus. It's difficult to imagine any beauty like this in a place where such an evil king ruled.

The stream winds through the airy corridors, and we walk alongside it until we reach an open terrace overlooking a lush green valley. The stream cuts under a massive mahogany table and beneath the glass railing, where it cascades over the terrace's edge.

"It's beautiful," I breathe without meaning to.

"Thank you," Misha says, pulling my gaze away from the steep drop. He's holding a glass of wine and lounging against the base of a massive sequoia that appears to be rooted in the terrace's stone floor. He straightens and steps toward me. "I wish I could take credit for it, but it was my ancestors, many generations before mine, who thought it fitting to allow the wilds to form our palace."

"I've never seen anything like it," I admit. "It's lovely."

"As are you, Princess." He looks me over slowly, his brows inching up his forehead with his perusal as if every bit of me is some new surprise. "Now that you're clean, I can certainly see the appeal."

"The *appeal?*"

His russet eyes are bright when they meet mine again. "As we speak, two of the most powerful males in our realm are fighting over you." He waves a hand up and down. "Now that you're cleaned up, I can see why. Perhaps I'll let them destroy each other and keep you for myself."

I gape. What a *pig.* "You will *not.*"

He arches a brow, the corner of his mouth twitching in amusement. "No?"

"First, I won't be *kept* by anyone. Second, you're a married man, and I'm sure your wife wouldn't appreciate—"

"My *wife* wouldn't bat an eye." He chuckles softly. "This isn't the mortal realm. Marriage doesn't come with the same *expectations* here. Especially not among the royalty."

"Right. Those silly peasant mortals expect *love* and *trust* from their life partners. That must seem so ridiculous to you faeries who put power and status above all else."

He cocks his head to the side and studies me. "Did I hit a nerve?"

I swallow hard and reel in my emotions. I've shown too much of myself. "No. I don't care what marriage means to you."

He scoffs. "Sure you don't. But you can relax. I'm not interested in anything from you but an alliance. Shall we?" He waves a hand, and a feast appears on the table. Piles of fresh-cut fruit, bowls of steaming potatoes, trays of thinly cut meats drizzled with aromatic sauces.

My mouth waters, and I'm suddenly famished. In the short weeks I've been in Faerie, I've become accustomed to regular, hearty meals, but I've only eaten once since leaving the palace. My stomach feels as if it might eat itself if I don't feed it soon.

I've trusted Misha this far. I might as well continue, so I take a seat and wait as he sits opposite me. We quietly fill our plates, and I'm careful to let him take several bites before I begin. A small amount of caution can't hurt.

But after I take my first bite, I nearly lose myself in the pleasure of it. The meat is tender and perfectly seasoned, and the fruit bursts with sweetness on my tongue.

I slow down only when I realize that Misha has leaned back in his chair and is watching me.

"What?" I put down my fork, my cheeks heating.

"I'm sorry I didn't feed you when you arrived. You looked like you might fall over, and given that you'd recently taken the potion, I thought sleep would be best." He glances at my plate, and I realize I've already eaten half of the food. "I may have chosen poorly."

"I'm fine."

"You're not, but you will be. A few hearty meals and some more sleep, and you'll feel nothing like you did when you arrived yesterday morning."

I frown. "Yesterday? You mean *this* morning?"

He shakes his head. "You slept for a day and a half, Princess, and it probably wasn't enough. I've heard stories of people sleeping for a solid week after taking the Potion of Life. Even after that, they're usually urged to stay in bed for several days so their bodies can recover from the transformation. But you did neither. You had one night's sleep before running across the Seelie countryside. Never mind the extraordinary amount of magical energy you expended to escape the Golden Palace and then help those children. By all rights, you should've collapsed before you made it past the palace gates."

"Yet here I am."

"Here you are. More powerful than I can explain." He looks me over slowly, and everything about his perusal feels like approval.

It's tempting to feel flattered by the attention, but I resist. It's undoubtedly some sort of manipulation.

Slowly and too conscious of the movement, I pick up my fork again and scoop a small bite. "Where are all your people?" I ask before popping the food into my mouth.

Misha glances around the quiet terrace. "Assuming that's not a literal question, you're going to have to be more specific."

"The courtiers," I say, waving my fork. It seemed Sebastian was never alone. If one of his potential brides wasn't with him, Riaan was at his side, usually along with several other sentries and members of his council. "Advisors, friends, the residents of your palace?" I pause. "Your *wife?*"

He folds his arms on the table and leans forward. "Amira, the *queen,* is looking forward to meeting you, but she's unavailable right now. As for the others . . ." He shrugs. "I wanted you to myself tonight. We have a lot to discuss, and most of it is far too important for me to invite other voices and ears into the conversation."

I grunt. "What could you possibly need to discuss with me? I'm no one but a foolish girl who was tricked into bonding with a manipulative prince." Again, more than I wanted to share. It seems I can't help myself.

His eyes blaze, and he tilts his head to the side. "Your anger is *intense.* I like it."

"You don't know the half of my anger, but if this is a trick somehow—if you're trying to force me to work with Finn or reunite with Sebastian—you'll soon find out."

He smirks. "Prince Ronan knows he cannot come to this palace, cannot come after you uninvited without risking a battle he would most definitely lose, but I'm tempted to invite him anyway — if only to let you unleash all the pent-up fury. It would be so much fun to watch."

I bow my head and blow out a long, slow breath. "Has anyone ever told you it's rude to rifle through another person's private thoughts and emotions?"

"I'm sorry," he says, sighing. "I'm being an insensitive brute, but I promise you I mean well. It's simply that it's been many centuries since two such powerful males fought over a female. Millenia since two brothers did, and this time seems no less significant than the last." He flicks his wrist, and a glass of wine appears on the table by my fork. "I offer a glass of my finest wine as an apology."

I ignore the wine and lift my gaze to his. "You keep saying two males are fighting over me. Why would you say that?"

"Prince Ronan and Prince Finnian? Ring any bells? Or are there other powerful males battling over you? If so, I'd like to know now. I don't like surprises."

I cool my glare to pure ice. "But wouldn't you know? Or are we pretending that you're *not* reading my mind now?"

He sighs. "Ronan and Finnian are fighting over you, obviously."

"And you know this *how?*"

"Because I have eyes in the Court of the Moon."

Of course. Everyone in this realm seems to have spies everywhere. It's a wonder there are any secrets at all. "Perhaps they fought, but that has nothing to do with me. Sebastian bonded with me because he knew it would kill me. Because of the curse, it would kill me, and when I died, he'd get the crown. This was all about the crown — about who is the rightful ruler of the shadow court — not about me."

"Are you so sure about that?" Misha asks, lifting his wineglass.

"Yes, I'm sure. And it's a relief. I'm done being a pawn. They can fight all they want over that damned court. It has nothing to do with me anymore."

He chuckles. "If only that were true."

"It *is* true." I wave to the top of my head. "See? No crown."

He cocks his head to the side. "Perhaps you'd like to see for yourself?" He whistles, and a large brown spotted hawk swoops down from the branches of the sequoia to perch on Misha's shoulder. "This is Storm, my familiar."

I frown at the hawk. "I have no idea what a *familiar* is."

"It means our minds our linked. He obeys me. Serves me."

I immediately think of the Barghest, the giant wolf-monster-creature that attacked me when I first came to this realm. Sebastian had said that sometimes the Unseelie take them on as familiars. He suggested that the attack may not have been coincidence.

"I had nothing to do with the death dog," Misha says. "My creatures don't attack — never offensively at least. If they're attacked first . . ." He shrugs.

"So what about this bird do I need to see?" I ask.

"Storm returned from the Court of the Moon this morning. If you look into his eyes, he can show you what he saw there."

"I don't need to know. It has nothing to do with me."

The corner of Misha's mouth twitches upward in amusement. "Humor me?"

The bird's eyes are just like Misha's — russet and glowing. The pupils dilate, then constrict as I look at them.

"I don't see any—"

I don't know how I expected it to work, but I'm not prepared when I feel as if my consciousness is yanked from my body, and suddenly — I'm flying. Flying like a bird of prey, circling a castle turret before swooping into a high window and perching on a stone ledge.

Below, Finn stands at the bank of windows, looking out onto a bright day. I instantly recognize the sprawling space with its crystal chandeliers and shining marble floor as the Unseelie throne room, even without Mordeus smirking from beside the throne.

CHAPTER FIVE

THE LAST TIME I WAS in this room, I plunged a knife into the false king's chest. I watched as his lifeless body collapsed next to an innocent girl — the one he'd killed to punish me for refusing to bond with him.

Now the room holds people I once called my friends — Finn, flanked by his sharp-eyed wolves, Dara and Luna; Jalek, the Seelie turncoat; Pretha, Finn's sister-in-law; and Pretha's daughter, Lark. Lark squeezes her mother's hand and lifts her gaze to the hawk. I wonder if she knows they're being watched, if she knew that I'd be seeing this scene for myself in the future.

Finn's speaking, but his sounds don't make any sense to me. The hawk, I realize, doesn't understand the sounds, only remembers them for his master. I watch their mouths and focus.

"I want everyone prepared to leave at moment's notice," Finn's saying, his attention still on the view outside the windows. I can't tell what he's seeing, but I sense his worry and grief. His utter exhaustion.

"What?" Pretha asks, her eyes hard. She folds her arms. "We've waited so long to get back here, and now you're just going to tuck tail and run?"

He sways on his feet and clutches the windowsill. His wolves, Dara and Luna, nudge his hands and whimper softly.

"Sebastian has the crown now," Jalek says, his dark green eyes sharp. "Finn's right. It's only a matter of time."

"So we're just giving up?" Pretha asks.

Finn's eyes flutter closed. Beads of sweat line his forehead. "The curse has been broken. And now Prince Ronan's on his way here to claim this throne. Once he does, we don't stand a chance against his power."

"If he's on his way, then we'll send our people out to greet him," Pretha snaps.

"You think he's foolish enough to come in the front door?" Jalek asks. "He'll have his goblin bring him right to the throne room—perhaps right onto the throne."

"Then we will wait on the dais with swords ready," she says, and the sadness and desperation in her eyes tears me in two. Before now, I hadn't realized just how much I missed these people—hadn't let myself think about it.

"What part of *he has the crown* don't you understand?" Finn rubs his temples. "I'm too tired to have this argument."

Pretha shakes her head. "You're not tired. You're ill. You need rest—rest in your own bed, in your own *home*."

Finn turns his back to the windows and tilts his face up, leaning his head back against the glass. Pretha's right. He does look ill. There's a worrisome pallor to his light brown skin and an uncharacteristic weakness in his stance. "Any minute now, this throne room will be filled with Sebastian's men and their goblins," he says. "They will come quickly, and they will be armed and prepared to kill. It was one thing to stand our ground when we thought the Cursed Horde would come out from hiding to have our backs, but without those forces, staying is suicide."

"They'll be here soon," Pretha says. "General Hargova wouldn't forsake you."

Finn shakes his head. "Too late is still too late — whether it's a minute or a century. We go."

"What about your court?" Pretha asks.

"We will do our best without the throne," Finn says.

The pain in his eyes is a punch to the chest. Finn and his people have probably been at the Court of the Moon since the day I killed Mordeus. Without the crown, Finn's rule would've been no more legitimate than the false king's. As long as I wore the crown, no one else could lay claim to the throne, but now Sebastian has the crown because of *me,* which means that Finn will never sit on the Throne of Shadows.

Somehow, despite everything he did to deceive me, I still believe Finn would make a good king.

"Pretha, the battle has been lost, but we will not lose the war."

Tears stream down Pretha's face, and my heart twists for the wretched grief I see there. She lost her husband — Finn's brother — to this fight, and now, because of me, it was all for nothing.

"We haven't lost forever," Finn says, forcing himself to straighten. "Just for now."

"It's too much." She hangs her head.

"Finn." Kane pushes into the throne room and takes a spot at

Pretha's side. Once, his red-on-black eyes terrified me, but then I got to know him and the rest of Finn's merry band of misfits. His people became my friends. Or at least I thought they were friends. It turns out they had their own agenda. *Just like Sebastian.*

"We're leaving," Finn tells Kane. "I was just telling Pretha."

Kane shakes his head. "We might not need to. There's been a disturbance at the Golden Palace."

Finn arches a brow, waiting.

"Abriella," Pretha says, smiling. "Please tell me she put that iron blade into Sebastian's heart where it belongs."

Kane winks at her, as if she's just said something suggestive. "Unfortunately, not that, but I like the way you think."

"The news?" Finn asks.

"The princess woke and didn't take too kindly to her dear prince's manipulations."

They're still calling me *princess,* even now. Though I supposed I proved them right when I chose to bond with Sebastian, despite their warnings. *I'm a fool.*

"What did she do?" Finn asks.

Kane's face twists into a wicked grin. "She threw the whole palace into darkness. Half his men were caged in by her power, and no one could get to them or see anything as Abriella left the castle."

Pretha smiles slowly. "Good girl," she murmurs.

Jalek grunts. "If she were so smart, she wouldn't have bonded with the boy to begin with."

"There's nothing we can do about that now," Finn says, keeping his eyes on Kane. "What does this have to do with Sebastian taking the throne?"

Kane's smile grows. "My sources tell me he's refusing to do the coronation without her. He wants to wait until she returns—to prove his devotion to her."

"Returns?" Pretha scoffs and wipes her cheeks dry. "As if she's out for a stroll and not somewhere raging about his betrayal?"

Lark smiles up at her mother. "He can't take the throne. It won't have him."

All eyes in the room go to Lark, and Pretha scoops her daughter into her arms. "Tell me what you mean by that, baby."

"Lark . . ." Finn steps forward, then stumbles back again, steadying himself on the wall.

Kane lunges for him, catching him before he can fall. "What's wrong?"

"He's *sick*," Pretha says.

Kane shakes his head. "That doesn't make sense. The curse is broken. I feel better than I have in years. You should too."

Finn draws in a deep breath. "I'll be fine." He turns to Pretha. "Send someone to the house and search it for any sign that Abriella's looking for us. If she shows up there, give her whatever she needs."

"Why?" Jalek asks. "The princess doesn't have the crown anymore. She's nothing to us."

Finn spins on him, eyes narrowed, and Jalek straightens and retreats a step, contrition on his face.

"Pardon me, Your Highness." Jalek bows his head.

She's nothing to us.

Jalek's right. Now that Sebastian has the crown, I'm nothing to *anyone,* and hearing it stated so plainly leaves me feeling hollow.

"Lark," Finn says, stepping toward her with more success this time. "Why won't the throne have Prince Ronan?"

"Queen Mab made the throne with her very magic. Magic isn't free. There are rules," Lark says. "Sebastian isn't following them."

Pretha and Finn exchange a look.

"What rules?" Kane asks.

"Mab's rules. She's been protecting her throne all this time." Lark smiles. "Sebastian can't take it without Abriella's power."

"I don't understand." Pretha shakes her head. "Abriella already gave Sebastian the crown when she bonded with him."

Lark rests her cheek on her mother's chest. "I know. She didn't want to die," she whispers.

"It's okay." Pretha strokes her hair. "Abriella's okay now."

"I told her she'd lose everything," Lark says, her eyes fluttering closed at her mother's soothing touch. "She didn't want to be queen, but I told her it was okay because she'd lose everything."

My heart tugs at the memory of that conversation. Lark had come to me in one of my dreams and told me that in some of her visions of the future, I died, and in others I became queen. I told her I didn't want to be queen and have so much when others had nothing, and she said that was okay because I would lose everything.

She was right. I lost everything the moment Sebastian betrayed me. I lost my human life, my chance to go back to my sister, and the male I loved. I've already lost everything, but she was wrong to believe I'd sit at Sebastian's side while he took the throne. *Never.* Not after all he did to me.

Pretha and Finn are talking, and I make myself focus to understand their words through the hawk's mind.

"If Sebastian somehow needs Abriella to take that throne," Pretha's saying, "then we need to find her first."

I don't have time to dwell on that thought before I'm being shown another vision. The hawk is perched in a slightly different location, but this time only Finn and Kane stand in the throne room.

Finn looks tired, but not as ill as he did in the last vision. He has a bit more color in his cheeks and stands straighter, as if he might stand a chance of using the swords sheathed at each hip.

"No sign of Abriella at the old house," Kane says. "Sources tell us she hasn't returned to the Golden Palace either."

Finn nods, his gaze steady on the view beyond the window. "She still doesn't trust him. Or us." He blows out a breath. "But I wonder where she is. Sebastian could easily track her with the bond."

"Thank the gods he hasn't," Kane says. "If he really does need her, as we suspect, this buys us a little more time."

"None of this explains what Lark saw. What if Lark is right and the throne won't take him? What if, when he got the crown from Abriella, he didn't get the rest of what he needed?"

Kane blinks at Finn. "Is that possible? Can the crown be cleaved from its power?"

Finn blows out a long breath. "She exhibited extraordinary power when she fled the Golden Palace."

"More power than the Potion of Life would grant to a human turned fae," Kane says, seeming to consider it. "Do you think he knows the throne won't accept him?"

"I'm not sure that *I* know," Finn says.

My head swims as I try to keep up. What exactly are they saying? What does my power have to do with Sebastian's taking the throne?

"If you're right," Kane says, "he'll want it back. What would that mean for Abriella?"

"Nothing good," Finn says, running a hand through his black curls. "I would put nothing past him. But he'll make his move soon enough — with or without the power the throne demands."

"The shield's around the palace, and we're gathering our forces to the mountains as we speak. Even without Hargova's guard, we'll be able to —"

"Finn!" Jalek's voice echoes in the cavernous room. "Lark says we're about to have visitors."

Kane's head snaps toward the window, and he scans the horizon. "I don't see any —"

"Hello, brother," Finn says softly.

Across the room, on a dais where no one stood before, a goblin at his side, stands Sebastian, dressed in a shining black tunic with silver piping. I've become so accustomed to seeing him in the gray and yellow of the Court of the Sun that he looks unnatural in the darker colors. Like a child playing dress-up.

Sebastian's eyes are wide as he stares Finn down. He wraps his fingers around the hilt of his sword. "I don't want to hurt you."

"Strange reason to pull your blade," Kane says, moving closer to Finn, a hand on his own weapon.

"My guard is on its way," Sebastian says. "Your shield may be slowing them down, but you forget that as soon as I sit on this throne, I can tear it down. I can flood this palace with those sworn to *me.*"

"So why do you hesitate, Ronan?" Finn asks, folding his arms. He cocks his head to the side. "Sorry—do you prefer *Bash,* as Abriella called you? Though I don't suppose she'll be calling you that anymore."

Sebastian lunges forward, but Jalek throws up a hand and Sebastian bounces back as if he hit an invisible wall. "I know you have her hiding in Misha's palace."

Finn smiles, and if I hadn't spent all those hours training with him, I probably wouldn't recognize the anger and impatience behind that smile. "Then you know she's safe," he says, as if he wasn't just discussing with Kane that he has no idea where I am.

They're *still* using me to manipulate each other.

Sebastian's eyes flash with anger. "Let me see her. I'll send my goblin. I'll—"

"If she wanted to see you, she'd be with you right now," Finn growls.

"Damn it, Finn," Sebastian snaps. "I don't want to hurt you."

"That's wise," Kane says, taking a step closer to Finn. "Because Brie isn't likely to forgive you as it is, but if you harm Finn, she may truly hate you forever."

"You're just angry that she chose me," Sebastian snarls.

"Oh, I'm angry all right." Finn's eyes glitter. "But she didn't choose *you*. She chose the work of fiction you created for her, the pretty little story you wooed her with—the poor golden prince with the dying mother and the dream of uniting two kingdoms after centuries divided."

"It wasn't fiction," Sebastian says. "You know the prophecy as well as I do—a king who appears as an outsider will balance shadow and sun, save Mab's people, and end the war. *I* am that king."

Kane coughs. "Bullshit."

Finn laughs darkly. "It's funny to me that you never mentioned to her how . . . *complicated* it would be to unite the Seelie and Unseelie kingdoms." He taps a finger to his lips and studies the ceiling. "No. Complicated isn't the right word. *Impossible* is more fitting. Our courts exist to balance each other. They cannot be joined without the blood of Mab, and your people saw to it that her line was killed off long ago."

"*You* didn't give her the full truth either," Sebastian says.

"Yes, but I never spouted such ridiculous plans." Finn's mask of amusement falls away. "You're a fool, *Sebastian*," he says, emphasizing the name like an insult. "A fool if you believe our world would be better off under one ruler. You might be young, but you know the history. You know how corrupt the royalty became with that kind of power."

"I suppose you believe that Mab's curse *saved* us?" Sebastian snaps.

"Yes," Finn says. "I do. The shadows bring balance to the sun, the dark balances the light."

"And war kills us all," Sebastian says.

Sighing, Finn strolls to the dais and takes the Mirror of Discovery from its place on the wall. "Was anything you told her true?" he asks, spinning the mirror in his hand. "Funny how you gifted her with such a precious artifact but completely neglected to mention its inaccuracies."

Finn grunts, and Sebastian takes a step toward him before stopping himself, clenching his fists at his sides.

"It suited your plans though, didn't it?" Finn went on. "She believed her sister was happy and healthy, that our evil uncle gave her all she needed while she stayed here." His gaze flicks up to Sebastian before dropping back down to the mirror. "You knew she'd see what she hoped to see. You knew her well enough to know that she was full of hope. And you did nothing to warn her."

"I wasn't the only one who lied."

"Perhaps not," Finn says, calmly replacing the mirror before turning back to Sebastian and staring at the tattoos visible above the prince's tunic. "Though I didn't hide as much either."

Sebastian's blade sings as he pulls it free of its sheath, but Jalek is there, moving faster than I can track and stepping between Finn and Sebastian. He keeps his eyes on the golden prince.

"Jalek," Sebastian says, as if he hadn't noticed him there before. His lip curls in a sneer. "Last time I saw you, you were in the dungeons, where you belong. Perhaps you can return once I become king. You can watch from there as your prince and all your friends bow to *me*."

"We bow to no one but Finn," Jalek growls.

Finn steps forward and puts a hand on Jalek's forearm. "Easy, friend. My brother's just here to take our father's throne." He waves a hand toward Sebastian and then the throne. "By all means, don't let us keep you."

Jalek turns wide eyes on Finn.

"What are you doing?" Kane grumbles.

Sebastian's gaze drifts from Finn to the polished ebony throne and back. "What did you do to it?"

Finn chuckles and steps toward the dais. "You know very well that I couldn't disturb the throne even if I wanted to. It's protected by Mab's magic."

Sebastian's eyes blaze. "You expect me to believe that you *want* me to take the throne?"

Finn widens his stance and folds his arms, his expression deceptively relaxed. "I never said that. But you wear the crown, so what's keeping you from it?"

Sebastian holds Finn's gaze for several pounding beats of my heart, the tension thick in the air. These males manipulated and deceived me, but I don't want to see them tear each other apart.

Sebastian lifts his chin. "I don't wish you any harm, Finnian. This throne was promised to me before I was conceived."

Finn scoffs. "Funny. Our father promised me the same thing."

"Oberon *wanted* me to rule. He wanted to unite sun and moon, light and shadow."

"Did he tell you that or did your mother?"

"This is my birthright. My fate."

Finn arches a brow. "Your birthright? Is that why he gave your crown to a mortal girl?"

Sebastian glares at Finn, and then, in a movement so fast I almost miss it, he sits on the Throne of Shadows.

The room floods with the inky black of a moonless night. The walls shake. The floor buckles. Terror fills me, but I am locked in this vessel, in this strange body, as the palace threatens to crumble around us.

The moment light fills the room again, Sebastian is launched from the throne to the dais steps and is left sprawling. He's panting and wide-eyed, but he doesn't look entirely surprised as he surveys the throne from where it has cast him onto the floor.

Jalek backs away from the dais as he stares at Sebastian, but he shifts his gaze to Finn when he asks, "What's happening?"

"The Throne of Shadows will not accept someone who doesn't possess the power of the crown," Finn says, strolling toward the dais.

"But . . . he has the crown," Jalek says.

"You *knew* this would happen," Sebastian says through clenched teeth, trying and failing to stand.

This is what I felt yesterday, through the bond. The throne tried to kill him.

Finn shrugs. "The possibility occurred to me when Abriella visited my dreams *after* bonding with you. You wore the crown, yet she still had powers unique to the Unseelie Court. And then there are these rumors about her throwing darkness onto your mother's precious Golden Palace, and I had to wonder. After all, no average fae would have the power to do what she did and walk away, let alone the power to do it without having the chance to recover from the potion."

"I'm not leaving," Sebastian says. "This palace is as much mine as it is yours, and my guard is marching through the capital now. They'll be here soon."

Finn shrugs. "Make yourself at home."

Kane gapes at him. "You're kidding me."

"Sleeping under this roof doesn't make one king. Mordeus proved that."

Jalek looks back and forth between Sebastian and Finn. "Would someone explain?"

Finn lifts his chin. "Sebastian may have taken the crown from Abriella, but Abriella still possesses its powers."

CHAPTER SIX

Like jerking awake from a dream, I'm back in my body, back at the table on the terrace with Misha. Nausea rolls over me, yanking my stomach into my throat. I push my chair back and stand, crossing to the railing, as if the sight of the drop might root me in my own body enough to let me catch my breath.

"I don't understand. Why can't Sebastian take the throne? He has royal Unseelie blood, he has the crown, how does he not have the power too?"

"Because you have it," Misha says gently. "When you bonded with Sebastian, the bond killed you, and since you'd never magically declared your heir, the crown followed that bond like a map to Sebastian."

"Then what's the problem?"

"Sebastian has the Crown of Starlight," Misha says. "And if he hadn't done anything but bond with you, he would have the power of the crown as well. But he didn't stop with the bond. He gave you the Potion of Life and made you fae, and in doing so, he tied the magic of the crown to your life before it could follow the crown."

Tied the magic to my *immortal* life. "Magic is life," I whisper, remembering those words Finn taught me. It feels like so long ago now, but it was merely weeks ago that I learned this about the fae.

"Without both the crown and the power, Sebastian can't take the throne."

It's not over. I shake my head to clear the thought away. "I can't have Oberon's power. I'm just a human girl." Before Misha can point out my error, I shake my head. "You know what I mean."

"Indeed, I do, but you're more than a human turned fae. Maybe you didn't notice that you swamped the palace in darkness when you ran? That you trapped the sentries at the refugee camp in cages of nothingness?"

"Yes, but I thought . . ." I swallow. *Magic is life.* I knew I'd gotten to keep my powers when I was transformed into a faerie, but I never considered how this would affect the crown.

"No one knew this would happen," Misha says.

"*You* seemed to."

"We all had hunches of how the crown might pass from a mortal to Court of the Moon royalty, but no one really knew how it would work or what would happen if, say, you died without bonding with anyone who could actually sit on the throne. If you'd bonded with a golden fae with no Unseelie blood, for instance, would the crown have gone to him upon your death? It would seem unlikely, since one must have royal Unseelie blood to inherit the crown and sit on the throne. But the way Oberon was able to save you—the way he was able to surrender his life and pass the crown to a mortal—broke all the rules we thought we understood. Then there was all the discussion of what would happen to the crown if you died before bonding with anyone—there were all sorts of ideas surrounding that possibility—yet no one ever questioned what would happen if you were given the Potion of Life upon bonding with an Unseelie."

I can just imagine them all sitting around and contemplating my death so casually. I toss a scowl over my shoulder.

Misha chuckles. "What's the problem?"

"You *knew.* That's why you brought me here. You figured it out before any of them."

"My spies told me of the power you'd wielded at the Golden Palace, and then I saw you in action at the camp. I didn't know for sure, of course, but my niece visited me in a dream the night we met at the refugee camp—she's a seer, as you know."

"Lark," I whisper. Funny how this vast new world seems so small. I'd already forgotten that Misha is Lark's uncle.

He nods. "Yes. She said Sebastian didn't have what he needed to take the throne and that you were running. She asked me to give you a place to hide until you were stronger. So between the great power you'd demonstrated and her prophecy, I drew the obvious conclusion. Once Storm showed me the throne rejecting Sebastian, my suspicions were confirmed."

"So when you say Finn and Sebastian are fighting over me, *this* is what you mean. They need my power." Just as they fought to win my loyalty when I wore the crown. *This will never end.*

"I think it's more complicated than that, but on the most basic level, yes. The throne wouldn't accept Sebastian, because he doesn't have the power, and it won't accept Finn, because he doesn't have the crown *or* the power. And obviously it won't accept you, because—"

"Because I'm barely even fae, let alone Unseelie royalty."

"Well, yes." He shrugs. "But even if you were, Sebastian still wears the crown. Regardless of how this ends, those brothers need you if the Unseelie Court is going to hold together."

"They need to kill me again?" I spin around and stalk toward the table, hysterical laughter bubbling from between my lips. "Once wasn't enough?"

Misha refills his wineglass. "That's not remotely what I'm suggesting."

"I never asked for any of this."

He narrows his eyes. "We've been over that already. None of us asks for the burdens we bear, but that doesn't make the way we handle them any less significant."

"Why can't they just make a new throne?"

He grunts. "A throne isn't just a *seat,* Princess. It's a metaphor, and its magic is stronger than you can imagine."

"That's why you're helping me," I say softly, resigned. I reach for the bottle of wine and refill my own glass. Maybe it's poisoned. Maybe this is all some wicked scheme to kill me so he can take my power and hand it over to Finn—Misha's sister was married to Finn's brother, after all. They're practically family. Or maybe Misha wants the power for himself. I look him in the eye and bring the glass to my lips, hesitating.

"It's not poisoned. I have no interest in killing you. As I mentioned, we're in uncharted territory here. It's hard to know what would happen if you died."

I roll my eyes and take a sip. "How reassuring."

"I need you, but even if Sebastian had the crown *and* the

power and were sitting on that throne right at this moment, I would still need you. The Unseelie realm is deeply divided. Mordeus's followers weren't loyal to *him* so much as to the way he ruled. His unfair laws and punishments favored the elite few, and that's exactly what they wanted."

"The elite few?" I frown. "I thought the masses were behind Mordeus, and that's why Oberon couldn't take his rightful place as ruler when he returned from the mortal realm."

"The masses weren't behind Mordeus," Misha says, sounding resigned. "The *masses* were dying in that damn war. But the vocal minority was behind him, and they had power and influence of their own. They supported Mordeus when he stole the throne from Oberon, because they knew Finn was dedicated to the commoners—his rule would've redistributed the power and privilege in their court. Mordeus's followers were willing to launch a civil war to avoid that, and I'd bet they still would be, wherever they are. Sebastian doesn't even have that."

I frown and try to bite back the question, but if I've learned anything from my goblin friend, Bakken, it's that information is power. "They still would be? What do you mean by that?"

Misha shrugs. "I mean they're in hiding. After you killed the false king, his followers fled, fearing Finn would bring his secret legions down on the palace. But wherever they are, they'll be back."

"Finn has secret legions? As in military?" Is that the Cursed Horde they mentioned in the vision?

Misha leans back in his chair and studies me. "What do you think Finn spent the last twenty years doing? He's been gathering his forces in the mountains, training them, preparing for the possibility that the crown might be lost forever and he'd have to oust Mordeus from ruling without it."

I study my wine. When I first met Finn, I accused him of living in luxury while his people suffered. But as I grew to know him better, I knew he would do anything for his people. Even now, despite everything, I feel guilty about my offhand attempt at cruelty.

"So there are those who supported Mordeus," Misha says, continuing with his explanation, "and then there are those who follow Finn. But there are also those who want to see Prince Ronan on the throne, who fought in the Great Fae War and think that only a ruler with both sun and shadow in his blood can unite the realm and save their children from endless war."

I shake my head, remembering the argument I saw through the hawk's eyes. "Finn said that couldn't happen, that it was impossible for Sebastian to rule over both courts." I frown.

"Finn's right, but the appeal of Sebastian's rule isn't that he'd rule both courts. The hope is that Queen Arya wouldn't go to war with her son's kingdom."

"Oh. But wouldn't she?"

Misha scoffs. "I've yet to find something she *wouldn't* do for more power, so I think those holding out for that are putting stock in an overly optimistic assumption. Regardless, the fact is this: the shadow court has never been as divided as it is now, and as long as it's so broken, it's weak."

"Okay, but you're king of the Wild Fae. Why do you care so much about the Unseelie Court?"

His eyes flash and his nostrils flare, his temper slipping for just a beat before he reels it back in. "A strange question from the former mortal who risked her own life to help dozens of Unseelie children escape the queen."

"Anyone in my position would've helped."

He hums. "I'm not so sure, but I find it quite endearing that you believe this, after all you've been through."

I look away, my face burning with embarrassment. I don't need Misha believing I'm some naïve girl, and I don't want him digging into why I feel this compulsion to help. The truth makes me vulnerable.

He sighs. "I care because what happens between the courts affects my lands and my people. I care because I know that as long as the shadow court is weak, the golden queen will capitalize on that weakness."

"Meaning what?"

"War is imminent," he says, "but this time instead of being locked into a centuries-long battle between two equally matched courts, the Seelie will be victorious. The golden queen will *win*, and the consequences will be catastrophic, not just for the Unseelie Court but for my territory and the human realm as well."

"What could she possibly want that's worth risking the lives of thousands?"

Misha turns up his palms. "What are all wars about? Resources, territory, power."

I narrow my eyes at him. "Specifically?"

"The Goblin Mountains that divide the courts are split down the middle by the River of Ice. The mountains to the east of the river are part of the Unseelie Court and the mountains to the west, the Seelie. The Great Fae War was waged when the golden fae tried to take the entire mountain range as their own."

"What about a mountain range is worth losing so many soldiers?"

"At first glance, nothing. The treacherous mountains are so sacred that the goblins themselves won't use their magic to bring fae beyond the foothills. But beneath those mountains, you can find our most precious resources." He nods at my chest, where the necklace from Sebastian still sits. I don't let myself think about why I haven't taken it off. "The fire gems."

I pull the necklace from beneath my top and study the softly glowing gem. "What do they do?"

"They make everything . . . better. Stronger. The fire gems are magical amplifiers." He holds up a hand and wiggles his middle finger, where a canary yellow stone sparkles in the evening light. "Wearing one can increase an individual's magical range and strength several degrees."

I scoff. "Knowing how the fae feel about magic, I'm surprised you're not all dressed head to toe in them."

He shrugs and looks almost bashful when he says, "I suppose we would be if there were benefits to wearing more than one, but wearing one fire gem amplifies an individual's power the same as one hundred."

"And what? There aren't enough to go around? Is that why they're fighting over them?"

"The fire gems found beneath those mountains are not abundant, nor are they infinite. For an individual, they are valuable, but in great amounts, fire gems are for far more than personal use. Our ancestors hoarded them, gifting them to their priestesses, using them to strengthen borders and to create tonics the likes of which could never be achieved without the fire gems."

"Like what?" I ask, tucking the gem back into my shirt.

"Like the Potion of Life, or the restorative potion the golden queen ingested to survive the damage of the curse. Like the toxin they injected into those children to steal their powers. As an amplifier, the magic of one gem serves us for hundreds of years, but those potions and tonics take hundreds of gems and are for one-time use. By all rights, the queen's reserves should've been depleted after the last two decades, but she's been vigilant in her efforts to gather more." Anger flashes in his eyes. "She's not satisfied with what's available on her side of the mountain range, so she's going to resume the mission of her grandfather, who started the Great Fae War to claim the Unseelie's side of the Goblin Mountains as his own."

"He didn't want the shadow fae to have access to the fire gems."

Misha nods. His eyes go dark as he turns his head to look out at the bright, sunny day. "Generations of Seelie rulers have sent their armies to fight for the land east of the River of Ice that cuts the mountain range down the middle, believing they could claim the land as their own. Countless golden fae have died for that mission, and countless shadow fae have died defending those lands. And now my sources tell me that history is repeating itself. I fear that this time the Court of the Moon will be too weak to protect their territory."

Has Arya always been like this—so cold and heartless? Or did Oberon's rejection break something in her?

"Perhaps a little of both," Misha says, answering my unspoken question, and this time I don't even complain about the intrusion. "She's the youngest ruler her kingdom has ever had. She never should've been allowed to take the throne when she did."

I shake my head. "War, fire gems, the queen—what does any of this have to do with me?"

"You alone hold sway over both Sebastian and Finn. You alone hold the power of the Unseelie crown. You could be the key to uniting the courts and helping protect future generations. If you will help me, help *them,* we can—"

"No." My chair screeches as I shove it back and jump to my feet. "I will not be manipulated again."

"No one is manipulating you. I am *asking* for your help. You think this is all about power. You think that nothing you do will help people like you—fae who are victims of their own circumstances."

"Get out of my head," I growl. I'm so mad I'm shaking. I'm angry and I'm frustrated and I'm so *sick* of being used so that these spoiled males and their twisted courts can get the power they crave.

"There's more I need to show you, Abriella." He extends an arm, and another hawk swoops down and perches on his wrist. "There's more to see. Don't you want to know what happened after the throne rejected Sebastian?"

I shake my head. "No. I don't want to see it. I don't care. I'm done with faerie politics. They can destroy the whole damn realm for all I care. Figure it out without me."

I turn on my heel and storm back to my room, even though it's not really mine. Nothing's mine, and I have nowhere to go.

I lied to Misha.

I said I didn't care, but we both know that's not true. I care more than I want to. My problem is I don't *trust*—not Misha, not Finn, not even the emotions I'm feeling through my bond with Sebastian. I don't trust anyone and don't plan on that changing anytime soon.

Unfortunately, unlike Misha, I can't read thoughts to find out someone's true intentions.

Since I'm not sure how Misha's power works, it's not like I can use my shadows to spy on him. For all I know, he'd sense my thoughts even if he couldn't see me in the room, rendering my ability to hide in shadows useless.

The second he mentioned that Finn was the one who wanted to help the commoners in the Unseelie realm, I felt myself softening, listening a little more intently. Then he spoke of protecting future generations, and I realized I was being played. Misha is no different from the others—telling me exactly what I need to hear to get me to act exactly as he wants me to act.

But I won't be played again. The only thing I can trust is that no one can be trusted.

I collapse on my bed, not bothering to remove my boots, and try to think. Part of me wants to listen to Misha's plan. That part wants to know how I can help Finn and Sebastian avoid another costly war. I want to know what I can do to keep the queen from claiming more power. An image of that awful "camp" flashes in my mind, and the reminder of the children in cages sends a surge of anger through me.

Rolling my face into my pillow, I release a muffled scream. I have nowhere to go, so if having a room here is contingent on helping Misha, I don't know what I'll do. I just need . . . *time.* Time to get more information. Time to make my own decisions.

Maybe I can't spy on Misha, but Sebastian doesn't have those powers. If I blend to shadow around him, I might be able to get some of the information I need.

I hop out of bed and rush to the door. When I pull it open, Misha's standing on the other side, his fist raised, as if he's about to knock.

I cock out a hip and fold my arms. "Why knock? Didn't you know I was coming to the door?"

Dropping his hand, he tucks it into his pocket. "I'm not a seer."

"Is that supposed to put me at ease?"

"I don't *try* to read your thoughts — well, not every time — but sometimes you shove them out there." He sighs. "I came to apologize for pushing you. My wife was kind enough to tell me the error of my ways. You've been through a lot, and as Amira pointed out, no one in your position would be ready to entertain the idea that they could help fix a problem that, at its roots, is centuries old."

My shoulders sag. "Thank you." I've never met Amira, but I like her already, not because I trust what she's saying, but because this is an excuse to buy more time while I figure out who I can trust. "Where is she — the queen? I'd like to meet her."

His brows lift in surprise — my interest in his wife seems to please him — but he shakes his head. "I'm afraid she's on her way out. She was heading to the Unseelie settlement in the valley for the evening."

"Oh." Maybe I can't trust Misha yet, but that doesn't change all the good he and Amira have done by bringing the Unseelie refugees here. "Does she spend a lot of time there?"

"A bit." He shrugs. "You were clearly on your way out just now. Do you need anything? I could escort you somewhere, or your handmaiden could take you if you've had enough of my face for one night."

I crack a smile. I might be bitter and hardened, but I suppose I'm not immune to Misha's charms. "Do you have a goblin in the palace? I want to go see Sebastian."

His eyebrows raise, but it's the only sign of his surprise. "Why?"

"Well, I'd like to . . ." I bite my lip, trying to think of a good way to explain that I need to gather as much information as I can.

"Ah," Misha says, cracking a smile. "We call that *spying*."

I glare.

He chuckles. "Please don't misunderstand. I absolutely approve."

"Fine. I want to spy. I want to see what he's doing now that he's realized he can't sit on the throne."

"He's taken up residence at the Unseelie palace. He's managed to get enough of his guard in with him that Finn and his people have . . . evacuated for the time being."

"Fine, but I want to know what he's saying when he doesn't think I'm listening."

Misha nods. "I'll send Storm."

I shake my head. "I need to see for myself."

He folds his arms. "Have you forgotten that you're bonded to Sebastian? That he has an awareness of how you feel and *where you are* at all times?"

"No. I haven't forgotten. I can't forget." I touch my fingertips to my temples. "He's here." I press my palm to my chest. "And here." *And I feel him when I curl up in bed to sleep.* But I can't bring myself to admit that part. "You said you could teach me to block—"

"It takes practice. And patience—and a whole lot of energy you simply don't have right now, but I promise to give you a lesson first thing in the morning."

He's right. I haven't been out of bed more than a couple of hours, and I'm already exhausted and looking forward to climbing beneath the blankets again. But with sleep comes dreams, and in dreams I risk opening myself up to Finn or Sebastian.

"Tomorrow," Misha says. "After you've slept and had a chance to digest what we've discussed today, we can practice blocking, but only with the caveat that most bonded pairs can feel each other's presence more powerfully the closer they are. Even after years of training, you might not be able to spy on your bonded partner undetected."

I nod. "Okay." Even if I can never spy on Sebastian, I want to learn whatever Misha can teach me. Feeling Sebastian right there all the time is making me weak. If he walked in the door right now, I'm not sure I'd be able to prevent myself from diving into his arms.

"As for tonight," Misha says, "would you like a proper tour of my palace?"

I would. I've never seen any place as breathtaking as the parts of Castle Craige I've seen so far. Yet that's not how I want to spend my evening. "Could I go with Amira? To . . . the camps?" I bite my lip. I want assurance that Misha is a good male, but do I want to know that for myself or for the sake of the vulnerable?

"Oh. I'm not sure." Misha says. He's silent for a long time, his gaze distant, and I wonder if he's trying to get me to backpedal and say I don't need to go.

"If you're trying to hide something—"

Suddenly he nods and smiles at me. "Amira's still in the stables. She said she'll wait, and we can all ride together."

I frown and look around. "You just . . . *talked* to her?"

His smile stretches wider. "Indeed." He taps his temple, as if that explains everything, then says, "Can you ride in that or would you like to change?"

I look down to the leather pants and boots I put on earlier. "This will do."

"Good." He nods, already turning and heading for the stairs. "Amira says to grab a cloak. It will be dark by the time we return, and it gets chilly when the sun sets."

I spot a black cloak hanging by the door and grab it before

jogging after him. He has such long legs that he's already at the top of the stairs by the time I reach him. "Will I be able to do that with Sebastian?"

I'm not sure how I'd feel about that. On the one hand, it's all I can do to ignore the constant hum of his emotions pecking at my consciousness. On the other hand, it would be pretty amazing to be able to have a conversation with *anyone* when they're not even under the same roof.

Misha shakes his head. "I'm not privy to the details of the golden prince's powers, nor do I truly know the extent of yours, but as far as I'm aware, you two can't speak telepathically."

"So how the bond works is dependent on one's powers?"

At the bottom of the stairs, he turns left, leading me out of the palace and onto another staircase. There are stairs all around us, I realize, all built into the face of the mountain. It's as if Castle Craige is built on the highest point in this area of the Wild Fae Lands, and to get to anything beyond it, once must descend.

Misha looks at me and cocks his head to the side. *This isn't a product of any bond,* he says in my mind, as clear as if he were saying the words aloud. *This is my gift. As is picking up your response.*

"Oh. That's . . ." *Creepy* is the first word that comes to mind, but I'm too polite to say it.

Misha chuckles, hearing the word anyway. "I'm curious, though," he says. "Yesterday it seemed like you wanted to cut off the emotional awareness between you and Sebastian, and now you're asking how you can make it more . . . precise—how you can have a conversation through it."

I shrug. "Can't blame me for my curiosity."

"But which is it? Do you want to shut him out or be able to communicate freely with him?"

My instinct is to declare that I absolutely want to shut him out—to never know his thoughts or emotions again, to never see him or think of his face again. But I realize that's the heartbreak speaking. "I think both," I say thoughtfully. "I want to be able to shut him out at will, but I'll admit I'm intrigued by the possibility of communicating with someone without speaking. For me it's about having the choice. *I* want to be the one in control of my own mind and feelings."

"That's fair," he says, nodding.

I straighten and have to bite back a smile as an idea occurs to me. "How far does your gift work?"

"It depends. If the mind I'm tapping into is weak or has made a choice to intentionally strengthen our mental connection, I've been known to speak mind-to-mind from one side of a court to the other. But if I'm trying to read the thoughts of a shielded mind, I have to be in the same room, and even that won't work if the individual has trained well."

"What about with humans?"

He smirks. "Human minds are typically easy to read."

"Could you . . . Do you think you could check on my sister? Make sure she's okay?"

He shakes his head. "My power doesn't work between realms, I'm afraid."

"Oh. Of course." I study the thin layer of dust on my boots.

"I could send Storm so you could see her for yourself."

I don't like the idea of having any of his creatures spying on my sister, and my mistrust must show on my face because he amends, "If you don't trust what you would see through him, you could send a letter through my goblin."

"Really?"

"It would be my pleasure. I know what it's like to be disconnected from a younger sibling." He gives me a sad smile.

"Thank you so much. Theoretically, I know she's okay, but now that I'm fae . . ." I search for the words, but my eyes burn, and I have to swallow hard to keep sudden unwanted tears from spilling over. "When I visited my sister with Sebastian, it never occurred to me it might be the last time I'd see her."

"Would you like to bring her here?"

Yes, please. The words want to burst out of me, but I hold them back. I want Jas with me more than I want anything, but I can't. I'll never forget the terror in her eyes when I suggested that she come back to the Faerie realm with me. Whatever she endured while imprisoned by Mordeus left a mark on her, made my cheerful, trusting sister fearful of all fae. I won't take away her choice the way Sebastian took away mine.

"No," I finally say. "No. She's where she wants to be. I'll send her a letter." I can't imagine what I'll say, but I'll find a way to reach out to her without making her worry about me.

Misha slows; then we stop walking altogether. When he turns to study me, there is such raw compassion on his face that I have to turn away from him for a beat to find my composure.

"It won't always be this way," he says softly. "The loneliness isn't unfamiliar to you, but someday . . . I promise someday it will be."

I stare at my boots. "I thought you weren't a seer."

"I'm not. But I *am* very, very old, and I recognize a good soul when I meet one, and good souls are never alone for long." He squeezes my shoulder, and then I hear the scuff of steps as he walks away.

CHAPTER SEVEN

I FOLLOW MISHA QUIETLY, EMBARRASSED that I let my emotions get the better of me. By the time we enter the stables, I've collected myself enough to pull back my shoulders and lift my chin.

"This is Amira," Misha says, waving his hand toward the tall female saddling her horse.

Tossing me a smile over her shoulder, his wife tightens a few straps before turning to me fully. I'm not sure if I'm more surprised by how genuine her smile seems or that she's saddling her own horse.

She's tall — as tall as Misha — with gentle brown eyes and skin as dark as the night sky. Her dark hair is cut short, cropped close to her scalp in a style that draws attention to her big eyes and the shining amethyst studs lining her delicately pointed ears.

Stepping forward, I extend a hand. "I'm Abriella. It's nice to meet you."

She takes my hand in both of hers. "It's my pleasure," she says, her voice low and melodious. "Finn and Pretha have told me so much about you."

I stiffen, thinking of her visit to Finn's house — back before I understood the curse and before I knew Finn and Sebastian were both after a crown I didn't know I wore.

"I'm glad to see you're well," she says, dipping her head with a deference that surprises me. She's *queen* of the Wild Fae. All I am is a former human who disrupted the future of an entire realm. If I'd never been saved by Oberon . . .

Misha clears his throat, and I flinch at the reminder of his gifts. I might as well wear my wretchedness on my chest for him to see.

"Are you sure you're okay with me tagging along tonight?"

Amira's eyes light up. "Of course! I'd love to take you, and the ride will give you a chance to see some of our lands as well."

"Thank you," I say.

"Pick a horse, Abriella," Misha says, lifting both hands, palms up, in the direction of the stalls. "Our stable hands are on their dinner break, but we can help you with your saddle if you need."

There are dozens of horses, but a black mare tosses her silky silver-streaked mane as I approach, as if she's trying to get my attention.

"That's Two Star," Amira says, hoisting a saddle onto her shoulder and heading toward me.

"She's beautiful," I say, stroking the mare's nose.

"She's very special, and she knows it," Misha says, saddling his own horse, a chestnut stallion I'd need a ladder to mount.

Amira lifts the latch and opens the stall. "She's named for the silver markings on her hindquarters. There are very few like her, all from the same line — descendants of Queen's Mab's steed."

That's the second time tonight I've heard mention of the old faerie queen from the legends. "Queen Mab was . . . real?" I ask, helping Amira put on the saddle and bridle. I'm only working from memory of all the times I watched this done in Sebastian's stables, but Amira quietly leads me through the steps.

"Oh, very real and very beloved by her people," Misha says. He saddles his own horse with the unconscious movements of someone who's done this thousands of times. Given how old these two likely are, they probably have. "It was her line that ruled from the Throne of Shadows before Finn's grandfather stepped in."

"Did Finn's family . . . overthrow them?" I ask.

Amira purses her lips and shakes her head. Her brown eyes look sad when she says, "Finn's grandfather Kairyn was second to Mab's last living descendant, Queen Reé, and he took the throne after she was assassinated."

How convenient for him.

"Kairyn was devoted to his queen," Misha says, leading his horse from its stall. "He was her tethered match and would've died for Queen Reé or any of her heirs."

I bow my head, ashamed for my assumption.

"It's okay," Amira says, her hand brushing mine. Her gentle smile puts me at ease even though I get the feeling that her gifts put her in tune with my emotions. "With what you've seen of our kind, no one came blame you for assuming the worst, but the loss of Mab's line was devastating for anyone in this realm who didn't want to see the Court of the Sun extend their rule beyond their own borders."

"Is that why the fae began having children with humans?" I

ask. "To have more heirs? To keep the lines from dying out so easily?"

"Mab had many children—some with humans, some with fae," Misha says. "And her children had children, and so on. The line was blessed with fertility."

I frown. "So what happened to them?"

Amira holds my gaze for a long moment, and I can practically see the heartbreak in her eyes when she says, "The golden fae killed them all. Even the babes."

We ride miles from the palace down a mountain path that is rocky, wooded, and so steep that my thighs and core ache from the work of keeping me atop my mount. Every time another wave of exhaustion hits me, I wonder why I'm not back at the palace, resting in my bed. I don't know how to decide who I can trust in this realm, but you can learn a lot from the way someone treats those weaker than they are, those who have nothing to offer them. Tonight will tell me volumes about my hosts.

On the ride down the mountain, the king and queen continually refer to the camps for the shadow fae as a "settlement," but it's not until we arrive that I understand why. What they've set up for the Unseelie refugees is more like a small village than a temporary camp.

I expected primitive conditions, but the small straw-roofed huts that sit in neat rows on either side of the road look far better than the "adequate" conditions Misha described.

When the road comes to a T, Misha dismounts before helping

his wife off her horse and then me off mine. Two smiling boys with tiny horns and long dark hair lead our horses away, leaving us in what seems to be the settlement's common area. There's a pavilion lined with tables — a common dining area, I imagine — and, beyond that, a playground where three children toss a ball between them.

"Our school is here," Misha says, leading me through the pavilion to a line of buildings on the other side of the square. They're made of stone and look very old. "And the infirmary is there. That's also where we do intake for the new residents, since so many of them need to see the healer."

"Is that where the children are reunited with their parents?" I ask.

Something like sadness flashes across Misha's face. "Only when we're very lucky."

"This settlement is one of many throughout our lands," Amira explains behind me. Turning, I see that a line of children has formed in front of her, and she's crouched down and hugging them one by one. The sight reminds me of my first schoolteacher in Elora, back before the fire, when our family was still whole. Mrs. Bennett was warm and kind, and anytime my friends and I spotted her outside of school, we raced to be the first to receive one of her hugs.

I wanted to use this visit to judge how much I could trust this couple, and if Amira had known that and planned accordingly, she couldn't have set a better scene. But this wasn't planned. These children aren't pretending. I can see that the Wild Fae queen spends a lot of time here, and the children are truly happy to see her. She doesn't rush them, but gives each one the moment they were waiting for.

Misha steps to my side. "When we open the portals to bring the refugees here, our goal is to remove them from the Seelie lands," he says. "Only once they're safe do we begin the task of reuniting families. It takes time, though, and often the children are too sick to travel right away."

"Why not keep the refugees in one settlement?"

Misha shakes his head. "Foolish."

Amira hugs the last child, then gives me a smile, as if she's trying to soften her husband's harsh response. "It would be easier in many ways," she says, standing and joining us, "but it would make it too easy for the golden queen to attack. We have members of our guard assigned to organize communications between the settlements and keep logs of the residents within them. Reunion is always the goal, but it's not always possible."

A little boy whom I'd seen getting a hug from Amira moments ago paces back and forth between us and the pavilion, a scowl twisting his face.

"Some of their parents didn't make it," Misha explains softly. "And many of the adults give us fake names. Their years under Mordeus's rule have made it too hard for them to trust anyone. The challenges are endless."

I swallow hard, imagining all the orphans wondering if their parents are alive. I know what that's like.

"There's a market over there," Misha says, pointing to a row of stalls in the distance. "It opens every morning and closes at high sun. The trade is healthy, and the stall rent helps us pay a portion of the costs to keep the settlement running smoothly."

"You should come back for market sometime," Amira says. "Whether you appreciate fine arts and crafts or just enjoy good food — there's something for everyone."

A female with golden skin and short-cropped white hair approaches us and drops into a low curtsy at the sight of Misha and Amira. "Your Majesties."

"Leta, this is our guest, Abriella," Misha says. "Abriella, I'd like you to meet Leta."

"A pleasure to meet you," Leta says, bowing her head.

"The pleasure is mine," I say, shifting awkwardly. I've lived most of my life in the shadows, avoiding notice. The deference of the maids at the Golden Palace always made me uncomfortable, and this is no different.

"Leta runs the infirmary here," Amira explains. "Many arrive from Arya's camps wounded, and Leta nurses them to health. We are lucky to have her."

Leta's cheeks flare red. "Thank you, Your Majesty. I'm honored to serve." She swallows. "I'm sorry to interrupt Lady Abriella's tour, but if you have a moment, there's something you should see."

Misha and his wife exchange a look, and then he nods. "After you."

Leta leads the way to the infirmary, and we follow into the stone building and to a room in the back, where a row of beds is filled with sleeping children.

Misha frowns as he surveys them. "Have so many younglings taken ill?" he asks.

Leta shakes her head. "We don't know what it is. It's like they're sleeping, but . . ."

He looks at her, waiting, and she turns up her palms. "They don't wake up. Their breathing is shallow, their body temperature low, like they've entered some sort of odd hibernation."

"Something contagious?" Misha asks. "Is it spreading?"

"Only among the children. The first were brought in yesterday and two more this morning. None of the adults show signs."

Amira crosses to one of the beds in the center of the row where a young boy with short dark hair sleeps, curled on his side. If it weren't for Leta's explanation, I'd think he and the others were napping.

These children are different from the ones Lark showed me in my dream, but I can't ignore the similarities, and I still don't understand what she was trying to tell me.

They're looking for you. You need to come home.

Did she mean this will be my home? That there's something I can do to help these children? Then why did the image she showed me differ so much?

Amira brushes the boy's hair from his forehead. "Hey, little one."

"That's Cail," Leta says. "He's three. He arrived at the settlement with his older sister about a month ago."

"How's the sister?" Misha asks.

"She seems fine. She's worried about her brother, of course, but she shows no signs of illness."

Amira drops to her knees so she's face-to-face with the sleeping boy. "Cail? Are you in there?"

"We've tried everything," the nurse says. "Perhaps it's some strange sickness, but I've never seen children sleep so soundly for so long."

Amira strokes the boy's hair one final time before standing. "I feel him in there," she says. "He's not hurting, but it's odd. I've never felt anything like it. Please keep us updated?"

Leta nods. "Of course. I am sorry to bother you, but I appreciate the time."

"It's no bother at all," Amira says, taking one of Leta's hands in hers.

Leta's shoulders visibly sag, and her breathing steadies. "Thank you," she breathes.

Outside, someone starts screaming.

Misha and Amira rush from the infirmary, and I follow them. The scowling little boy from earlier is standing alone in the street, screeching, as if he's being attacked. The moment I see him, his terror washes over me as if it were my own.

Amira drops to her knees before him and wraps him in her arms. He continues shrieking, but he buries his face in her chest, as if he's searching for comfort there.

The people around us look their way once or twice but don't seem particularly alarmed by the child's outburst.

Amira doesn't pick him up, doesn't tell him to be quiet. She strokes his back gently and repeatedly as he continues to shriek and scream.

Fear swirls around me, caging me in, and I feel . . . *helpless.* Utterly helpless at the sound of this child's devastating cries. "What can I do?" I ask Misha.

He places a hand on my arm, and Amira meets my eyes and gives a subtle shake of her head.

Nothing. I can do nothing. Like always.

I step to the side. If I can't do anything else, at least I can be out of the way.

The boy finally stops screaming, and as the silence falls, the fear in my blood washes away as if it were never there. Amira brings him into her arms, resting him against her shoulder as she stands.

"Be right back," she mouths to me.

I nod and watch as she carries the boys into a cottage several doors down. "What's wrong with him?" I ask.

"We were able to rescue some children before they were put into the camps," Misha says, watching her go. "That was always the plan—to find them as they came through the border and open the portal to transport them to safety here before the Arya's guard could capture them. But Mordeus and the queen were both watching us. Mordeus didn't want his subjects leaving, and the queen wanted any shadow fae caught in her lands to be working in her camps or dead. Our efforts at organization were undercut at every turn by our need for secrecy." He nods at the house where Amira disappeared with the child. "Far too many of the children ended up spending weeks in the camps before we got to them, and some have never recovered from those days."

"What did she do to them?" I ask.

He shakes his head. "We don't know everything, but I know she sent them down into the mines."

"The mines?"

He studies me for a long beat, and I wonder if he's reading all my thoughts, seeing all my heartache over the reality of these divided families. "I told you what's to be found beneath the Goblin Mountains."

"Fire gems," I whisper.

Misha rocks back on his heels, crossing his arms. "She's been sending Unseelie children into those mines for twenty years. If she hadn't maintained her supply, the price of her curse would've killed her long before you broke it. She claimed that she captured the Unseelie as a warning—that she was trying to keep them out of her lands to protect her people—but the truth is that she needed those children to retrieve the gems so she could survive the curse."

"Why Unseelie children?" I ask. "Because they're small? Aren't they defenseless?"

"It's not just that children are small, although that helps. It's that the young have an innate ability to sense the fire gems' presence within the walls. It's an awareness that fades with years. And why Unseelie? Perhaps because of their gifts with the darkness, or perhaps because her heart is filled with vile hate. Some never made it back out, and the ones who did . . ." He shakes his head and speaks the rest directly into my mind. *Most adults would die in the face of the terrors beneath those mountains.*

I'm almost afraid to ask, but the residue of the child's fear still clings to me. "And what's that? What's waiting in that darkness?"

"The monsters that dwell beneath the Goblin Mountains . . . well, one cannot access great power without facing great horrors."

"But she didn't face them. She sent in children to do it for her," I say darkly, and rage boils in my blood. In the mortal realm, children are tricked into contracts that lock them into lives of servitude, and here children are sent underground to face unfathomable monsters. Is it so unreasonable to believe the powerful should be *protecting* those most vulnerable?

Maybe Misha is manipulating me for his own political scheming. Maybe I truly cannot trust anyone in this realm. But that child's fear was real, and I'll do anything to keep the golden queen from gaining more power and exploiting more children. In the human realm, I always wished I had some way to protect the weak and vulnerable — I still think about that stack of contracts in Creighton Gorst's vault. Here, I actually do have a way, and I refuse to waste it just because I'm struggling with my own broken heart.

"She sent in *children,*" I say again. "Sacrificed children."

"Yes," Misha says gravely.

"Death is too good for her," I breathe, not even thinking before letting the words out of my mouth.

But Misha smiles. "It certainly is." Blowing out a breath, he shakes his head, as if clearing away some haunting image.

And what more might she do if she's successful in expanding her territory into the Unseelie lands? What might come of the children in that part of the territory if her greed goes unchecked?

I frown. "It seems like everyone suspects that the queen killed her parents. I've never understood that."

"Mmm." Misha's eyes go wide, almost intrigued, but his response is carefully noncommittal.

"That can't be true, right?" I ask. "I was told that a crown couldn't be passed to the heir if the heir murdered for it. So if that's true, then how did Arya get the crown?"

"That's the question," he says. "And many believe that if we could find the answer, we'd know Arya's weakness. But we don't know." He shrugs. "I somehow doubt she just got lucky."

I swallow hard. "I should've killed her when I had the chance."

He shakes his head. "You never had the chance, Abriella. Don't let brief proximity fool you. She goes nowhere without dozens of the most powerful and fiercely loyal guards. If you'd tried, particularly as a human, you would've failed."

I sigh. Maybe I shouldn't find that comforting, but I do.

"Come with me." He leads me several doors down to the school he pointed out earlier. Its doors are wide-open, and there is a cluster of children playing in the little flower bed out front.

Inside, a dozen chairs face a large chalkboard, and in the corner a silver-haired female sits at a large desk that faces the room. She stands when she sees Misha, and he waves.

"Hello, Della. We're just here to look at the children's art."

"Anytime, of course." Her cheeks are bright pink, as if his presence alone is both elating and embarrassing. She can't seem to make eye contact, but I don't think it's because she's not allowed. I think she's just awed by the presence of the Wild Fae king.

He nods to the wall behind the desks, where pictures of all

shapes and sizes hang. I step closer, fascinated by what I see. Drawings of families, of starry night skies, of mountains and rivers and flowers. But the ones I can't stop staring at are of monsters — drawings of eyeless and sharp-toothed beasts that are rudimentary yet also look like they're emerging from the paper.

"This is Abriella," Misha says, and I force myself to look away from the art and turn to greet her.

The woman steps forward and offers a hand. "It's always lovely to meet a friend of Misha's."

"She's not just a friend," Misha says. "She's the one who killed Mordeus."

The teacher's eyes go big. "Oh gods! I didn't realize . . ." She drops to one knee, still clinging to my hand, and brings my knuckles to her forehead. "This is such an honor. Thank you, thank you. You have no idea what you've done for my people. We are so indebted to you. Please tell me how I can honor you on this day and each day ahead."

"I . . ." I look to Misha, unsure what to say. I thought Leta's greeting was uncomfortable, but this . . .

Misha shrugs, as if he's not personally responsible for putting me in this awkward situation.

"Please stand," I say. "You owe me nothing."

"I owe you everything. Mordeus killed my parents, my brothers, my bonded partner, and my . . ." She chokes on the word, but I already know it without her saying. Mordeus isn't just the reason she had to leave her home. He killed her child.

Would she be kneeling if she knew that more unrest was coming? Would she thank me if she understood that by taking the path that allows me to stand here, I've doomed her people to more of the same? Perhaps the villain will be different this time around, but without anyone on the Throne of Shadows, the Unseelie Court doesn't stand a chance against the queen.

"He was a monster," she whispers.

"There are many monsters in this world," I say, thinking of the creatures under those mountains, of the queen. "I killed only one, and while I'm glad he's dead, he's not the last. Please stand."

She obeys, reluctantly, but her head remains bowed. "The prophecy told us you would come, but I wasn't sure I'd live to see it."

I cut my gaze to Misha. *What prophecy?*

I'm not sure what she's referring to. Could be a distorted version of several different tales about mortals born to slay wicked kings.

Huh. Misha's magic may be creepy, but it's convenient.

Isn't it? Misha's deep voice asks in my head.

Amira steps into the schoolhouse and smiles when she spots us. "There you are."

"Is everything okay?" Misha asks his wife.

Amira nods, and when the silence stretches, I realize they're having a silent conversation of their own.

Della finally releases my hand and steps back, her head still bowed.

"Do you ever need help?" I shift awkwardly, unsure what I'm offering.

Della finally lifts her head. "Help with . . . what do you mean, milady?"

Misha and Amira are staring at me now, and I feel foolish, but I continue. "In the classroom. If you ever needed someone to read with the children or—"

"Oh, you don't have to do that," Della says at the same time Misha says, "That would be amazing, Abriella. Why don't you return tomorrow?"

Della's cheeks are bright red, but she nods. "It would be an honor."

"Come, Abriella," Amira says, leading me from the building. "Allow us to show you the rest of the settlement."

"It was a pleasure to meet you," I call over my shoulder to Della.

"The pleasure was mine, milady."

I hustle away as fast as I can.

"They always need help in the classroom," Misha says, joining us outside.

The three of us walk together, and I try to breathe, but the more I think, the smaller my lungs become. The sky is colored by the vibrant rainbow of pastels that trails in the wake of the setting sun, but as beautiful as it is, I wish night were here. I wish I could see the stars.

"She thinks I saved her," I blurt when we've walked a good distance from the school. "But it's my fault they can't go home yet. It's my fault their throne—their whole damn kingdom is broken."

Amira stops in front of me, turns, and takes my hand. "Abriella," she says, and with her voice, her touch, my anger and self-loathing washes away, replaced by warmth and . . . *peace.*

My eyes go wide, meeting hers, and she smiles.

It's a lovely gift, isn't it? Misha's voice asks in my mind, and I nod without thinking how odd it might look.

"Do you think these people would be better off if you'd let Mordeus live?" Amira asks. "If you'd never come to our realm in search of your sister?"

I shake my head. I can't think about Jas. Saving her wasn't a choice. I simply had to. But what happened after—

Amira's eyes remain locked on mine. "No one knew what would happen. This is *not* your fault."

"They want to go home. Can't you feel it?" I swallow hard, not even sure what I'm saying. I don't understand this feeling. I didn't even realize I had it until just now.

"*I* can feel it," she says, cocking her head to the side. "But that's my gift. I'm an empath. But you're saying you can too?"

"It's in the air, like a cry for help."

She looks to Misha, and they exchange a long look before she turns back to me. "And what am I feeling right now?" She holds my gaze, and when I shake my head, she takes my hand and presses my palm against her chest. "Do you feel *me?*"

"No." I shake my head again. "I'm sorry. I . . ."

"It's Oberon's power," Misha says. "The power of the crown must give her a connection to them."

"That's one theory," Amira says. She looks to the setting sun for a beat. "We should head back. It will be cold soon."

As we collect our horses, I let myself feel the emotions in the air. There's heartache and loneliness, homesickness, but there's also joy here. A feeling of security. *They're safe.* And that tells me more about Misha and Amira than any conversation ever could.

As the stable hand helps me mount my horse, I catch myself thinking of Finn. He's Unseelie. Does that mean I'd be able to feel him too?

I wonder if I'll ever get to find out.

CHAPTER EIGHT

MISHA'S LIPS ARE SOFT AGAINST my knuckles when he stops at my door back at the palace. "Sleep well, Princess," he says, slowly releasing my hand.

Ignoring the awkwardness I feel at his gesture, I shake my head. "I'm not sure I can. There's too much going on in my mind." Between the realization that I could feel the Unseelie at the settlement, my own emotions, and what I'm constantly picking up from Sebastian, I was reeling the entire ride back. "It's so overwhelming, I can't even trust my own thoughts. Did you know—that I could *feel* the Unseelie like that with Oberon's power?"

He slides his hands into his pockets. "Not at all, but there's a lot I don't understand about your magic. I do know this: you're more powerful than you realize. More than even I would've guessed."

I cut him a look. "Obviously."

He snorts. "And so humble too."

I shake my head. "That's not what I mean. My power comes entirely from Oberon, from the Unseelie throne. I'm not being pompous. I'm simply agreeing that I know nothing about the depth and extent of this power." Before tonight I didn't even know

I had any empathic abilities at all—though I suppose I'd used them at the queen's camps.

"Hmm." He takes a step back and looks me over. "That's an interesting assumption."

"It's an accurate assumption. Where else would it come from?"

"Honestly?" He draws in a deep breath. "I don't know. But I'm trying to figure it out. Finn wondered the same thing."

I straighten at the name. I can't think of the shadow prince without my chest becoming a tangle of conflicting emotions. "But he knew," I whisper. "He knew where my power came from."

"He knew his father's magic. Was quite familiar with it. So he was the first to recognize that you wielded something different. Something . . . more."

I somehow doubt it. I think I surprise these people so much because they never expected a human girl to have any sort of power, but I don't feel like arguing. "I'm tired."

He nods. "I asked Genny to draw you a bath. It's waiting."

"Thank you. For that and for taking me along tonight."

"It was my pleasure."

"I'm not sure I ever properly thanked you for giving me a place to stay." I bow my head. "You didn't have to do a thing for me, but you have anyway."

He chuckles. "I have my own reasons."

I'm sure he does. They all do.

"Sleep well, Princess."

I step inside my room but hesitate before closing the door. "Why do you call me that?"

Misha's eyes light up, and he grins. "Only because calling you

Queen would be inaccurate," he says, then turns and disappears down the corridor.

"What nonsense," I mutter, turning into my room. A fresh sleeping gown waits on the bed, and I can feel the humidity in the air from the warm bath that waits in the connected bathing room.

I quickly strip out of my clothes and head to the tub, where I sink into the hot water, sighing as it envelops my aching thighs. When everything goes quiet around me, I feel Sebastian so intensely—his grief and sadness—that I want to cry. I miss him. I miss believing that he loved me, that I could trust him.

Hoping to keep my hair dry, I tie it up as best I can, but several locks are too short to stay and they fall in my face and around my neck. The curls tighten in the steam rising off the bath. I wash the rest of myself quickly, as if getting out of this tub will help me escape these emotions and this overwhelming loneliness.

By the time I've dressed in my sleeping gown and am under the covers of my bed, the light of the rising moon slants into the bedroom windows. Exhaustion pulls at me, but every time I close my eyes and try to relax, I picture that little boy screaming in the middle of the road, remember his horror racing through my own veins.

I don't know why Misha thinks that I, of all people, could unite a divided court. Any loyalties Sebastian and Finn feel toward me are just complicated by the fact that I have something they both need. That doesn't mean I could get them to work together, or that I would have any idea how. But I can't deny that the queen can't go unchecked. Not after seeing those camps. Not after hearing that little boy's screams of terror tonight.

So maybe I can't do everything. Maybe I can't heal a broken land or mediate power struggles, but I could do something about those camps if I knew where to find them. And *that* would be worth asking for Sebastian's help.

I finger a loose strand of hair at my temple and smile as the light catches on the threads of the goblin bracelet Bakken gave me. Dozens and dozens of thin silvery threads visible to no one but me glitter iridescent in the moonlight. I hop out of bed and find my knife. Using the sharp edge against the back of my scalp like a razor, I sheer off a short lock of hair and snap a thread on my goblin bracelet.

Bakken appears almost immediately. It's the first time I've seen him since that night at the Unseelie palace. Then, with blood still on my hands from slaying Mordeus, I'd had to sheer off all my hair up to my jaw to get the goblin to take me to Finn's catacombs.

I'm hoping tonight he'll work for less.

"Fire Girl," he says, grinning at me. "What do you have for me?"

I open my palm to show him the tuft of short hairs I've shaved from the back of my head.

Bakken scowls. "Don't insult me, Fire Girl."

"I'm mean no offense," I promise. "But this is all I have, and I need to go to the Unseelie palace."

"I don't work for free."

"Consider this a deposit," I blurt, then swallow, hatching a plan on the spot. "How would you like a lock of Prince Ronan's hair for the return trip?"

Bakken narrows his bulging eyes. He wants what I'm offering. "How do you intend to obtain the prince's hair?"

"Leave that to me," I say, a little breathless. I think this is going to work. "Please?"

It's only as Bakken reaches for my wrist that I remember I'm dressed in nothing more than a thin sleeping gown.

Bakken brings me directly to a low-lit bedroom and vanishes again before I've even fully materialized. This isn't the lavishly furnished bedroom I appeared in when going through the portal in the queen's armoire. This one overlooks a rushing river flowing through a mountain pass, but it's not the view that strikes me most intensely. It's *him.*

The utter essence of Sebastian slams into me.

"Abriella!"

I turn to the sound of Sebastian's voice. He launches himself out of bed. Before I can say a word or even brace myself, he's gathered me into his arms and lifted me off the floor. He's shirtless and warm, and it would be so easy to melt into him. Not just because I miss his warmth and love. Not just because I'm lonely and don't want to live in this awful realm without him.

I want to melt into him because here, in the same room, this connection between us is more than a conduit of emotion. It's as if he's half of me, and I cannot bear the pain he's feeling. It reminds me of myself seven years ago, of my grief in those days after I'd recovered from the fire. I'd almost died, yes, but my father *had* died that night, and the weight of that loss had been a constant pressure on my chest and shoulders, a grip around my lungs that made it impossible to take a deep breath.

Feeling that now—knowing Sebastian's suffering in that way—I want nothing more than to ease his pain. With my kiss. With my body. With my forgiveness. *Anything* to crawl out from under the weight of all this grief and guilt and worry.

But I can't. Instead, I press my hand against his chest and pull away. "Put me down."

"Gods above and below, you came back to me," he says, nuzzling my neck. His lips graze my skin, and it feels incredible—a buzz of awareness both from my own body and from his. "I knew you'd come back."

I'm perilously close to dissolving under his touch, and I grapple for my control. "Put me down *now,* Sebastian." Darkness floods the room with a deafening boom.

Sebastian obeys, slowly lowering me to the floor, and I grasp for control over my magic even as the darkness lifts. "I'm sorry," he says, scanning my face. "I just . . . I've been so worried and have missed you so desperately. I tried to visit your dreams, but you pushed me out."

"I know. Because you're not welcome there."

I don't need to see the hurt flash across his features to know I've struck a blow. I *feel* it. It's like breaking my own heart with every word. He shakes his head, and the pain abates—*all* of his emotions weaken, as if he's somehow put a damper on them or thrown up a wall.

"I understand why you're angry," he says, "and I deserve that, but—"

"I'm not here to talk about us. I don't forgive you, and I'm not looking for a reunion."

His face pales, and those beautiful sea-green eyes lose their luster. "I didn't want things to go the way they did," he says.

I set my jaw. I thought I was ready to face him, that I could focus on my mission, but it's harder than I expected. "You had choices. You could've told me."

"Could I?" he asks. "What would you have said?"

I would've gladly given him the crown if I could. Except . . . it required me to die or to become fae to survive. The truth is, if I'd known what he needed from me, I would have run.

"Did you ever really love me?" I ask.

"You're my bonded partner," he says, cocking his head.

I huff. "Judging by the tattoos all over you, it seems to me that you bonded yourself to everyone who'd have you, so forgive me if I don't take that as a sign of your undying love."

His eyes grow cold. "My point is that since we're bonded, you don't have to ask. You already know exactly how I feel about you."

Because I feel him in my blood. I feel his heartache and his longing and his love, even through whatever shield he's put up to soften those feelings. "How could you do this to someone you love?" I draw in a sharp breath. I will not cry. "Was I supposed to wake up and be okay with everything? Did you expect me to put it all together and then happily march to your coronation?"

"You were supposed to give me a chance to *explain*. That's how it's supposed to work when you love someone. But you ran. Just like you always do."

I flinch, because he's right. Every time things have been hard between us, I've run, but that doesn't free him of responsibility for his decisions. "You can't put this on me. You chose the crown over my *life,* and you're upset that I didn't hang around to *chat* about it?"

He shakes his head. "Have you thought about why I asked you not to come to Faerie? I told you to stay put in Fairscape. I needed another year."

"And what would've happened in a single year that—"

His eyes blaze. "She would've died!"

"The queen." His mother. He wasn't broken because she was dying. He was hoping to hide me until her death. I draw in a shaky breath, remembering what he'd said to me when he visited my dream.

I knew I couldn't do it. I knew I'd rather watch my mother die than betray you. But I ran out of choices.

"When I turned nineteen, my mother sent me on a mission to find you, to find my father's crown. She would've done it herself, but she was too weak. The curse had ravaged her. So she sent me to do this one thing I was born to do. To claim the crown Oberon had promised her would go to their child." He swallows. "And then I met you. I knew she'd destroy you, and I couldn't let that happen. All I could do was hide the truth. Bide my time until the curse finally stole her last breath. Only then would you be safe."

Such pretty words. He always has such pretty words for me.

"All I wanted was to keep you safe."

"Me or the crown?"

"You," he growls, eyes blazing, and his frustration spikes through whatever shield he's placed between me and his emotions.

"But you wouldn't listen to me, and you came here anyway." He shakes his head. "I had to do the best I could — the only thing I could."

He steps closer and cups my face in one big hand, grazing his thumb across my cheek.

I close my eyes, trying not to fall under his spell. Between the gentle sweep of his calloused thumb and his heat — so close I might be warm again if I just curled into him — I'm weakening. His love for me is everything I need. It's bigger than anything I fear, stronger than any enemy. I'd never have to be alone again if I'd just accept it. I'd —

I grit my teeth. "Stop this."

"Stop what?"

"You're making me *feel* this . . . this pull. You're projecting so I'll stop thinking for myself."

"I'm letting you feel what I feel. We are *bonded.* Whether you like it or not. Everything you feel through the bond is real. It's part of me."

"But you're masking some of your emotions," I say. "You're choosing to let certain pieces through more than others."

He shrugs, as if this is completely normal behavior. Maybe it is. Maybe this is how bonded pairs endure the overwhelming nature of so many emotions. Or maybe he's just a manipulative bastard who doesn't deserve the benefit of the doubt.

"What would've happened after the queen died?" I ask, grappling for reason over emotion. "How would that have changed anything?"

"What would've changed? There would've been one less

threat against you. One less faerie willing to take that crown and its power at any cost." He swallows hard. "I needed time."

"For what?"

"Time for the prophecy to play out, time for you to love me enough to understand that I didn't want *any* of this. We were falling in love." He makes a fist and presses it to his chest. "I didn't want to trick you out of anything. I wanted to find a way to tell you the truth. I wanted you to love me enough that you'd *choose* to take the potion without being cornered into it."

"Nothing was keeping you from telling me."

His nostrils flare. "You were falling for him. As long as Finn had a chance to trick you out of the crown, you wouldn't be safe. That's why we needed to bond. That's why I deceived you — because taking the crown for myself was the only way to keep you safe, and withholding the truth was the only way you'd bond with me."

It's such a pretty explanation, and I want to swallow it whole, to believe that everything will be okay if we just trust each other again. But I can't. "You knew I'd die, that the bonding ceremony would kill me."

"I knew you'd die, and I knew you'd take the potion. I was okay with that because —"

"You were *okay* with it?" I seethe. The selfish faerie *arrogance.*

His eyes flash. "Yes. Because it meant you'd become fae — and better yet, you'd no longer be wearing a crown so many in this land would go to war for. It kept me up at night, imagining what my mother would do to you if she found out, imagining how close Finn was to gaining your trust."

"Don't you understand?" I whisper. "You didn't just take the crown. You took my life. You *killed* me."

Sebastian squeezes his eyes shut. "I *love* you."

I shake my head. Because I know it's true. I know he believes it. "Love means nothing without trust."

He swallows. "I know you're hurt right now, but do have any idea how much it broke me when you left? And you went to *him?* After everything?"

I frown. "Who? Misha?"

"Finn," Sebastian growls. "You want me to understand why you can't forgive me, but you forgave him for the same thing."

"Finn has nothing to do with this. I haven't seen him since that night in the catacombs."

"But . . . you're in the Wild Fae Lands." Confusion flashes through the bond before he muffles it. "You're staying with Pretha's brother . . ."

"Misha offered me refuge when I needed it. A place where I could get away from you *and* Finn." I shake my head. "Don't turn this around and pretend I've betrayed you. You don't get to do that."

His brow wrinkles. "Tell me what to do to earn your trust. You know I love you, so tell me how you can trust me again."

There it is. My opening. The reason I'm here. "You want to earn my trust? Help me dismantle your mother's *camps.* Free the Unseelie who are trapped in the Seelie Court and send them home."

Sebastian blinks twice, then shakes his head. "It's already

done. She released the Unseelie to return home once Mordeus was gone."

Does he really believe that? "Not the children. She still has the children. I saw it for myself. She's drugging them to suppress their magic and keeping them alive so she can send them into the mines at the border. She's using them to collect fire gems."

He squeezes his eyes shut and curses. "She promised," he whispers, shaking his head.

I close my eyes against the devastation on his face, but it doesn't help when I can feel it tearing through my chest. "Promised what?"

He looks out the window, a dozen emotions flitting across his features. "Shortly after you came to the palace, I visited one of her camps and met two children who'd been taken to the mines. They were . . ." He swallows and shakes his head. "I confronted her, and she promised they were the only two she'd sent, that she'd had to send them to get the fire gems the healer needed to keep her alive."

"She told you it was just the once? And you believed her?"

"I knew she was dying and I knew she was desperate, but I hoped . . ."

"She's not dying anymore, and still she holds the children—thousands of them. Still she uses them to gather fire gems to make herself more powerful. You can't trust her promises. And if you do, I'll never be able to trust you."

He turns his gaze to mine and searches my face. In this moment I know he'd give me anything I asked for. I know it as surely as I know my own thoughts. "I'll dismantle the camps," he says. "Consider it done. I'll assemble a team first thing in the morning."

"I'll be ready."

He shakes his head and swallows. "I can't let you go with them. I won't risk you like that."

"You can't control me. I am not human anymore. I have this power, and I'll use it."

"But if she finds out you have it . . ."

"What? She'll kill me so the power transfers to you? Isn't that what you want?" I stare at him unblinking, daring him to lie to me.

His eyes blaze, and he loosens that hold on his emotions, lets them flood over me in a powerful wave of hurt and disbelief. "You don't believe that." It's not a question. He knows I can't bring myself to believe it, even if I want to. His gaze skims over my face again and again, as if he's trying to read more from me than this bond will give him. "I don't know what she'll do, Brie, but I won't risk it. Not for anything."

"It's not your risk to take. This is *my* life, and this is the only way I can . . ." *This is the only way I can live with myself.*

No. I won't say those words. I won't show that weakness. Not to him.

It's all been too much. Oberon gave his life to save me, and in doing so, he sacrificed the future of his entire kingdom. Then, because I took the Potion of Life, the power of the crown was tied to me, and every member of the shadow court is in danger yet again.

All for me, for *my* life. I may hate the fae, may loathe being trapped in this new fae body, but I will never believe that my life is more important than the lives of so many.

If I don't fight for these children—these *innocents*—how am I supposed to live with myself?

I don't have Sebastian's skills, though, and I have no shield to keep him from unearthing this secret truth from whatever he's receiving through our bond. His eyes go wide, and I wonder what he's processing. The self-loathing? The grief for everyone who sacrificed for my miserable life? The futility of this immortality I don't even deserve?

"Brie," he says softly.

"I know what it's like, Sebastian. I've lived to serve the whims of a greedy debtor. I've been trapped and worked until I collapsed and still found myself further from freedom each day."

"But you hate our kind."

I lift my chin. "I will *never* be like her. So bigoted and self-righteous that I think my life is more important than *thousands* of lives. That the children are fae is irrelevant. They are *children,* and she is a monster."

He swallows, and the echo of his heartache rolls through me as he says, "Can you blame me for loving you so desperately?"

I stiffen my spine. "So tomorrow I help?"

"Do you want to risk the children like that?"

"What do you mean?"

"I haven't spoken to my mother since before we were bonded, Brie. I don't know what she's doing, what she knows or what she has planned."

"Why won't she meet with you?"

His jaw twitches, and he directs his hard gaze at the wall when he says, "Secrets? Scheming? I don't know, but whatever it is, it's not good. I'm worried about what's to come."

"You should be. Your mother cannot be trusted."

"I already knew that, but with so many unknowns, I worry about what she might do if she caught you in her lands. She wouldn't hesitate to take out an entire camp of refugees to get to your power."

I was prepared to fight for this, but his point makes me pause. Why attempt a rescue if my presence risks their lives? "If I let you do this without me, do you promise to return them home?"

His shoulders sag and his relief slides over me like cool water. "Trust me with this, and I will take you to see the children myself when they're returned to the shadow court where they belong. I promise."

Releasing a breath, I nod. "I'll hold you to that, but work quickly. And whatever you do, Bash, don't let her convince you to look the other way."

He shakes his head. "You have my word."

"Thank you." I step forward, closing the distance between us, and reach up to slide my fingers into the hair at the base of his neck. The strip of leather tying it back falls to the ground, and his breath catches.

Sebastian's gaze drops to my mouth. "Abriella," he murmurs, lowering his mouth to mine.

In a move so swift he doesn't see it coming, I use my knife to slice off a lock of his white-blond hair, then back away before his mouth can touch mine.

Sebastian blinks, then narrows his eyes at the lock of hair in my fist. “What’s that for?”

“It’s fare for my transport back to Castle Craige.”

His eyes go wide, but before he can respond, I’ve snapped another thread on my bracelet and handed the lock of hair to Bakken.

“Abriella,” Sebastian calls, but we’re already gone.

CHAPTER NINE

"You're sure there's nothing else I can do for you?" Holly asks, refilling my coffee cup for the second time. I should really make her stop that. I'll be jittery the rest of the day. But better jittery than dead on my feet, I suppose.

I was a mess when Bakken dropped me in my room last night, but I made myself get into bed, and despite my thoughts going in a hundred different directions, I fell asleep the moment my head hit the pillow. I didn't wake until this morning, when a rush of anger and betrayal hit me so intensely, I launched myself out of bed, prepared to fight. Only to realize that I was feeling Sebastian's emotions and not my own.

There's a soft knock at the door, and Holly rushes to answer it before I can stand up from the little table where she served me my breakfast.

"Your Majesty," she says, dipping into a low curtsy. "Good morning. What can I do for you?"

"Good morning, Holly," Misha says, nodding his head in greeting. He's dressed in leather pants and a loose white tunic, a single sword strapped across his back. Storm is perched on his shoulder. "I'm just here to speak with Abriella a moment. Would you give us some privacy, please?"

Another curtsy. "Of course, Your Majesty. I'll be in the hall if you need anything."

"Thank you." He watches her go, then softly shuts the door behind her before turning to me. "Did you sleep well?" he asks.

"Like a rock." I allow myself one more sip of coffee before pushing it away. "You said that after I rested, you could teach me to block."

Misha nods. "You're sure you have the strength for this?"

"I'd like to find out."

"It's difficult, and of course, in the purest execution of the bond, you'd never *want* to block it."

"Never?" I ask. It's so hard to imagine wanting to be aware of what someone else feels at all times. More often than not, I want to hide my emotions, not advertise them.

Misha shrugs. "It's a soul-deep, lifelong connection. Forever and always is the *point.* In fact, there are some couples for whom the connection of the bond isn't enough."

"What more do they want?" I don't try to hide the horror in my voice.

"They want forever. They want the promise that the bond can never be undone and they'll never have to live without each other. These couples travel to the River of Ice beneath the Goblin Mountains and swim in the waters, tying their lives together for eternity."

"But why?"

Misha scoffs. "No one can accuse you of being a romantic."

"Don't you ever just want to be *alone?*"

He arches a brow. "If *I* want to be alone, I can be alone."

I shake my head. He doesn't understand what I'm asking. "You're saying that you walk around completely aware of Amira's feelings at all times?"

His perpetually amused smirk falls away. "What makes you think I'm bonded to Amira?"

Oh. *Oh.* "She's you're wife. I just thought . . ."

"Our marriage was for political advantage, not a love match," he says. "I needed her as my wife. And while most assume we are bonded, since that is the tradition of ruling spouses in my court, it wasn't necessary. I had no interest in forcing my bride to partake in something so intimate."

Swallowing, I stare at my feet. It's so easy to think of Pretha as the losing party in their tangled relationship. She was in love with the female who was betrothed to her brother, and when her parents found out, they sent her away. I never gave much thought to how that must've been for Misha, marrying a woman who didn't love him, who wanted his sister. "I'm sorry," I say, but when I look up again, the amusement has returned to his expression.

"Why?"

"I just . . . The whole situation. I'm sorry you didn't get to marry someone you love."

"I *do* love her, Abriella." He pours himself a cup of coffee. "Maybe not in the way husbands love their wives in your world, but she is dear to me. She's my best friend, as you humans might say it."

"Will you two have children?" The question flies out of my mouth before I can stop it. I'm overstepping. It's practically obscene to ask such a personal question, and it's absolutely none of my business.

"Amira has lovers," he says with a shrug. "As do I. Perhaps one day we'll be blessed with a child, but if not, there are many others in my line who would serve as capable rulers."

They both have lovers, but not each other? I've pushed far enough already, so I don't dare ask. It's not like it'll change anything for Pretha, even if I do want my friend to be able to be with the one she loves.

My friend? Is she still that? Even now?

"For what it's worth, I believe my sister considers you *her* friend," Misha says with a sad smile. "You'll just have to decide if you'll allow her to be yours."

I clench my jaw, but instead of scolding him for reading my thoughts, I shake my head. "Tell me how to block."

He sighs, and I wonder if he was hoping to talk me into trusting his sister again. "I'm trying to think of a good path for you." He taps his index finger to his lips. "How about this? I want you to think of the difference between being mortal and being immortal."

"The difference?" I ask.

"It's hard to say what that means for you. After all, you had power even before you became immortal. But even so, your connection to that magic is different now, isn't it?"

I nod. "Completely different." I could tap into it before, but it was usually a conscious choice. A decision. Now it's just *there.* All the time. Now it's more like I have to consciously choose *not* to use it.

"Tell me," he says.

I shrug. "It's just *there* now."

"Describe it. Before. How was it not *there* before?"

"It's almost as if magic is right in front of me now. All around me all the time. I don't have to search for it or even open my eyes to know it's present. Whereas before, using it was more like . . ." I try to think of a way to explain. "It's the difference between looking at something right in front of you and looking at it through a grimy window."

Misha's eyes light up. "Perfect. I can work with that."

"What do you mean?"

He stares into the distance, as if we had all the time in the world. "I mean we'll be using what you envision to put a wall up in the middle of your bond with your prince. You just need to think of that grimy window, as you call it. Take that window and black out the glass. Now imagine it not between you and your magic, but between you and Sebastian's emotions."

I shake my head. "They're inside of me," I say, pressing my hand to my chest. "I feel them almost as if they're mine."

"Close your eyes," he says, and I reluctantly obey. "What's he feeling now?"

It's not that simple. His emotions blur into mine and make this muddled mess in my mind that leaves me feeling spent and exhausted.

"Shhh. *Focus.*"

I exhale slowly and focus on the very thing I've been trying to ignore since I fled the Golden Palace. What I feel. What he feels. "He's sad, and he's . . . worried. He's very worried about something." He's also hopeful. Hopeful that the team he assembled this morning will be successful and he'll be able to earn my trust back.

I flick my gaze up to Misha, worried that he might be reading my mind and know I visited Sebastian last night, but he seems lost in his own thoughts.

"Okay," Misha says. "Now keep your eyes closed and follow those emotions. You feel them inside you. Trace them back to their roots, as if you're following a thread that's tangled up in your chest. I want you to find the end of that thread, and I want you to pull slowly. Bit by bit."

I pull at the sadness, little by little.

"Keep pulling," he says, "until it's all cupped in the palm of your mind's eye."

The sadness detaches from me like a cat retracting its claws from my skin, and my eyes fly open. "It worked."

"Close your eyes," he says. "Finish."

I do as I'm instructed, pulling at the rest of the sadness as if I'm physically extracting it from my chest. It's a relief, and also a reminder of how alone I really am. Feeling Sebastian was keeping my loneliness at bay, and now it's returning like an old, unwelcome housemate. But I continue, doing the same with his worry, that gnawing torment that worry has become for him. This one's harder, but I keep tugging until, in my mind's eye, I'm holding the strings in my hands.

"Good," Misha says, seeming to sense that I've reached the

end. "Now place them on the other side of the window." I open my eyes again, but he says, "Stay focused. This is your mind. You decide what gets in and what stays. Place them on the other side of your darkened window where they belong."

Focusing, I crack the dark window and toss the balls of string through. The second I slam the glass back down, my body feels lighter. My eyes fly open as I smile, but at the same moment, Sebastian's *there* again. All his worry and sadness back as powerfully as before.

I shake my head. "It's not working."

"You're not *focusing,*" Misha says. "Try again."

I close my eyes and repeat the steps, visualizing the balls of string and the darkened window. This time when we're disconnected, I focus on keeping my guard up, but when I open my eyes, Sebastian's emotions snap back into place with mine.

"You're trying to make this easy," Misha says. "Stop thinking of the connection as something malleable and start thinking of it as something unmovable. The bond is there, whether you like it or not. You're simply pulling a heavy curtain to make it harder to see in and out. Try again."

I try. Again. And again. I envision a blackened window and it turns to air. Other times the glass cracks under the intensity of my focus.

"What are you darkening your window with?" Misha asks, pacing in front of me. From the look of him, he thought this little training session would be easier than it has been.

I shrug. "I'm painting it black."

He stops pacing and turns to me, smiling. "Not paint. *Night.*

Place your shadows—the deepest, darkest you have—between you and your prince."

I'm exhausted, practically shaking from the mental energy required to do this again, but I try. This time when I open my eyes the shield holds. Sebastian's emotions are still there, but they're muted. Distant. I could lift the darkness, open the window, and retrieve them, or I could choose to leave them on the other side.

I draw in a deep, relieved breath. "It's working."

"For now," Misha says, and I scowl. "You'll need practice if you want any sort of stamina. Be patient with yourself."

I shrug. "I have nothing but time."

Misha treats me to a full smile. "Good work, Princess," he says. "Don't expect this to ever completely negate your connection. Your shield will get better over time as you become stronger, but it will always be difficult to block the bond during highly emotional, intense, or painful situations."

I nod. "I understand." I take a breath. "And will the same technique work for blocking *you* out?"

He chuckles. "It will. But again, it takes practice. Be patient with yourself, and remember that even when you have me blocked, you can choose to use my *creepy* talent to communicate with me if you wish."

"Even if I have you blocked? How?"

He studies the ceiling thoughtfully. "Think of it this way—you and I have connected, and I've chosen to keep a bit of my mental energy locked on you. Since I've done so, you can tap into it. Try visualizing a thin tunnel of energy between us that will allow me to speak in your mind."

I focus, visualizing it. *Like this?* I ask.

He smiles. *Exactly like this. Well done. Now shut me off.*

I throw up a wall of night in my mind and focus hard.

That's enough to keep your thoughts from flying at me when I'm minding my own business, but not enough to keep me out.

I growl, and his lips twitch. "Keep working on it," he says. "It's a muscle, like anything else."

"I don't want just anyone in my mind without my consent."

"Then practice. Every day. Train your mind as you'd train your body, and you will improve."

I feel guilty for asking, but . . . "When I get stronger, will this work for when I'm in the settlement as well? When I'm feeling the children's emotions?"

Misha turns up his palms. "That, I can't say. I'm not familiar with a gift that allows the bearer to tap into the emotions of an entire court."

I chew on my bottom lip. When he puts it that way, it sounds too big. Too *important.* Again I find myself questioning what kind of king Oberon must've been. He loved my mother, yes, and at first glance, saving me from certain death sounds like a good and kind choice. But handing his crown and power over to me was reckless and irresponsible. He warned my mother that there would be a cost, but I wonder if either of them knew the cost would be far greater than just his life, that his act of love would threaten his entire kingdom.

It's hard to judge him for his choices when they're the reason I still breathe, and yet . . .

Misha takes my hand and lifts it to his lips. He presses a soft kiss there, just as he did when he brought me to my room last night. "Whether you know it or not, you are a gift to that court. Stop thinking of yourself as a curse."

Over the next two weeks I fall into an easy routine in the Wild Fae territory. In the mornings I help in the schoolhouse at the Unseelie settlement, sometimes lending a hand at the infirmary before I ride back up the mountain. In the evenings I have dinner with Misha and Amira — sometimes both, sometimes one or the other. The time in between, I spend exploring the castle grounds, riding Two Star, or holed up in the library, reading. Unable to contend with the emotions that flood into me when I don't shield against Sebastian, I work diligently to block him and try to ignore the loneliness that haunts me when I'm successful.

Misha says I'm improving faster than he expected, and I can even block him out much of the time now.

I sleep more than I ever have in my life — twelve or more hours at night and often a nap in the afternoon. Misha says it's because I'm still recovering from the metamorphosis, and it will get better with time. But I don't mind the sleep. Unconsciousness is a refuge from my thoughts. Sometimes Lark visits my dreams. She looks at me with those shining silver eyes and tells me to hurry home. At least I think it's her. Maybe it's just my subconscious showing me something that feels comforting. And when Sebastian or Finn appear in my dreams, I shove them right back out.

The library has become my favorite place in Castle Craige. The room is circular, with twenty-foot-tall walls lined with books and a glass ceiling that floods the space with natural light. In the center of the circle of shelves are various work and lounging areas. Tables with plenty of room to work, sofas with ottomans, chairs arranged in cozy groupings facing each other. I like to sit in here at night best of all—there's something peaceful about lounging with an open book on my chest as I gaze up at the stars—but this morning I'm enjoying the warmth of the sunlight pouring in.

"How'd I know I'd find you in here?" Misha asks, strolling in through the arched doorway from the hall.

"Because this is where I spend most of my waking hours."

"Right. That." Grinning, he settles into the chair across from me. "How are you feeling?"

I shrug. Mentally and physically I'm better every day, but I can't say my heart has recovered from all I went through this summer. I miss my sister, I miss Sebastian, and even though Misha and Amira have proven to be excellent companions, I'm lonely. "I'm . . . fine."

Misha's face twists in sympathy. Whether through my thoughts or deduction, he knows that's a lie. "It's only been a couple of weeks. Even a faerie's heart needs time to heal."

I blow out a breath and change the subject. "How are you?"

"I'm fine. I have news." He retrieves a letter from his pocket and passes it to me. "My goblin was able to deliver your letter to your sister, and she sent this back. He said she seems well. Spends her days making dresses and her evenings watching a child. She appears happy and healthy."

My heart aches as I finger the envelope's soft pink seal. I miss her so much, but I couldn't bring myself to tell her about my transformation. I kept the update on myself simple. I missed her and hoped to visit one day—all true—and focused mainly on questions about her welfare. I long to open her response now and see her words in her own writing, but I'll wait until I'm alone.

"I have other news as well," Misha says. "My sister has sent word that she, Finn, and his people have arrived in my lands. They're headed to the palace and should be here by tomorrow morning."

I stiffen at the mention of the people I once considered my friends. *So much for my safe place to hide.* "What brings them here? I thought Finn had forces in the mountains and people all over the Unseelie Court who'd give him refuge."

Misha nods. "He does. That's not why they're coming. We need to make plans for the queen's first attack."

"You're sure it's coming?"

"Her guard has been spotted moving east through the Goblin Mountains."

"So Finn is coming to request your help? And . . . you'll give it?"

Misha's brows shoot up. "Have I given you any reason to think I'd be willing to let that monster have any more control than she already does?"

"No, but—"

"Even if I didn't care about the atrocities she's committed in her short life, I have my own people to think of. The queen will no longer settle for extending her territory to the other side of the Goblin Mountains. Now she wants the entire Unseelie Court as part of her own, and if that happens, my own lands will be next. It's my duty as a king to protect the Wild Fae, but it's my duty as a faerie to do everything I can to stop the queen from getting even one more ounce of control. And I plan to, Abriella, with or without your help and with or without the Unseelie Court's alliance."

I frown. "I thought you already had an alliance with Finn."

Misha arches a dark brow. "With Finn, yes, but as we've established, Finn is no more in control of that court than Mordeus is from his grave."

Which is why Misha needs me. When I arrived, I couldn't imagine aligning myself with another member of faerie royalty, but now that I know more about the queen, now that I've seen her camps and Misha's settlements, now that I've heard the terrified screams of one of the children she's sent into those caverns, everything's changed.

"They don't know you're still here," Misha says. "Though they suspect. They wouldn't have known at all if Sebastian hadn't accused Finn of bringing you here. What happens next is up to you. If you'd like, you can sit in on our meetings, listen as they share what they know, and help us make a plan. Or, if you're not yet ready to assume a role in our discussions, I can hide you temporarily. I think you could be an important part of the meetings—both because of your power and your perspective—but it is your choice. Either way, Finn and the others are unlikely to stay long. The Lunastal holiday is quickly approaching, and it will be the first in twenty years that Finn's been able to spend in his homeland."

"Why?" I ask.

Misha arches a brow. "Why what? I'm afraid I don't understand the question. Your shield is working rather well today, I might add."

I acknowledge the compliment with a smile. "Why give me this choice? It's been two weeks since you first told me that you want me to help Sebastian and Finn work together, and I haven't agreed to anything. Why are you being so kind to me? Why would you deceive your sister and your allies for my benefit?"

He lifts his chin. "Ah. That." With a sigh, he leans back, somehow still looking regal as he settles into the chair's fluffy cushions. He's quiet for a long time, and I think he might not answer at all when he finally says, "I need your alliance as much as I need Finn's. I don't know what the queen is planning, but any course of action that gives her more power is one that hurts my kingdom. I need people on my side who will fight against her, and whether you're ready for that fight now or months from now, I know you're going to be part of it."

I cock my head to the side and study him. "And how do you know that? You barely know me."

"Like you said, we all have our motives." He gives me a gentle smile. "And don't forget I had access to your thoughts those early days of your visit."

"And sometimes now," I say. We both know I'm still learning and not that skilled at shielding yet.

"And sometimes now," he admits, shrugging. "It's not the same as knowing someone's heart, but it's the next best thing." With that, he pushes himself out of the chair. "You don't have to decide now. You can tell me in the morning."

I stare at the words of my book as his steps grow distant, but they all blur together. "I've already decided," I say, then turn to see if he heard me.

He stops in the library's arched doorway and slowly turns back to me. "Don't leave me in suspense, Princess."

"I want to be part of the meetings."

"Even if it means trusting people who have deceived you in the past?" He tucks his hands into his pockets. "I wasn't sure you could forgive Finn."

"Finn used me, but he's not the one who broke my heart."

Misha arches a single brow, and I brace myself for an argument, but instead he says, "Join me for dinner so we can plan for this meeting? I have some ideas."

I nod and watch him leave. I'm anxious to get to Jas's letter.

As soon as I start reading, I can hear her voice in my head as if she's talking to me. It's a comfort and an ache deeper than any homesickness I've ever felt.

CHAPTER TEN

EVERYONE'S GATHERED IN MISHA'S PERSONAL meeting room. Their voices are low murmurs from the hall, so I can't tell if I'm choosing a good time or a terrible one to interrupt — Misha would likely argue that they are one in the same. Finn may be his ally, but he's set on showing Finn that *I* am *Misha's* ally.

Lifting my chin and straightening my shoulders, I swing the door open and stroll inside. Finn's wolves lounge in the far corners and perk up at my entrance before laying their heads back down.

There are eight seats around the massive polished oval table, which has room for many more. Misha and Amira sit at opposite ends, and Pretha and Finn sit with their backs to me, Tynan, Kane, and Jalek opposite them. The lone available chair is to Finn's right, and I can't help but wonder if Misha planned it that way. He already asked me to join the meeting late for the purpose of throwing Finn off guard, but is he seating me next to the shadow prince an effort to rock Finn or *me*?

Jalek spots me first, and his green eyes go wide. Then Kane, who pushes his chair back with a squeak and rises to his feet. The room goes silent, and seven heads turn in my direction.

Pretha's jaw drops, gasping as if the sight of me is some monumental relief. "Brie."

But it's Finn's reaction I can't move on from—not that he's giving anything away. His face is stoic, his sharp eyes assessing as he looks me over, taking in my boots, my pants, the belt of knives slung around my hips. My power purrs in his presence, and I don't bother reining it in. Tendrils of shadow slip from my fingertips and coil around my wrists before snaking up my arms. Finn follows their path, impassive.

"Ah," Misha says, not even trying to hide the delight in his tone. "My guest has joined us."

"You said the princess was no longer in residence," Finn says coolly, still not standing to greet me, but not taking his eyes off me. His silver gaze has drifted from my shadows and settled on my face. I wonder what he's thinking, wonder if he's angry that I've pushed him away when he visited my dreams.

"Did I?" Misha asks with a shrug. "I stand corrected. She's here."

Finn's eyes glitter, and when he turns them on Misha, I almost feel sorry for my new friend.

"We've been worried about you," Pretha says to me, standing and stepping closer.

I arch a brow. "About me or about the power I still carry?"

Pretha straightens. "I care for far more than your magic, Abriella."

"Is that so?" I cock my head to the side. "Do you plan to kill everyone you care about, or should I feel special?"

She closes her eyes and sighs. "Brie—"

"Don't. It doesn't matter."

"It matters to me," Pretha says. "What you think of us, of the decisions we made . . . that matters a great deal to me."

I swallow hard, thinking of what Finn said in my dream after I'd taken the potion. He said he'd found me in the mortal realm two years ago, and instead of trying to trick me out of my power, he'd worked on finding another way. Not that it made a difference.

"Did you know this would happen?" I ask Finn. "Could Sebastian have known that giving me the Potion of Life would end this way?" I've already heard it from Misha, but I want to hear it from Finn.

"We didn't know," Finn says. "No one knew anything. It was all speculation. But it makes sense — the potion saved your life, and in doing so bound your life to your magic." He shrugs, as if this is as inconsequential as who drank the last of the coffee and not a matter tied to the destruction within his own realm.

The empty chair beside Finn backs away from the table on its own. Misha says, "Please join us, Princess. We speak of the future of your court."

Kane whips around to glare at Misha. "*Her* court?"

Misha shrugs. "Sorry. Would you rather I call it *Prince Ronan's* court?"

"It's *Finn's* court," Kane says.

Finn props his elbows on the table and steeples his fingers. "It's no one's court so long as the crown and the power are divided. Sit, Princess. It seems you're to join this little planning session, so let's get started."

I'm tempted to remain standing just to spite him, but my

stubbornness wouldn't serve anything but my own childish satisfaction, so I take the seat.

Across the table, Tynan meets my eyes and gives me a gentle smile. "It's good to see you're well, Abriella."

I swallow hard. "Thank you. You too, Tynan." Tynan's the quietest one of the bunch, and I always liked him. He and Pretha are both Wild Fae, but Pretha married into the Unseelie Court, whereas Tynan had no connections to the shadow court other than his friendship with Finn. Now that I've met Misha, I have to wonder if Tynan's purpose was less about helping Finn and more about being an intermediary between Finn and the Wild Fae king.

Of course, Misha says in my mind. *I trust Finn, but I'm not naïve enough to think he wouldn't wreck all my plans for the sake of his own court. We all have our priorities, Princess.*

I shoot Misha a glare for poking around in my mind, and he winks at me.

Look at how jealous he is. If you'd like to make him absolutely mad *with jealousy, I'd be happy to help.*

Don't hold your breath. I give him a pointed look to drive the thought home, and Misha grins.

Beside me, Finn growls and sends a glare of his own in Misha's direction. "If you two are done, I'd like to return to the subject at hand."

Misha shifts his smile to Finn, not intimidated in the slightest by the shadow prince. "Perhaps we should bring the princess up to speed."

Pretha folds her arms on the table and leans forward, looking past Finn to meet my eyes. "We have teams working in the

Seelie Court to dismantle the queen's camps and get the Unseelie refugees to safety, but the last dozen we've found were already handled before we reached them."

Sebastian. I hold back my smile, but the warmth in my chest is real.

"And before you think that the queen dismantled them out of the goodness of her black little heart, we should be clear that they weren't just disbanded," Jalek says, narrowing his eyes at me. This one has never trusted me, not completely, though he was certainly nicer after I rescued him from the golden queen's dungeon. "These camps were brought under siege. Bodies of golden guard members litter the sites."

"Sounds like someone was trying to help," I say innocently. "Do you know who?"

You were behind this? Misha asks in my mind. *I should've known, but look at you, keeping secrets.*

"Sebastian, much to our surprise," Finn says, and shakes his head. "Before he arrived at the Unseelie palace, he managed to assemble a contingent of the Golden Military that pledged their loyalty to him. He's dismissing anyone who won't act against the queen's camps. Rumor has it that he's sent so many teams to free the prisoners in the Court of the Sun, he's down to a bare-bones army in the shadow court."

He's left himself vulnerable for the sake of the refugees. I swallow hard. Sebastian has betrayed me more than once, but it's a relief to know that on some level, he's still the male I believed him to be. Still the male I loved. "You know he never liked those camps."

"Yes," Finn says, his eyes narrowing as he studies me. "And now he's proved it. And he's winning loyalties as he does it. He has Unseelie joining the ranks at the palace now."

Pretha says, "Sebastian is likely hoping his actions will prove that he can be the king they've needed for so long."

Is that why you did it? Misha asks in my mind. *To help him gain favor with the court his mother promised him?*

I shake my head. "He can't be king. The throne rejected him."

"Mordeus managed to rule without a throne or a crown," Finn says. "But pledging our allegiance to my uncle was never an option."

"Neither is allying ourselves with the golden prince," Jalek snaps. His jaw is hard as he meets Finn's gaze. "Trusting him is no smarter than trusting that bitch queen. I won't do it."

"And that's just how Queen Arya wants it," Amira says, leaning back in her chair. She's been so quiet, I almost forgot she was here. I wonder how much she learns simply because others forget she's present.

Pretha settles her hands on the table in front of her and keeps her focus there instead of turning to Amira. "Jalek's not wrong to be cautious," she says. "Sebastian may be dismantling camps, but we have no reason to believe that when push comes to shove, he wouldn't choose his mother over the Court of the Moon. We don't know his true motivations."

Amira nods in my direction. "Abriella might know something."

All eyes at the table turn to me, and I shake my head. "She raised Sebastian to believe he could unite the courts and rule them both. Because he is of both courts, he believes he can save thousands from dying in another war."

"He thinks he's the promised child," Kane growls.

"She raised him on lies and pretty stories," Jalek says. "Even if the courts could be ruled as one—which is another issue altogether—letting him rule both would mean she had to hand over her power. We all know she's not going to do that."

I know it's wishful thinking, but I'd like nothing more than to see the queen relinquish her power, but I ask anyway. "Do we know this for sure?"

"We do," Finn says softly. "Otherwise she wouldn't be moving her forces into the Goblin Mountains."

Of course. If she planned to give her son power over both courts, she wouldn't be readying for war. "Do we have any hope of holding her back without anyone on the throne?"

"No," Jalek says darkly.

"Finn should be wearing that crown," Kane says.

"*Should* won't get us anywhere," Pretha says.

"Can Sebastian give it to him?" I swallow. "Sebastian *cares* for the people of the Unseelie Court, and he's proved that by helping the refugees. If he could help by giving Finn the crown—"

"The transfer of the crown requires a forfeiture of life," Jalek says, "so unless you're suggesting that he sacrifice himself so that Finn may wear it—"

"Sounds good to me," Kane says.

"What do you mean?" I ask. "Wouldn't it be the same as a king passing a crown to his heir?"

Misha shakes his head. "It doesn't work here the way it does in the mortal realm. When the rule of a Faerie court is passed on — whether it's the golden court, the shadow court, or my own — the prior ruler forfeits their life on this plane and moves on to the Twilight. Since the power is tied to their lives, the only way they can pass on the power is to yield that life."

Finn cocks his head to the side and studies me. "You know this. It's how my father saved you."

"Yes, but I . . ." I thought it was different with me. I thought what Oberon did for me was some strange, unused magic, not the tradition of generations of rulers. "I didn't realize."

"This whole line of thought is a waste of time," Jalek says. "Prince Ronan's been raised to believe that throne is *his.* If you think he's going to cut his life short so Finn can have it —"

Finn meets my eyes. "It wouldn't matter anyway. The throne would reject me without the power, just as it rejected Sebastian."

Jalek looks at me. "Are you ready to end your days to pass over the power?"

"I . . ." I don't know what to say. One life versus thousands. I can't say no, but —

"That's not an option," Finn snaps. "As you pointed out, Abriella has no Unseelie blood, so we don't even know how that would work. We could risk losing the power of the throne altogether."

"I'm not sure I trust Sebastian on the throne anyway," Kane mutters. "I don't care how much he claims to want the best for the shadow fae. I don't trust anyone who's been close to that bitch."

Finn swallows. "We might not have a choice, Kane. If I have to choose between allowing an imperfect boy to rule and watching my kingdom die, there's no choice at all."

"Then what have we been fighting for all this time?" Jalek asks, and at the same time, Kane says, "Think of the future of the court. Think of—"

"Sebastian's a good male," I say, cutting them all off.

Everyone goes silent, and all eyes in the room turn to me.

"You're the last person I'd expect to defend him, after all he did," Pretha says.

"And you of all people should understand *why* he did what he did." I shake my head. "I'm not defending the decisions he made, but I would venture that you'd have done the same in his position."

"*I* wouldn't have given you the damn potion," Jalek says, his voice deadly soft. When I meet his glare with my own, he says, "Never doubt my appreciation for the way you saved me from the queen's clutches, Princess, but with all due respect, there are bigger things at stake here than your broken heart."

"Don't be a dick, Jalek," Pretha says.

Jalek shrugs. "I won't change who I am or what I'm willing to sacrifice for this fight just because you think she's too fragile."

"I'm not," I say quickly, straightening, all too aware of Finn's heavy gaze boring into me. "I'm not fragile, and I'm not worried about my broken heart." Don't they understand that Sebastian's betrayal isn't the only reason for my heartache? "My very existence may mean the destruction of an entire court. Every Unseelie child who is vulnerable to the queen is at risk simply because I breathe. Because of a decision that was forced on me. Trust me when I say I understand the stakes."

———•———

The meeting with Finn and his people leaves me feeling dizzy and overwhelmed. As everyone stands from the table, Pretha turns to me, but I dodge her and leave the room, heading straight to my chambers.

As the subject turned to the various locations and numbers of their forces and allies, I tried dropping my shield to see if I could feel Finn and Kane the way I feel the Unseelie children in the settlement, but all I accomplished was feeling Sebastian. He's in trouble. I don't know why, and I'm not familiar enough with the workings of this bond to be able to say where he is, other than *far*, but an undeniable sense of dread crept over me. Now I can't stop thinking—worrying—about him. And I don't want to worry about him. I don't want to give in to this temptation to drop my shields altogether so I can monitor him throughout the day.

When I reach my bedroom, Holly's waiting just outside the door. Her eyes light up when she sees me. "May I bring you fresh coffee, milady?"

I shake my head, marveling at how odd it is that attentive servants are a normal part of my life now—not that anything about this situation is normal. "No, thank you," I say. "I just need a few moments before I head to the settlement."

"I'll prepare a lunch basket for you to take along."

I open my mouth to tell her that's not necessary, but then snap it shut again. I need to let her do her job, no matter how uncomfortable it makes me. "Thank you, Holly. That would be wonderful."

As I step into my room, a weight lifts from my shoulders and

I let out a long breath. I shut the door behind me and collapse against it.

"Stressful morning?" an all too familiar deep voice asks.

I don't bother to straighten or open my eyes. Honestly, when it comes to him, I'm better off without my sense of sight. "What are you doing in my room, Finn?"

"I was simply waiting for you, Princess."

Now I do open my eyes so I can narrow them at him. He's standing at the window, hands tucked into his pockets as he stares out at the view. My gaze sweeps across his broad shoulders of its own volition. He's removed his cloak and tied back his dark curls in the time since our meeting, as if readying himself to work—or fight. "How did you get here before me?"

"I believe you call it *magic*?"

My eyes widen, too shocked to be annoyed by his sarcasm. "You can travel—like a goblin?"

He grunts and turns to me. "Goblins would be offended to hear you suggest anything of the sort. I can move from one part of a room to another or from one floor to the next. However, if you'd like me to magically whisk you away from here and take you to Unseelie palace so you can visit your beloved, I'm afraid I can't help you."

I set my jaw, determined not to take the bait. "Why did you leave the palace? Why give it to him?"

He strolls toward me, and the room suddenly feels far too small for the two of us. Dreams aside, the last time Finn and I were alone together, I was holding the knife I used to kill Mordeus and trying to convince myself to use it on Finn. I couldn't. Part of me knew, even then, that he was no villain.

"The palace belongs to no one but the land, and sleeping there doesn't make one significant. No more than sleeping in a witch's cellar makes one insignificant." He shrugs, those eyes scanning every inch of me. "As you already know."

A protective instinct surges in my chest. "Sebastian's not . . . *insignificant,*" I spit.

Finn's eyes widen in mock innocence. "I didn't say he was."

Growling, I stomp to my armoire. I wanted to have a few moments of peace to digest everything. Not only do I need to think about what I learned during the meeting, I need to consider what I want to do about what I felt from Sebastian when I lowered my shields, but I guess that's not happening.

I pull out a cloak. I'll need it if I end up lingering at the settlement until after sunset, and I might as well get on my way. "How long until you *leave*?" I ask, slamming the armoire closed a little harder than necessary.

When I spin around, Finn's blocking my path to the door. He cocks his head to the side. "Already dreading my departure?"

"Not in the slightest." But as soon as the words leave my lips, I recognize them for the lie they are. Gods, I hate how conflicted I am when it comes to Finn. I miss our friendship, that feeling of belonging I had when I trained with his misfit faerie crew, but it wasn't real. The only reason he befriended me to begin with—the only reason any of them gave a shit about me—was because of that damn crown, and I'm too proud to let my anger go so easily.

But now that he's so close, I'm reminded of the way my power purrs in his presence. My power and . . . *other things.*

Maybe this physical attraction was never real. Maybe the way Oberon's power responds in the presence of Unseelie royalty messes with my head, makes me *think* there's attraction — *chemistry* — when what I'm really feeling is a great magic I'm still not able to control.

"I should've known Misha would take advantage of the opportunity to scoop you up." He smiles, and for once it's not the cynical twist of his lips I know so well. "He always was one of the smarter ones."

"I had nowhere else to go," I say, folding my arms. "It's not like I rushed headlong into some sort of alliance. I've already made that mistake once."

"Is that what I am to you?" he asks, stepping close. "A mistake?"

He's so tall and broad, and when he's this close and looking down on me with soft eyes, I feel . . . *safe.*

None of this is real. They need Oberon's power. Nothing's changed.

"Excuse me," I say, sidestepping even though there's not enough room between him and the bed for me to move around him. "I'm running late."

"I'm coming with you."

"What?" I shake my head. "No. I go to the settlement every day. I can manage on my own."

Finn arches a brow. "I don't doubt that, but I'd planned to visit today anyway and figured we could go together." He steps to the side, finally allowing me through. "After you, Princess."

CHAPTER ELEVEN

LESS THAN TWENTY MINUTES LATER, I'm riding Two Star and trying not to admire the way Finn looks trotting along in front of me. I'm failing. The truth is, Finn looks absolutely *regal* on horseback. He rides like he was born atop a horse, as if adjusting to the creature's canter is second nature. He looks like the king he should be.

"What are you thinking about so hard back there?" Finn asks, glancing over his shoulder.

"The children," I lie. Though they're never too far from my mind. "Many in this settlement have yet to be reunited with their families."

Finn bows his head, as if he took the words as a reminder of his failings. "Misha told me what you did," he finally says.

Frowning, I nudge Two Star forward to ride alongside him. I don't like the idea of Misha talking to Finn about me — especially since the king has all too frequently been privy to my most private thoughts. "What I did *when?*"

Finn keeps his eyes on the trail ahead. "When you were running from the Golden Palace, you stopped to help with an escape at one of the queen's camps. You freed those children even though you hate the fae and were angry with Sebastian—and with *me,* for all I'd done, for my trickery and . . . for what I'd planned."

"The children are not responsible," I say. "For any of it."

"I know that, but . . ."

"You thought I'd hold it against them? They did not choose to be born fae, and I do not blame them for the decisions of those who came before them."

He arches a brow, as if he finds my response intriguing. "Perhaps not, but there are many who believe themselves good people who avert their gaze from injustice every day. You could've done the same."

I look away, unable to handle the intensity in his eyes. "I know what it's like—to be powerless like that. There are children in the mortal realm who are tricked into unfair contracts and end up spending their lives in servitude. I always told myself that if I had the power, I'd free them. For years, I would look at the night sky and send that wish up to the stars, but I remained trapped and powerless, and I stopped believing."

"No, you didn't," he says softly. "You told yourself you didn't believe, because that hope made you feel weak, but you never stopped believing."

I shrug. He's probably right, but back in Elora I was too busy surviving to give it much thought. "I helped because I could. That they're fae hardly matters. They're innocents, and they deserve someone to fight for them."

"Just like you and Jas needed someone to fight for you?" he asks.

I swallow hard. "*I* fought for us. We were okay."

"I'm *grateful* for what you did." He turns his head and studies me as our horses trot along. "But not surprised. I know who you are, Princess."

I roll my eyes. "Obviously not if you're still calling me *Princess.*"

"Would you prefer I call you something else?"

"I do have a name."

"And a lovely name it is," he says. "But I can't resist the instinct to give you a title. It's the least you deserve, considering all you've done for my people."

I snort. "Right. The *mess* I've made for your people is more like it."

The silence stretches between us for several heavy beats of my heart until Finn asks, "Do you want me to pretend that I think raiding the camps was Sebastian's idea? That little act of heroics had your name all over it."

I swallow hard. "I didn't do anything. I simply made him aware of the problem and asked him to help."

Finn grunts. "Yes, and now he's reaping the benefits of that decision."

I shift in the saddle. "Does that bother you?"

"Yes . . . no." He shakes his head. "My first priority is my people, and as long as his actions are in their best interests, I don't really care about the rest."

"But . . ." I prod. He doesn't answer, so I add, "Emotions aren't always as simple as what we should and shouldn't feel."

When he turns his head to look at me again, his eyes are like a caress. Or maybe that's just me and this blasted attraction I can't shake. His voice is rough. "Nothing's ever simple."

There's no answer to that, so I stroke Two Star's dark coat instead of replying.

Finn watches the movement. "I see you've already found a friend here."

"She's beautiful, isn't she?"

"Yes," he says, his voice a little gruff. "She suits you."

Not trusting myself to look at him after he says things like that, I bow my head, but I feel his eyes on me as we continue toward the settlement. I've traveled this path many times since arriving in the Wild Fae Lands, and I'm always so distracted by the scenery that the time passes quickly. Today the journey stretches out, as does the silence between us. I'm aware of Finn watching me intently, aware that his attention never strays for long.

"Do I look that strange as a faerie?" I finally snap.

He chuckles softly. "Not at all."

"Then why do you keep staring?"

"Just . . ." He shakes his head. "I'm glad you're okay. When I learned you were bonded to him, I feared . . ."

"You thought he'd let me die." And maybe he should have. I hate that it comes down to that, but no one can deny that everything would be simpler right now if Sebastian had been able to take that throne.

"I didn't know what to think," Finn says softly.

"Sebastian's made mistakes, but he's no different than you are. You two wanted the exact same thing and were planning to get it in the same way."

Finn's nostrils flare. "I'm *nothing* like him."

"If that's what you need to tell yourself."

"I . . ." The trees open up just ahead, and the path turns wider as it stretches into the settlement. Finn shakes his head. "We'll discuss this later." He leans forward on his horse, spurring him into a gallop.

I follow him down the path and into the stables, where we hand our horses over to the young males on stable duty for the day.

"Have you been here before?" I ask as we meander toward the main square. The market is wrapping up for the day, but several of the vendors wave politely and others bow their heads as we pass.

"Several times," Finn says. "Over the years, I've made it a priority to visit each of the camps as often as I'm able."

"That must be difficult. Misha said they're spread throughout his territory and shielded from goblin travel."

"It's worth it," Finn says. "Anything to reassure my people that they haven't been forgotten is worth a bit of inconvenience."

My heart tugs. Despite what he may have intended for me, Finn's love for his people is true. "I'm going to make a quick stop at the infirmary; then I'll be helping in the schoolhouse most of the day," I say. "Don't feel like you have to wait for me when you're ready to go. I travel the path alone frequently."

Finn grunts. "Your trips up and down that mountain alone will be a conversation for another time."

I roll my eyes. No doubt he's more interested in protecting this power I carry than in my personal safety, but I'm happy to push that argument off until later.

"Now tell me what you're doing in the infirmary. Are there so many sick they need your assistance?"

I shake my head. "They don't need me, but I like to help where I can. There's a strange illness passing through the settlement. We're not sure what it is, but the healers have their hands full, so I offer what I can."

When we step into the brick building, we're met at the door.

"My prince," Leta breathes. She drops into a low curtsy, bowing her head. "It's an honor to see you again, Your Highness."

"Please stand, Leta," he says.

I study the discomfort on his face. It must feel terrible to have people acknowledge him as their leader when that position's been taken from him.

"I hear there are sick children," he says.

She nods. "Seven more just this morning," she says.

I gasp and stop dead in my tracks. That means the number of sick children doubled overnight.

Finn frowns at me. "Are you okay?"

"Yeah. I'm fine." I roll my shoulders back, determined to offer any assistance I can for as long as I can but feeling helpless anyway.

"Come this way," Leta says, waving us toward the back.

We follow her into the infirmary, but once we get into the door of the sleeping room, it's Finn's turn to freeze.

"Explain," Finn says.

The female nods. "They're . . . sleeping and do not wake. There's no sign before they go down. They just go to sleep. Parents are terrified to put their children to bed each night."

"We might need to consider quarantining the children," I say, taking in all the new faces. "Perhaps they're contagious before they go down, and if we could—"

"It wouldn't matter," Finn says. He's gone pale beside me. "It's not contagious."

The nurse frowns. "Can you be sure?"

"I've seen this before," Finn says. "We'll make arrangements to take the sleeping ones back to Unseelie Court. I'll be in touch with more information when we have it."

"Are you sure it's wise to move them?" I ask.

"Yes," Finn says. "Being back on native soil is the best thing we can do for these children right now. Speak with their parents and whatever adults are caring for the orphans. Tell them to prepare to go first thing tomorrow."

"Yes, Your Highness," Leta says.

Finn turns to me. "We need to go. The sooner we return these children to the Court of the Moon, the better." He strides out of the infirmary without waiting for me to acknowledge his command.

"Finn," I call after him. Leta's eyes go wide, and I realize she probably thinks it's strange that I'm using his given name. I ignore her and chase after him. He's already at the stables by the time I catch up to him. "Finn, slow down."

He hands me Two Star's reins. "We need to go."

"Why the rush? Tell me what you're thinking—what you know."

"The sleeping children are the first sign of a dying court. If we want to save them, we need to get them home to buy more time, and then we need to put someone on that damn throne."

I open my mouth to object, then snap it shut again.

"We *must* reunite the crown, the power, and the throne. And do it as quickly as possible. We're running out of time."

"How?" I ask.

Finn takes a long, shaky breath. "I don't have the answer, but I know who does."

We find the others on the dining terrace when we return. Judging by the empty plates scattered about the table, they've just finished lunch.

"Back so soon?" Misha asks, sipping a glass of dark red wine.

Finn shoves his hands into his pockets and rocks back on his heels. His jaw is hard and his silver eyes glitter with rage. "You didn't tell me about the sick children."

"There are sick children?" Pretha asks. Worry twists her mouth.

"Yes," Finn says.

Misha's eyes go wide. "I wasn't aware that you needed detailed updates about what's happening at the settlements, Finnian. Children are frequently unwell when they come to us, and then, after that, they fall ill from time to time, as children sometimes do. I will have Leta keep a log for you if you like."

"This is different," Finn snaps. "Surely you must have thought it was odd enough to mention."

"Someone explain," Pretha says.

Misha sighs. "Odd, yes, but it was no secret. We don't know what's wrong with them. It's like they're sleeping, but they do not wake. I've never seen anything like it."

"I have," Finn says.

Misha's gaze snaps to him. "When?"

"Twenty years ago, when Oberon was locked in the mortal realm and Mordeus declared himself king of the Unseelie Court. Children started . . . falling into what we called the Long Sleep."

"I remember," Pretha says. "They looked so peaceful, but they were locked in stasis."

"I never heard anything about this," Misha says.

"We didn't speak of it," Finn says, his voice low. "We kept it quiet."

I step forward and catch Finn's eye. "If you've been through this before, then you know how to help them."

Finn shakes his head. "It's not that simple. Children are the future of our court. They are the sign of all the good things that are to come, so when a court is dying, it hits the children first." He turns to Pretha. "We were so busy celebrating that Sebastian couldn't take the throne that we didn't stop to consider the cost of it remaining unoccupied."

"Mordeus ruled for twenty-one years," I say. "No one has sat on the throne in all that time. Why is this happening now?"

"It's true that the throne has been unoccupied since my father was locked in the mortal realm," Finn says, his gaze focused on some distant point. "But there was less than a year between the time when Mordeus took over the rule and the golden queen cursed the Unseelie. During that time our court withered and weakened and scores of children fell into the Long Sleep, but then the queen's curse ironically reversed our course. That curse made *her* weak, and that weakness brought a sick sort of balance between the courts."

I shake my head. "I don't understand what one has to do with the other."

Misha lifts a hand and summons an hourglass filled with sparkling grains of sand, turning it on its side and balancing it on his palm. The grains settle to the new bottom of each half. "Imagine this hourglass as the Seelie and Unseelie courts. The grains on each side represent the courts' power. There is most peace and calm when the two sides are balanced." He shifts his hand from side to side, and as the glass moves, the sand shifts from one side to the other. "There's room for some temporary imbalance, but if the imbalance is too great" — he tilts the glass to a more dramatic angle and the sand starts flowing to the other side — "one side can end up with everything and the other with nothing."

"When you broke the curse," Finn says, "the queen's power returned. Her court is no longer weakened, but since no one can take the Unseelie throne, we've been thrown into a power imbalance again. The longer it remains this way, the more children will fall and the greater chance there is that they won't wake again. If we don't act quickly, the whole court will die."

"So we kill the queen," Kane says. Finn flashes him a look, and Kane shrugs. "It's worth a shot. Assuming Prince Ronan doesn't take her crown and her place, a vacant golden throne would buy us time."

"That's a big assumption," Finn says. "Besides, if we couldn't kill her for the two decades that she was weakened by the curse, what makes you think we can kill her now?"

"A male can dream," Kane mutters.

"The bottom line," Finn says solemnly, "is that the Throne of Shadows cannot remain unoccupied. We need to find a way to reunite the power with the crown so that *someone* can take the throne."

Kane waves toward me. "The princess has the power and is bonded to Prince Ronan. He hasn't declared an heir, so perhaps, if we could manage a way for him to meet an untimely end, the crown will shift back to her."

I flinch. "You can't kill him." I find Misha's eyes. "Right? Because the magic of the crown prevents anyone from killing for it?"

"We'd be more clever than that," Kane says before Misha can answer.

"First of all," Finn says, "we can't risk it."

"Even if it worked, Brie can't take the throne," Pretha says. "She's not Unseelie."

Misha smirks and holds my gaze for a beat before swiveling to Finn. "And yet she sat on the throne and it didn't reject her."

"Impossible," Kane says.

Pretha shakes her head. "You *sat* on the throne?" she asks.

I roll my eyes. Of course they hate the idea of a lowly *human* sitting on their precious throne.

Kane shakes his head. "No way. The magic is as old as Mab and stronger, too. It wouldn't have allowed that."

I shrug. "I was wearing the crown, so I was able to sit."

Finn's face pales, but he remains quiet.

"What do you mean by *sat*?" Kane asks. "Just stepped close or—"

"No. I sat. I had to put the crown back where it belonged to fulfill my part of the bargain and save my sister. So that's what I did."

"And what did the throne *do* when you sat on it?" Pretha asks.

I laugh. "What do you mean?"

"Perhaps she wasn't there long," Finn says, studying me now as if he's never really seen me before. "Or never *fully* sat."

My mind latches onto the memories of that day. The woman Mordeus killed to punish me, to show me he could control me even once the bargain was fulfilled and Jas was back home. "I didn't stay long," I say. "Just long enough to save my sister."

"The throne must've sensed that she didn't intend to claim it," Kane says.

Finn is still watching me, still so quiet, those eyes calculating. "That's one explanation. But regardless, it doesn't solve the matter at hand."

Everyone's silent for a long time. Misha studies his wine, Pretha toys with an orange in her hand, and Kane examines the edge of his blade.

Finn watches them all and is the one to finally break the silence. "If anyone will know how to fix this mess, it's Mab. She created the Throne of Shadows, and she's our best hope of finding a solution."

Kane grunts. "Good luck with that."

"I'm not joking," Finn says.

Pretha curses. "Do you have a death wish?"

"Of course not. But I won't watch Arya destroy my court or my people," Finn says. "Even if it means I need to visit the Underworld." He turns to Misha. "In the meantime, we need to return the sleeping children to Unseelie land. They have their best chance of a full recovery if they're on native soil. I presume you'll help make the arrangements, Misha?"

Misha nods. "Of course."

This conversation has taken a turn, and I don't think I'm keeping up. "The Underworld?" I look around the table, as if the explanation might be right there in someone's eyes. I've heard talk of an Underworld in myths and legends, but is Finn saying he plans to *go* there? "That's a real place?"

Pretha's hands curl into fists on the table, but she doesn't raise her head. "It's a sort of intermediary space between here and where our rulers go . . . *after*."

"After . . ." It clicks, and I gasp. "You're saying the afterlife is a physical place?"

Finn shakes his head. "Our past rulers don't reside in the Underworld. They reside in the Twilight, where we cannot visit. But we can, on occasion, visit the Underworld, and so can they. It's the only way to speak with Mab."

"It's a suicide mission," Pretha says.

Finn shoves his hands into his pockets. "It's been done before. More than once."

Pretha pushes out of her chair and stands. "And more than one has tried and failed — tried and *died*."

I'm still trying to wrap my mind around the idea of a member of the living visiting the Underworld, but I ask, "Why do people die when they go there?"

"It's always about balance," Misha says, tilting his hourglass from side to side. "If our great leaders who are no longer on this plane can visit the Underworld, so can the great monsters that we've cast out of this world."

Finn looks at Misha and cocks his head to the side, but there's nothing playful about the hard gleam in his eyes. "Thankfully the princess broke the curse, and I'm no longer the helpless waste of space you had to protect for the last two decades. I am heir to the Throne of Shadows. My magic walks the line between life and death. I am the best candidate for this job. Mab will know how to save our court, and I intend to get those answers."

"We don't even know where to find the portals to the Underworld," Pretha says. "And the last time you tried to get the High Priestess to open one, she wouldn't meet with you."

Finn nods. "I remember, but I have a plan for that." He turns to me and meets my eyes for a long, tense moment. "Assuming the princess will be kind enough to accompany me into the mountains for Lunastal."

"I'll go where I'm needed," I say, but I shake my head, still feeling miles behind in this conversation. "What's in the mountains? And what's Lunastal?"

Finn smiles. "That's where the High Priestess resides. On major holidays she resurfaces from her deep meditations and takes audiences for several days. And I'll need her, as she's the only one who can open a portal to the Underworld."

"You're going to ask her to send you to your death?" Kane asks.

Pretha shakes her head. "It's too risky."

"Enough." Finn's command is sharp and clear, silencing everyone in the room. "Abriella and I will see the High Priestess, and if she grants me access, I will go to the Underworld to talk to Mab." He sweeps his gaze over the group, daring anyone to contradict him, then settles his eyes on Amira. "There are four days until Lunastal. We need to move."

"We couldn't possibly make the necessary preparations in time," Pretha says. "There are procedures in place for when the prince attends a celebration. Never mind that we need time to prepare Juliana. If you show up with Abriella and Juliana senses that she holds the power of the crown, there will be hell to pay."

"Too bad."

CHAPTER TWELVE

I WAS INSTRUCTED TO PACK bare necessities for a week or two and told that Pretha and Misha would be working together to open a portal from the settlement into the Unseelie Court. They said I'd need to be ready to head out before dawn.

No one told me why Finn needs me with him to see this priestess, nor did anyone explain what Finn's trip to the Underworld would entail. As much as these people pretend that I'm part of the team now, the truth is, they still don't trust me completely. It's a reminder that while I may have power and a new immortal body, I don't truly belong. But I can live with that. I have reasons of my own to want to see this priestess. If she's able to open portals to the Underworld, perhaps she knows something about this "reverse Potion of Life" Misha once mentioned. Even if it no longer exists, perhaps there's another way for me to become mortal again.

Finn, or one of his people, put wards around their wing of the castle, but I slip through them like water through the cracks of a mountain. I hide in the shadows, let myself be one with the darkness, and slink noiselessly toward the sound of their voices.

Pretha and Finn are on one of the castle's many terraces. Finn's arms are braced on the railing, a wineglass cupped loosely in one hand, while Pretha paces behind him.

"—missing something important," Finn's saying. "It just doesn't add up, but I'll be damned if I let fear keep me from finding the answers we need."

"There has to be another way." Pretha rubs the center of her chest with her palm. "Who else might have a solution?"

"No one." His voice is calm, almost lazy, but I feel his worry. It's a vibration that roils just under the surface of this inexplicable connection between us. "There's no one else, Pretha. I'm doing this."

Pretha summons a bottle of wine and pours herself a healthy serving. The dark, velvety red liquid seems to gobble up light. She drains half the glass in one pull and immediately refills it. "What about your responsibility to your people? We've protected you for twenty years so you could lead them, and now—"

"Now that's off the table. I'm not the one wearing the crown, so we need to find another way to protect them." With a sigh, he turns to her. "I don't have a choice. It's not like I'm looking forward to taking her back to him. He'll have her eating out of his hand in no time."

"I'm not so sure about that." Pretha takes another sip of her wine. "What if Mab says the only way to do this is for Brie to forfeit her life and let Sebastian rule?"

"There has to be another way," he says, but he seems to be talking to himself.

"Why do I think you're more opposed to Brie's death than to seeing Sebastian on the throne?"

He cups his forehead in one big hand and squeezes his temples. "The last thing we need right now is my ego getting between us and the cure for my dying court."

Pretha blows out a breath. "We'll find a way. I have to believe it."

Turning, he lounges against the rail and studies his sister-in-law. "How are you doing with all this?"

"The pending destruction of our entire realm?" she says, her eyebrows inching up. She hoists her glass in the air. "Oh, just great."

Finn shakes his head. "This is the first time you've stayed at Castle Craige since your parents sent you away. How does it feel to be home?"

My heart sinks. Pretha's such an assertive, capable member of Finn's team. It's easy to forget that she was once a girl in love with her brother's betrothed.

"It's . . . fine. Good. It's good." Her expression goes distant as she looks out at the sprawling valley beyond the terrace. "I miss this place, but I didn't realize how much until we stepped foot in the palace." She bites her bottom lip, and her big brown eyes brim with tears. "I have a lot of happy memories here."

Finn reaches for her wrist and squeezes. My heart tugs at the rare sign of physical affection from the shadow prince, but at the same time an uncomfortable feeling wraps around my heart. Jealousy, I realize. I've been jealous of Pretha's relationship with Finn from the day I met him. At first, because I thought they had a romantic relationship, but now because of their connection. They have each other to lean on. I've been so lonely since running from Sebastian. I have all these people around me who claim to want to be my friend, but how can I trust them when they care more about this power than they'll ever care for me?

If I could shed this power like an unwanted cloak, would any of them care about me? Would I even have a place to stay or would I still be running?

"Your brother and Amira's relationship isn't a romantic one," Finn says, releasing Pretha's wrist. "Rumor has it that he's trying to impregnate one of his consorts to carry on the family line."

Pretha scoffs. "I'm pretty sure he's been trying *that* since he came of age."

Finn grunts and flashes a rare grin. "I knew Misha back then, and I hate to break it to you, but he wasn't after an heir when he took all those females to his bed."

"Trust me. I've heard the rumors." Chuckling, Pretha studies her wine. "Brace yourself. I think he has his sights set on Brie now."

Misha wants me to be his . . . consort? Or is that what he wants them to think? My instincts tell me it's more of the second than the first. Misha is kind and gorgeous, but more likely he wants access to this power or has some plan to use any perceived relationship with me to increase his own standing in Faerie politics.

Finn arches a brow. "And what does that have to do with me?"

"You're protecting her. Everyone knows it."

"It's the least I can do." He turns back to the view and leans his forearms on the railing. "After everything."

"Has she visited your dreams again? Since . . ."

He shakes his head. "No. I don't think she intended to that time. Her magic was surging through her transformation, and her mind latched onto me as a way to make sense of everything." He drags a hand through his curls, making a mess of them. "Sebastian really loves her—deceit or not."

"Yes, well . . . what did love ever do for us but mess with our plans?" Pretha asks, and Finn grunts in agreement. "I should go," she says. "I need to say goodbye to the female I love and pretend that I'm okay sleeping alone while she's under the same roof."

Finn arches a brow. "You don't have to sleep alone," he says softly. "Amira has her own chambers. Everyone knows she'd happily make room for you in her bed."

Pretha closes her eyes and swallows hard. "I decided long ago that I would rather be lonely and miserable than be her mistress. I can't fault anyone who would've chosen differently, but for me . . . it wouldn't be enough. It didn't seem fair to enter into an arrangement that would leave me feeling angry and bitter toward her and my brother."

Finn gives her wrist a final squeeze. "Sleep well."

After Pretha leaves, I find my way back into the corridor and wait several minutes before stepping out of my shadows. I take a deep breath as I feel myself turning corporeal again, and then I join Finn on the terrace, my boots clicking against the stone floors with every step.

"I forget how beautiful the nights are in these lands," he says before I have a chance to explain my presence or why I snuck through his wards — not that I have a good explanation.

I join him at the rail. "They are stunning. Better than home?"

A small, sad smile curls his lips. "No. Nothing's better than home."

"I bet you're anxious to get back there."

His eyes meet mine, and the wariness I see there is like a stone settling in my gut. "I'm anxious to be doing something that gets us closer to a solution. The palace itself . . ." He shakes his head. "Going home is always an emotional quagmire, one I'm never eager to rejoin."

"Why's that?"

Finn's mouth twists unhappily. "It's irrelevant. All that matters now are answers."

"Answers about what?"

"About the children. About my people. About what we do now. We are a court in shambles."

And that's all my fault. I let the words sink into me, let them settle like stones in my gut. "You really think Mab will have a solution?"

He nods. "I think the Great Queen would go to untold lengths to protect her court, but especially to protect it from Seelie rule."

"And you'd accept her solution if it involved letting someone else sit on the throne? Even after . . . everything?"

He swallows. "Believe it or not, I want what's best for my people more than what's best for me. Right now, what's best is a kingdom that survives." He shakes his head. "My life is less valuable than that of an entire court. If I didn't know that, I should be ashamed to ever believe I could rule."

"You must really despise me then," I say softly.

Straightening, he turns to me slowly. "Not even a little, Princess."

"You should. My life is no more valuable than yours, yet my beating heart is the reason your court is in shambles, as you say."

"I don't see it that way." Lifting his face, he turns his attention back to the night sky, and the silence sits heavily between us. "Are you prepared to see him again?" he asks.

"I saw him once already."

Finn arches a brow. "Let me guess—when you asked him to dismantle the camps?"

Nodding, I lean on the rail and watch a bat circle in the distance. "Does it ever get easier? Being connected to someone like this?"

He narrows his eyes, as if the answer is out there in the dark and he need only focus to see it. "Does it *feel* difficult?"

I huff. "Always having to cut myself off from his emotions? The constant distraction of feeling what he's feeling and the vigilance necessary to keep my shields up?" I sigh. "Difficult. Exhausting. Yes."

"Hmm." He squeezes the back of his neck. "You're shielding against your bonded partner? Interesting."

I glare at him so hard I can't believe he doesn't shrink from the force of it. "It's not your business."

"I don't think it's supposed to be a hardship. Ideally, it would be a comfort, but you two . . ."

"Were cursed from the start?"

He huffs out a laugh. "It's complicated, I guess." He looks down at his arms. The sleeves of his black tunic have been rolled to his elbows, exposing his strong forearms and the rune markings covering them. "Not that I'd really know."

I study the tattoos on his arms and then the ones peeking out from his collar. Since I've seen him shirtless, I know there are many, many more where those came from, and each represents a unique bond. "Are any of them alive?" I ask. "Or were they all tributes from the time of the curse?"

He blows out a breath. "I never saw the point in bonding to my servants. And of course the moment I bonded with the tributes . . ."

"They died," I finish.

He nods.

"And what about Isabel?"

He flinches. "She was the first human I killed." His voice is so low I can barely hear the words. "The first human whose life force I got to feel pumping through my veins."

I want to be disgusted, but there's something in his expression that only makes me feel *sorry.* "But you loved her?"

His eyes connect with mine. They're haunted. "I did," he says. "So don't ever fool yourself into thinking love is enough, Princess. Maybe that's true where you come from, but it couldn't be further from the truth in this godsforsaken place."

I open my mouth to argue, but I'm cut off when Kane rushes onto the terrace.

"Word has arrived from the Unseelie palace," he says.

I squeeze my eyes shut, hating the interruption but feeling grateful for it at the same time. I wish my feelings for Finn weren't so conflicted. I wish I could simply slot the shadow prince into the "enemy" category in my brain, the way I did with Mordeus, and move on, but no matter how much I try to convince myself he's no better than his evil uncle, my heart refuses to believe it.

"There are riots outside the palace," Kane says.

Finn frowns. "In response to what?"

"Prince Ronan ordered the Midnight Raiders to move into the mountains, and let's just say they weren't open to the golden prince stepping into a position of authority. Reports say they want his head."

"Well, that's convenient," Finn mutters.

I gasp at Finn. "Are you serious?"

Kane turns those creepy red eyes on me. "I thought you loathed the golden one. Didn't he deceive you?"

"That doesn't mean I want him *dead,*" I snap.

"We wouldn't be in this mess if he were," Kane mutters, and I glare at him. He turns his attention back to Finn. "For the time being, his guard is keeping them at bay, but the crowd grows. They're demanding to see their true king."

At least now I understand what I felt from Sebastian earlier. His worry was undoubtedly in response to the riots.

Finn grimaces. "Whoever the fuck that is," he mutters.

"They want you on that throne," Kane says.

"What can we do?" I ask.

"We?" Finn asks.

I turn up my palms. "Surely this isn't what you want—seeing your own court descend into chaos."

"What I *want,* Princess, is to repair the damage Mordeus did to my *home* over the last two decades. What I *want* is for the parents of the sleeping children to be able to see their bright eyes again. I *want* to figure out how to fix this before we lose more children to the Long Sleep, before every member of the next generation of my court is lost, trapped in their own slumber."

"They want *you,*" I say softly. "That's what Misha told me. He said that many silently supported you through Mordeus's rule and that if you and Sebastian formed an alliance, if you worked together, the majority of the court would be united."

"Misha talks too much." He blows out a breath. "All those people want is someone they can trust. They don't know anything about Prince Ronan except for who his mother is and what she did to them. How are they supposed to take him on as their prince, as their king? How are they supposed to trust anything he says?"

"Don't let them kill him," I whisper.

Finn's eyes flash and his nostrils flare. "It's tempting." His gaze rakes over me, and he shakes his head. "But as we already established, if Sebastian dies, we don't know what happens to the crown. I have no intention of letting a mob get at him, as satisfying as it may be."

"How noble of you," I snap.

Kane clears his throat and glances longingly toward the corridor. "I can leave."

"Stay," Finn and I bark at the same time, neither of us taking our eyes off the other.

Finn lifts his chin. "What do you want from me, Princess?"

Kane groans behind Finn, looking back and forth between us like we're two bombs about to explode.

"I want you to *go,*" I snap. "Be that person. Be the one who rules and protects them. Prove that you want what's best for them by forming an alliance with Sebastian. It might not fix the court, but it will make it stronger while we search for a long-term solution."

He folds his arms. "What makes you think your prince is interested in an alliance?"

I shrug. "What makes you so sure he's not?" After everything Sebastian explained to me, it's hard to know what to think—to know what was true and what was manipulation—but in my heart I still believe he is good, that he wants what's best for his father's people. He had so much hope for these courts and for the continued peace between them that he betrayed me to make it happen. He and Finn aren't so different.

"I'm going with you anyway," I say. "I might as well help convince him while I'm there. We'll figure this out together."

"The only thing your presence will help us figure out is how much he's willing to grovel to get back into your bed."

"Even so," Kane says, "having Abriella on our side might work to our advantage."

Finn scowls at him.

"You can't deny she has a way with you princes." Kane turns up his palms. "Kings too, it appears. She even has Misha wrapped around her finger."

First Pretha and now Kane? I flash him a glare. "I do not!"

He chuckles. "Don't worry. He hasn't noticed yet."

"Misha's a *friend*."

"You're excused, Kane," Finn growls, and Kane doesn't waste a moment before disappearing into the castle.

When we're alone again, I turn back to Finn. "Let me do what I can to help you convince Sebastian."

"You'll make it sound like he's doing us a favor. Let me handle this."

"You told me once that he wasn't your enemy. What changed? Why do you wish him ill now?"

"That was before he destroyed my court with his reckless decisions," he snaps.

"You mean before he saved my life."

He closes his eyes. "That's not what I said."

I lift my chin. "Your court is in trouble because he saved my life and chained the power of the crown to my existence. Say it however you want. That's the truth."

His eyes glitter in the moonlight, and his jaw goes hard. "Stop it. Stop thinking that this world would be better off without you."

"You said yourself that you'd put Sebastian on the throne before seeing your court fall. That's exactly where he would be if it weren't for me." I step back, shaking my head. These are the thoughts that haunt me. "If I hadn't taken that potion—"

Before I know what's happening, Finn spins me around and presses me against the wall. He stares down at me, his silver eyes hard. "But you did. You took the potion, and in doing so, you salvaged one beautiful thing in a world full of ugliness. I, for one, will *never* be sorry for that."

I can barely process his words before his mouth is on mine and—*gods,* the heat of his hard body pressed against me, the feel of his lips sipping at my mouth, like I'm the finest wine and he's fighting between warring instincts to savor and devour.

When he sucks my bottom lip between his teeth, I open for him. I kiss him back with equal hunger. This isn't just a kiss. It's all the words we haven't said written with our mouths, with our bodies. It's unbridled anger and hope and fear and lust—all woven together and electrified. There's no loneliness here. No regrets. Just the taste of him, like rich red wine, and the feel of his strength wrapping around me, surging inside me.

My arms loop around his neck and my hands dive into his hair, freeing it from the tie so I can feel the silky curls between my fingers. Finn tears his mouth from mine and trails hot, open-mouthed kisses along my jaw and beneath my ear until he finds the juncture of my neck and shoulder, where he bit me not so long ago. His tongue sweeps across that spot, and I gasp as the sting of pleasure floods my blood and the memory blooms in my mind.

Finn groans and positions his thigh between my legs as if he's remembering too. "I thought I'd made it up," he murmurs. "But you taste even sweeter than I remember."

Stop. I love you. Stop. Please. Please, please, please.

An ache swells in my chest, terrible and desperate and not my own, but it makes my head clear just enough. *This a mistake.* This kiss. These touches. Melting at the sound of his sweet words. It's all a terrible mistake, and I've already made too many of those.

I shove him away and haul up my shields, blocking out the sudden surge of Sebastian's feelings.

Finn doesn't resist. He doesn't even stumble. He simply takes three steps back, as if he'd been bracing himself for the moment I'd come to my senses.

Chest heaving, he stares at me. I wonder if I look as untethered as he does, if my lips are as swollen, or if the hunger I see in his eyes is mirrored in my own.

"You can't kiss me." My protest sounds weak. Forced. Probably because it is.

Finn draws in a long, shaky breath, and I can practically see him pulling himself back together. "Sorry to break it to you, Princess, but I wasn't the only one doing the kissing."

"Well, I can't kiss you either."

He arches a brow. "And why is that?"

Because I can't think straight when you touch me. Because I won't be a fool again. Because it would be too easy to believe your sweet words and let myself fall for you. Because I still have something you want, and I can't trust that you want me more than this power.

I'm too shaky, too vulnerable to share any of those reasons with him, so I go with the one I know will hit him the hardest. "Because I'm bonded to Sebastian."

Finn doesn't move, doesn't physically bristle, but I see the change in his eyes. Like a door being closed. "Interesting."

I press my lips together, but I can't help it. I take the bait. "What?"

He shrugs. "Misha's under the impression that you no longer want the bond. That you're hoping to find a way to sever it."

I huff. "You're right. Misha does talk too much."

"Is it true? Do you wish to undo the bond?"

I set my jaw. "Sebastian didn't exactly enter into it under honest pretenses."

"And you think there's some exceptions clause allowing you out of it because he deceived you?" Finn finally turns away from me and strolls to the railing. "You have so much to learn about this world, Princess."

Of all the pompous, condescending bullshit—

I turn to leave but stop, my back to the stars. "Don't confuse ignorance for naivety, Finn. I'm no longer the foolish girl who could be so confused by physical attraction and pretty words."

"I'm sure Sebastian will be more than happy to put that theory to the test."

I look over my shoulder. He's studying me like he wishes he could get into my mind. "I was talking about you."

He swallows. "Be ready to leave before dawn," he says. "It will a long day."

CHAPTER THIRTEEN

THE MOMENT FINN MATERIALIZES IN the Unseelie throne room, Riaan grabs him from behind and puts his sword to the shadow prince's neck. "Tell me why I shouldn't slice you open right here and right now."

Finn's goblin disappears in a blink, and I stay in the shadows, just as we planned. This morning, we rode our horses through the portal and into the Unseelie capital. While Misha, Pretha, and the others helped transport the children to infirmaries in the city, Finn's goblin brought Finn and me straight to the palace throne room.

I scan the room now. Sebastian's on the dais, narrowed eyes on his half brother and Riaan, but the large room is otherwise empty.

Finn smiles. He doesn't even try to evade Sebastian's sentinel, even though he could. I've seen him evade attack after attack when he trains with Jalek. He could've had Riaan on his back without so much as touching his magic. Instead, he remains entirely still as Riaan presses the blade into his neck. The only movement is from his cold, silver eyes as they lift to meet Sebastian's. "I believe he's waiting for your order," Finn drawls.

"I'm hoping," Sebastian says, "that it won't come to that."

Finn's brows arch and he laughs. "Really?"

"Riaan, put away your blade."

The male's nostrils flare, and he tugs Finn's head back for a moment—as if he might disobey his prince and slice Finn's neck open anyway—but then he thrusts a knee into the shadow prince's back, shoving him forward as he releases him.

Finn's all grace on his feet and doesn't even stumble. He simply strolls up the steps toward Sebastian. "It appears you've found yourself in a bit of a dilemma with the natives," Finn says, glancing toward the bank of windows that line the side of the throne room.

All I can see from my perch in the corner is a sunny morning, but we all know that hordes of unhappy shadow fae wait beyond the gates. I could hear them protesting when we came through the portal.

"It's a *temporary* dilemma," Sebastian says. "Once I sit on this throne, they'll accept me."

Folding his arms, Finn rocks back on his heels. His smile is anything but cheerful. This is the smile of a male promising death to anyone who hurts those he loves. It's the smile of an exiled prince who had his only chance at the throne stolen from him. "I'm delighted to hear you have a solution," Finn says. "Though I'm curious what it could be."

"You think I'm going to tell *you?*"

Finn shrugs. "I'm just thinking it through. You know the power won't shift to you if you murder your princess, and now that you've made her immortal, you can't count on her dying naturally anytime soon." Finn cocks his head to the side. "Perhaps you're hoping she'll choose to join our elders at a remarkably young age and pass the power off to you that way. Perhaps you're counting on her love for you being strong enough to overcome the fact that you lied to her and manipulated her to get that crown . . ." He studies his nails for a beat and hums softly, as if he's thinking this possibility over. "Of course, that plan would rely on her forgiving you, and if I remember correctly, she's sworn she won't."

Sebastian lunges forward and shoves Finn, palms flat against his chest. Again, Finn doesn't even stumble. Sebastian and Riaan are boys, I realize. They're children compared with Finn. Amateurs drawn into a game of chess with a master. "I have *advisors,*" Sebastian growls, his teeth clenched. "They're working to find a solution that won't harm Abriella."

Finn laughs. "So when you say you *have a plan,* what you really mean is you're hoping your *advisors* will come up with a plan. Makes you wonder, doesn't it, what would've happened if you'd told her the truth back when you were painting me as the villain?"

Sebastian roars, and darkness creeps up the walls and the floor quakes.

"Was that supposed to scare me?" Finn asks, his gaze flicking about the room as the shadows recede. "Don't stress. I've been playing with my Unseelie power all my life, so it's hard to impress me. I'm sure your Golden Military sentinels will be awestruck."

Sebastian's face twists in anger. "Shut your mouth or get out of my throne room."

"*Your* throne room?" Finn asks. "How do you figure it's yours?"

"It's more mine than it will ever be yours."

Finn rubs his jaw, as if considering this. "See, that's where I think you're wrong. So many believe that power is about the crown or the magic itself. But those people outside the palace gates? Many would argue that the power of a kingdom comes from them—belongs to them. That's where Mordeus went wrong. He failed to understand that when you rule this kingdom, you serve everyone. The weak and the strong. The subservient and the rebellious."

"I *know* that," Sebastian growls. "I have no interest in ruling like Mordeus did. You forget that I did all this to remove him from power—to save this kingdom from *him*."

Finn steps closer, his face inches from his brother's. "And *you* forget that while you spent the last two years playing human boy and trying to steal Abriella's heart, *I* was working to make sure my people knew I hadn't forgotten them, to make sure they knew that no matter who took over this palace, no matter who pretended they belonged here, they would have their basic needs met, and if they weren't, there would be an army to fight for them."

"I don't want to hurt them, Finn." Sebastian swallows hard. "You claim I lied to Abriella, but I didn't lie about what matters. I want what's best for both kingdoms. I want to protect both kingdoms from rulers who would destroy everything for more power."

"You mean your mother?" Finn asks.

"Yes!" Sebastian roars. "Of course I mean her." He shakes his head. "Do you forget that I am Unseelie too? Like it or not, *brother,*

Oberon's blood pumps through my veins the same way it pumps through yours, or this crown would never be on my head. And I know I've failed them. In so many ways I failed them. But I want to help them. And I think you do too." He holds Finn's gaze. "Help me do right by them. Help me protect them. Help me *organize* our forces so we're not torn apart from the inside before my mother even strikes."

"Hmm." Finn narrows his eyes, studying the top of Sebastian's head as if some strange creature sits there and not an invisible crown. "I just don't see what's in it for me."

Sebastian swallows. "Help me."

"But why should I? If this kingdom falls apart while you pretend to rule it, doesn't that make *me* look good? If Mordeus ruled without the throne, I can too."

I clench my jaw from the shadows. This is why Finn didn't want to ask Sebastian for an alliance. He doesn't want to reveal that he needs Sebastian as much as Sebastian needs him. He doesn't want Sebastian to know that the shadow court is dying until Sebastian promises whatever it is that Finn is after.

"Finn," Sebastian growls. "I can't—" He shakes his head. "You know I need you. To resolve this peacefully, I need you."

"Not necessarily," Riaan says. "We have ambassadors in meeting with the Midnight Raiders now. They'll convince them—"

"It's not working," Sebastian growls, his eyes flaring bright. He turns to Finn. "Name your price."

"Abriella."

"What?"

Finn's face is the picture of ambivalence. "My price is Abriella.

If you want peace at your palace gates, if you want me to convince the Raiders to join your forces in the mountains, you have to give me your princess."

"Excuse me?" I bark. I don't care what I promised. I don't care what kind of game Finn is playing trying to keep me in the shadows. I let them all fall away, and Sebastian's eyes go wide as he takes me in.

"Brie." Sebastian rushes toward me. He's a step away when I hold up a hand, and he stops. "How long have you been here? And why don't I—" He presses his fingertips to the rune tattooed on his wrist. "I've barely been able to feel you. Are you okay?"

"I'm fine." I turn and glare at Finn. "You're out of line," I hiss.

Chuckling, Finn shrugs. "That's my price," he says, holding my gaze. "If Sebastian wants me to help him with his little problem, then he'll give me *you*."

"I hate you," I bite out.

Finn holds my gaze for a long, loaded moment and smiles slowly. "Whatever you need to tell yourself, Princess." He turns back to Sebastian. "It's only fair. After all, our father made the same promise to both of us—or so your mother claims. This way, you get the crown. I get"—he waves toward me as if I'm am a stray weapon they're fighting over after battle—"the other half."

I want to scream, but I bite my tongue. I don't know what Finn's playing at here, and if I say too much, it could fall apart. As much as I don't trust him, I believe we have the same goals.

"Simply dissolve the bond between you so she can bond with me. She'd certainly enjoy that more."

"You've lost your gods-damned mind," I mutter.

Finn winks at me. *Winks.*

Sebastian searches my face. "You want this? You—no, it doesn't matter," he says, his voice cold as he turns back to Finn. "Brie is *mine.* She bonded with me, not you. You can't have her."

"I don't want to be bonded to *either* of you!" My shadows swirl at my feet and wrap themselves around my arms, and I don't bother to pull them back in.

Finn's gaze sweeps over me hungrily, and his smile suggests that I've just handed him a gift.

Sebastian, on the other hand, looks like I've slapped him. "I won't let you go. Not until we've had a *chance.* I love you."

"Is that what you said to the human girls at the Golden Palace who were clamoring to be your bride?" Finn asks. "Did you pledge your love before they bonded with you so you could have more power?"

I frown and look back and forth between Finn and Sebastian. "What is he talking about?" I say.

"Oh," Finn says, shaking his head. "Sorry. I forgot you told her that you 'sent them home.' Oops."

Images of those girls faces flash in my mind, and my stomach cramps. I was so jealous of them. So jealous of the chance I thought they had to be Sebastian's bride, when all along they were being duped as badly as I was. "How could you?" I ask, thinking of all the times he used magic just to impress me, just to show me he could. Those girls. Those innocent lives fueled each needless magical act.

"I was just trying to survive." Swallowing, Sebastian holds my gaze. "All I want is to take care of you."

Finn wrinkles his nose. "That crown on your head suggests otherwise."

"This crown is *useless* without the power!" he shouts.

"Indeed." Finn rocks back on his heels. "If only you'd known this would happen."

"Even if I'd suspected," Sebastian says, nostrils flaring, "I would've given her that potion."

My heart squeezes. Is that true? Would he have saved me at the cost of ruling the shadow court—or is that his pride talking?

Sebastian's chest heaves, and when he closes his eyes, I can see him reining his temper back in. After several long, deliberate breaths, he tells Finn, "As you know, ending our bond is not so simple. Even if . . ." Swallowing, he finds my gaze and holds it. "Even if we *both* wanted that. And I certainly do not. You'll need to come up with something else."

"You have nothing else to offer me," Finn says.

"Think of something," Sebastian growls. "Since Abriella's uninterested in sharing the bond with you anyway," he says, with no small amount of satisfaction in his voice, "asking for her bond is moot."

I swallow. I might not know what game Finn's playing, but that doesn't mean I can't play my own. "What if Sebastian just dissolved the bond between us," I ask Finn. "Wouldn't that be enough?"

"No," Sebastian barks. He closes his eyes for a beat, then shakes his head, and when he speaks to me again, his voice is softer. "I know you think that's what you want, but it's off the table."

Finn taps a finger to his mouth, considering. "There's a

ritual — an old one that my maternal grandparents used in the war — that allowed a member of a bonded pair to shift the bond to someone else for a time. You see, when couples were divided during wartime and one was left at home while the other went to fight, the idea was to protect the individual at home from the pain and anguish of the front lines. Transferring the bond could also protect the bonded partner should the warrior become a captive — as those connections were often used against the Raiders to get them to reveal proprietary information. So some priestesses came together to create this ritual that would enable the bond to be temporarily shifted from one individual to another."

"I'm . . . familiar with the concept," Sebastian says cautiously.

"Then you know it's possible, and that there's no way for me to use it to permanently steal your bond with Abriella."

Sebastian folds his arms. "Why?"

Finn shrugs. "The people outside your gates aren't the only problem. As I mentioned, I worked to ensure that my people would have the protection of a fully functional army should I never recover the crown. Now those forces wait at the ready under the command of General Hargova."

"The Cursed Horde," Sebastian whispers, something like awe in his voice. "They're real?"

Finn chuckles. "They may be near invisible, but they are real. They trust me to a degree, but they trust the power of the crown more. If Abriella and I visit them as a bonded couple, we could convince them to join the Raiders and your guard — to be a united front against any future attacks by the Seelie Court."

"Abriella and I can go," Sebastian says. "We already *are* a bonded couple. And I have the crown."

Finn arches a brow and remains silent a moment. "The problem is, while they may only trust me to a degree, they don't trust you at all. And as you mentioned, that crown, in its current condition, is useless."

Sebastian looks at me and holds my gaze for a long time, so long that I realize he's trying to communicate something.

The moment I lower my shield, I'm slammed with the impression of jealousy and fear. He's afraid that if he does this, he'll lose me. And that if he doesn't, he'll lose his father's kingdom.

"I need to think about it," he says softly. He tucks his hands into his pockets and strides toward the throne room doors. He stops with his palm pressed against them and turns to look at me. "Abriella, I have a meeting, but I'll be taking lunch in the dining room in two hours. I hope you'll join me. We have a lot to discuss. I think you'll be pleased with all I have to report."

When I climb the palace's highest turret, it's my first chance to see the teeming throng beyond the distant gates.

Somehow I'm not surprised to find Finn already here, standing stoic in the midmorning light as he looks out to where his people are protesting. When he turns to me, his face is lined with worry. Gone is the male who was laughing in Sebastian's face and ambivalent about the fate of the court. In his place is the shadow prince who would sooner die than see his court fall.

"Don't you dare do that again," I say softly. "I am not for sale.

Nor am I his to give. I am not something to be bartered or sold or—"

"Obviously I know that." His jaw ticks.

"You're an ass. You never wanted me to stay hidden the whole time. You knew I'd get angry and come out of the shadows. That was part of your plan."

"It worked," he says, shrugging. "If you'd been by my side from the start, he'd think we were working together—that you were in on my plan—and he'd be suspicious of even a temporary arrangement."

"I don't understand what game you're playing."

His expression turns stony. "I've told you from the beginning. My priority is my people."

"And you somehow need to be bonded to me to protect your people?"

"I need answers, Princess. I need to see the High Priestess, and she won't be obliged to see me without the power from my father's throne. *You* happen to be carrying that power."

"You've already explained that you need me with you to see the High Priestess, but why do you need the bond?"

His eyes go hard. "Maybe I just don't want him to have it."

"Aren't you, like, hundreds of years old? Why are you acting like a spoiled child who doesn't want to share his *toys?*"

His grin is smug, and his gaze is pure wicked intention as he looks me over slowly. "I don't consider you a *toy,* Princess, but if you'd like to play, all you have to do is ask."

Flames of embarrassment lick my cheeks, but I refuse to back down. "You wish."

"When you aren't blocking him, Sebastian can sense where you are through the bond, and I don't trust him enough to reveal the location of our High Priestess's sacred temple."

"So everything you said about needing me to convince this general of yours to join forces with Sebastian's legions?"

Finn grunts. "A convenient excuse. General Hargova's Cursed Horde answers to their general, and General Hargova answers to me, the crown and its power be damned. He already has legions stationed in the Goblin Mountains to defend the border, and if I want them to continue to do so alongside Sebastian's warriors, I need only meet with the general. We are weeks, maybe days away from all-out war with the golden queen's kingdom. I can't fathom why she hasn't attacked already, but it's only a matter of time. Maybe she doesn't know or understand what a mess the court is in." He shrugs. "The real reason I need you by my side is so the High Priestess will tell me how to find the portal to get to Mab."

"I think it's a mistake to play these games with him," I say. "Sebastian *cares* about the Unseelie Court. He just said—"

"I don't care what he *says*." He blows out a breath, exasperated. "The High Priestess can't deny the power you carry, and when you ask where to find a portal to the Underworld, the oath she swore to Mab will compel her to answer you as a part of the Great Queen's throne. I fear what kinds of information Sebastian, wearing the crown, could force her to answer if he knew where to find her."

"You could've told me all this before we came here. You could've asked *me* instead of asking Sebastian, as if I'm nothing more than a horse you want to borrow for a few days."

He shrugs. "It was more fun this way."

Sighing, I turn my gaze to the gates and the throng of fae beyond them. "There are so many of them," I say. "What keeps them from rushing the gates?"

"They could if they truly wanted to," Finn says. "Sebastian's guard holds a shield of protection around the Midnight Palace. Those beyond it are prevented from coming in—though if they worked together, they could probably get through it."

I arch a brow. "Midnight Palace? That's really what this place is called?"

"The Court of the Moon pulls its power from the night. What better name for the palace than one that honors the moment the moon reaches its highest point?"

"I suppose," I say, but my mind's busy contemplating the protesters. "If they could get past the gates, why don't they?"

Finn sighs. "Right now, their presence is a protest, not a declaration of war. They don't want to lose any more loved ones. They might not trust Sebastian, but his inaction—the fact that he doesn't attack or allow his sentinels to go out there and handle them with force—that keeps the protest peaceful. He could wipe out dozens of them with a single strike from behind the safety of this shield."

I frown. "He won't."

"I hope you're right about that. Your boy's certainly powerful enough now that the curse is broken." Finn studies me. "Though not nearly as powerful as you."

"How will you handle them?" I ask, changing the subject. "Assuming he agrees to my terms?"

I set my jaw and nod. I expect Sebastian to agree — he'll do it for those people out there — but I'm not sure yet what I think of the cost.

"I'll go out there myself," he says. "They won't believe it if we send a messenger. They need to see me. To feel my presence and trust that the ruler they've waited so long to bring home hasn't forsaken them." There's a sadness in his voice that melts away all the anger from earlier.

"You think you failed them," I say.

His throat bobs, and he keeps his eyes focused on the horizon. "I know I did."

I want to argue with him, to convince him that this mess wasn't his making, but I can tell by the set of his jaw and the distant look in his eyes that there's something heavier weighing on him. More that I don't know.

"They want a sign that the power of their court hasn't been lost." He turns to me and studies me for long moments before saying, "You could give them that."

I take a deep breath and stare out at the crowd beyond the gates. With half a thought, I cast out night over them. I make it soft — a blanket of black velvet instead of the abyss of nightmares. Above them, I hang stars so bright they feel close enough to touch. Shivers run up my arms and down my spine — not just because I, too, love the image I've given them, but because it feels *good* to use this power that's trapped in my veins. Especially when I'm around Finn and I feel so filled with it.

A hush ripples through the crowd as they all look up. I give it everything I can, feeding details from the beautiful nights in my memories—at the beach with my mother, the tail of a shooting star easing my worry. And then I slowly pull it back, letting the sun creep back in as I wind my power back into my center.

When I look at Finn, he's watching me slack-jawed, something like wonder in his eyes.

"What?"

He shakes his head, and that cocky smirk reappears. "You are . . . incredibly inefficient."

I gape. "Excuse me?"

He waves into the distance. "What you just did there? That should barely skim the top of your power, but instead of using what you need and saving the rest, you throw it all out there. Like dumping a vat of wine over the whole table just to fill a small glass."

"I'm so sorry that the way I use my magic isn't to your liking."

Finn grunts. "The way you use your magic is wasteful, bordering on irresponsible." He presses two fingers to the center of his chest. "It comes from here and should be used with focus and precision. You're spilling energy from every inch of you. It's like wielding a battering ram when you only need a needle."

"I haven't exactly had a lifetime to practice, like some people," I grouse.

He steps closer and crouches until he's eye-to-eye with me. "You don't understand what I'm saying. Magic is life. You need to conserve it. It's self-preservation."

"I get it," I snap.

His expression softens. "I'll teach you. If you'll let me."

I look away from the tenderness in his eyes. It's too confusing.

"Why bother? This is temporary, right? Mab will tell you how to take it from me, how to reunite it with the crown?"

"I don't know," Finn says. "I'm counting on her for a solution, but it's futile to predict what that might be."

I fold my arms. Futile as it might be, Finn's clearly bracing himself for Mab to put Sebastian on the throne. He's said too much for me to believe otherwise. And if Sebastian's going to be the ruler of this court, we need to let him in on its secrets. "I want to tell Sebastian," I say. "About the sickness, about the dying court."

Finn's jaw goes hard. "That could be a mistake."

"It's not. He cares for these people. He is more like you than you know. Trust me on this."

He closes his eyes. "Princess—"

"I don't need to tell him that you plan to see Mab, but let me explain how dire the situation is. Then you'll get your temporary bond. You'll be able to keep your priestess's location a secret. But the rest Sebastian deserves to know."

He meets my eyes. "Do what you think is best."

CHAPTER FOURTEEN

THE DINING ROOM IS EMPTY when I arrive, and rather than sit and wait at the table, I melt into the shadows and enjoy the moment of quiet. My head spins with the games Sebastian and Finn are playing.

I understand Finn's reasons for wanting to take over Sebastian's bond with me for our trip into the mountains, but I can't pretend I'm looking forward to being bonded with another male, even temporarily.

Sebastian enters the dining room right on time and closes the double doors behind him. "I know you're here, Abriella."

So much for my shield. I wonder if I would've had any chance of remaining undetected in the throne room if he hadn't been distracted by Finn.

I let my shadows fall away, and he gobbles me up with those sea-green eyes, looking me over again and again, as if he's afraid I'm not real. Tension stretches between us. It reminds me of when I was young, going fishing at the creek with my father, the way the line drew taut as we reeled in the catch. Tighter and tighter the connection grows through this bond. But I'm not sure which one of us is on the hook.

"I'm so glad you're here," he whispers. He takes a step closer, then stops himself.

I swallow. "I'll be leaving with Finn in the morning."

"We need to talk before you go," he says. "I've done as you asked. We dismantled the camps, and I'm glad for it, whether you care or not."

"I know. I'm grateful."

"You never came back," he says.

"There's more work to be done. The Court of the Moon is in danger."

"You think I don't know that? I don't have to be sitting on that throne to understand what's happening outside those gates. We can't afford a civil war now any more than Oberon could when he returned from the mortal realm."

"Then you understand how important this mission is. How important it is that you and Finn present a united front."

He slowly crosses to me. "If I let him do this, if I let them spell me so he can carry the bond, you'll be able to feel *him* like this when he touches you." He slides one hand onto my hip and the other into my hair. "Is that what you want?" His beautiful eyes search mine, and I feel my shield fall away, as if dissolved by the weight of his heartache.

The bond glows to life between us, bright and uninhibited, but the devastation that awaits me on his side of this connection is dark and tormented. It makes me want to curl onto the floor and cry, to apologize a million times for making him hurt, to forgive and forgive and forgive. "Bash," I whisper.

"Tell me what you want. Anything." He closes his eyes and swallows. "Anything but *him*."

I flex my fists in frustration. "This isn't about Finn. It's about the Unseelie Court and the future of the entire realm."

He loosens his grip on my hair and touches his forehead to mine, cupping my face and stroking my jaw with his thumb. I should pull away, but the contact feels so *nice*. I just want one moment to pretend that life doesn't have to be as lonely as it has been, that my future isn't one endless stretch of purposeless days before me. Just for this moment.

"How am I supposed to trust him? How am I supposed to let you go for even a minute? Don't you realize he'll take this as an opportunity to steal what I have—what he wants?"

I stiffen. "How could he steal my power?"

"Not your power. *You*."

He can't steal something you don't have. I bite back the words and shake my head. "This isn't some scheme to win my affection. *I* am unimportant in this situation."

"Never." Sebastian tilts my face to his, and before I realize what he's doing, his mouth is on mine. I'm so blindsided by what I feel in my mind that it takes me a moment to react to what's happening physically. I feel . . . *him*. Everything. Even more than before.

His heartache and anguish. His grief and his longing. I feel how much he misses me and wants me so deeply that I become it and it becomes me until I am erased and rebuilt with his broken pieces. I so desperately want to put him back together that my hands go to his shoulders and my mouth opens under his.

I love this male. Or I thought I did. Maybe I don't anymore, not the way I did, but I can't bear to be the source of his pain.

He groans in approval and threads his fingers through my hair, tilting my head to the side to deepen the kiss. His arousal is potent, and it latches onto me through this bond, becoming my own.

"It never takes you long to forgive him, does it?"

The sound of Finn's voice snaps me back into myself, and I jump away from Sebastian.

Finn looks me over, but his carefully schooled expression gives nothing away.

Sebastian is panting. Lips parted, eyes foggy with lust. He shakes his head just barely. I'm not sure what he means—don't listen to Finn? Don't walk away?

"So *predictable,* Princess."

Sebastian's gaze snaps to Finn and his jaw goes hard. "Mind your own business."

"This *is* my business," Finn says. "The two of you are the business of my whole damn court. I'm just trying to fix your mess."

A muscle flickers in the side of Sebastian's jaw. "I'm not going to explain myself to you."

Finn scoffs. "No need. But maybe you should explain yourself to the parents of the dying Unseelie children."

Sebastian frowns. "What?"

Finn grunts and turns to me. "I thought you wanted to tell him. I guess you were so busy reuniting with your lover that you couldn't be bothered."

"I—"

Finn doesn't wait for my explanation. He simply *disappears.* As if he were never there.

"I'm going to kill him," Sebastian growls, but instead of going after Finn, he pulls me close again. "Forget him."

When he lowers his mouth back to mine, I press my palm to his chest and gently push him away. "Sebastian."

"He's always coming between us," he says softly, but he steps back and blows out a breath. "Is what he said true? Are the Unseelie children dying?"

I nod. "Many have fallen into the Long Sleep."

"The long what?"

I swallow. Of course he wouldn't know. "It's a symptom of a dying court. The children don't wake, and might not ever if we can't fix this. The numbers are growing, but it's happened before—right before the curse when Oberon was stuck in the mortal realm and there was an imbalance between the courts. That's part of why Finn needs my bond. He wants to talk to the High Priestess about what to do." I bite my bottom lip. I hate lying to Sebastian, but this is at least more of the truth than Finn gave him.

Sebastian tips his face to the ceiling and closes his eyes. "And he needs you because she's only obligated to talk to the one who holds the power of the court."

I shrug. "Something like that."

"I don't like the idea of your traveling in those mountains. They're dangerous. The High Priestess is difficult to reach for a reason."

"But if there's any chance it will help, I'm going to go."

Sebastian studies me for a long time. "No one in this court or this realm deserves you, Abriella."

The sincerity in his words echoes through me, and I bow my head. This would be easier if I could believe Sebastian was the villain. If I could believe he tricked me and didn't care about the consequences. Thanks to this bond, I know that's not true. Slowly, I lift my shields again.

"You need Finn," I say. "This court needs you two to work together."

"And what about you? Do *you* need Finn? Is he what you want?"

He felt something through the bond when I kissed Finn. He might not know exactly what was happening, but I see in his eyes that he suspects.

I shake my head. "I don't want anyone."

"You're sure about that? You light up when he's around. I suspected it before, but now that we're bonded, I *feel* it."

"It's not because I'm pining for him." I cringe because that's only partly true. "My magic is stronger when Finn's around. It's been that way since I came to Faerie. I used to think it was because of his connection to the crown, but I . . ." Suddenly finishing that sentence seems very cruel.

"But what?" Sebastian asks. "But you don't feel the same surge of power around me? Is that what you were going to say?"

"I'm sorry," I whisper. "I don't understand it, but it wasn't something I *chose.* It just is."

"Tell me what you want." He means for me to tell him how he can win me back, but I don't have an answer for that.

"I want peace. I want what's best for this kingdom."

"I do too." Sebastian presses a hand to his chest. "I just don't want to have to give up everything else that matters to me in order to find it."

I swallow hard. After having a similar, yet opposite conversation with Finn, Sebastian suddenly seems very young. "Do you want to be king, or do you want to be a great king? Sacrifice is what makes great kings. That's what great leaders do."

Wincing, Sebastian bows his head. "Right."

A servant brings in a tray of food and sets it on the table before ducking out again just as quietly.

Sebastian pulls out a chair and gestures for me to sit. When I hesitate for too long, he says, "Please?"

"I'm not hungry." I twist my hands. In truth, I need to get away. Seeing Sebastian, kissing him, *feeling* him, it's too much. "I need to head into the city. I want to see that the sleeping children are settled in before we leave tomorrow."

"It's not safe to travel through the palace gates right now. I'll send Riaan with you. He can take you another way."

I nod. It's easier to accept the escort than it is to argue, and probably wise as well. "In the meantime," I say, "you can meet with Finn and decide what you want to do."

"The answer's no." His voice cracks on the words. "I won't allow him to hold the bond. Not even temporarily."

I hold my breath. "Are you sure? That was his offer in exchange for helping you."

He glances toward the windows, as if he can see the unhappy crowds that wait beyond the gates. "He needs me as much as I need him. As for the bond with you . . . The priestess will want to talk to you, not him. The bond is irrelevant."

"I hope you're right about that," I say softly, and I hope Finn's wrong not to trust Sebastian with the location of the priestess's temple.

"Finnian's jealous that I have you and he doesn't. Don't let him get in your head."

Even though I know it will hurt him, I say, "You don't *have* me, Bash."

His throat bobs as he swallows. "I did. For a minute."

And because it feels impossible, I don't bother blocking the impact of his emotions as they come at me right through my shield—his sorrow, his regret swelling inside me as if they were my own.

"I love you," he says. "I still, forever, and will always *love you.*" Silence stretches out between us, and he searches my face again and again. He draws in a ragged breath. "Say something."

"There's nothing I can say."

"You felt it too," he says. He reaches for me, but I step from his grasp. "I know you felt it too. I know you meant every word you said when you took the bond. You loved me."

"I loved the male I thought you were. Twice. And both were a lie."

"Where do you think you're going?" Finn asks.

I let the stable boy help me up onto Two Star and take her reins. "Sebastian said no. He won't transfer the bond."

Finn grimaces. "He's a stubborn *child.*"

I shrug. "Maybe so, but his mind's made up. You'll have to find a way to work together without that part of the agreement. Your court is counting on you, so maybe that could be reason enough." I nudge the mare with my heels, leading her out of the stables.

Finn grabs the reins. "You didn't answer my question. Where are you going?"

"I'm going into the city to check on the children."

"I'll go with you," Finn says.

"No. Stay and work it out with Sebastian." I cock my head to the side. "Unless you're going to be just as stubborn as he is."

Finn scowls. "You can't go alone. It isn't safe."

As if on cue, Riaan trots out of the stables and pulls his stallion to a stop beside Two Star. "She won't be alone."

Finn looks back and forth between us, then sighs. "Fine. Tell Misha and the others we leave at first light. When you return, Sebastian and I will have a plan on how we can work together."

I give him a stiff smile. "See, was that so hard?" I don't wait for a response before I nudge Two Star into a gallop and take off down the path toward the gates. Riaan easily catches up with me and takes the lead before we head out.

The Unseelie capital is situated all around the palace grounds, just beyond the gates. I used to believe that the Unseelie Court would be a showcase of torture and sadism, with every corner occupied by cruel fae doing wicked deeds.

I know better now, and it comes as no surprise to me that the capital is a city more vibrant and thriving than any I ever visited in Elora. The cobblestone streets are lined with stalls of merchants selling their wares — beautiful fabrics, fragrant pies and pastries, and coffee that smells better than any I've ever tasted.

If someone had dropped me here without telling me, I'd have no way of knowing this was the Unseelie Court and not the Seelie Court. The landscape is similar, as are the half-timbered homes and the creatures who walk the streets. It strikes me as sad, somehow, that two places that have so much in common have made enemies of each other.

By the time we reach the infirmary, I am so enamored with this little city that part of me longs to wander through the market, soaking up the details and investigating the merchants' offerings. But I don't. I duck into the infirmary, where I can't fix anything and am probably not even needed.

I help Leta wash the children's faces, their arms and hands. We drape them in clean blankets and turn them so they don't get bedsores. I like helping, but it doesn't do much to ease my guilt. Knowing I'm the source of the problem means I can never do enough.

When the children are all clean and turned and there's nothing more to be done, I settle into a chair and tell them a story about a peasant girl who slayed a wicked king to save her sister. I have no idea if they can hear me, but if I were trapped in an endless sleep, I would want someone to tell me stories. When I finish weaving the tale that's part truth and part fantasy, I find Misha perched by the window, watching me.

When I meet his eyes, he gives me a sad smile. "If love and devotion were enough to heal these children and this court, they'd have the savior they need in you."

I flinch, then bow my head. I know he meant it as a compliment. "Instead, the opposite is true."

"You keep telling yourself that the court would be whole if you were gone, but you forget how reluctant these people are to follow a ruler with Seelie blood." He tips his face up toward the ceiling and takes a deep breath. "Don't blame yourself for fissures in a world that was broken long before you were born."

I cock my head to the side, trying to figure out his mood. "Why so morose today, friend?"

Other than the children, we're alone in the room, but Misha scans it anyway and then looks over his shoulder before stepping closer. "Something's off." He shakes his head. "Lark is at Castle Craige with Amira, but she sent a goblin with a message when you first arrived at the infirmary. She warned that she saw fire. I sent Kane and Tynan on patrol through the city, but they didn't find anything."

I swallow hard. The last time Lark warned about a fire, I almost died. "Did she say where?"

He smirks. "You know my niece. Her prophecies sound like half nonsense."

And yet she's so often right. "What were her words?"

"Fire, not from Abriella's mind, but from their—"

A sudden *boom* rocks the infirmary, then another. Like a tree falling? Misha and I look at each other. Leta runs back into the room, eyes wide.

"What was that?" she asks, heading toward the window.

A boy rushes in behind her, his eyes bright, his pointed ears poking through his mop of curly black hair. He could be a cousin of Finn's, a brother even, and I wonder if he knows how much he resembles his prince.

"What's happening out there?" I ask.

Misha has that faraway look in his eyes that tells me he's already inside the minds of our friends and allies, calling for help.

"Eli told me to come tell you it's raining fire," he says.

Leta frowns and glances over her shoulder at him. "What do you mean it's—"

The next boom is so loud, my ears feel like they're bleeding, and before I can pull in a breath, there's another—right on top of us—and the ceiling is falling in, rolling flames pouring in with it.

"Get out of here!" I scream to the boy. Then I turn to Leta. "We need to move the children."

Misha grabs my arm. "Abriella, go. Lark said you need to *run.*"

I shake my head. "Not without the children." The room is heating as fast as an oven as the flames race across the ceiling. How many times will I live this nightmare—the fire, the falling beams, the suffocating smoke that presses in too fast?

I scoop up the nearest child, holding him to my chest, then throw out my power, wrapping the rest of these innocents in a cocoon of shadow to protect them from the flames. "We have to get them out."

Misha hoists a child onto each shoulder, and Leta grabs a small girl from the bed closest to the door. Together, we run toward the exit.

Outside is pure chaos. Blazing balls of fire fly through the sky, turning thatched straw roofs into kindling. People scream and run in every direction, trying to escape the fires that seem to be everywhere. White-bodied water fae emerge from the river and redirect the water, blasting streams onto the burning homes. One stops to douse the flames that are burning a young merchant's dress. The merchant drops to her knees, wet and sobbing.

"The infirmary," I shout to a water fae who's emerged from her river home, her iridescent scales glistening. "Can you work to control the fire there while we get the children out?"

She doesn't bother to answer but goes running toward the building, running on webbed feet as she whistles for others to follow.

"Over here!" a woman calls, throwing her arms out. A shimmering dome the size of a small house snaps up around her. "The fire can't penetrate this shield."

I shift the child in my arms and head toward the dome. "Can you hold it?" I ask the faerie who's inside.

She nods. "I'll try."

I lower the child to the ground inside her shield and turn back for another.

Someone grabs me from behind, and strong male arms wrap around my center. "Don't go back in there," Misha shouts. "This court *needs* you."

I growl, and I dissolve into shadow—into *nothing*—and dart

back into the fray, weaving like mist through panicked people as I return to the children. It's hotter now, and smoke is thick in the air. I won't let myself think about how helpless these children are, how much smoke they've drawn into their lungs without knowing it. I won't let myself remember what it's like to be trapped and helpless while fire burns around you.

I snap back into solid form so fast my stomach heaves, but I don't slow down. I grab two children this time—twin toddlers who are deadweight in their unnatural sleep—and I hold my breath as I race back out through the smoke to the safety of the shield.

With every breath, I draw from that seemingly endless well of power, reinforcing the cool cocoon of shadow that I have wrapped around the children, praying it can hold when the flames grow too hot.

When I return, there's a boy lumbering toward the exit, a child thrown over each shoulder, Misha right behind him.

The boy stumbles outside and coughs fitfully, swaying on his feet. "You can't go back in there," he says.

"It's too bad," Misha agrees. "Let the water fae smother the flames before you go back in."

I shake my head. "I won't leave them."

Misha's eyes blaze. "You go in there, and you might not come back out."

I push past him into the thick smoke.

Misha's right. The building is falling. Inside, the walls burn bright and the smoke crowds every inch of the air. Outside, people are screaming. The cacophony of destruction fades into the back of my mind while I scan the infirmary, where the only sound is the snap and hiss of the fire and the creaking of the weakening ceiling joists. I weave my way through the flames, gritting my teeth through the pain as they lick at my skin.

The last two children are holding hands in their sleep, a small girl and her older brother. I couldn't carry them both on my best day, but right now, already dizzy from the smoke, my lungs burning, I know the odds are stacked against us.

I wrap an arm around one child and then the other. My power wavers, the shield I have wrapped around them threatening to dissipate, but I need more. Just a little more.

I focus on shadow and darkness and the cool, soothing night until the back wall is nothing but shadow and flame. Then I heave and thrust the children through to the other side with the last of my strength.

Like the string of a bow stretched too tight, my power snaps and retreats to just beyond my grasp. I collapse, flames licking my legs.

I'm coming for you, Princess. Don't let go.

Misha's voice forces my eyes open. The flames around me are too close.

No! I shout the word in my mind. I can't let my friend come in here. I can't risk him being trapped, can't risk more devastation to save my life.

I reach for my power again. It feels like swimming through sand, but I keep reaching, gathering up every little bit I can until the wall ahead of me gives way to shadow and I can crawl through to the other side.

I take a deep breath of blessedly cool air. It's a balm on my lungs.

A black-cloaked figure lunges for me.

"No," I cry, dodging. But I'm too slow, and I feel a needle slide into my arm, the burn of the toxin racing through my veins.

I grapple for my power, but it's like tipping over an empty cup. There's nothing there.

I know this feeling.

Then I'm lifted into someone's arms and carried away from the flames, away from the desperate cries for help. I'm belly-down on the back of a horse and riding fast.

"Heal her now!" someone shouts. "Before we lose her. Orders were clear — she lives."

"Calm down," a softer, more feminine voice says. "She's going to be fine."

I don't recognize the voices, and when I try to talk to Misha through that connection in our power, it's like hitting a wall.

I'm dizzy and drained. Weak. I need to know where I am — to see where they're taking me — but my eyes refuse to cooperate, and unconsciousness grips me.

CHAPTER FIFTEEN

When I come to, the sky is pitch-black. The moon is hiding behind clouds and there are no stars in sight, but my eyes adjust quickly. In the distance, a modest temple's been built into the side of the mountain.

We're still riding. I'm slouched in front of a large body—male if I had to guess. I count three males and a female around us, but hear others close by.

These are the people who rescued me from the fire. The ones who healed me. The ones who want me alive. But I know with every inch of my being that they are *not* allies. I try to move and wince. My wrists are bound, and my muscles ache.

"I think she's sore," the male riding behind me says. His meaty palm gropes my thigh. "I can make you *real* sore, honey."

"Back off," the female riding beside us says. She sneers as she looks at my riding buddy. "The queen wants her alive and unscathed."

The male behind me grunts but moves his hand from my thigh. "I'd only leave a few marks—just enough to show the girl what we do to traitors."

These people healed me to take to Queen Arya. Was the fire a trap? A way to make me drain my power so I'd be easier to capture?

Misha. I think his name as hard as I can, but I hit that wall again. Our connection must rely on my magic on some level, but they injected me with that toxin when they snatched me from the capital, and until it leaves my system, my power is gone.

In the far distance, the thunder rolls, and just beyond that . . . hoofbeats. *Someone's coming.* Sebastian? An ally of my captors?

The female beside us perks up in her seat and glances toward the trail behind us. I'm not the only one who heard it.

"We have company," she announces, squinting off into the distance.

"How far?" a male in the front asks. He's tall and has the same white-blond hair as Sebastian. I bet he's part of the queen's Golden Military. Maybe they all are.

She shakes her head. "The storm makes it hard to tell. Less than half an hour."

Her friends stand and peer back in the direction we came. "Who else would be this deep in the mountains at this time of night?"

"Could be anybody, now that the unclean ones have their power back. Whole world's gone to hell."

I narrow my eyes on that temple in the distance, closer now. Can these fae see in the dark like I can? Can they see the ravens circling the temple steps? When they chose this path, did they know they'd be riding through a pack of Sluagh? I doubt it. Sluagh are too powerful to risk in the dark.

Maybe that is Sebastian riding toward us, but if he's alone, we'll be outnumbered. I need to give him a chance, but I have no weapons, no allies, no magic. Nothing but Sluagh lurking too close for comfort.

If I can't use my magic, I'll have to rely on theirs.

I wait until we've almost reached the temple steps, then clutch my stomach and bend forward. "Gonna be . . . sick." My voice sounds like my body feels — beaten, pulverized.

"What is she muttering about?" the male ahead of us asks.

"She feels sick," the female says, barely sparing me a glance. "Those injections do that, honey, but we can't let you have your magic, now can we?"

"No. It's not —" I rock back and forth, parting my lips and miming dry heaving.

"Aw, shit," the male behind me says. "She's gonna hurl."

"So let her," the female says.

I gag and lean into the male I'm riding with.

"Nah, I'm not doing this," he says, jerking his horse to a stop in front of the temple. He hops off, then swings me off the horse, practically dropping me on the ground.

The others stop, and the one in the lead groans. "We don't have all night."

I gag again, louder this time. If I can just keep them focused on me, maybe they won't notice the ravens that circle so close.

I crawl onto the marble steps and get a boot to the gut. "Get up," grunts the male standing in front of me. "We aren't going in there. Finish your business; then we're back on our way."

"So sick." I stumble to my feet, then collapse again, trying to look weak—not that it's hard. My body's wrecked, and with my hands bound, it's tough to get my balance.

The female hops off her horse, and my riding buddy winds a rope around his hand and yanks hard. I stumble forward, only now realizing that they don't just have a rope around my wrists, but one around my neck as well. Like a leash. Or a noose.

This could end very, very badly.

They climb on their horses. The male holding me snaps the rope. "Enough. You're just stalling."

"I could knock her out again," the female offers, stepping toward me.

I swallow hard and pray my captors are too distracted to see the ravens I feel circling closer.

Suddenly the male holding my rope looks around wildly. "Shit! Over there!" He drops the rope and the horse's reins and darts into the woods.

"What the—" the female ducks, as if something's attacking her from the sky. "No! Please!"

Abriella! My mom's voice. Like a siren call in the distance. Crashing waves fill my ears, and cold water licks my shins.

It's not real. Do not *engage.*

Another male slumps on his horse and weeps. "No. Please don't! I'm so sorry!"

A small part of me regrets dragging anyone through this mental torment, but I shut it down.

The final males stumble off their horses and scramble toward the temple steps. One cradles his head in his hands and claws at his hair as if he's trying to rip it from his head.

Abriella! Hurry. The water's getting too deep.

Ignoring my mother's voice is like ignoring the need to breathe.

Abriella, please. Hold my hand.

I know if I turn my head, I'll see her. I know if I offer my bound hands, she'll free them and hold me close. I'll get to look into her eyes again. Everything will be okay.

I can't help but hesitate. My feet refuse to move.

It's not her. My mother is gone.

I squeeze my eyes shut, blocking out the Sluagh's siren call.

"Brie, over here!" Sebastian's voice is so close. But has he come for me or are the Sluagh making me think he did? "Brie, let me help you."

I want to see my mother's face just one more time, and when I turn, I'm treated to her beautiful smile, her kind eyes—right before a wave crashes over her and pulls her under the sea.

"Mother!" I shout, diving in after her.

Hands claw at my legs, pulling me under, but I fight them and swim toward her. My mother's chestnut hair floats around her in the water and her eyes close.

No.

Teeth like razor blades dig into my legs, my arms, rip into my gut, pulling me back from her. I fight them with the last of the air in my lungs.

"Abriella, *breathe!*"

I force my eyes open to see Sebastian's face backlit by the morning light pouring into the temple's sanctuary. He's bending over me, and those beautiful sea-green eyes are ravaged with worry.

"I knew you'd come," I whisper, but I can't keep my eyes open. Then a soft wind picks me up from the ground and I'm in his arms, being carried away from the temple and down the mountain.

"I'll always come for you," Sebastian whispers.

I'm vaguely aware of the voices around me. Sebastian's frantic requests and a low voice I somehow know belongs to a healer.

"There's nothing more I can do," the healer says. "The toxin is everywhere in her system, and any attempts to actively heal strengthen the poison."

"She's hurting," he says, his voice raw.

"All we can do is wait. She needs rest. She needs to be *home.* Put her close to anything she naturally draws power from. Take her to the roof and let her rest beneath the stars."

"We're bonded," he says, gasping. "Can't I do something? Can't she pull from me somehow?"

"The bond doesn't work like a tether. You know this, Prince Ronan."

My muscles scream as I'm scooped into someone's arms.

"I'm sorry," he says. "Abriella, I'm so sorry. I know what to do."

And then I feel weightless, like I'm leaving my body. And it's a relief, even as I fight it. I need to be in my body. I'm afraid if I leave it, I'll never come back. If I disconnect from this physical pain, I'll never find the courage to return.

I'm thrown back into myself in a rush, and I feel the arms around me shift, feel Sebastian stumble.

"Thank you," Sebastian murmurs, and then I hear the sounds of a goblin thanking Sebastian for his payment.

"What happened?" Finn's voice.

"I found her outside a temple in the Goblin Mountains. The others were dead, and she was like this — as if some creature tried to tear her apart."

"Pretha, send for my healer."

"No!" Sebastian shouts. "My healer already tried, but there's a toxin in her system that fights back — it's made stronger by any effort to heal her. She needs to be surrounded by her darkness. She needs . . ."

I force my eyes open. I'm in Sebastian's arms, and he's staring at Finn. I turn to see Finn's face — I desperately need to see that face after being locked in my own nightmare — but I don't have the strength.

"She needs everything she can draw power from, and she told me her power is stronger with you."

"I understand," Finn says softly. "I've got her."

I whimper as they shift me into Finn's arms and pain tears through me. When I open my eyes again, Sebastian's backing out of the room, tears streaking down his cheeks.

"Please," Sebastian says. "Please do whatever you can."

"Thank you for bringing her to me," Finn says.

Consciousness comes and goes, but I'm aware of the soothing darkness, Finn's heat, and the leather and fresh pine smell of him.

"Shhh," Finn whispers. Was I crying? "Shhh, you're home now."

"Home," I say softly, burying my face in his arms. I don't know where we are, but home feels right.

"I've got you," Finn says. "Don't give up. Don't you dare fucking give up. You're safe now. You're home."

I feel myself being lowered into a bed, and I cry out, afraid he's going to leave me here. I can't find the words, but I don't want him to leave, I don't want to be alone. Because I'm dying.

"Shhh, I've got you." Then I feel the mattress shift as he climbs onto the bed behind me and wraps himself around me. "Just rest, Abriella."

When I open my eyes again, I'm in a big, soft bed and the night sky stretches endlessly above me. I brace myself as I roll to my side, shocked when nothing hurts.

"Is this a dream?" I ask the wall. I know Finn's here. Even though I haven't set eyes on him, I feel him.

"No," he says. "You've been sleeping, but this is real."

I force myself to sit up, but the effort sends me into a coughing fit.

"You should rest," he says, but his eyes are red and his skin's pale, as if he's the one who should be resting.

I shake my head. "The children?"

"Safe," he says. "Thanks to you. Pretha was able to work with Hannalie, and together their shield held. They kept the sleeping ones safe until we got the fires under control."

I swallow hard and look around. We must be back at the Midnight Palace, but I don't recognize this room. The massive bed is centered on the longest wall, and there's no ceiling—as if whoever created this space couldn't fathom sleeping anywhere but beneath the stars.

Looking around, I shake my head. "What if it rains?"

He chuckles. "Magic protects the room from the elements while still allowing it to feel like the outdoors."

I lift a hand, feeling the breeze brush my fingers. In the corner, Finn's wolves, Dara and Luna, lift their heads and sniff the air and cry softly in my direction. I smile to reassure them. "What happened?"

Finn blows out a breath and settles into a well-worn chair next to the bed. "Which part? The one where you almost got yourself killed by running into a burning building?"

I scowl. "That's not what I'm asking, and you know it."

"Seems like you make a habit of it."

"I had to."

He swallows. "I know. And I'm grateful—more grateful than you know. But the way you spent your power, exerted so much of it without properly tapping into its depths? That was dangerous, Princess. More dangerous than any smoke or flame."

I scoff.

"You're immortal now. Your skin will heal, your lungs will recover, but you spend your magic that hard and fast and no healer can bring you back."

Maybe that would be for the best.

Finn frowns at me, and I'm suddenly grateful that he can't read my thoughts.

"Tell me more," I say. "Who was behind the attack?"

"A contingent of the Golden Military ambushed the city. A legion of the queen's fire fae attacked from the mountains." He looks tired, his face haggard. "Thanks to Sebastian's connection to the golden court and Riaan's knowledge of their military tactics, we were able to locate and stop them relatively quickly, but . . ."

"But not quickly enough."

He shakes his head. "We didn't see this coming. We've been preparing for her forces, watching her armies to prepare ourselves for a military attack, but we were so focused on the legions assembled in the mountains, we missed the signs on this one."

"Do you think the queen knew this would happen to the Unseelie Court if Sebastian gave me the potion?" I ask, frowning. Breaking the curse on the Unseelie should've helped the shadow court, but without someone to sit on the throne, it helped the Seelie queen most of all.

"Possibly," Finn says. "It's hard to say, but it's fair to assume that she knows now. That's why she wants you alive. If she can capture you—hold you somewhere alive but unreachable—then there's a chance we won't be able to reunite the crown and its power."

I glance toward the night sky. "How long was I out?"

"It's been a day and half since the attack. Misha, Sebastian, and I have taken turns keeping watch over you, but"—he averts his eyes and smiles slightly—"you seemed to fare best with me, so I've been with you almost round the clock."

I glance at the bed, then arch a brow at him.

"Not to worry, Princess. I've been in this very chair since right after you fell asleep."

Maybe that's why he looks so ragged. "Do you think your connection to the crown helped me heal?"

He opens his mouth, then closes it before trying again. "I think there's a connection between us that I don't have an explanation for."

My gaze snaps to his. He feels that too? "Before I became fae," I say, "my power always felt stronger when you were close. I thought it was because you were Unseelie royalty and I was carrying the power of the crown, but if that was it, wouldn't it have flared in the same way when I was near Sebastian?"

"That would make sense," he says. Lifting a tentative hand to my face, Finn swallows. His fingers brush my cheek so lightly it could be the breeze. "I feel it too, you know. This connection between us. This . . . *awareness* of you."

"Like the bond?" I ask.

He shakes his head. "I can't track you or sense your emotions so directly. But it's almost as if your power's connected to me."

"Your power's stronger when I'm around, like mine is when you are?"

"No. Not stronger, but linked somehow." He shrugs. "I don't have any answers, but I won't deny that I take a bit smug satisfaction knowing you feel it too. Even if it's a bit different on your end."

I study the stars. "I'm sorry if I delayed your trip to visit the High Priestess."

"You didn't. Lunastal hasn't begun, so we have time."

"I should be fine to go by morning."

"Brie . . ." His silver eyes find mine. "I've changed my mind about you coming with us into the mountains."

I sit up in bed, and the room spins a little. "What? No. Finn, you can't go without me. You said yourself that she'll only meet with someone who has the power of the crown." I press a hand to my chest. "That's me."

"I won't risk them snatching you while we ride through the forest, and neither Sebastian nor Jalek can come with us because of their Seelie blood."

I shake my head. "I don't need Sebastian. I'll have you." The words make me feel more vulnerable than I like, so I duck my head and add, "And the others."

Finn studies the dark bedsheets. "There's something else I need to talk to the priestess about," he says, worry hanging on every word. "Another reason I'm hesitant to take you with us."

I grab a pillow from beside me and clutch it to my chest. It's soft and smells like pine and leather. Like Finn. "What is it?"

He closes his eyes, and I take advantage of the moment to study his face in the moonlight—the sharp line of his jaw, the high cheekbones, his thick, elegant brows, and those dark curls that beg for my fingers. He's always beautiful, but somehow more so in the starlight. When he finally opens his eyes again, he holds my gaze for a long moment before speaking. "Something's wrong with me, Abriella. I don't know if it's connected to the disease that's affecting the children or if it has something to do with the crown being tied to another heir."

"What do you mean? What's wrong?"

He studies me with such intensity I can practically feel his eyes pass over my neck, my jaw, my cheeks, and settle on the bow of my lips.

A warm shiver passes over me at the intensity in those silver eyes.

"I've become weak," he whispers. "Not always. Sometimes I feel fine — most of the time, even. But I've been having these spells where I feel like the very life has been sucked from me. I have no magic to draw on and very little strength."

"Like when you were cursed?" I ask.

"No. It's different." His brow wrinkles as he considers. "With the curse, the magic was still here, just finite, scarce at times. What I've been feeling since Sebastian took the crown — it's more like having the valve on my magic opened. As if it's leaving me too fast, and for no reason."

Life is magic. Magic is life. My chest aches as I imagine Finn's power — his *life* being ripped from him. "Have you told anyone else?"

"Pretha and Kane know. I tried to hide it, but they've known me too long and too well. The days following a spell, my strength rebuilds, and I feel okay again." His gaze drops to the blankets. "But I was powerless to help while those fire fae attacked. I couldn't defend the city or get to you. I couldn't do anything. If you were endangered in the mountains while I was having another spell, if you were hurt or captured because my magic failed me?" He shakes his head. "I don't want to risk that."

"Will the priestess be able to fix it — whatever's wrong with you?"

"She's not a healer, but I hope she'll be able to identify what's happening. If we know that, perhaps we can find a solution."

"You don't sound confident."

"Each time I've had one of these episodes, I'm surprised to wake up the next morning. I keep expecting . . ."

My stomach twists painfully. "You think you're going to fall into sleep, like the children."

"I don't know. Maybe."

I wish he'd look at me. I suddenly need the reassurance of those silver eyes on mine. "Is it happening to anyone else?"

"No one has spoken of it, but I can't exactly go around letting everyone know that their prince is—"

"Dying," I whisper. "You think you're dying."

"Maybe." The word is rough, like it's jammed in his throat and he has to force it out. "In an ideal situation, the rulers of our lands will never die. They will simply choose to pass on to the Twilight. When rulers approach the time to pass their power to their heir, there are signs that force their hand. It's believed that the gods do this so the courts don't grow stagnant, so that no one ruler has power for too long. My father was nearing his time when he passed his power to you, and everything I remember, everything I've read about it sounds uncomfortably similar to what I'm experiencing."

"We'll fix it," I whisper. My eyes feel suddenly hot and wet. "We'll find a cure for you and the children. We'll figure this out."

When he finally looks at me, he treats me to a soft smile, but it never meets his eyes. "As much as I appreciate your concern, that's not your job. I'm only telling you because I want you to understand that I might not be able to protect you—especially if Sebastian doesn't bend on the bond."

"I understand." I swallow. "But I'm not worried about myself."

His brows draw together. "We very nearly lost you — again. If they'd gotten a goblin to take you to Arya instead of taking you through those mountains, or if Sebastian had arrived an hour later . . ."

"I'm not staying behind, Finn." I wrap my hand around his arm, and power flares inside me, filling me up. I gasp at the strength of it and watch as his lips part. He said it's different for him — not a flare, but a connection.

"We will travel to Staraelia on horseback, so consider the physical toll of the journey as well."

"We won't use goblins?"

"No. In part because that becomes difficult when traveling with a group, but more so because of the perceptions. In many parts of this land, goblins aren't trusted, and traveling with their magic can send the wrong impression."

"I can handle it, and I promise not to put Oberon's power at risk. I will be as well-behaved as your wolves. Just let me come."

His lips part and his nostrils flare in exasperation. "You truly think my primary concern is my father's power."

"Well, yes." I shrug. "I can't blame you for that."

He cups my jaw in one big hand and skims his thumb across my bottom lip. A shiver runs through me and I lock my gaze with his. "I think we should try to seek an audience with the priestess without you."

"You —"

He presses his thumb against my lips, silencing me. "But the decision is yours. All I ask is that you're honest about how you feel, and if we need to delay by a day or two, then we will. I have other reasons for wanting to be present for Lunastal, but if we need to, we can go straight to the priestess." As if suddenly realizing how intimate his touch is, he drops his hand and stands. "I'll see you in the morning."

"Finn," I say, stopping him before he reaches the door.

He turns, his dark brow arched. "Yes, Princess."

I fold my arms and give him the most self-assured smirk I can manage. "Use your thumb to stop me from speaking again, and I will bite it."

His smile is slow and wicked, but it brings light into his eyes that I'm hungry to see. "Is that supposed to be a threat?"

I grab a pillow and launch it at him, but he disappears, and it falls to the ground.

CHAPTER SIXTEEN

A FEW HOURS LATER I'M awake again, bathed and dressed and dying for a cup of coffee. When I open the door to exit my unconventional bedroom, Sebastian's waiting just outside, and he spins around at the sound. He's stiff, fists clenched at his sides. Worry is all over his face. For a moment my defenses fall, and I feel it. Terror, worry, concern.

Heartache.

All those feelings of his I've been working so hard to block out.

"How are you feeling?" he asks. I can almost see how badly he wants to touch me. How much he wants to pull me into his arms. But he's holding himself back. Instead, he looks me over again and again, as if he wants to make sure I'm okay and gobble me up all at once.

"I'm fine. Better. Thanks to you."

"I felt you," he says softly. "In the fire. I couldn't get there fast enough, and by the time I tracked you down in the mountains, the Sluagh—"

"I'm better," I say. "Finn said I used too much power at once, but I feel as good as new this morning." And it's almost true.

He nods. "Good. I'm glad to hear it."

"Thank you for coming to save me." I shift awkwardly. "I know you aren't very happy with me right now, that I've hurt you, but you still came."

"Of course I did." He takes me by the shoulders and turns me toward him. "I said I would always come for you, and I meant it."

My heart twists as I look up into those eyes and see the ache and longing there. I felt those same things not so long ago.

His gaze drops to my mouth and he leans in, but I press a hand to the center of his chest and nudge him back before he can come closer.

"Bash, that's not who we are anymore."

"I don't agree," he says, his voice rough. "It's who *I* am. Loving you is part of who I am. Do you know what it was like? To not know if I'd get there in time? To have to let *him* help you when we returned? Do you have any idea what that does to me?"

"I do. And I'm sorry."

I drop my gaze to the polished stone floor. It's too hard to see his face, to look into those beautiful eyes and block him out. "Finn told me you were the one who was able to track the fire fae in the mountains—that you saved so many people."

"With Riaan's help, yes. But so many were still lost, Brie." He stares toward a window at the end of the corridor and watches the rising sun with tired eyes. "They died because of her. Because of my mother. I need you to believe me when I tell you I'm not working with her. That I will go to war with her kingdom before I let her destroy the Unseelie."

"I know." I swallow hard and drop my voice. "I feel it. I feel you. I know you."

He swallows. "I'm so sorry if any of my decisions ever made you think I'd support her in any way. But now it's as if she's trying to punish me — trying to turn my court against me before I even have a chance to take the throne. And I . . . I don't understand why."

I squeeze his forearm. "You're doing the right things. Just keep working with us — with Finn and his people, with me. We'll figure this out."

"Good," Sebastian says, then eyes the room behind me. "Now that you're better, we can move you to my room."

"We probably shouldn't share a room, Bash." I bite the inside of my cheek, then force myself to meet his eyes. "I want us to work together. I want us to be friends, but I can't offer anything beyond that."

His fair cheeks flush, and his eyes darken. "But you don't mind sharing a room with *him?*"

Blinking, I look over my shoulder. I didn't know this was Finn's room, but it makes sense — the way his wolves lounged in the corner, the way the sheets smelled like him. The Midnight Palace would've been his home before Mordeus stole the throne, and the palace is big enough that Finn's chambers were probably untouched when he returned.

When my thoughts stall on how I just slept in the same bed

where Finn's spent countless nights, I cut them off and shrug. "It doesn't matter. We're leaving today."

He slides his hand down my arm and squeezes my fingers. "Come back to me — after? Give me a chance to win you back?"

"Are you two coming?" Pretha asks from down the hall. She's smiling, but her expression is tight. "The others are waiting in the briefing room."

I gently extract my hand from Sebastian's. "We should go."

We follow Pretha into a room I've never been in before where Finn, Misha, Kane, Tynan, Riaan, and Jalek are gathered around a large table. There's a glass of water at each spot, right next to an empty glass. Down the center of the table are three separate decanters of amber liquid, as if this is some sort of whiskey-tasting party and not a meeting to plan our strategy to protect this court from a power-hungry queen.

Good to see you on your feet again, Princess, Misha says in my mind.

I flash him a quick smile. *Glad to be on my feet.*

"Nice of you two to join us," Finn says, his gaze skipping over me and stuttering for a beat on my hand — which Sebastian has taken in his again. Finn turns to Riaan. "What's the status of the queen's forces in the mountains?"

"They're in a holding pattern right around the border," he says. "Their numbers are growing, but there are no signs of them advancing."

"And why should we listen to him?" Jalek asks. "He served Arya."

Riaan's eyes blaze with anger, but he leans back in his chair. "I served my *prince*," he says. "And continue to."

Sebastian releases my hand and approaches a vacant chair. "I think Riaan proved himself when the capital was attacked. Without his help, we wouldn't have been able to end that fire fae legion as quickly as we did."

But you don't trust him, Misha says in my mind as the others continue to talk.

I don't trust anyone, I tell him.

Liar.

Can you get into his mind? I ask. *See if we can trust him?*

I already tried. He's too well shielded.

Is that suspicious?

No. It's just good sense.

"—now that the Midnight Raiders are positioned in the mountains," Finn is saying.

I jerk my attention back to the conversation at the table. "They are?" I ask, taking the chair beside Sebastian. "I thought they were protesting."

Sebastian shakes his head. "Finn and I met with the captains and made it clear that we're working together." He reaches for the hand I have resting on the table and squeezes, and Finn follows the movement.

I give Bash a polite smile before gently extracting my hand from beneath his and placing it in my lap. "If the Midnight Raiders are in the mountains, who will protect the capital?" I ask.

The table returns to discussion of military strategy, and I try to ignore the ache of rejection I feel rolling off Sebastian. Misha was right, the bond is much harder to block when we're close.

"I thought we were headed into the mountains to see the High Priestess," I say to Finn as Kane leads us off the mountain trail and toward a small village. I didn't expect we'd be traveling with a caravan, but Kane, Misha, Pretha, and Tynan all joined me and Finn on our journey. Even Finn's wolves are traveling with us, though they spend most of their time out of sight, investigating off the trail.

Finn and I ride side by side just behind Kane, with the three Wild Fae following behind us.

"We are," Finn says, "but she won't meet with us before Lunastal."

I turn on my horse and arch a brow. "I thought that's why I was here with this"—I wave my hand around my head—"almighty power of mine. So we'd be welcome?"

Finn snorts and shakes his head. "We're heading first to Staraelia, a town in the foothills, where we will meet with the locals and let it be known that we plan to meet with the High Priestess. If we're lucky, she'll see us on Lunastal rather than making us wait until later in the week. And then we need more luck if we're going to convince her to open a portal to the Underworld."

"Pretha and Misha create portals for you all the time. Why can't *they* do it?"

In front of us, Kane snorts.

Finn smiles at his friend before turning to me. "The portals to the Underworld cannot be opened by just anyone. Our ancient guardians wanted us to be able to reach them, but only with the approval of those deemed most worthy among us."

I took for granted that Finn would be able to speak with Mab. Now this all seems like a wish and a prayer. "You're sure the High Priestess will grant you this?"

"If Mab wants to allow our visit, the High Priestess will be required by her oath to the land to open the portal for us."

Pretha clears her throat behind us. "This might be a good time to tell her who she'll be when we get to Staraelia."

I frown at Pretha over my shoulder. "What do you mean by that?"

Finn rolls his shoulders back. "I haven't been there in a long time. I don't want to assume that everyone is trustworthy. Since I'm not bonded to you, the next best excuse to stay close enough to protect you is to claim we have a relationship."

"Who are these people? I thought they were Unseelie? Why do you need to stay close to me?"

"There could be moles working for Mordeus's followers," Kane says. "Or even those who've been paid to work for the queen."

Finn nods. "Most are Unseelie and proud—they will recognize me as their prince regardless of whether I ever get to be king—but some among them will also be able to sense the power you carry, and that could be dangerous if they don't trust you. So we need a way to make them trust you." His gaze shifts away from me and tracks across the cottages growing closer on the horizon.

"Will they resent me for having the power of the crown?" I ask.

He blows out a breath. "Not if they think you're with me."

I swallow. "You want me to pretend that we're . . . *together?*"

Ahead of us, Kane chuckles. "Can't get anything by that one," he snarks.

I toss a ball of shadow at his shoulder, knocking him off-balance for a beat. He looks over his shoulder and winks at me.

Finn squeezes the back of his neck. "I've thought this through. I can't come up with any other way to do it. Since I don't have the bond to keep you safe, this is the next best thing. We already know Arya's after you. The last thing we need is my own people coming after you because they think it will help *me* in some way."

"Why don't you just tell them—"

"What would you have me tell them, Princess?" he asks softly.

I realize the problem and flinch as if I've been slapped. I can't explain that I inadvertently gave the crown to the golden prince or that I broke the throne—the whole *court*—when I took the Potion of Life. They'd hate me, and rightfully so.

"I know why you bonded with Sebastian," Finn says softly, "and I do not blame you for your decisions, but these people might. They had to abandon their homes and live in the caves beneath the Goblin Mountains during Mordeus's rule. After all they've suffered, we would be wise to be cautious. If we're together, they'll sense the power, but they won't question who it comes from. Anyone who's tuned in enough to realize the power's coming from you will believe it's because I've bonded with you. They'll assume they're picking up on that bond."

"Won't they ask if we're bonded?"

He shakes his head. "To question our relationship would be considered rude."

I sniff. "Fine, then. If I pretended to like the queen those weeks in the golden palace, I can certainly pretend to find you tolerable."

He chuckles, and the tension between us is broken. "I appreciate that, Princess. Now, let's spend the next couple of hours working on using that considerable power of yours without leaking so much."

I scowl at him. "Are you serious?"

He arches a brow. "What's wrong? Embarrassed for me to see just how little you've been training in our weeks apart?"

I shoot out a hand of shadow and put it over his mouth to shut him up.

Chuckling, Finn nips at it. I shiver as I feel the scrape of those teeth on my own skin. After that, I choose other targets for my magic.

Spirits lift as we pass through the gates of a country manor and ride our horses right up to its wide stone steps. Dara and Luna run past us to sniff the flower garden and the stairs.

Finn jumps off his horse and tosses the reins to Kane before stepping over to help me off Two Star. I want to decline, but the last thing I need is a broken ankle before we venture into the mountains. And anyway, I have a role to play here.

The feel of Finn's hands on my waist is an unwelcome reminder of what I've felt for him since the day we met. A reminder of how it felt to have his body pressed to mine when we kissed. A reminder that I unknowingly spent the last two nights sleeping in his bed.

He holds me too close to his body as my feet settle to the ground. "You okay?"

I nod, wetting my lips as I look up at him, at those gentle silver eyes. He's so tall, and when I haven't been close to him in a while, I forget just how broad he is.

"Are you sore?" he asks.

"I'm fine."

"I know you didn't do much riding in Elora."

I try not to cringe at the reminder of my commoner roots. In Elora, horses are for the wealthy, and I was little more than a slave in my last nine years there. "I got a lot of practice in the Wild Fae Lands."

The sound of boots on stone has our heads turning toward the house, and a woman with long, wavy brown hair appears on the front steps. She's wearing a dress the color of cherries, which makes her cheeks glow a healthy pink. If she were human, I'd guess her to be my age, maybe a little older, but those elven ears peeking up through her hair give her away.

"About time you came back, Finnian." She grins widely, then takes off into a run right toward us.

Finn drops his hands from my waist and turns, catching her just as her body collides with his.

She wraps her arms around him and squeezes tight, squealing. "It's been an age. I was beginning to wonder if I'd ever see you again."

When she pulls back, he smiles down at her, and unwelcome

jealousy claws at my chest, replacing the warmth I felt when he helped me from my horse. "How have you been?" he asks. "Still making your mother crazy?"

"If I didn't, she'd think there was something wrong."

Finn chuckles, flicking her nose before stepping back. "Juliana, this is Abriella."

"This is the one who'll be posing as your betrothed?" she asks.

My gaze shoots to Finn and I stiffen, shocked that he's shared this information with this female I don't even know, and a little hurt that she knew about his plan before I did.

Finn meets my eyes and gives a curt nod, as if to say it's okay. "Yes. At least until we can meet with the High Priestess, this is the best way to keep her safe."

She swings her attention to me, and I can't help but notice that her smile falls a bit as she does. "Abriella, it's nice to meet you. I'm happy to welcome you to my village."

Her village?

The question must be clear on my face because Finn explains, "Juliana is the Lady of Staraelia. She presides over these lands."

A female in charge. *How refreshing.*

"We might be rural lands," Juliana says, "but we're wise. For generations, the people of these parts have understood that leading is best left to the females."

"And they've prospered for it," Finn says, smiling, and the niggling jealousy rears its head again. "Could we bother you to show us to our rooms? It's been a long ride, and we could use a moment of rest."

"Sure. I'll call for help with your bags," Juliana says, and as if she shouted for them, half a dozen fae emerge from the house. "I've put Abriella down the hall and you across from me, Finn. It'll be just like old times."

"Abriella will stay with me," Finn says.

Juliana's smile falls away. "She's safe here."

"I believe so, but maintaining appearances is important. I promise that you and I will catch up tonight." He leans forward and gives her a wicked grin that sends jealousy running wild through me. "Just like old times."

"Better this way," Pretha says, stepping up beside me, her voice low. "The last thing Finn needs is Juliana getting her claws in him." She flashes me a smile. "With you in his room, he'll forget she exists."

CHAPTER SEVENTEEN

"OH, IT'S VERY . . . NICE," I say, turning in a slow circle and trying not to stare at the single bed framed by two large windows.

"Don't worry, Princess," Finn says. "I don't expect you to share your bed with me tonight."

I frown and turn to him. Didn't he just insist that we share this room? "Then where will you sleep?"

He grabs the blanket that's draped across the foot of the bed and throws it on the floor. "That spot looks fine to me."

I shift awkwardly. "Finn . . . you can't—"

"Don't insult me, Princess. I was raised camping in these foothills and sleeping on the ground every night. I can handle it."

"But . . ." I shake my head. "Let me sleep on the floor. I don't mind."

He chuckles. "My mother taught me better than that. Enjoy the bed. I'll be fine right here." When I open my mouth to protest, he holds up a hand. "Trust me, with all the togetherness we'll have this weekend, you'll probably want to take advantage of the moments you don't have to be so close to me."

I have to bite hard on my bottom lip to keep myself from

arguing about our sleeping arrangements again. "Juliana seems . . . nice."

He snorts. "Don't let her fool you. She's only nice when it serves her or her people."

Could've guessed that, I think, but I keep my mouth shut.

"Luckily, in this case, what we're after happens to serve her people." He opens the wardrobe and sorts through its contents before nodding in approval and turning to me. "You should have everything you need here, but let your handmaiden know if you need anything else. She should be here shortly to draw you a warm bath." He turns for the door.

"Where are you going?" I ask.

"I'm meeting with Juliana. We need to discuss a few things before I meet with my general."

Jealousy rears inside my chest, making me feel ugly and small, and I bow my head to hide it. "Be careful."

He chuckles. "Watch out, Princess. I might start to think you care."

Juliana leans across the table, refilling all our glasses before straightening and hoisting her own in the air. "I'd like to make a toast," she says, flashing that dazzling smile all around the room before letting it rest on Finn. "To our prince, who we always knew would come home." She hoists her glass higher. "May the road take you exactly where you need to go and always bring you back to us."

"Hear! Hear!" Kane shouts, pounding his fist on the table.

We all gathered for dinner at a large table situated on the

beautifully landscaped stone terrace behind the house — Finn, Pretha, Kane, Tynan, Misha, Juliana, and me. The food was delicious, especially after the day's long ride, and everyone seems to be having a great time, but the whole night has left me feeling lonely.

I smile politely and take a sip of my wine. I'm the odd man out here. The only one who doesn't understand how Finn fits into this world, the only one who hasn't known him for decades or more.

I'm focused on my thoughts, so I barely realize that Kane has leaned closer until I hear him whisper in my ear. "You don't need to be jealous, Princess."

I stiffen. "What? I'm not —"

He chuckles. "He doesn't look at Juliana the way she wants him to. Never has." His voice is so quiet, I'd never be able to hear him if it weren't for these fae ears. Still, I look around to make sure no one else is listening.

"I'm not jealous about anything," I say, but then Juliana makes a liar out of me. Instead of returning to her seat, she plops herself into Finn's lap and loops an arm behind his neck. Finn grins at her, as if having her in his lap is the most natural thing in the world. I give Kane a tight smile and push back from the table. "Excuse me. I need to stretch my legs."

Kane shakes his head and mutters something under his breath about females.

The air is cool and the sky is clear, and the minute I'm out of sight of the rest of the group, my muscles loosen. I know I'm being childish. My jealousy is unreasonable and unwanted. I shouldn't feel this way, but feelings very rarely care about *should* and *shouldn't.*

Kane was trying to help, but he doesn't understand my emotions right now. Sure, I'm jealous, but not just of Juliana and whatever relationship Finn has with her; I'm jealous of the rest of them too. Of the community and friendships they have that I never will. I'm jealous that they get to see their family when my only family is in another realm where I'll never be welcome. I'm jealous that they can give something back to this world when the best I can hope for is to fix what my very existence has broken.

I'm at the stables before I even realize where I was headed. Two Star neighs and tosses her head when she catches sight of me. "You think I brought you treats, sweet girl?" I ask, reaching into my pocket. I open my palm and offer her one of the sugar cubes I snatched from the tea setting.

Two Star gobbles it up, and I stroke her nose before bending to grab her brush.

Juliana's stable hands have taken good care of her, but I let myself into the stall anyway. I brush her soft coat, enjoying the ritual of grooming her — the soft swish of the brush and the flick of her tail in the night breeze. I may not have any family or friends in this whole realm, but I feel a little less alone out here with my horse.

"How'd I know I'd find you in here?" Finn asks.

I don't have to turn to know who it is. He could've entered without speaking and I would've felt him. My power *hums* when he's around. I smile a bit, happy with the new knowledge that he feels this connection too. "This girl's got me wrapped around her finger," I say.

He comes to my side and strokes her velvety black coat. "You were quiet at dinner."

I cut my eyes to him without turning my head. "I thought we weren't putting on airs for this group. Did you need me to give a speech?"

"No. Of course not. I was just worried that you were . . . uncomfortable."

I shake my head. Tears burn the back of my eyes. How can I explain this to him? In light of everything else that's happening, it seems so foolish, petty even. How can I complain about my loneliness or my fears for my future? How I fear that now I've turned fae, I'll never fit in anywhere. The only thing more embarrassing than that would be complaining that I never have.

I swallow it all back. "They call this place your home. You weren't raised in the palace?"

He stares at me a long moment, and I can see him contemplating whether to push me about dinner. Instead, he sighs and lets it drop. "Yes and no. My mother was raised here and kept a home here, but we visited only occasionally while she was alive."

"And after she passed?" I ask.

"After she passed, my father left my mother's sister in charge of raising my brother and me, and she believed we would grow to be better leaders if we were raised in our mother's home. Vexius and I spent more time here than anywhere else."

I drop to my knees to inspect Two Star's hooves. Or maybe I

just want to put some distance between me and those silver eyes that seem to see right through me. "You liked it here?"

"More than anywhere else. For that reason, Staraelia will always be my home, even though I haven't been back in a very long time."

I look up at him. He's leaning against the stall door, watching me as I work. "Since the curse?" I ask.

"Since Mordeus began to rule." He tips his head back and closes his eyes. "When my father was locked in the mortal realm, I wasn't ready to be king, and rather than step up in his absence, I convinced myself that Father would find a way home sooner rather than later. That decision — that hesitation to step up to my responsibilities — it cost my people." He opens his eyes, but his gaze is distant. "I failed them by staying here when I should've gone straight to the palace. I didn't realize that Mordeus was gathering his followers, his sycophants, those traitors who would do anything my uncle said just for a chance for a little more power, a little more wealth. And by the time I realized what was happening" — he blows out a breath — "it was already a mess."

"But your father hadn't passed on his crown to you," I say, standing. "Would it have mattered if you'd returned to the palace sooner?"

"I didn't have any more right to the throne than Mordeus did, but I gave him a chance to get a foothold, and that made all the difference. I was so focused on . . ." He grimaces and swallows hard. "I was so focused on my life here that I couldn't be bothered to consider what might be happening at the capital."

His life here? Does he mean with Isabel? I want to ask how he met her, when things changed between them, and why he was willing to sacrifice her for his own power, but I bow my head and finish grooming Two Star.

I return the brush to its basket and wipe my hands on my trousers before leaving the stall.

Finn steps close, right between me and the exit. He takes my chin in his big hand and scans my face. "Are you ready for tomorrow?"

I swallow hard. I haven't been this close to him since we were on the terrace at Castle Craige. Since he kissed me, and I wanted him to do so much more. Even when he sat next to my bed at the Unseelie palace, there was more room between us. Or maybe I'm just feeling particularly exposed and vulnerable tonight.

I look away, fearing my expression might betray me. "I'll be fine. Exactly what kind of event is this?"

Dropping my chin, he shoves his hands into his pockets. "It's a celebration of the bounty of the harvest," he says. "And everything that represents it."

"You're being cryptic."

The corner of his mouth quirks into a mischievous smirk. "I'm afraid you might take offense if I explain."

I fold my arms. "Now you have to tell me."

"We celebrate our females on Lunastal. We celebrate their work in the fields and in the home, but also because" — he tugs his bottom lip between his teeth for a moment before releasing it — "because females represent fertility — the continuation of our bloodlines."

"I'm afraid to ask just how you do that," I say, but my cheeks are hot as my imagination latches onto any number of ways I could celebrate fertility with Finn.

"Maybe it's better that it's a surprise," he says, grinning.

I shove against his chest with a flat palm. "You can't do that to me! I won't sleep. I'll be too worried."

His gaze dips to my mouth again. "I promise not to do anything that makes you uncomfortable." He winks. "No matter how much I might want to celebrate the way Lugh intended."

Just as I warned Finn it would be, my mind is too full of thoughts of what might happen tomorrow, and I can't sleep. I roll over and punch my pillow, but the sound of laughter behind the house drags me from bed and to the window.

Juliana and Finn are seated on the patio, drinking wine. Finn's smiling at her, and she has her head thrown back as she laughs. Gods, I'm so envious of her — of that smile Finn's giving her, of her history with him, and — as shallow as it might make me — even of that lush, dark hair cascading down her back.

I've never been particularly beautiful, but I was always rather proud of my long red locks. I miss them, if I'm honest. As petty as it is, I kind of wish I could chop Juliana's hair off to even the playing field. And then, because I'm more sensible than petty, I'd like to keep it for payments to goblins when I need them.

"I'm no better than my catty cousins," I mutter, shaking my head.

On the patio below, Juliana's face goes serious and she leans in.

I want to know what she's saying, and I don't let myself overthink it before I slip into shadow and head down the stairs.

I creep onto the patio and become one with the shadows. Dara's and Luna's heads perk up in unison, looking in my direction from where they lounge in the moonlight, but if they sense my presence, they must not consider me a threat, because they almost immediately lie back down.

"That's the last of the bottle," Finn's saying. He pours the final drops from the bottle into her glass.

"Then we should open another," Juliana says.

Finn laughs. "That was the last of the *second* bottle. Any more, and tomorrow's hike will feel like torture."

"It's just that I hardly ever see you," Juliana whines. She swirls her wine and frowns at him. "I was honestly surprised you joined me tonight."

Finn arches a brow. "I told you I would."

She chuckles softly. "I underestimated your ability to resist the beautiful female in your chambers, I suppose."

Finn bows his head and studies his wineglass. He takes a long swallow before speaking. "I won't pretend it's easy."

"I'm surprised you can stand the sight of her, knowing she's the one your father chose," Juliana says softly, as if contemplating this. "Knowing he passed his power to her—a *human*—rather than to you."

Finn's head snaps up. "I didn't tell you that."

"Come now, Finnian. I may not be a priestess, but I *am* the daughter of one. I'm not without certain powers of my own. I feel it in her. My only question is how the curse was broken when the queen still lives and this one has the power of the throne."

Finn takes another long pull off his drink and sighs. "The curse was broken when she bonded with Prince Ronan, died, and passed the crown — not the power — to him. That is why Prince Ronan's at the castle — not just because the curse is broken, and not just because he has a birthright to the throne, but because he wears the crown."

She flinches. "I was worried it might be something like that."

"Unfortunately, but at least he seems to be genuine in his desire to do right by the shadow fae. He helped defend the capital during the attack, and he dismantled the queen's camps as well. He brought hundreds of children home."

"As grateful as I am for that" — Juliana blows out a breath — "it won't work, Finn. He can't be king. Our people will never accept him. He could lead us in war and win, and there are still those among us who would refuse to accept him just because he's Arya's son."

He sighs. "This court is dying, and an imperfect solution is better than no solution."

She cocks her head to the side. "Will you let him have *everything* you want so dearly?"

Finn's jaw ticks. "What do you mean by that?"

"Abriella. She's bonded to him, yet you look at her like she is the stars and the moon. Like she's rain at the end of a long summer drought. You look at her the way all the young females in Staraelia dreamed you might one day look upon them." She pauses for a beat. "You look at her the way you looked at Isabel."

His grip tightens on his glass. "Don't."

"You deny it?"

"I don't appreciate the parallels."

She snorts. "Is that why Ronan beat you to claiming the crown? Because you'd already fallen for the human? I bet every time you thought about bonding with her, you remembered Isabel dying in your arms."

"You push me too far," Finn says. His voice is quiet but as sharp as the blade I plunged into Mordeus's chest. "Do you forget that I don't need your permission to speak with your mother?"

She sighs. "I'm not trying to be cruel, Finn. I'm trying to understand why this happened. How is this girl bonded to Prince Ronan but here with you?" She stares, clearly waiting for the rest of the explanation.

"She's with me because she won't forgive him for his deception, and because she wants to find a way to save these lands and their people."

"She's *human*." Juliana tosses her hair over her shoulder. "You believe that?"

"She's fae now, not that it's relevant."

"She and the prince could be playing you. Maybe she wants the throne for herself."

I bare my teeth and nearly lose my shadows. It's all I can do to keep from growling at her. Why would I want the throne? How dare she put those ideas in Finn's head?

"I suppose that's possible," Finn says, the edge in his voice gone now, "but everything she's said and done indicates that she views the power as a burden, not a blessing."

"What a fool," Juliana mutters.

Finn shrugs and takes another sip of his drink. "Perhaps *we're* the fools."

Nodding, she hums. "You still haven't explained how she kept this power she supposedly doesn't want."

"The golden prince gave her the Potion of Life to save her and turn her fae, but in doing so, he inadvertently tied the power to her life."

Juliana presses her fingertips to her mouth. "Why would he risk such a thing? He had to have known there was a chance."

"Because he was in love with her — *is* in love with her."

"Hmm," she says. "You said he gave her the Potion of Life because he loves her —"

"He does."

"Then do you truly believe he'll sever the bond?"

"No," Finn says softly. "I don't."

"Interesting."

Finn groans. "Out with it."

"I was just thinking that the last time two brothers were in love with the same female, Faerie was split down the middle."

"It's not the same."

"You're not in love with her? You didn't bring her here to introduce as your betrothed because you want to make sure the people from your homeland accept her by your side? There's not a part of you that's hoping to get Mother's blessing on your relationship to your *brother's* bonded partner?"

Finn remains silent and reaches for a fresh bottle of wine. He refills his glass. "You know what brought me here."

"I know what *should've* brought you here. I know how

desperately your people need to see you after all these years. Those who weren't forced into hiding were scared, praying that their prince would come home, but you didn't even visit. Not once."

"Coming here would've put the entire village at risk. Mordeus would've loved an excuse to lay siege to Mother's favorite place. I stayed away to protect everyone here."

She swallows. "I know that, Finn, but not everyone understands. There are some who feel abandoned." She shakes her head. "You truly intend to celebrate Lunastal by honoring your brother's bonded partner?"

"He's not my brother."

"Oh, I suppose that's true," she says, draining her own glass. "Since your father disowned you."

"You press your luck, Juliana."

"I speak the truth." She takes the crystal goblet from his hand and drinks from it. Handing it back, she lifts her gaze to meet his. "You are my prince and the rightful heir. Long ago, I pledged my allegiance to you and swore to put your future on the throne before my own life. That hasn't changed. But I also know that you're here looking for solutions, and you might not like what you find."

"You might be surprised by what I find," he snaps.

Juliana cocks her head to the side. "What do you mean by that?"

He's quiet for a long moment. "What do you know about the tethered?"

"Your line?" she asks.

Finn swallows hard. "My line back before we were on the

throne. My line before Mab's line died out."

She shakes her head. "Not much. They were servants to the crown. Highly powerful, trusted, honored, but exploited as well. Vessels for our rulers."

"Have you heard of anyone being tethered since—to the crown or otherwise?"

"Why are you asking, Finn?" Her face pales. "Surely you don't believe— It's impossible."

"I don't know. I dismissed the possibility for weeks after she arrived, but I've felt it from that first moment I stepped close to her. It's there—a connection that's unlike anything else. And she draws from me. Has from the beginning. I blamed it on the crown before, but . . . that's not it."

"But she still has the *power* of the crown, if not the crown itself. Perhaps it's rooted in that—rooted in your destiny to carry that power yourself."

"Have you ever heard of such a thing happening?" he asks.

"No. But it's more reasonable than to think the gods would've tethered you to some random human." Juliana's jaw goes slack and she shakes her head. "Tethered," she repeats, as if the word itself is a wonder. "I don't believe it. I think you're fixated on her and trying to excuse your lustful thoughts."

Finn grunts. "Trust me, I have plenty of those, but that's not what this is about. I can't explain it. When she uses extraordinary amounts of power, she pulls from me. I get weak. When she first became fae and used her power to escape the Golden Palace and lock everyone she left behind in darkness, I thought I was dying."

"This has happened again? Since?"

Finn nods. "Yes. She used a great deal of power when the capital was attacked. At the same time, I was in the palace suffering one of these spells. I've been searching for another explanation, but I keep coming back to the same thing."

"I almost thought it was a myth. An excuse the old queens used to keep their lovers close." She blows out a breath and shakes her head. "I think you're out on a limb. If you're tethered to anything, it's the throne." She meets his stare and holds it. "And you are not meant to serve that throne, Finn. It was made to serve you."

"It was made to serve Mab's line, not mine."

"But her line is gone, and she trusted your father's line to rule in their stead. Don't doubt our Great Queen's will."

"I don't."

"So if Mab tells you to kill them both—the girl and Ronan—and claim the throne for yourself, you'd do it?"

Finn stares at her for a long time, and I throw my hand over my mouth and bite the inside of my cheek as I wait for his reply. I know I shouldn't trust anyone—that I never can as long as I have this power—but I can't accept that Finn would consider killing me and Sebastian to claim the throne for himself. The idea hurts too much. But could I accept it if it would save thousands?

"She won't," he finally says. "The magic of the crown would keep it from passing to me even if I were willing to consider it, so don't make me answer an impossible question that will never be relevant. If I'm right, and I am tethered to Abriella, you understand what that might mean for the throne."

Juliana sneers. "I'm insulted that you're even asking me to

consider it. You've lost your mind, Finn. Do you forget how our throne works?"

"I haven't forgotten a thing, but since Oberon passed his crown to her, it seems we've been working under a new set of rules."

"Maybe *you* have, but the old rules matter to the rest of us. Bloodlines and Mab's will matter to us. You forget how terrible it was for us under Mordeus's rule."

"I never forget that," he says, his voice solemn.

"You're asking me to protect Prince Ronan's bonded partner. To consider that she might be worthy of a power that was made for the greatest among us."

"She *is* worthy."

Juliana's eyes flare with anger, but she sets her jaw and stares into the distance. "I won't argue with you about this. I have faith that Mab will have the answers we need."

"As do I," Finn whispers.

When she turns back to him, her face softens. "I'm sure I seem horrible to you, but I don't mean to be. I want you on that throne where you belong, and despite any illness you might be suffering or any quirks in the magic from Oberon's ill-fated choices, I believe that's where you'll end up."

He reaches across the table and takes her hand. There's such a tenderness between them that I slip back into the house, more confused than I was before and feeling guilty about spying on Finn.

Maybe I'll tell him tomorrow. It would be better, wouldn't it? To just be honest about the fact that I'm a terrible friend who eavesdrops on private conversations?

This one, like so many others, has left me with more questions than answers. *Tethered.* Where have I heard that term before? I'll have to confess to Finn tomorrow; that way he can tell me what it all means.

When I crawl back into bed, my mind is spinning. There are so many more important things to ponder, yet alone in this room we'll share tonight, my thoughts snag on the most insignificant parts of their conversation.

I underestimated your ability to resist the beautiful female in your chambers.

I won't pretend it's easy.

I think you're fixated on her and trying to excuse your lustful thoughts.

Trust me, I have plenty of those.

The snippets play on repeat in my mind. They don't matter. It's not as if this attraction between me and Finn is a revelation. Or that it's even meaningful. Yet part of me always assumed he was just teasing. Flirting to win my favor. Part of me really likes the idea of Finn struggling to resist me — the same part that likes to imagine him sleeping in this room with me tonight and struggling with those lustful thoughts he admitted to having.

I dream of being nothing more than shadow — a dark penumbra who doesn't hide or cower. Who takes what she wants and laughs at anyone who gets hurt along the way.

I'm nothing more than a silhouette of myself as I creep quietly out of the bedroom I'm sharing with Finn and down the hall to another room. He smiled at her. He laughed and confided, let her sit in his *lap* at dinner. He probably thinks she's so beautiful, with that feminine grace and her long dark hair. She doesn't deserve him.

Her door's closed. *How cute.* I slip right through it and walk through the darkness to Juliana's side of the bed. Her hair is fanned out around her on the pillow. She's so peaceful, hands folded on her stomach, chest rising and falling in the easy rhythm of sleep.

With a smile, my shadow takes a handful of her hair and uses the knife I didn't realize I was holding to slice it off. She'll still be beautiful. She'll still have that smile and those sparkling eyes. She'll still know exactly where she fits in this world, but I will have her hair for the next time I need to bribe a goblin.

I'm grinning as I return to my own room and drop the hair and the knife on the bedside table with a thunk. When I spot my body in the bed, the dream blinks in and out of existence. In my body again, I roll over and burrow a little deeper under my blankets. In the next moment, I'm disconnected again, watching myself from the foot of my bed, where I smile into the night and stretch my arms overhead.

It feels *good* to be free of my own skin. Feels good to be alive and know Finn is so close. Because he's the one I want. In the dark of this dream, with nothing but my shadow for my body, he's *all* I want.

I slink through the darkness to his makeshift bed by the window. He's beautiful, sleeping on his back, with one hand behind his head and the other resting on his bare chest. I study the planes of his face in the darkness. It feels so natural — so *good and wicked and delightful*—to straddle his waist and lower myself onto him.

He feels perfect under me. *Warm. Solid. Strong.* He likes it too. He releases a contented groan, not opening his eyes. Hot and solid and powerful even in his sleep.

I take the hand from his chest and place it on my stomach, watching with rapt attention as his eyes flutter open.

"Abriella?" He sounds confused, as if he doesn't expect me to be here—as if there's anywhere else I'd want to be. Pulling his hand from behind his head, he blinks up at me, then rubs his eyes. "What is this?"

"I . . . *want,*" I say, shifting, sliding down his body until my thighs are cradling his hips. I can feel him through the sheet, hard and thick against me.

With a curse, he draws in a ragged breath. "Do you know what you're doing right now?" he asks.

"I'm taking what I *want,*" I whisper, and I rock my hips to show him exactly what I mean. "And giving what you want."

Finn's neck arches as he groans, his hips lifting off the floor and seeking more. Seeking *me.* "Brie," he breathes.

I graze my shadow fingers over his bare chest, over his navel, and along the soft line of hair that disappears beneath the sheet.

"Gods above and below," he breathes. "Is this even real?"

"Does that matter?" I purr.

Suddenly he sits up, and I grin in delight at the heat of him coming so close. His gaze darts to the bed, then back to me. "What is this?"

"Don't worry about *her.*" I'm annoyed. I want his focus. His whole attention on *me,* not that girl in the bed.

He shoves at my shoulder, but his hands go right through me, and I chuckle. "I just want to have some fun, Finn."

He scrambles away from me and stands, backing toward the window. He's wearing fitted black shorts and nothing else, but there's fear in his eyes as he shifts his gaze between me and the bed. "What are you?"

Reluctantly, I follow his gaze, and my body jerks. Like I've been doused with a bucket of cold water, I jerk upright in bed and look around.

"Brie." Finn stares at me, breathing heavily, mouth ajar. "Are you okay?"

I glance at the foot of the bed, where I was just standing, where I was just . . . there's nothing there. But then I catch sight of the bedside table — and the locks of luscious brown hair I dreamed of cutting from Juliana's head.

CHAPTER EIGHTEEN

THE CONFUSION IN FINN'S EYES mirrors my own.

"What was that?" he asks.

My heart is racing, but my body . . . my body is tingling as if I really was just straddling Finn and not sleeping in this bed, under these blankets. "I was dreaming. I was . . ."

Finn is breathing hard, and his gaze shifts back and forth between me and the mess of blankets on the floor where we were just . . . "I've never seen you do that before. I've never . . ." He curses under his breath and shakes his head. "Tell me that was you."

It wasn't me. I was in this bed. I was sleeping. But . . . I look Finn in the eye. "I thought I was dreaming."

He stares at me for a minute; then all at once that spooked, worried expression falls away and his mouth twists into a lopsided grin. "You thought you were *dreaming?* What else do we do in your dreams, Princess?"

I grab a pillow and throw it at him.

Dodging, he chuckles before his face goes serious again. "How long have you been able to do that? How often does this happen?"

"Never before. I—" Memories come at me in gruesome

flashes. The orcs around the fire. The bloody knife. The way their guts oozed when I cut them open. "I don't remember."

He takes a single step closer. "What aren't you telling me?"

I close my eyes and remember that night. "The night I met Misha at the refugee camp, I was captured. They injected me with that toxin, and I couldn't access my magic. My arms were in shackles. I was outnumbered and *so tired*—from the metamorphosis, from the way I used my magic as I stormed out of the palace, and from helping those children get to the portal." I swallow hard, and my insides shiver. I haven't thought much about that night, haven't stopped to wonder who slayed my captors. I realize now that I never let myself think about it. "I went to sleep wishing them dead, and when I woke, they were. Gutted in their sleep. And a bloody knife—*my* knife—lay on the ground beside me."

"You think you did it?" he asks. "But you don't remember?"

I squeeze my eyes shut, not wanting to admit it even to myself. "I've gotten flashes of their panicked eyes as they were sliced open," I finally say. "I told myself I was imagining it. That it was just my mind trying to make sense of something I couldn't explain."

"Shit," Finn mutters.

"What does it mean? I've turned myself to shadow countless times, but never while leaving my actual body."

He tips his face up and blows out a breath. "There are legends about Unseelie who could control their shadow selves. Generations ago. There's a story about Mab. That she was captured once, locked in an iron room that nullified her power, yet she was still able to send her shadow self to destroy the guards and free herself from that prison."

"Even though she couldn't access her magic?"

"The idea was that her shadow self wasn't bound to her corporeal body." He shrugs and blows out a breath. "So much of it is legend. I'm not sure I ever believed it was real."

"Is there any other explanation for what happened with us tonight?" I ask.

"I saw you—*felt* you—on me. I touched you, and you were as real as anything. But then once I spotted your sleeping form on the bed, you weren't corporeal anymore. My hands just went right through you."

"You don't know anyone who could do this?" I ask, but I'm still shaking.

"No," he breathes. "My father wanted to, actually. He trained with a special priestess trying to access his shadow self, but he never could. Just be careful, Princess. With you, we don't—"

"—know how my magic works and why, because I'm a mortal who was turned immortal and holds the power of the Unseelie crown that Oberon never should've been able to pass to me to begin with."

He shrugs, but his expression is apologetic. He glances out at the dark night outside the window and pulls the curtains closed. "We should get some sleep."

I settle back against the headboard and cringe at the sight of the lock of hair and the knife on my bedside table. I'm so spooked, I'm not sure I'll be able to sleep.

"What's that?" Finn asks, following my gaze.

I shake my head, still staring at it. "I don't really know, but I think it's Juliana's hair."

Finn barks out a laugh. "You cut off Juliana's hair?"

"I thought it was a dream."

His chest shakes in silent laughter. "You thought you were dreaming, so you let yourself slice off her hair, but it just so happened that your shadow self was doing the same thing in the waking world."

I shrug again. That about sums it up, but it doesn't make it any less creepy.

"Remind me to stay on your good side, Princess."

I cut him a look. "I'm not sure you've even met my good side."

His gaze slides over my face to my neck and the low-cut top of the sleeping gown, then down to the blankets that cover my legs. His gaze smolders so hot I might as well be naked. "I *have* met your good side," he says. "She came out to play that night in the shower. She was a lot of fun." I throw another pillow at him, and he snatches this one out of the air, grinning. "Thanks. Looks like I have all your pillows now. Does this mean you'll be joining me on the floor?" He grabs the other off the ground before lifting them both in the air. "Or would you prefer I join you on the bed?"

"What happened to staying on my good side?"

Chuckling, he tosses a pillow back to me before climbing back onto his pallet of blankets on the floor. We're both quiet for a long time.

I close my eyes and listen to his breathing, but I know he's not sleeping, and neither am I. With visions of those gutted orcs flashing through my mind, I'm not sure I will.

"You're shaking," Finn says. "I can feel it from here."

"I hate feeling like there's this part of me that maybe I don't control." I bite my lip. "I'm scared."

He's quiet so long that I think he might've fallen asleep, but then I hear him stir, and in the next moment, my sheets rustle as he pulls them back. The bed shifts under his weight. "I'm here," he whispers, and his hand finds mine under the blankets. "Right here. I promise I'll wake you before your shadow self can seduce me." His words are laced with mischief, and I can't help but smile.

I pinch the back of his hand. "How do you know she wasn't just after a lock of your hair?"

Chuckling, he rolls to his side to face me. His lips press against my shoulder, warm and sweet. "Next time you straddle me," he murmurs, "wake up first. I want all of you, not just some dark and twisted secret corner of your mind."

A shiver runs through me, but I'm not shaking anymore. At least not from fear.

Light hits me like a physical blow, and I roll over in bed, burying my face in the pillow. "Close the curtains," I groan.

My demand is met with a feminine chuckle. "It's time to wake up, sleepyhead," Pretha says. "If you don't get dressed now, they'll have to leave without you."

"Let them leave," I mumble. "I need sleep."

The blankets are ripped off me, and I whimper. "Why do you hate me?"

"I don't hate you. Not even a little. But today is important. Get up."

I sit up, but only because I smell coffee, then freeze as memories from last night slam into me. Closing my eyes for a beat, I let myself remember how it felt to straddle Finn, to wake him, his hungry growl when he realized it was me . . . even though it wasn't. Not *really.* The memory brings nothing more than embarrassment and more questions about this world and my powers.

But then I recall the way he fell asleep holding my hand. How nice it was to have him close. And his words before he fell asleep? *I want all of you.*

I make a beeline for the coffeepot steaming on the corner table. I'm going to need it if I want to process any of what happened last night. After Finn fell asleep beside me, the night seemed to stretch on forever as my thoughts ran in circles. By the time I drifted off, the sun was beginning to rise. "Tell me again what we're doing today?" I ask, pouring myself a cup.

Pretha studies the contents of the wardrobe thoughtfully. "Today and tonight, we celebrate Lunastal," she says, smiling over her shoulder at me.

"Tell me what that entails." Finn's explanation left a lot to be desired.

"It's a celebration of the beginning of the harvest. In these parts of the territory, it's considered bad luck not to celebrate, and it's believed that the god Lugh will cast a blight on the crops of those who fail to pay him homage."

I swallow my first sip of coffee and give myself a moment to let it warm my chest. "Is this celebrated all over Faerie?"

She nods, pulling out a dark red dress the color of crisp autumn leaves. "Yes, but more ardently in the rural areas, where they rely so much on crops for their livelihood."

"And where is Finn?" I didn't hear him this morning, didn't feel him leave the bed.

"He woke early to pay a visit to an old friend," Pretha says.

I wonder if he's meeting with Juliana again. Letting her touch him at every opportunity. Making her laugh. Jealousy makes my coffee settle uneasily in my stomach.

Pretha chuckles. "You are so transparent it's laughable."

"What?"

"You're jealous."

"Am not. Just curious where he might be."

She doesn't bother to hide her grin. "Well, you should know that this old friend is coming up on his thousandth year and rarely leaves his cottage by the river, so I don't think you need to worry about his friend doing anything that would make Finn stop pining for you."

"He doesn't *pine* for me."

She snorts. "Whatever you say."

But he doesn't, does he? There's physical attraction on both sides for sure, and last night he made it clear that he's open to acting on that attraction. But that's where this ends. Anything beyond that would be too complicated. "I take it this celebration begins in the morning," I say, if only to change the subject. "That's why you're dragging me out of bed so early?"

She chuckles and tosses the dress on the bed. "It's all day. We'll begin with the traditional trek up Mount Rowan, which will take most of the morning."

I frown at the dress. "Hiking all morning, and I'm supposed to wear *that?*"

She smooths the bodice and smirks at me. "You're here as Finn's betrothed. Regardless of what happens to the Throne of Shadows, this makes you their future queen in their eyes. They'll expect to see you dressed accordingly."

Grumbling, I refill my coffee cup. "I think you know me well enough to believe me when I say I can't even *pretend* to be a lady."

"Just be yourself. The only pretending you need to do is about your relationship with Finn—though I don't expect that will be much of a stretch."

I freeze, my coffee cup halfway to my mouth. "What's that supposed to mean?"

Pretha snorts, then cocks her head to the side. "You think none of us notice the way you look at each other?"

"Pretha, don't."

She sighs and rolls her eyes. "Once we reach the crest of the mountain, we'll settle in at the campsite, then travel to the sacred spring farther north."

"Aren't we in a hurry to get to the priestess? I thought we were going to her temple."

"That was the plan, but we won't be able to see her until tomorrow. Word arrived this morning that in light of the attack on the capital, she's not seeing anyone who hasn't made an offering to Lugh."

I stiffen, thinking of the human "tributes" the Unseelie took through the years of the curse. "What kind of offering?"

"Stop looking at me like I'm going to make you tear out a puppy's heart. We offer Lugh grains and corn. Nothing your delicate sensibilities can't handle."

"I'm not delicate."

She chuckles. "Regardless, we'll return to the celebration before nightfall."

"And what happens tonight?" I ask.

"There will be a bonfire with dancing, drinking, matchmaking ceremonies, and general merriment."

"You love this," I say, studying her. Even if she weren't grinning, her sparkling eyes would give her away.

She shrugs. "I have a lot of good memories from this time of year. My husband was raised out here, and Lunastal was one of his favorite celebrations." She looks lost in her memories. "He was strong and athletic, and he liked to show off during the competitions, but he also liked . . ." She swallows and lifts her gaze to meet mine. "He loved the community, the people. He loved knowing he'd always have a home here. There's a certain loyalty among these people that you don't find at the capital, and Vexius appreciated that."

"Is this where Finn met Isabel?" I ask, remembering what Finn said in the stables last night about being distracted by his life here when Mordeus stole the rule of the Unseelie Court.

Pretha nods. "Yes. And I imagine that's why returning is so bittersweet for him."

"How did they meet?" I ask. "She was a human, right? Was she a servant?"

"You are full of questions this morning. Let's get you dressed." She comes around the bed and unzips the red dress. She waits for me to strip out of my sleeping gown before helping me step into it. "Yes, Isabel was human," she says, zipping me up. "Well, a changeling, technically."

I glance over my shoulder. "What's a changeling?"

"There are those among the fae who take special interest in sick human children. They can't stand to see them suffer and believe it's their duty to use the magic of Faerie to heal them."

I spin to face her. "They just *steal* them from their parents?"

Her face grows serious as she studies me. "I don't expect you to understand these traditions, but I do ask that you believe me when I say that any child that's brought here as a babe has its death already written on the wall. It is not easy, and there is much sacrifice to bring a human child to live in our realm."

"So Isabel was a changeling," I say. "What does that mean, exactly? Did she have shifting abilities?"

"No," she scoffs. "Heavens, no. She was just a human raised in Faerie."

I take another sip of my coffee and remember the woman in the white dress from the catacombs. "And she was very beautiful," I whisper.

"Yes," Pretha says. "She was a quiet kind of beauty. The kind of person who looked out for those less fortunate than she was, who always put others before herself."

Shame swamps me. That wasn't the kind of beauty I was asking about, but I know Finn well enough to know that *who* she was would've mattered more than the rest.

"She was physically beautiful too," Pretha says. She pulls a pair of silky stockings from the wardrobe and tosses them on the bed.

"Enough so that many believe her adoptive father knew exactly what he was doing when he put her in Finn's path."

"But Finn wasn't supposed to fall in love with a human."

"No." She huffs and shakes her head. "I take that back. No one cared who he fell in love with. He just wasn't supposed to spend his life with a human, wasn't supposed to put one on the throne beside him. But that was his plan. He'd marry her, make her his queen, and after she gave him a few heirs, she'd take the Potion of Life and become fae."

"Of all the humans who bear children for fae males, why are so few are given the potion?" I say, grabbing the stockings and sitting on the edge of the bed to put them on. It would've been easier to do this before putting on the dress, but Pretha must understand that I'm too modest to want to be so exposed for long.

"The potion isn't used often. It's quite valuable and rare. The ingredients come from the caves beneath the Goblin Mountains, in the magical gems that are found there."

Both stockings on, I stand again and smooth my skirts. "Misha told me about the fire gems."

"Good. Then you understand why the potion isn't something we simply have on hand."

"Humans speak of it as if the fae have a limitless supply."

Pretha shakes her head. "You're the only human I've ever known to have been turned. I've heard of others, but in all my years, you're the only one I've met."

"What about Finn's betrothed? Would she have taken the potion?"

"Finn was trying to procure the necessary ingredients when

they planned their vows, but with the war raging over control of the mountains, he couldn't get what he needed. He was hoping to have it by the time their children were born." She sorts through a bag of cosmetics. "His father was so angry when Finn told him about the wedding. Oberon had planned for Finn to marry . . . another. Someone who would strengthen the power in their lineage. But Finn refused. It was very dramatic, but Finn was a lovesick male who refused to put politics before his own heart."

Jealousy grips me. No, not jealousy. How could I be jealous of a dead woman? A woman who got to see the very worst side of Finn's kind — of Finn himself.

"Seems like you would've been sympathetic to that," I say.

"Of course." She nods, pulling a palette and small brush from the bag. "Close your eyes."

I obey and let her sweep a tiny brush across my eyelids. "Were you jealous that they got to choose when you didn't?"

She sighs. "By then I was in love with Vexius. I believed the gods gave me two great loves. I don't regret my marriage or my decision to bond with my husband, and I didn't then either. Vexius truly brought me joy, and if I'd refused to marry him, I would've never known what it was like to have his love. I wouldn't have Lark."

"That's true." And very mature. I'm sure her emotions aren't anywhere near so simple.

"You can open now," she says after a final sweep of her brush. I do in time to see her produce a necklace of tiny pearls. She loops it around my neck, and I touch my fingers to the gem Sebastian gave me.

"Should I remove this?"

Pretha shakes her head. "We all wear a fire gem somewhere. It's expected."

But how would Finn feel about me wearing this one if he knew it came from Sebastian? It's probably better not to ask.

"When Oberon and Finn were at odds about Finn's future, I worried for Finn more than anything. I understood what it was like to have your individual wants and needs destroyed by the political ambitions of your parents, and I knew how much that hurt."

I lift my hand to the pearls. They're as smooth as silk beneath my fingertips. "You've been a good friend to him."

"He's easy to love." Shrugging, she fastens the clasp. "Now your hair."

I tug on a lock that falls just past my ear, pulling it until it's straight. "Not much you can do with it, I'm afraid."

"You might want it pinned back. For the flowers," she says, her eyes mischievous.

Flowers for the ceremony I still know nothing about, but rather than ask more questions, I nod and reach for my mug again. "Will you keep me company on the hike?"

She shakes her head. "No. The official journey is more of an act for newly bonded couples."

I cough and nearly spit out my coffee. "Is that so?" I knew I needed to act like Finn's betrothed this weekend, but I'm beginning to worry that I should've asked more questions about why.

"Plenty of singles trek up the mountain as well," she says, "but the ritual is considered the prime time for matchmaking, and

I'm . . ." She shakes her head. "Although it's been long enough that I'm expected to move on, I'm not ready."

And how could she be? She loved her husband and lost him, but never stopped loving Amira either. I can't blame her for not inviting more heartache.

"Anyway," she says, sliding pins into my hair, "Kane will hike alongside Juliana, and Misha, Tynan, and I will follow on horse-back a little behind the official trek."

I nod, though my mind won't stay on the details of the day. "When did it change between Finn and Isabel?" I ask, even though Pretha seems to be done with the subject.

"What do you mean?" she asks warily.

"How did he go from rebelling against his father for her to deciding it was worth sacrificing her?" I'm so busy avoiding her gaze that I don't even notice how quiet she's gone until a few moments have passed. I lift my gaze and see that she's frowning at me, something like disappointment in her eyes. I cringe, but I don't take the question back.

"There are some stories you need to hear from Finn," she says. "But I can tell you that whatever you're feeling for him shouldn't be dismissed because of what you *think* you know. Talk to him."

I swallow hard, shame making my skin feel too hot and tight. "It doesn't matter what I feel or what answers he could give me," I say softly. "I shouldn't trust anyone. Not anymore."

She doesn't speak again until she's done with my hair, and even then she waits until I meet her eyes. "Did you ever ask yourself why Finn didn't try to get you to bond with him that night when you were drugged?"

The heat in my cheeks turns from shame to mortification as I remember that night. The shower. My *begging.* "Because he knew I would've said no," I say.

Pretha gives me a sad smile that seems to say she understands me better than I understand myself. "I'm not sure that's true."

"I would have. I wanted Sebastian." But I wanted Sebastian to be the male I thought he was. The male whose top priority was protecting me, not cheating me out of the crown.

"Well, you got him." Her face twists in irritation.

"Don't act like Finn's reasons for wanting me were any more noble than Sebastian's," I growl. "They wanted the same thing for the same reasons — still do."

"At first that was true. At first, you were just a pretty girl who had what he needed." Sighing, she steps back and looks me over, surveying her work. "Then you became something else."

"Became what?"

"My friend, among other things," she says. "And as a friend, I'll share this with you. When my parents found out about Amira and me and sent me away, I was broken and angry. I prepared to spend my life in a political marriage and for my heart to always belong to someone else. I wasn't prepared for Vexius. I never knew I could love two people in that way — romantically, completely, and simultaneously. My feelings for one always felt like a betrayal of the other, yet one never diminished the other."

I think about how I've somehow fallen for two faerie princes — romantically, completely, and simultaneously. But unlike Pretha, I shouldn't trust either one.

By the time we head downstairs, rain is tapping against the window in a steady rhythm. A look outside reveals Finn, Kane, Juliana, and a group of fae I don't recognize all standing around and talking in the rain. None of them seems the slightest bit concerned about the drizzle wetting their clothes or the droplets of rain rolling down their faces.

Pretha opens the door for me and nudges me onto the front stoop.

"And then he said he would—" Finn stops in the middle of his sentence when he spots me, and his eyes trail over me, from the short red curls Pretha pinned out of my face all the way down to the hem of the red dress that sweeps the damp wet stone of the stoop. His face is solemn when he lifts his gaze to mine. "Good morning, Princess. You are absolutely stunning, as always."

My stomach does a giddy flip at those words, even as I realize that they're more for the crowd that's waiting here than they are for me. Even so, some visceral part of me desperately wants to believe them.

He steps forward and takes my hand, drawing me out from the overhang and fully into the rain. "Are you ready for our trek up the mountain?"

"We'll be soaked through," I say, tilting my face up toward the sky. I don't mind, truly, but suddenly the idea of hiking through the rain at his side, of pretending to be a couple, makes me feel far too vulnerable—as if the rain might wash away the last of my willpower where Finn's concerned. Perhaps that's ridiculous after last night, but at least last night there was no one watching us, no one trying to dissect what we feel for each other.

Juliana steps forward. She's dressed in a shining yellow and gold dress that reminds me of the sunshine, and she has marigolds woven into the curls pinned off her neck. One chunk of curls, I notice with a shameful flash of satisfaction, is a great deal shorter than the rest. "A gentle rain during Lunastal is considered a blessing by Lugh," she says, handing a basket of flowers to Finn, who accepts them wordlessly.

He takes a handful of flowers from the basket before placing it on the porch and standing to face me. "May I?" he asks, combing two fingers through a curl that's broken free of the pins.

"It's tradition," Pretha says behind me. "To allow your partner to put flowers in your hair. You'll wear them to the top of the mountain and then bury them at the door to your tent."

"It is believed," explains a horned male I've never met before, "that by burying the flowers at the door to where you'll share a bed, you ask the gods to bless you with fertility and a healthy pregnancy."

My eyes go wide, and flames of embarrassment lick my cheeks. Finn's eyes dance with amusement as they meet mine. I almost swat the flowers right out of his hands and ask him what he's thinking, but I can't with all these people watching.

"May I?" Finn asks again, stepping even closer.

I nod, not sure what else I can do. It's not as if there's any risk of this ritual resulting in pregnancy anyway, so I nod, and Finn places the flowers in my hair, one by one.

The air is chilly in the rain, but Finn's body is warm, and his big fingers are gentle, almost soothing, as he uses the pins to form miniature rosebuds and mums into a crown atop my head.

"It looks beautiful," Pretha says when Finn steps back.

"Truly lovely," Juliana agrees, and I wonder if anyone else notices the disapproval in her tone.

Kane grunts and nods. "Appears our prince has finally found something he's good at."

Finn cups my jaw for a beat. "She makes it easy," he says roughly before stepping back.

When his hand is gone, I long for it to return.

CHAPTER NINETEEN

OUR "CELEBRATORY" HIKE UP THE mountainside was more like an endless slog through mud and rain. The good people of Staraelia don't allow inclement weather to prevent their celebration of Lunastal, so even when the rain was coming down so hard and cold that it felt like being stabbed with a million tiny needles at once, we trudged forward. Finn was quieter than usual on the trek, always by my side but touching me only to offer help over particularly steep terrain. Every so often I'd catch him staring at me, as if he was trying to figure something out.

I like to consider myself tough, but by the time we reached the top of the mountain, I nearly whimpered in relief. I've let my training lapse in my weeks in the Wild Fae Lands, and I could barely keep up with these happy, sun-kissed fae from Staraelia. Perhaps instead of helping at the infirmary and school at the settlement, I should've worked the fields.

Someone hands me a canteen of cold water and I gulp it down while scanning our destination. We're not so much at the top of the mountain as we are at a rocky plateau near the top. There are dozens of tents already set up and servants darting about with food and wood.

"Your tents are ready," a male announces from in front of a roaring bonfire. "Please retire at will."

"Which one's ours?" I ask Finn, trying to keep the exhaustion from my voice.

"Anxious to get him alone?" a strange male asks. His low chuckle makes me wish I could take the question back. It's better, though, I suppose, that all these people believe Finn and I are madly in love. Better that they don't understand that my desire to find our tent has more to do with the muscles in my thighs trembling from that climb than it does with what will happen once we're alone together.

"I promise to show you soon, but first you need to take a seat," Finn says, taking my hand. The idea of *sitting* sounds so glorious that I happily allow him to lead me toward a seat beside the fire.

I barely have a chance to enjoy the heat of the flames before I realize that all the fae who marched up the hill with us are congregating behind Finn and smiling as they watch us.

Finn winks at me. "Don't move," he says.

As if I could. Now that I'm sitting, exhaustion weighs more heavily on my shoulders—in part from the exercise, but also undoubtedly from my inability to get back to sleep last night. No, now that I'm sitting, I may never rise from this spot again.

Finn takes a two large bowls from beneath the bench and turns to the fire, where he fills them with water from a black metal pot. He winks at me before sprinkling bits of dried flowers into one and adding droplets of oils to the other.

His movements are so precise, they could never be mistaken for anything but ritual, as much a part of this tradition as the flowers in my hair. The watching crowd grows as he works — my self-consciousness right along with it.

Finn returns to my bench, settling his bowls on the ground before kneeling between them. The water steams, and I can't wait to sink my aching feet in it, but I wait, all too aware of the many eyes watching to see if I make a wrong move.

Finn reaches beneath my dress, and my breath catches. His hands wrap around my shin and slide up. The heat from his skin seeps through the leather of my boots. "It's my honor to wash the feet of my future queen," he says softly, his fingers beginning to unlace the boots beneath my skirt. "To show my reverence and to prove my subservience."

My cheeks are on fire again. It seems so wrong to partake in these rituals when we're not actually a couple, when I'm not on my way to the throne, but in the way of the throne accepting a new king. More than that, his touch feels far too intimate. One big hand holds my leg behind my knee while the other removes my boots from one foot, then the other. It feels, embarrassingly, like a seduction, and if we weren't being watched so closely, I'd surely ask him to stop.

Or maybe I'd encourage him to go on.

The fact that I don't know for sure either way makes my cheeks burn hotter.

When Finn moves higher up my skirt, his calloused fingertips find the top of my stocking at the middle of my thigh. Eyes locked on mine, he hesitates there, trailing his finger right along the edge of the silk, as if he's fascinated by the contrast between my skin and the thin fabric. I can't breathe.

"What's the problem, Finnian?" Juliana calls from her spot at the side of the gathered crowd. I *must* have been distracted by Finn to not notice her there. "Have you forgotten how to undress a female?"

My cheeks blaze with embarrassment at the reminder that we're not alone, but Finn seems unfazed by her comment. Not even bothering to look her way, he flattens his palm on my leg and brushes my inner thigh with his thumb. "Are you okay?"

Okay? With his thumb stroking there? With his hands so far up my dress that he could— "I'm fine." I'm a liar. *Fine* isn't the right word. I'm burning. I'm aching. Half of me wishes we were alone, and the other half is grateful that we're not.

He gently curls his fingers under the top of the silk and slowly rolls it down from just above my knee all the way off before going to the other leg. He doesn't take as long on this side, but his fingers sweep far higher than necessary when searching for the top of the stocking.

When I shiver, he frowns. "The day will warm once the sun comes out," he says, placing the second stocking neatly on top of the first. "But I promise there's a hot bath waiting when we're finished here."

A bath sounds glorious, but waiting where? In front of all

these people? "Should I brace myself for a special tradition in the tub as well?" I mean the question to come out flippant, but instead it sounds like I'm suggesting something indecent.

Finn only winks in response as he dips a washcloth into one of the prepared bowls of hot, fragrant water. He slips back under my skirt and washes my feet and ankles, trailing the washcloth all the way up the front of my leg to my knee, then around and back down my calf. And I can't decide if he intends his touch to be sensual, or if he is going through the motions of the ritual. Perhaps it's *my* mind and *my* desires that are responsible for the way his hands on my skin warm my blood. Or maybe the words he spoke in the dark last night are to blame. *I want all of you.*

But does he? Or does he really want this power and nothing more? It's becoming harder and harder to convince myself that the latter is true.

With Finn on his knees in front of me, his soapy hands sliding up and over my skin beneath my skirt, it's hard to think straight, but the truth is, any remaining suspicions I had that his motives might not be pure crumbled last night, when he fell asleep holding my hand. If I'm trying to hold on to that belief now, it's only a desperate attempt at self-preservation.

I already have feelings for Finn, and it would be all too easy to fall so hard that there would be no coming back.

Someone hands Finn a dry towel, and he sweeps it over my legs and feet, drying the skin he just washed, his eyes still on mine. I shiver, but not with cold anymore. I'm imagining what's waiting for us in the tent—*our* tent. A bath, he promised.

"Next," Finn says when I'm all dried off, "the flowers." Standing, he begins to pull the flowers from my hair, dropping the buds into the bowl of herbed water he used to wash me. When he pulls the last one free, he passes the bowl to the horned male from earlier, then sweeps me into his arms.

I squeak and throw my arms around his neck. Finn grins, and the crowd cheers.

"Is this really necessary?" I whisper in his ear.

"Relax and enjoy it, Princess. It's tradition." He carries me around the fire and then to a large tent behind it, but when he reaches the door, he doesn't carry me through. Instead he turns to the horned male, who's waiting behind us with the bowl of water, herbs, and flowers.

The male bows his head and murmurs a few words over the water, then offers it to us.

"If you will, Princess?" Finn asks softly.

I release one hand from behind his neck to take the bowl.

The male smiles and reaches for a shovel from beside the tent. The soil is soft and loose as he digs, murmuring something in a language I don't recognize.

Once the hole is several feet deep, he steps back and drops to a knee.

I look to Finn.

His face is solemn. "Now you pour the contents of the bowl into the earth." He shifts me in his arms, making it easier for me to aim as I pour.

As I overturn the bowl, a rush of power tingles through

me, and when Finn draws in a sharp breath, I know he feels it too.

"May the gods bless you, your queen, and your children, Your Majesty," the kneeling male says.

"Thank you, Dunnick," Finn says, and then he steps over the muddy pits of flowers and herbs and into the tent, letting the flaps fall closed behind him.

The tent is larger than I expected. Tall enough even for Finn to stand. In its center, a large cushion the size of our bed at Juliana's manor sits on the floor, piled with soft blankets. There's a chair in the corner, with two piles of clothes atop it—his and hers.

"You can put me down now," I tell Finn.

He studies me for a long, intense moment, and I think he might kiss me, but then he lowers me to my feet.

When he steps back, his breathing is uneven and his gaze goes to the floor. "I need to check in with Misha and Pretha and make sure everything is set for our visit to the sacred spring this afternoon. A servant will be in soon to draw you a warm bath; then you might consider a nap. Today's ride through the mountains won't be an easy one."

"Okay," I say softly. I feel him pulling away and wish he wouldn't. The ache in my heart seems too big to stay contained in my chest. "I don't want Sebastian," I blurt.

Finn's head snaps up, his eyes wide, as if he's surprised I said it. I am too, if I'm honest, but that doesn't make it any less true.

"You've made comments—more than once—implying that I'm eager for some sort of reunion with him."

"I saw you kissing him," he says softly. There's no judgment in his voice.

I swallow. "That was a mistake. He caught me off guard, and the bond made it . . ."

He closes his eyes, as if this explanation makes it worse. "I imagine it was quite intense with the bond. I've heard . . ." He sighs and shakes his head. "It doesn't matter why you kissed him or if you plan to do it again. Contrary to any comments I may have made that day or after, it's not my business."

"Maybe not, but I wanted you to know. Nothing's changed since the day I left the Golden Palace. He deceived me twice, Finn." I shrug. "I'm not sure if our relationship could ever come back from that. Even if I wanted it to."

He cocks his head to the side and stares at me. "Why's that?"

Because he's not you. Because I can't stop thinking about our kiss or the way you comforted me last night. Because though my bond with Sebastian might heighten the things I feel about and with him, none of it compares to the way I feel when I'm close to you.

But I don't tell him any of that. Finn's been honest about what he wants — about his motivations and his priorities. He's attracted to me, yes, and maybe he'd even welcome me into his bed. But he's here for his people, not for me, and it's not fair for me to wish for anything different from him. "I don't trust anyone," I finally say.

Finn nods and turns to leave, but he stops with his hand on the tent flap. He doesn't turn around as he speaks. "You *can* trust me, you know. I realize my word doesn't mean much to you, but it's still true."

I bathe, eat some of the bread and cheese prepared for us, and attempt a nap, but every time I drift off, I hear something outside the tent and jerk awake, thinking Finn might be returning. There's so much we need to talk about. I still haven't confessed that I spied on him and Juliana last night or asked about what the tethered are.

But he doesn't come. Instead, the servant who helped with my bath returns to the tent in the late afternoon and tells me that Finn would like me to dress for our outing and meet him at the stables. This afternoon we travel to a sacred spring and make an offering to Lugh so that the priestess will agree to see us tomorrow.

I let the servant help me into one of several dresses that were waiting in the tent when we arrived. It's the same red as I was wearing this morning, with thicker sleeves and a higher neckline.

I'm dreading a return to the rainy day, but when I step out of the tent, the sun is shining. I wonder if I'll regret the heavy dress and the extra layer of socks beneath my boots.

The servant directs me toward the stables, and the moment I see Finn standing next to Two Star, I remember why the term *tethered* as a relationship between two people sounded familiar.

Misha and Amira told me that Finn's grandfather Kairyn was the tethered match of Queen Reé, the last ruler from Mab's line. I didn't ask what that meant and had assumed it was some sort of pledge between a queen and her second. But if Finn thinks *we* might be tethered, it can't be that.

"Did you have a nice nap?" Finn asks.

"Yes, thank you," I say, smiling through the lie. Admitting

that I spent the whole time wishing he'd join me will only sound pathetic.

"Good." He pulls the saddle cinch tight and pats Two Star's flank. "Kane and Pretha will be joining us. We can be there in an hour if we move quickly."

The other two mount their horses, and I frown. "Where's your horse, Finn?"

He grins at me and strokes Two Star again. "You and I are riding together."

I scoff. "You're kidding."

Finn arches a brow and shifts his gaze to the servant waiting at attention behind me. *Right. Because we're supposedly betrothed.*

"I'm just saying," I say, schooling my features, "I don't mind riding alone."

"It's safer this way," he says. "I'm not taking any chances after what happened in the capital."

"Lucky for us, the sun came out," Pretha says from atop her mount, tilting her face toward the sky. "Feels like summer again."

Kane nudges his horse forward and comes to a stop beside Pretha. "You probably should've dressed in something cooler," he says, looking me over.

I shrug. "I'll be fine. How hot can it get in the mountains?"

Really damned hot. Especially considering my too-thick clothing and the heat of Finn riding behind me. The sun beat down on us as we rode along the mountain paths, and by the time we stopped at the spring to make offerings to Lugh, I was flushed, sweaty, and miserable.

The human in me wanted to mock the foolishness of the simple ritual, but when we walked sunwise around the small stone-encircled pool in the mountainside, dropping handfuls of grain into the water, I felt the magic flow through me as sure as I feel the presence of the night sky.

When we were done, Pretha asked that we go on ahead and give her some time alone.

We ride only a short way before stopping in a clearing. "We'll wait here," Finn says, dismounting. When he helps me off the horse, he holds me close a few moments longer than necessary, the corner of his mouth twitching up in a smile, as if he knows exactly how riding so close to him affected me.

I wiggle from his arms and step back. Looking over my shoulder. We've traveled just far enough that Pretha's out of sight, but not out of earshot. "Why did she want to stay?"

"She scattered Vexius's ashes around that spring," Finn says softly. "This is the first time she's been back to visit."

My heart tugs for my friend and her grief. "Are you sure we shouldn't have stayed?"

"We're sure," Kane says, taking a seat on one of several fallen logs arranged in a circle. "She wants to be alone. Let her."

I follow his lead, but I settle onto the dirt in front of my log so I can lean back against it. The heat has taken too much out of me.

"Are you okay?" Finn asks for the third time since we left the spring.

"I'm fine. I can handle a little heat."

"You could take off the dress," Kane suggests, smirking. "We don't mind."

I roll my eyes. "Don't be a pig."

"Ignore him," Finn says, shooting Kane a look.

Kane shrugs. "She's uncomfortable. I'm just trying to help."

"It's the season," Finn says. "This part of the court could bring you snow in the morning and a warm enough evening to go swimming."

"It's true," Kane says. "The only thing reliable about the weather here is that it's unpredictable."

"It's not so different in Elora," I say, remembering how volatile the weather could be at the end of the summer. I laugh. "Did you know that some humans blame you for any unexpected, unseasonal weather?"

Kane grunts. "Blame the fae? For the weather in an entirely separate realm? How powerful do they think we are?"

"The better question," Finn drawls, "is why would we care enough to bring an early snowstorm or a winter heatwave to the human realm?"

I laugh again — so much of what I thought I knew about the fae was wrong — but then my smile falls away. "They also believe the Unseelie are wicked and cruel," I say, shaking my head. "But even Mordeus couldn't compare with the cruelty of the supposedly benevolent golden queen."

"That was no accident," Kane says. A fly buzzes around his face, and he waves it away. "Back before the portals were closed, the Seelie used the fear of the Unseelie to get humans to trust them."

"Queen Mab used their fear to her advantage, though, like she did everything else," Finn says.

"Was Mab the first Faerie queen?" I ask.

Kane pulls his canteen from his mouth and coughs.

"Not at all," Finn says, shaking his head at Kane. "But she was the first shadow queen. She created the Throne of Shadows and provided a refuge for those the Seelie Court tried to enslave."

"How did she create her own court?" I ask.

"This realm existed for millennia as a whole," Finn says. "Faerie was one kingdom united by one king and one queen, but everything changed when Queen Gloriana came to rule. She did something unprecedented at the time: she took power before ever choosing a husband. Her parents passed the crown and its power to her and allowed her to step into the position before she chose her king, believing she hadn't found her heart's match yet. In truth, she was in love with two males—both were sons of a faerie lord but born of different mothers. One son, Deaglan, was born of the lord's wife, and one, Finnigan, was born of the lord's peasant mistress."

"Finnigan?" I ask. "Another Finn? Are you named for him?"

Kane arches a brow. "She's quick, that one."

"He's an ancestor, then?" I ask, ignoring him.

"Not by blood," Finn says, "but you're getting ahead of me. Legend says that Queen Gloriana loved them both and would've preferred never to choose, but the brothers were jealous and possessive, and together they demanded that she pick one to put on the throne beside her. Tradition would dictate that she choose Deaglan, since he had a royal mother and was of noble birth, whereas Finnigan was a peasant's son, a bastard who would have to fight for the respect of the kingdom. But Gloriana's advisors saw the extent of the males' jealousy and told her that choosing either was dangerous. They told her to allow Deaglan and Finnigan to be her consorts but to choose someone else to sit beside her on the throne. Her advisors presented her with many options, and she determined to follow their advice, causing the brothers to believe that all hope was lost."

I bow my head, hoping to hide my burning cheeks. This was what Juliana was talking about last night when she said the last time two brothers were in love with the same female it tore their realm in two.

Finn continues, "Although she was a peasant, Finnigan's mother was also a priestess. Unbeknownst to any of her peers, she was the most powerful priestess in the history of our kind. Now she's known as Mab."

"I thought Mab was a queen, not a peasant."

"She was a peasant first," Kane says. "And she was a loving but mightily protective mother — of Finnigan and then of the court the gods gave her."

Finn flashes him a look. "You're getting ahead, Kane."

"So Queen Gloriana was urged to choose someone other than the brothers," I prompt.

Finn takes a stick from the ground and begins absently breaking off pieces. "The queen may have chosen one of the royal-born males brought before her, but she found herself pregnant with Finnigan's child. Children are so rare among our kind that Gloriana took it as a sign from the gods that she was to marry Finnigan. He was delighted, and they began to plan for their wedding and bonding day, but on the morning of the event, she was poisoned, causing her to fall onto her sickbed, where she lost the baby."

"Oh no," I whisper. "That's terrible."

"Deaglan whispered into the ears of all the queen's court, and even the ill queen herself, blaming her betrothed for the poisoning," Finn says. "Deaglan claimed that Finnigan had been after the throne and the queen's power for himself."

"Why would he poison her before the wedding?" I ask. "If he was really out for the power, that doesn't make any sense."

"That's partly why the lie was so clever," Kane says. "Deaglan claimed that Finnigan had intended to poison her on her wedding night, but the queen had found the chocolates before the ceremony, ruining Finnigan's plans."

"For whatever reason," Finn says, "the people believed the lies and demanded that Finnigan be hanged for treason."

Kane shakes his head in disgust. "He declared his innocence until the moment his neck snapped, but no one listened."

"Mab was distraught," Finn says. "She'd lost her son and her grandchild within a week's time, and she knew Deaglan was responsible. She sent a warning to the palace, alerting them that she'd cast a powerful curse that would break the kingdom if the one responsible for her son's death came to rule beside Queen Gloriana. The curse, as she cast it, said that the kingdom would suffer endless days, so the wicked rulers could never hide their misdeeds under the blanket of night."

"But Deaglan didn't realize how powerful Mab was," Kane says. "He dismissed her as a peasant and proceeded to worm his way into the queen's court."

"In the months that followed Finnigan's execution," Finn says, "Queen Gloriana fell deep into her grief and abandoned all her duties as ruler of the kingdom. Deaglan carried the load, helping her keep her head above water so the people didn't rebel against a neglectful queen and take her throne. After a time, she agreed to marry him, if only out of gratitude for what he'd done for her kingdom while she was too tangled in her grief to serve her people.

"But Mab's curse was still in place, and the moment Gloriana bonded to Deaglan and had him sit on the throne beside her, the kingdom was cursed to endless days. Deaglan's sentinels tracked Mab down and dragged her into the Goblin Mountains. They couldn't risk killing her outright, so they left her bleeding in the mountains. Her blood drained out of her, along with her tears, forming what we now know as the River of Ice. And when the last drop of her blood spilled, her curse was broken, bringing night to the kingdom for the first time in weeks."

"If she died, how did she become queen?" I ask.

"Mab never intended to rule," Finn says, drawing two lines in the dirt. "She never intended to do anything but seek justice for her wrongfully accused son, but the gods rewarded her for her deep love in a world that had too little of that. They resurrected our Great Queen and presented her with a choice. She could choose magic, keep her immortal life, and have more magical power than anyone in the history of the realm. If she chose the power, it would pass down to every generation after her. Or she could relinquish her immortality and her magic altogether. In exchange, the gods would create the Court of the Moon and allow her to rule with the remaining years of a mortal life span."

"But Mab was too clever for choices," Kane says. "She wanted both, and both is what she got."

"How?" I ask.

"She convinced the gods that two courts were vital to the realm," Kane says, "and she made them see how Deaglan's duplicity could spread like a sickness if he were allowed to rule over all the land. The gods saw the truth of her argument and divided the land into opposing courts. They fractured the kingdom in two, right down the center of the Goblin Mountains and along the River of Ice."

Finn nods. "Thus, they presented her with the Court of the Moon, which would draw power from the night, the stars, and the moon. For balance, they gave her enemy the power of the day and the sun and called it the Court of the Sun."

"But Mab had tricked the gods," Kane says. "She hadn't *chosen* the court with its curse of mortality, merely explained the merits of two courts. Once the kingdom was already divided and she wore the Crown of Starlight, she made her choice. She wanted to be more magically powerful than any fae in history and have her offspring gifted with the same power.

"She was a priestess who'd tricked the gods, who'd died and come back to life," Kane adds, "so naturally the Court of the Sun painted her as the doer of dark magic, as someone wicked, someone to be feared and avoided at all costs."

"It worked, too," Finn says. "Droves of fae left what's now known as the Unseelie land. They declared their loyalties to the Court of the Sun. Perhaps Mab wouldn't have had a kingdom to rule at all, but Deaglan was a cruel king, casting out anyone who didn't have something to offer him, demanding tithes from the poor and building that shining quartz palace through the labor of slaves. All those Deaglan cast out of his court, Mab gave refuge; those he persecuted, she rescued."

"That's why she was so beloved," I say. "She literally saved them."

"Exactly," Finn says. "And won over the hearts and loyalties of many others while doing so. Some refused to claim loyalties and escaped to the far west — the territory now known as the Wild Fae Lands. Those who remained in Deaglan's lands were the Seelie, a title they gave themselves to claim their pride at being part of the original court. They believed themselves better than those who were cast out, and because those in the east would never be ruled by those who shared the original royal blood, the golden fae called them *Unseelie,* seeing it as an insult and weaving tales of the wicked queen and vile deeds in the kingdom to the east."

"But those in the east embraced the title," Kane says. "Mab ruled the misfits, the dreamers, the rebellious, and those dedicated to truth and integrity. They didn't want anything to do with King Deaglan and his lies, his manipulations. They were *Un*seelie. They were better than Seelie because their royal line would never be tainted by Deaglan's traitor blood."

Finn nods, and I can tell they know this story as well as they know each other's faces. This is part of their history. Their heritage. "The Seelie said that the proof of our evil hearts lay in that we draw our power from the darkness," Finn says, "but they don't understand that those of us who love the night revel in it because of how clearly it allows us to find even the smallest points of light.

Whereas they deny that darkness exists, even while the sun they worship throws shadows in every corner."

"That's why it's so hard for the Unseelie to see Sebastian in the palace," I say softly. "That's why Misha says they may never accept him. Because he's a descendant of Gloriana and Deaglan."

Finn stares off into the trees and nods. "The rivalry between the courts began with their creation. And though it changed over time, it never lessened. The Seelie were prejudiced against those to the east and against Queen Mab, believing she'd won the land through dark magic. They would weave tales of the wickedness of those in the east, giving the Unseelie queen and those who served her the reputation of being cruel and evil, even though there were many cruel and evil among the fae who remained in Queen Gloriana's court."

"And then they killed off Mab's line," I say, remembering the story Misha and Amira told me. "They killed off every descendant of her bloodline to rob her of that great power the gods had bestowed on her and to destroy the shadow court."

Finn swallows hard. "They did, but it didn't bring the court down the way they planned. We're stronger than they realize. Thanks to the Great Queen."

"Or we were," Kane mutters, "until King Oberon decided he'd seduce the Seelie princess to destroy their court from the inside."

My head snaps up. "What? I thought he loved her."

Kane barks out a laugh. "You think the king of the Court of the Moon just *happened* to fall in love with his greatest enemy's daughter and impregnate her?"

"I . . ." I don't know what I thought. "That's the story."

Finn hangs his head. “The Great Fae War had raged on for years,” he says. “Arya was part of my father’s plan to destroy the Seelie kingdom from the inside, but he didn’t count on her parents locking him in the human realm. And he didn’t count on his own brother trying to steal the throne.”

He never loved her. “Gods,” I mutter. “At least now I understand why she’s so angry.” And I hate it. I hate the similarities between me and Arya. We were both betrayed by males we thought loved us, both romantically manipulated for political gain. Both bitter and angry.

Finn’s watching me carefully, and I’m as grateful as ever that he can’t read my pathetic thoughts.

“Were the gods not angry for being tricked?” I ask, if only to get my mind off the differences between myself and the vile golden queen. “Did they hold it against Mab? Against her court?”

“Oh, yes,” Finn says, “and like in all things, the gods value balance. That’s why they created the fire gems and the bloodstones to represent her choices, if in lesser measure. The fire gems would amplify the magic of any fae, Seelie or Unseelie, and though their users would never be as powerful as Mab, they could do great and terrible things with the aid of those gems.”

“Are these the same fire gems that are used today? Like the one I wear?” I ask, pressing my hand to the gem between my breasts.

Finn nods.

“What about the bloodstones?”

Finn’s face goes solemn. “The bloodstones were the real punishment for Mab’s trickery. They allowed their user to steal the magic and immortality from one with Unseelie blood and funnel its power into something else. Those stones made Mab and her entire court vulnerable, as they allowed the Seelie to steal our power without any of the consequence that Arya's court suffered when she cursed our people."

I swallow hard. "Do people use them?"

Kane rolls his eyes. "Are you asking if we have a magic stone that could turn you mortal again? No, Abriella, we do not. Mab destroyed them so they could never be used against her or her court."

I wait for the disappointment to hit. My only chance to be a mortal again was lost thousands of years before I was even born. And maybe . . . maybe I was never meant to live out my days as a human. Maybe I was meant to be something different, meant to find another way to help those who've been exploited the way Jas and I were as children.

I feel Finn staring at me and lift my head to meet his eyes. There are countless questions in those silver eyes, and I wonder if he thinks I'm wishing for a bloodstone for myself.

The sound of hoofbeats pulls our attention to the rocky path. Pretha draws back on her horse's reins as she nears the clearing, then dismounts in once smooth motion. "You found shade," she says, fanning herself. "I'll take some of that."

Kane guzzles from his canteen before wiping his mouth with the back of his hand. "I suppose we should head back then."

"Do you mind if we take a little break first?" Pretha asks. She ties her horse to a tree near the others and collapses on a log. She yanks at the top of her dress. "I'm overheated, and I need to cool off or I'll be an unbearable grump tonight."

"How's that different from usual?" Kane asks.

Pretha glares at him, then turns to me. "Would you mind waiting a bit, Brie? I promise I won't make us late for the festivities."

I shrug. "It's fine. If we can't see the priestess until tomorrow, there's no reason to rush." I don't mind at all, actually. I'm not eager to get back on that horse with Finn, and the hot afternoon is only part of the reason.

"We don't have to be back for a few hours," Finn says. "If we're all in agreement, there's no rush."

"Thank the gods," Pretha says, hiking up her skirt and unzipping her boots. "I swear, I'm melting. I take back everything I said about it being too cold this morning."

Kane waves toward the trees. "Go cool off in the lake. I can hear the waterfall from here."

Pretha shakes her head. "I can't even be bothered to strip. Heat makes me lazy."

A *waterfall?* Hopping to my feet, I turn toward the woods, practically salivating at the thought of cool water flowing over my skin. We certainly have enough time.

"Where do you think you're going?" Kane asks, standing.

Turning to him, I set my jaw, annoyed that I have to explain myself. "You said there was a lake," I say, waving in that direction. "Thanks to this heat, I probably smell like I haven't bathed in days. I thought I'd use the time to freshen up."

Kane grunts. "If you think we're going to leave you alone after — "

"I'll go with her," Finn says.

CHAPTER TWENTY

I SPIN ON HIM. "EXCUSE ME?" All I want is to sink my body in that water, to feel the waterfall on my hair and scrub the sweat off my skin.

"We don't know where the queen has people—who's following us, who's watching. It would be foolish to swim alone."

"I'm not swimming, I'm *bathing*."

He folds his arms. "Your point?"

"Why not Pretha?" I ask.

Pretha's eyes go wide, and she looks back and forth between me and her brother-in-law. "I mean, I guess I could—"

Finn turns on his smolder. "What's wrong, Princess? Do I make you nervous?"

"Fine," I grouse, turning on my heel toward the water. I hear his soft chuckle behind me, his footsteps crunching on the fallen leaves.

The lake looks beautiful in the afternoon sun. The light sparkles off the water, and the rush of the waterfall fills my ears.

"I think you had the right idea," Finn says. "When we're done,

I'll send Kane and Pretha for a turn. Beats smelling them for the rest of the journey."

"We?" I ask, propping my hands on my hips. "When *we're* done?"

"We," Finn says. "You're not getting in that water alone."

"Because some creature lurks in its depths?" I step forward and peer into the crystal-clear pool. "I don't think so."

"Who says I don't need a bath too?" Finn's gaze rakes over me and leaves happy little shivers in its path. I know I don't look like much now, but judging by the heat in his eyes, I might as well be a siren calling from the deadly rocks along the sea. I've always been a conflicted mess when it comes to Finn, and apparently today is no exception.

My stomach knots. I planned to bathe under the waterfall, to let it shower me. Showers are a rare luxury in Elora, and I've been in one only a few times in my life—the last time being at the house where Finn was staying after I'd been drugged. My skin heats as I recall the way he held me under the spray, trying to get my body to cool from its reaction, as I recall the way I begged him.

Amusement curls his lips, and he glances at the waterfall before looking back to me. He might not be able to read minds like Misha, but right now he doesn't need to. "Afraid you might beg me to touch you again?" he asks.

I scoff. "Do you get tired carrying that ego around with you everywhere you go?"

"You better hurry," he says, glancing over his shoulder. "They'll come looking for us if we take too long. I'd hate to lose the little privacy we can get."

I swallow hard, not wanting to let my thoughts linger on why we might want *privacy.* "Turn around," I say.

He doesn't. Just folds his arms and keeps his gaze locked on mine.

I scowl. "So I can undress?"

He still doesn't move, except for his lips, which slowly curve into a mischievous grin. I tug off one boot and hurl it at him.

He snatches it from the air, chuckling, but finally gives me his back.

I'm all too aware of his presence as I unzip my dress, careful to drape it over a rock so it won't get dirty; then I peel out of my thick socks and stockings. I'm greedy for the feeling of cool water on my skin, but I leave my undergarments on. At least they'll provide me with a bit of modesty, and I can slip them off before putting my dress back on.

Only when I'm in as deep as my neck do I realize my mistake. "Stay there," I shout before Finn can turn around.

"Is there a problem?" Finn asks, amusement curling his words.

I glance down at the clear, clear water and the very thin, now translucent material of my undergarments. I might as well be naked. "Why don't you wait on the shore," I say. "We'll take turns."

Slowly, he turns to face me. "Then who would wash my back?"

"You should ask Juliana. She seems like she'd like to wash any part you asked."

His lips part, and he blinks at me. "Jealous, Princess?" He

stalks toward the shoreline, shedding his tunic and unbuckling the bandolier of knives from his waist.

"No. You can do what you please, with whomever you please."

"What I please? So, joining you in this lake—"

"Still wouldn't be . . . *proper.*"

That grin grows wider, and he comes closer, discarding another item of clothing with each step. "And since when did you care about propriety?"

I bite my lip. The reasonable thing is to insist that he stay put. He *would* respect my wishes if I pushed the issue . . . But after all those hours riding in front of him on his horse, feeling the heat of his body and the strength of his legs cradling me? The reasonable thing doesn't even resemble the thing I want.

So I don't object. But I am feeling a little shy, so when he moves to peel off his pants, I dive under, distancing myself from the shore. When I surface, he's in the lake, three feet from me, his curls wet, rivulets of water rolling down his face. That grin falls away as he studies my expression, and his eyes turn hot as they trail down to the water—to everything I know is all too exposed beneath the surface.

I splash him, and he jerks back, as if yanked from a stupor. "Eyes to yourself," I say.

"But the view is so lovely out here," he says. "I should thank you for not using that impressive magic of yours to hide it from me."

My magic. *Of course.* With a single thought, I cast shadows around myself, weaving a gown of darkness from above my breasts to below my knees.

He brings his gaze up to meet mine. "That wasn't a suggestion."

I shrug, then turn away from him, swimming toward the waterfall and the steady thrum of the water pounding the rocks. A moment later something grabs my foot. I draw a big breath of air before I'm pulled under. I spin beneath the surface to see what — *who* — has ahold of me, and Finn's silver eyes glow back at me, somehow sparkling even down here.

He smiles as he swims toward me, catching me around the waist before he pushes us both back to the surface. I pull in a breath, but don't have a chance to say anything before his mouth crushes down on mine. One hand grips my waist, holding me close, and the other slides into my hair as he tilts my head and slants his mouth over mine.

The water is cool, but my skin is warmer than it was on the sunny ride here — hot and needy all at once just from the brush of his tongue against mine and the feel of his hand wrapping around my hip.

When he tears away, he's panting, dragging in big gulps of air, as if we were underwater for much longer than we were. His gaze drifts to the shore and stays there for a beat.

"What is it?" I crane my neck around. Just beyond the shore, in the tree line, red eyes glow in our direction. My fae sight allows me to just make out the sight of Kane's imposing figure leaning against a massive oak. "Voyeur," I mutter.

Finn chuckles. "More like a worrywart," he says. Beneath the water, his fingers intertwine with mine and he tugs my hand. "Come with me." He releases me, and we swim side by side toward the waterfall.

Kane's appearance is a reminder that I should bathe and head back to my clothing, but I haven't been able to stop thinking about Finn's hands on me since the incident with my shadow self last night—maybe since long before that—so I follow.

Finn dives beneath the waterfall, swimming under it. The water pounds so hard, I can't hear anything else, but I dive after him. When I surface, he's already pulled himself up on the rock ledge. He extends a hand for me and helps me out of the water. I should feel awkward, exposed as I am, but I don't. I want this moment badly enough that I don't have the energy for any self-consciousness.

The sound of the falls is almost deafening, but the water makes a screen, hiding us here, giving us privacy.

Finn cups my face in his hands, studying me. "Are you okay?"

"I'm . . . I'm fine." I'm not fine. My heart hammers manically in my chest and anticipation skitters along my skin.

Finn swallows and tips his head down, touching his forehead to mine. "I've wanted to kiss you again every day—every minute—since I got to at Castle Craige. I can't stop thinking about it." He skims his thumb over my bottom lip. "Tell me you want this—that you wanted it before this moment."

"I want this." I slide a hand behind his neck and pull him with me as I lower myself to lie on the rock. He presses his mouth to mine, gently at first, sucking and tasting, before his tongue sweeps inside.

I moan beneath him as need and desire ignite in my blood. He deepens the kiss, groaning with a hunger that matches my own. My hands roam over his shoulders and down his powerful back. I taste the desperation in his groan, feel it in the hand he has wrapped around my hip. He slides it to my waist. To my breast. His thumb lightly brushes the underside through the thin, wet fabric, and I gasp at the pleasure of such a simple touch. Arching my back, I press into him, willing his hands to explore and—

Agony. I jerk out of Finn's arms and push him away. I'm swamped with pain. Heartache. I let out a cry, but it has nothing to do with physical sensations and everything to do with the ache in my chest.

"Abriella?" Confusion warps Finn's features as he studies me. "What is it? Are you hurt?"

I press a palm to my chest, and my eyes fill with tears. "I—" I sob.

"Talk to me."

Dragging in a ragged breath, I focus on what Misha taught me. To ground myself. To shield. "It's . . ."

Understanding flashes in his eyes as he pulls away from me and settles into a crouch on the other side of the rock. "Sebastian." He mutters a curse. "Of course. He feels you—knows you're here with me—and you're experiencing his reaction to that."

"How . . ." I shake my head. "I thought I'd blocked him."

"It's hard to feel anything intensely and block it from that bond." He scoots close enough to reach me and brushes his fingers over my cheek, down my neck. "I'm sorry."

I shake my head. I'm the one who's sorry. I'm the one who bonded with Sebastian for the wrong reasons.

"I'll let you finish bathing and meet you back on shore." He lowers himself into the water, then slips beneath the surface and swims away.

I open my mouth to call him back, but what can I do? What can I say?

I'm bonded to Sebastian. I made that choice despite Finn's warnings, and now it can't be undone.

The ride back to camp is tense and painfully quiet. I ride in front of Finn again, but instead of the proximity feeling sensual and decadent, it's an uncomfortable reminder of what happened under the waterfall. Finn keeps his hands wrapped around Two Star's reins and nowhere else. Somehow that only makes it worse, and I'm grateful when camp comes into view.

Soon I'm alone in my tent, changing into yet another dress. This one is the palest silver, the color of the moon. It's strapless, with a heart-shaped bodice that barely conceals the rune marked on my breast, and the soft fabric flows in layers from the high waist.

I linger as long as I can, hoping we'll have a chance to talk in private, but Finn doesn't come.

The clear skies remain through the evening, and when the sun sets, every star looks like a precious jewel glittering in the moonlight. The Lunastal celebration weaves between tents and around the bonfire, even down the side of the mountain.

Musicians play all around us, dancing and singing as their fingers fly over the strings and keys of their instruments. There's food and laughter and so much dancing. These people are so excited to welcome their prince that my heart aches for the role I played—even unintentionally—in keeping the crown from him.

"Are you having fun?" a deep voice asks beside me.

I turn to see Misha's smile, his big brown eyes scanning my face as if he's trying to read my mind through my shield. "Sure."

He huffs. "You seem awfully sad tonight, Princess. This is supposed to be a party."

"I guess I'm just lost in my thoughts." My throat goes tight. "I heard about what happened to these people during Mordeus's rule, how they had to abandon their homes and their lives here to hide from him."

Nodding, Misha scans the crowd. "I imagine that's why they already love you."

"They don't love me."

He chuckles softly. "Everyone does, Abriella. Everyone here at least." His gaze scans the faces of the happy, dancing people around us before landing on Finn. The shadow prince is leaning against the side of a tent and has a hand tangled in his own dark curls as he smiles down at Juliana, who's gesticulating wildly, telling some exciting story, no doubt.

"They love *him,*" I tell Misha. "They accept me because they think we're a package deal."

"You realize what he did this morning, don't you?" he asks.

I frown at him. "What do you mean?"

"When the shadow king—and do not be fooled, that's what Finn is to these people—when he kneels before his partner and washes her feet, it's a very powerful symbol. He's declaring that you are worth serving, and if *he* will kneel before you, then they must too."

I shake my head. "It was just a ritual. It didn't mean anything."

"It *is* a ritual. One that means everything to these people. If you hadn't been here, he wouldn't have been kneeling before another female. He *chose* to show his deference to you as a sign to these people that you are valuable and are to be honored from here forward."

My stomach flips. "Why would he do that?"

Misha huffs. "I can think of a few reasons, though maybe you should talk to Finn about that. But they would've honored you anyway. You killed Mordeus. You're responsible for breaking the curse."

As if I need to be reminded. "And for destroying their throne."

He nudges my side. "Quit thinking about such matters. This is a celebration." He grabs a glass of sparkling pink wine from a passing servant and hands it to me. "Drink."

I frown. The last time I drank faerie wine at a party, I ended up drugged and in a shower with Finn.

"Oh really?" Misha says, eyes bright and lips curving.

I glare at him and fortify my mental shield. "Would you stay out of my mind?"

"I *like* your mind," he says. "It's so sweet and charming, and sometimes . . . deliciously devious." He takes the wine from my hand, sniffing and sipping it before handing it back to me. "It's safe to drink, but I promise to take care of you myself if you end up drugged tonight."

I narrow my eyes. "You'd like that, wouldn't you?"

The corner of his mouth hitches up in a grin. "Let's just say I'd be more *accommodating* than your shadow prince."

I throw a ball of shadow at his chest, and he stumbles back, still chucking. My cheeks burn. "You are so bad," I growl.

Misha comes close again, undeterred. "I've been told," he says, "that I'm actually quite good."

Rolling my eyes, I take a big drink from my wine. Bubbly and subtly sweet, it tastes like crisp summer apples with a hint of sour plum.

"Finish it quickly so we can dance," he says, watching me tilt the glass to my lips.

I swallow and relish the warmth in my chest. "You want me to dance with you after *that?*"

"Trust me. I know my place," he says. "In truth, I value your friendship too much to ruin it with a night in your bed. However enjoyable that might be. Anyway, I've had my fill of chasing emotionally unavailable females."

My jaw goes slack. *Chasing?* Did he pursue Amira once? "Do you mean—"

"Don't." Misha's face hardens, revealing nothing. "I don't want to talk about it tonight. I just want to dance with the prettiest girl at the party." I melt a little at his flattery, and he sighs. "But since *she's* not available, I'd settle for a dance with you."

I cackle. "What a pest!" I take another sip, if only because Finn is still grinning at Juliana like she's the most amusing creature he's ever encountered. My undeniable jealousy makes me question every decision I've made since arriving in this realm, and as that's not a very productive way to spend my evening, I might as well get drunk on Faerie wine and enjoy the dance.

"Thatta girl," Misha says when I drain the glass. He takes it from my fingers and plops it onto a nearby table before pulling me out onto the dance floor.

The song is fast, the kind of beat that makes me feel lighter—or maybe it's the wine. Misha positions me at his side and patiently teaches me the choreography. It's quite simple, but looks gorgeous when everyone does it together. A side step, a shuffle, a cross behind, with some waving arms and an occasional bow, then a quarter turn before doing it all over again in the opposite direction.

Sprites with glowing wings swoop through the air in their own dance, leaving streaks of light above our heads, and soon enough I'm grinning and keeping up with the new steps.

I'm so out of breath by the time the dance ends that I don't complain when Misha wraps his arms around me and pulls me against him to sway to the slower beat of the next song. The moment I think our position might be too intimate, he leads me into a dip so deep my short hair nearly touches the floor. I laugh as he pulls me up again, and his eyes sparkle with amusement.

"Don't look now," he whispers into my ear. "But I think there's someone here who doesn't appreciate seeing me dance so close with you."

I turn my head, but Misha stops me with a big hand on the back of my neck.

"I said don't look."

"But I don't know who you mean," I say, frowning at him.

He throws his head back and laughs again. "If I really have to answer that question for you, you two may be more hopeless than I realized."

Finn.

In the next moment, Finn steps up beside Misha and gently nudges his shoulder. "I'll take the next dance. She's supposed to be *my* betrothed, after all."

"Oh, is *that* why?" Misha asks. "To keep up the *ruse?* I thought it was something else."

I expect Finn to argue, but he surprises me by winking at his friend. "Can't a male have more than one reason to dance with a beautiful female?" Without waiting for a response, he steps between us, taking my hand in one of his and sliding the other to the small of my back.

"Enjoy," Misha says, bowing slightly before walking away.

Finn watches him go, then turns his attention back to me. "You've been avoiding me tonight."

"I figured you were too busy dancing with Juliana to notice." I immediately regret that glass of wine. There's no way Finn would ever miss the jealousy in a statement like that.

He grins, as if my outburst pleases him. "I haven't danced with her even once." His grin grows. "But you know that because—despite avoiding me all night—you've barely taken your eyes off me."

I open my mouth to argue, then decide it's not worth it.

"That is," Finn says, "until Misha got you in his arms." His grin falls away as he searches his friend out in the crowd. "It seems he's grown quite fond of you."

"He's become a good friend."

"I envy that," Finn says.

"You have it." Laughing, I pull back enough to look Finn in the eye. "You've known him much longer than I have."

"Not your friendship with him," he says, watching me. "I envy his friendship with you."

I swallow. "You and I *are* friends, Finn."

"Hmm." He pulls me closer and tucks my head under his chin.

I can't resist breathing him in. He smells like leather, pine trees, and the endless night sky.

"Perhaps we are friends again," he says. The small circles he's tracing on my back send delicious shivers down my spine. "But I think I had your trust once, back when I didn't deserve it. I grieve that loss."

"I don't trust anyone," I say softly, but even as I say the words, I realize they're not true. Not anymore. And that terrifies me. "How are you feeling?" I ask. He's so hard to read most of the time.

"Fine, I think—good, actually. I haven't had a spell in days."

I release a breath. "That has to be a good sign, right? That it's getting better?"

"I hope so."

This would be the perfect time to ask him about the tethered and why he thinks that might explain the connection between us, but I'm reluctant to ruin the moment with a confession of my spying ways, so I keep my mouth shut. We dance in silence for a while, and I let myself enjoy the moment—his warmth, his touch, his closeness.

"You look really beautiful tonight," Finn says.

I wish I could see his face. I want to see his eyes when he says things like that. I want to know if it's a polite observation or something more. I want it to *be* something more, and the shame of that makes me put a little distance between our bodies.

He sighs. "You're allowed to take a compliment, Princess, even when you're bonded to another male."

"I know that," I say. But Finn's words feel different than a compliment from someone like Misha. Maybe that's the problem. *I'm* the problem. "And . . . thank you. That was a very nice thing to say."

I don't hear his chuckle so much as note the shake of his chest against mine and feel the puff of air in my hair.

"Don't laugh at me," I say.

"You are really *the worst* at taking compliments."

"I said thank you!"

"Hmm. I suppose. Not the same as believing what I said, but it'll do." Stepping back, he squeezes my fingertips and motions toward a quieter spot just beyond the dancing crowd. "Come on. I want to show you something."

CHAPTER TWENTY-ONE

KEEPING HOLD OF MY HAND, Finn leads me away from the celebration and the music, toward the summit beyond our tents. I wonder if we're going to talk about what happened at the waterfall. Or if he might try to kiss me again. I wish he would. And I wish I could kiss him back without hurting Sebastian.

"Where are you taking me?" I ask.

"Somewhere I think you'll like."

We walk in silence for a while. I don't pull my hand from his, and he doesn't let me go. It's not until we approach a steep, grassy incline that I hesitate. "Finn?" I glance down at my gown and consider my slipper-clad feet beneath. "I'm not exactly dressed for hiking this evening."

"It's not far," he says. "And if you get too tired, I'll carry you."

That just makes my cheeks burn hotter, but I nod and let him lead me up the hill. I don't complain once about being tired or about how useless these slippers are. I don't dare. I'm trying to resist temptation here and I don't think I'd succeed if Finn scooped me into his arms.

"I'm sorry the priestess made us delay our visit," I say, if only to distract myself. "I'm sure you're anxious to get to Mab."

"I am," he says softly. "But more than that, I'm worried that the priestess might refuse to see me altogether."

"Why? I thought that was why you brought me. As long as the power of the throne is with you, she'll agree to an audience."

"She can't refuse the power of the crown—not without risking the wrath of Mab and having the very magic of her position turn on her. But she could make it difficult or refuse to let me stand by your side. To spite me."

"Why?"

"Remember when I told you that I blame this whole mess on myself for not stepping up when my father was in the mortal realm?"

How could I forget? Finn's guilt is so heavy. That night in the stables at Juliana's estate, I finally understood a piece of why that is. "I remember," I say softly.

"Well, it's a little more complicated than that. I'd been rebelling against my father for years—ever since I fell in love with Isabel and decided to make her my bride. My father didn't care that I was involved with a changeling—many of the nobility have affairs with humans. But when he found out that I planned to marry her, all hell broke loose. I was to be king and needed a proper queen by my side."

He focuses on the path ahead, but I know that if I could see his eyes, there'd be pain there. "I wanted to spend my life with Isabel. To rule beside her." Finn sighs. "My father forbade it, but I was young and in love, and I didn't care. My stubbornness cost me in so many ways—with him, with my court, and with the High Priestess."

"Why did the High Priestess care?" I ask.

"Because I was supposed to marry her daughter."

I frown. Isn't the priestess's daughter— "Juliana?"

"The one and only. She's the one my father picked for me to marry. We practically grew up together, and our parents were thrilled when we became good friends. I knew I was lucky. In a world like ours and in positions like ours, friendship in marriage is more than most get. Sometimes it's built over time, but too often . . ."

I watch him, waiting, and his jaw ticks. "Too often what?"

He sighs. "Too often, the hate ruling couples feel for their spouses rivals what they feel for their kingdom's enemies. I saw it in my grandparents, and Pretha will tell you the same about hers. But after I met Isabel, I knew I couldn't marry Juliana. I couldn't do that to either of them."

"You loved Isabel from the first moment you saw her?" I ask.

He takes my hand and helps me up over a rocky ledge, and when I'm on level ground with him again, he's smiling. "I think *lusted* might be a better word. She was the most beautiful thing I'd ever seen."

Finn doesn't release my hand as we start walking again. Instead, he laces his fingers with mine. "You'd never seen a human before?" I ask.

He laughs. "Oh, I'd seen plenty of humans, and I'd met plenty of changelings, but I'd never met any like her. Attraction is strange like that. It's like we don't even get a say in it. Just—*boom.* It didn't hurt that she looked at me like I was a god. Her own personal salvation."

"Hero worship does it for you, huh?" I ask, arching my brow.

"Apparently not anymore," he says, winking at me.

I nudge him with my elbow. "I'm sorry I don't stroke your ego to your liking."

He rakes his gaze over me. "It seems I find you irresistible nonetheless."

My cheeks burn, and I bow my head. "So you loved Isabel enough to rebel against your father?" I prod because apparently I *am* really bad at taking compliments.

He blows out a breath. "I was young and stubborn and probably a little spoiled too. My entire life I'd gotten everything I wanted, and when I wanted Isabel, I didn't see why that should be any different."

When a small cottage appears over the next rise, I'm breathing hard and my slippers are soaked from the dewy grass.

"We made it," Finn says, flashing me a smile as he pulls open the front door.

"What is this place?"

"This is what I wanted to show you," he says. "Or part of it at least."

The cottage is dark and a little musty, as if it's sat empty for a long time, but when Finn casts a ball of light in the corner, I see that it's lovely. Warm and cozy, with a fireplace and the kind of furniture that invites you to curl up and spend the day reading.

"That was not a short walk," I argue as I follow Finn up the stairs. "For future reference."

He opens the door at the top of the stairs and takes me by the hand to pull me out onto a rooftop terrace. "But it was worth it, wasn't it?" He drops my hand and turns his palms up. "Just look."

I turn a slow circle, taking in the view. It's lovely up here. In one direction, I can see Staraelia, the lights of the lanterns burning on the cobblestone streets. And then, closer, the lights of the party. Opposite the party, the deep forest rolls into the hills and valleys beyond. "It's stunning."

Finn places two fingers beneath my chin and meets my eyes. "Look up, Princess."

I don't want to. I want to keep looking into those hypnotizing silver eyes. I want to step closer and revel in this connection between us that never seems to dissipate but always seems amplified in the moonlight.

When I don't immediately obey, he smiles, as if he knows exactly what I'm thinking, but then he tilts my chin, directing my gaze skyward, and I gasp.

Never have I seen so many stars shine so brightly in such a clear, lush sky. All I can do is stare for a long time as memories from my childhood niggle at the back of my mind. My mother's voice. She's in the next room, speaking to a woman who scares her. She scares me too. Her mouth is too big for her face, her eyes too pale. Then my mother's holding my hand and pointing to the most beautiful starry night I've ever seen.

Abriella, make a wish.

Then the wind in my hair as we race on horseback on the beach away from . . . *something.*

"Are you okay?" Finn asks.

Like grains of sand between my fingers, the memory slips away before I can make sense of it. "I'm fine."

"You left me for a minute there," he says.

I shake my head. "I was just . . . remembering a day from my childhood. Thank you for bringing me here." I don't dare take my eyes off the sky, too afraid I might miss something.

"It's yours," he says softly.

I smile at a shooting star. "The sky belongs to everyone. And we all belong to it."

"Abriella." His voice is firm enough that I pull my gaze back to meet his. "This cottage is yours. The cottage and the land it sits upon — the whole damn mountain belongs to you."

I shake my head. "I don't understand."

He blows out a breath. "Mother left this piece of property to me. I think she knew I needed a place of my own away from the Midnight Palace. Now I'm giving it to you."

"You can't do that, Finn."

"I already did," he says softly. "It's done. I finalized the paperwork before we left the capital."

"But . . . why?"

He swallows. "Because I know you think you don't fit in this world. I know you think that by giving up your human life, you also gave up your only chance of going home." He takes my hand and squeezes my fingers. "I can't change what happened, and I can't make the mortal realm a safe place for you, but I can give you a place to call home. The most beautiful place in my whole court. It's yours."

"In exchange for what? What do you want from me?"

"Many things, but nothing in exchange for this." He scans my face again and again. "It's a gift — yours, whether you end up in the palace or not and whether you stay with Sebastian or not." He huffs out a dry laugh and gives me a wry grin. "All we have to do is keep the queen from destroying it."

"Why not keep it for yourself?" I ask. "What if Sebastian ends up on the throne? You need a home as much as I do."

Finn lowers himself to the floor, leaning back on his elbows as he watches the stars. There's a subtle, pulsing energy that rolls off him in the starlight, as if he draws his power from the night itself. It's stronger since the curse broke, stronger still here in the Court of the Moon. It's not anything I can explain with the vocabulary I have, but it's there — and I can sense it as surely as I can see the moon shining above.

I follow his lead, taking a place beside him on the cool, tiled rooftop.

"Do you remember the night you helped me rescue Jalek?" he asks. "We sat outside together afterward and you told me your mother taught you to wish on stars."

Abriella, every star in that sky shines for you.

I swallow hard. The physical attraction to Finn was there from the first moment, but that night was the first time I realized there was something more than that between us. "I remember."

"That night I realized how much I wanted to bring you here." He blows out a breath. "I was trying to figure out a way I could do it safely, without being detected by Mordeus. Jalek and Kane both thought I was crazy. I told them it was a way to earn your trust so that when I finally suggested the bond, you'd say yes . . . but I knew. Even then, I knew I couldn't do what I needed to."

"You mean you couldn't kill me."

Turning his head, he meets my eyes and nods.

"I hate that I'm the reason for this mess," I say softly. "This is all my fault."

"It's not. Not at all."

"Seems like it's a lot more mine than it is yours."

Turning, he narrows his eyes at me. "How many times did you tell me no?"

"What?"

"How many times did you refuse to bond with me?"

"You didn't—"

"I didn't ask. I never asked. I never even tried to make a compelling argument. I was so damn busy trying to think of a solution that didn't—" His mouth snaps shut, and he turns his face back toward the sky.

A solution that didn't involve hurting me, I realize.

He lies flat on his back and closes his eyes for a beat.

"I don't understand, Finn."

He takes several deep breaths before he turns his head and looks at me, his eyes so bleak. "What don't you understand?"

"You are *covered* in tattoos," I whisper. "You are forever marked by the evidence of the sacrifices you made to save your kingdom."

He grimaces. "How do you know I wasn't just worried about saving myself?"

Because I know you. Because you're better than that. But I won't let him distract me with that argument. "Why was I different?" I ask. I know I shouldn't. I know it's tacky to fish out someone's feelings like this. I shouldn't want him to feel anything for me, let alone pressure him into saying it out loud.

"You would've said no. It doesn't matter."

"Probably," I whisper. "But you could've done more to make sure I never said yes to Sebastian. You could've lied to me and made me think he supported those camps. You could've bought yourself so much more time. Kept a wedge between me and the other male trying to steal the crown. It would've been easy for you. You had every opportunity."

He huffs out a breath. "Now you sound like Jalek. He laid into me that day you found out about the camps. He said I acted like I didn't even want the throne."

"Didn't you?"

He opens his mouth, then snaps it shut again, taking a few more moments before he replies. "I think part of me has always known that I have a role to play in protecting my court, but maybe I'm not meant to be on the throne."

My heart tugs. Has he had to convince himself of this? Because of me? Because of Sebastian?

"But that day wasn't about the throne. It was about you. Jalek couldn't understand why I had to defend your prince, but he wasn't looking into your eyes. He didn't see how crushed you were to hear what the queen was doing." He swallows. "I didn't want to lie to you."

"And you didn't want me to die," I say.

He squeezes his eyes shut. "That's true."

"And somehow that makes you a bad guy? How's that supposed to make me feel?" It's my turn to look away. I understand the logic. It would've been better for everyone if I'd died while handing the crown over, but I feel too much for Finn to hear that while I look into his eyes.

"Brie," he breathes. "Look at me." I don't, and his fingers find my chin again and he turns me until I meet his eyes. "Wanting to keep you alive doesn't make me the bad guy. I've told you already that I'm glad you took the damn potion. But I'm an idiot for not figuring out sooner that you were in love with him. For not figuring out sooner just how deeply you trusted him. I was *blind.* I'm not mad at myself because I didn't end your life. I'm mad at myself for not finding a way around it."

"You told me yourself you'd been trying for years—to find a way to get the crown that wouldn't bring me harm. Was that true?"

"Of course it was true."

"So why are you to blame for not finding a solution that doesn't exist?"

He releases my chin. "I'm to blame for allowing my father to get things to this point to begin with."

"So now you're responsible for his actions?"

"No," he growls, his voice echoing in the night. He drags a hand through his hair. "I'm responsible for mine. I told you, I was spoiled, and I got what I wanted. I wanted Isabel, so she and I planned to be bonded in secret and begin our lives together. If it meant my father's refusing to pass me the crown, so be it. She wanted children, so we planned to have our family first, and I'd give her the Potion of Life before I took the throne from my father. We were in no hurry. If anything, I wanted more time before taking the throne. I wanted us to enjoy a life together before the pressures of ruling changed our lives. This was after Mordeus stepped in to rule, but I was sure it would all be handled quickly. My father had returned from the mortal lands and was weak from his many months there, but once he regained his power, I was sure he'd find a way to be rid of Mordeus without pulling our court into an internal war." He blows out a breath. "I was so naïve. About the hold Mordeus had over his followers, but mostly about the queen's power. Her rage and resentment. We all were."

"What happened?" I ask.

Finn takes my hand, as if he needs the comfort of my touch to tell his story. "The day Isabel and I were to be bonded, my father showed up and asked me to help him. He'd planned a scheme to reclaim his role from Mordeus. I don't even know what it was, though later I wished I'd listened, wished I'd had the details to remove my uncle from the palace and his tenuous position of power. I denied my father. Isabel had planned the day out, and I would've given her anything. But I did it out of spite too. I was bitter that he wouldn't support my future with Isabel, and I wanted him to suffer for it."

I squeeze his hand, and he cuts his eyes to me and grimaces. "I'm ashamed that I didn't put my court first that day. If I had, everything would be different."

"Tell me what happened."

"Isabel and I had our special day leading up to the ceremony, and as we said our vows . . ." He swallows and turns away, and when he looks at me again, his tear-filled eyes sparkle in the moonlight. "I felt *off* that afternoon. Not sick, but weaker in a way I couldn't explain. I had no way of knowing that the queen had just cursed all my people — cursed *me.* The moment my bond with Isabel was complete, she died in my arms." He shakes his head. "We were in a secluded cabin in the mountains, just north of here, completely alone. I didn't have the potion. I hadn't sourced the ingredients yet, and we weren't planning to use it for years. I wasn't prepared. And she died in my arms. Pure terror on her face."

And I had judged him. I judged him so harshly for killing her. For taking her life to hold on to his magic after the queen cursed his people. I judged him, and he didn't even know what he was doing. "Finn, I'm so sorry."

He swallows. "When the power from a human life is transferred to you, it's a physical rush. I thought there was something horribly broken inside me. I sat there with the woman I loved dying in my arms and felt more alive than I had in my entire life, and I hated myself for it."

I feel sick imagining it, and I want to curl my body against his and offer him physical comfort beyond intertwined fingers, but I'm not sure he'd find it comforting at all, so I don't.

"After that, we started putting together what had happened," he says. "Curses don't come with announcements explaining what they are or how they work. We had to figure it out for ourselves. Had to feel our magic weakening us and never refilling itself. Had to watch our people bleed out from wounds that typically would've healed on their own in minutes. At first we didn't know it was a curse. We just had to put it together over time and then, after that, had to find out for ourselves how bonding with humans figured into it. The worst part was that the curse prevented us from talking about it, which meant that every one of us had to figure it out on our own."

I never thought about that — how they discovered the ins and outs of the curse, how the discovery of each facet would've been traumatic in its own right.

"I was already angry with my father," Finn says. "But then we put it together and realized we'd been cursed by the golden queen, and my anger grew hotter. It was *his fault* that the woman I loved was dead. His fault that all my friends were dying.

"I told him I wouldn't help him get Mordeus off the throne. He'd made the mess. He could fix it." He rakes his hand over his face. "By the time he handed his life over for yours, I hadn't spoken to him in eleven years."

"Finn." I roll to my side, reaching my arm over my head and resting on my shoulder to study him. "Mordeus was only a small part of the problem. You weren't responsible for the Great Fae War, for your father's actions with the golden queen, or for the curse."

He turns to his side, mimicking my position. "If we'd gotten Mordeus off the throne, these people would've had only the curse to contend with, and they could've done so from the safety of their own homes. Instead, they were forced to run while they were at their weakest."

"I'm so sorry. I didn't have a choice in what your father did for me, but I am sorry for the havoc my survival has brought to your kingdom."

"I'm not sorry," he says. "Not for that part. When you came into my life, you were a bright star in an endlessly dark night. I needed to see there was still something worth hoping for. And maybe that proves I'm still a spoiled, selfish child, but I won't be sorry for any choice that brought you here or kept you here. Please don't ask me to be."

"Okay," I whisper.

He just stares at me, and the hands above our heads find each other. He strokes his thumb along the back of my palm, never taking his eyes from mine.

With a single, tentative finger, I trace the sharp tip of his ear and the hard line of his jaw. When I reach his mouth, his lips part and his eyes float closed. I want to kiss him. I want to let him kiss me. I want to pick up where we left off under the waterfall and learn how those hands would feel if they finished their journey up my torso and to my breasts. I want to feel his mouth on mine again, and this time I would memorize every facet of his taste and the feel of his lips.

Finn squeezes my hand, as if he feels it too and wants the same. But he doesn't kiss me.

"Maybe you didn't realize I was in love with him . . . because I never really was."

"You don't have to say that," he says softly. "Having feelings for one person doesn't negate what you feel for someone else."

Finn's talking about what I might be feeling for him. "I know that, but that's not what I mean. With Sebastian . . ." I squeeze Finn's hand, embarrassed to admit this. "I was in love with what he represented. After years of struggling all on my own to survive, he offered me companionship and security. That's why I bonded with him. I wanted his protection. I wanted not to be alone ever again."

He swallows. "You wanted someone you could trust."

"Desperately," I whisper, and the word is so raw that I feel more exposed than I did under that waterfall, dressed in nothing but my wet undergarments.

"Someday you'll have that." With that whispered promise, he rolls onto his back to look up at the sky, and I follow his lead.

We lie there for a long time, staring up at the stars, the quiet night wrapping around us like a comforting childhood blanket, the only sounds the music and laughter floating up from the party on the mountain far below. Our futures are so unsure, but in this moment, with our fingers intertwined, I feel peace. I feel *hope.*

When we return to the campsite, he brings me to our tent, but he's distracted. As much as I want him to come inside with me, I can tell he needs time alone with his thoughts. He needs these moments of reflection and silence before we see the priestess tomorrow.

"Good night, Finn," I say. "I'll see you when you come to bed." Solitude is all I can offer him right now, and I wish I could do more.

CHAPTER TWENTY-TWO

THE NEW DAY BRINGS MORE sun, but my mood is as dark as a moonless night.

If Finn ever came back to the tent last night, I missed it, and this morning he popped in to leave me a tray of coffee and let me know that we'll be leaving in an hour for our meeting with the priestess. Now he's busy elsewhere — probably speaking with Juliana again, but I try not to think too much about that. Or about where he may have been all night.

The same servant from yesterday has drawn me a bath and left me alone, and I'm determined to soak in the fragrant water until my ugly mood washes away. I strip off my sleeping gown and undergarments, tossing them in the corner.

The tent flap opens, and I spin around, arms crossed over my bare chest, eyes wide. Finn steps inside and lets the flaps close behind him. When he turns, he freezes at the sight of me. He looks so shocked, I half expect him to race back out of the tent. He doesn't.

Instead, he leisurely looks me over, an expression on his face that I can't begin to make sense of. He prowls forward, closing the space between us and making my heart race. He stops a step away, and our eyes meet. He smells like rain. Like earth and sky and . . . lust.

I hold my breath, unsure if I really want the heat of his hands on my bare skin, unsure if I can handle the complication of his mouth on mine right now — and wanting it all anyway.

He reaches around me, the sleeve of his tunic brushing my arm as he takes a robe that's hanging on the side of the tent. He holds it open for me, and my cheeks blaze.

I just stand here.

Naked.

In front of him.

Just stand here and wait for him to touch me. To take me. Just like I waited in that bed for him last night. And he was only grabbing a robe.

"You might be more comfortable in this," he says when I don't move.

"I'm sorry. The bath is warm, and since there's time before we need to leave, I thought I might as well . . ." I'm rambling, so I bite my bottom lip and make myself shut up. I haven't made a move to put on the robe. I'm far too self-conscious to drop my arms now that I know he only wants to cover me.

Finn drapes the robe around my shoulders and does his best to close the front. "For the record," he says, his voice a little rough, "you don't ever need to apologize for greeting me like that. But while there might be time for a bath, we don't have nearly enough time for" — I hear the smile in his voice even if I'm too much of a coward to look at his face — "*more interesting* activities. So unless you want us to be *very* late to meet the High Priestess, you should probably stay covered."

I quickly shove my arms through the sleeves of the robe and tie the belt. "Thanks," I whisper, still avoiding his gaze.

He takes my chin in his hand and lifts my face until my eyes meet his. His expression is serious, his eyes searching. "What's wrong, Princess?"

"Nothing. I . . ."

"You're being uncharacteristically quiet."

I scoff. He's barely been around to know. "You're the one who was out all night, my supposed betrothed—" I cut myself off with a shake of my head. I'm sick of hearing myself talk, so I loop my arms behind his neck and lift onto my toes, pressing my mouth to his the way I wanted to last night.

He groans softly and sweeps his lips over mine. I'm grateful for the excuse to stop rambling, but it's nothing compared with the relief of finally feeling his warm mouth on mine again. I plaster my body against his.

He grips my shoulders and steps back, putting space between us.

"Why are you pulling away?" I ask softly, even though I don't have the right to ask. Not when everything's such a mess. Not when I don't even know what I want from him. But if nothing else, Finn is my friend, and the thought of losing that makes my heart ache. "Why didn't you come back last night?"

He drops his hands and stares at the pitched roof of the tent for a long beat before rubbing the palms of his hands against his eyes. "You really don't know?"

I swallow hard. "Don't know what?"

He huffs, the muscle in his jaw ticking. He closes his eyes as he says, "There's nothing in the world I want more than to peel that robe off you. I want to lay you on that bed and see if the rest of you tastes as sweet as your lips and neck."

My stomach pinches tight and flips. He's saying these things that, gods help me, I want to hear, and at the same time he's taking another step back.

His eyes trail over my face, down to my robe, then up to my neck. "I'm haunted by your taste. By the sounds you make when you're turned on."

Heat races through my blood and my breathing turns choppy.

"I remember the way it felt to have you fall apart in my arms. I think about it every day."

I can't breathe. I've thought about that night too. I was drugged, but the lust, the desire, the attraction to Finn — that was there without the wine. It always has been. I step forward, close enough to touch. "Finn —"

"I'm not interested in pretending I don't want you, that I don't think about you constantly. It's insulting to us both." He swallows, and his gaze dips from my face to the V of my robe. His hand follows the same path, grazing down my neck and over my collarbone to between my breasts, where he nudges the silky fabric to the side.

He strokes his thumb across the swell of my breast, and pleasure whips through me, so intense that it takes me a moment to realize what he's doing — *where* he's touching. His thumb circles the rune tattoo that symbolizes my bond with Sebastian. "I want you so much, Abriella. More than I ever thought was possible. More than I should admit. But as long as you're bonded to him, you'll never be completely mine." He lifts his gaze and locks his silver eyes on mine. "And I am just as selfish as the males who loved Queen Gloriana. I don't want pieces of you. I want all of you, and I won't share."

Because he looks so sad, so devastated by this, I lean forward and brush my lips against his again. The kiss isn't passionate or hungry like the one we shared in the lake. It's a kiss that says I hear him, and I understand, that I feel it too.

When he pulls away, I lean into him, instinctively chasing more.

He groans and tucks an errant curl behind my ear. "I could take you right now, Princess. But I want you mindless with pleasure — lost to it. And if I do my job right, those shields of yours wouldn't stand a chance. He'd feel you, and you'd feel him, and in the end, it would be painful for all of us. *That* is why I didn't come back to the tent last night." He drops his hand and takes another step back. "Enjoy your bath."

The High Priestess of the shadow fae is, in a word, a bitch.

We arrived at the temple eight hours ago and were told she'd see us soon. Pretha and Kane left, and Finn and I were escorted into a cramped, stuffy room inside the temple and made to wait. Then we were left alone and locked inside. We waited. With no water or food, without a chair to sit in or even a window for fresh air, we waited for what felt like an eternity.

By the time a servant comes for us and leads us into a vast, window-lined sanctuary, the sun is setting. The sneer hasn't left her face since we stepped into the room, as if she's being forced to converse with the dirt on the bottoms of her shoes.

"High Priestess Magnola, thank you for seeing us," Finn says, bowing his head to the dark-haired, finely dressed female before us. She's seated on an ornate throne of sorts on the dais at the front of the sanctuary. It's studded with jewels and pearls, as is the priestess herself. They're everywhere—around her neck, her wrists, and up her arms, even woven into her hair.

"Finnian," she says, inclining her chin. She cuts her eyes to me for a fraction of a second before turning her gaze to Finn again. "You know I can't deny an audience with the rulers of this court."

"Yes," he says. "That's why I brought Lady Abriella."

"She is no lady," the priestess says, her lip curling as she looks me over. "She wasn't a lady when she was a human servant, and she's no lady now. She's a *mistake*." Her nostrils flare. "Nothing more."

"With all due respect," Finn says, but I put a hand on his arm and shake my head. I don't like this female. I don't like the way she's treated us or the way she's looking at me, but mostly I don't like the feeling of something crawling beneath my skin when I'm in her presence. Finn wants to defend me, but she doesn't deserve his explanation.

Those cold, bitter eyes narrow in on my hand on his arm. "When I was young, a soul bond *meant* something." She glares at me, and I want to wipe that sneer right off her face.

I clench my hands into fists and focus to control my power.

She continues. "It wasn't something done on a whim. We

bonded only with those we loved, and we were true to that bond until the day we died. But you stand here before me, bonded to one male while smelling of another."

For the first time since we stepped before her, I bow my head, unable to look into those angry eyes while she shames me. I might not care about being a *lady,* but my complicated relationship with Finn and Sebastian and the choices I made along the way? I consider that a failure. An embarrassment.

Finn stiffens beside me. "Abriella didn't know that Sebastian—"

"I don't want your excuses," she snaps. "It's been corrupted. Just like the crown, just like the court. It was never meant to be like this."

"I agree," Finn says softly. "Which is why we're here. The court is dying. The crown and its power have been cleaved, so no one can sit on the throne. There are children falling into the Long Sleep, more and more by the day. And Queen Arya will launch an all-out attack on our lands at any moment. The Court of the Moon needs to be at full strength if we're to have a chance at surviving this war."

She swivels her gaze to me, and I fight the urge to cower under its intensity. "You have the power of the crown, but no Unseelie blood," she says. "The court is dying because you still breathe."

Finn's anger rolls off him, and he steps forward, but I stop him with a hand on his arm. "I didn't have a choice," I explain. "I was dying, and Oberon—"

"I know the story," she snaps. "I simply find it disappointing."

Of course she does. I lift my chin. "Is there a way for me to shift the power to Sebastian?"

"Yes, but he cannot rule," she says. "This land is full of fae who would see the whole court fall before allowing Seelie blood on that throne."

I swallow hard. This is what we were afraid of—this stalemate.

"Convince the golden prince to surrender his crown to the girl," she tells Finn.

"No," I whisper. There has to be another way. "I can't sit on the throne anyway. It would be a pointless loss."

"His death would be step one." Her smile is wicked and angry. "Then you'd forfeit your own life to pass the power and crown to Finnian, where it belongs."

Next to me, Finn snarls. "That's not an option."

I swallow hard. *Maybe it should be.*

"Dear Prince, you know how this works. The power becomes one with the life, and only once the life is surrendered does the power move on to the heir. Isn't it time you made a sacrifice for your kingdom? For once?"

I can feel Finn shrink, and I want to claw her eyes out for hitting him in such a tender spot.

"Not before we've exhausted all other options," he says. "Open a portal to the Underworld so that I may ask the Great Queen Mab herself how to save our kingdom."

The priestess stares at him for a long time, and I hold my breath. I know the others have been planning for a way to proceed without whatever divine intervention Mab might offer, but I also know that if they'd come up with a true alternative, we wouldn't be here and Finn wouldn't be planning a treacherous trip to the Underworld.

The priestess holds Finn's gaze. "No."

Finn flinches.

"You were supposed to be king," she says. "You were supposed to rule alongside Juliana. She is worthy. You were once worthy. Prove that you are again. You've failed our kingdom, and now that white-haired Seelie trash lives in our palace and this human filth holds the power of our crown. I will *not*—" She gags, grabbing her throat as if she's choking, and then blood spills out of her mouth and her eyes roll back in her head.

Finn's arm darts out in front of me and he urges me to step back, away from the throne.

"What's happening?" I ask him.

"The High Priestess swore an oath to Mab when she took residence in this temple," he says. His eyes are wide as he watches her convulse. "There are consequences to taking that oath and then refusing to act in the best interest of the court, refusing to do Mab's will."

The High Priestess suddenly stops convulsing, and the air in the room shifts as something else, something *other* slides into her body, and the hairs on the back of my neck stand up.

Blood spills out of her mouth and splashes onto the marble floor as she leans forward and stares at us with the whites of her eyes. "At the northernmost peak of the Goblin Mountains," she says, but it's not the priestess's voice. This is a voice from far away and all around. It's the voice of *all* the shadow priestesses, and it sends chills racing across my skin and my heart stuttering in my chest. "In the cave beneath the roots of the Mother Willow, the portal waits." She turns her head and stares into my eyes, globs of clotted blood falling to the floor with each word. "Go there, Abriella, child of Mab."

Finn's snaps his gaze to me, wide-eyed and staring, but I can't take my eyes off the dead woman speaking to me.

"The Great Queen waits for you. Bring your tethered match," she says, "and the power of your blood combined will open the gates to the Underworld. Go learn how to save your kingdom." The priestess falls forward to the floor, into a pool of her own blood.

"Mother!" Juliana appears at the back of the sanctuary and races to her side, rolling the priestess to her back. "What did you do?" she shouts at Finn.

"Nothing," he says, but he doesn't take his eyes off me. "I did nothing but ask for a portal to see Mab."

Juliana presses her hand to her mother's chest. "Please, Mother."

"I'm sorry, Jules," Finn says, flicking his gaze to her briefly. "I didn't know this would happen."

She lifts her head, and tears roll down her beautiful face. "I don't understand."

"She swore an oath to protect this land and to serve the court. I don't think the gods liked her refusing me—us." He takes my hand and squeezes hard. "It seems that Mab wants to see her descendant. Abriella is a child of Mab."

Juliana's head snaps up, and she stares at me in shock. "That can't be. She was *human*."

"It appears there's more to the story," Finn says reverently.

Shaking her head, Juliana strokes her mother's cheek with bloody fingers. "Leave. Just leave me."

Finn practically pulls me out of the temple, leading me past the guards and down the steps, where Pretha and Kane are being restrained by guards, as if they'd sensed something wrong and had been trying to get to us.

"What happened?" Pretha asks, shrugging out of the grasp of the guard holding her.

"We're leaving," Kane growls at his guard, pulling out of his hold and following us toward our horses.

"We need to get back to the Unseelie palace," Finn says. He grips my hand tightly, as if he's afraid I might disappear.

"Explain," Pretha says. She tugs on Finn's arm and makes him stop. "We felt something awful. Something big, but they wouldn't let us in."

Finn looks at me and then back to Pretha. "The High Priestess denied us. She refused to open a portal. And then . . . something else took over her body to deliver a message — to tell us where to find a portal and tell us that Abriella and I will be able to open it."

"How?" Pretha asks.

Finn looks at me for a long moment, and his throat bobs as he swallows. "By using her blood mixed with my own. My suspicions were right. I am her tethered match."

Pretha and Kane exchange a look. "How?" Pretha breathes.

"Because my magic responds to the power in her blood. Abriella is a descendant of Mab. She is —"

"Our rightful queen," Kane murmurs.

"I don't understand." My head is spinning. They're throwing out these words—*tethered* and *portal* and *queen*—and my mind is still back in that sanctuary watching a dead priestess speak to me. "That . . . *thing* called me a child of Mab, but I've never met her. It doesn't even make sense. My mother was human. My sister is human. I was human until I took that potion."

"We didn't understand," Finn says. He's still watching me with that stunned, awe-filled expression. "There was always a reason Oberon was able to pass her the crown."

Kane slowly lowers himself to one knee and bows his head. "My queen," he murmurs. "It is an honor."

Pretha follows his lead, kneeling and bowing her head. "We will serve you."

I half expect Finn to burst out laughing, but there is nothing but reverence in his eyes as he lowers onto one knee, still holding my hand. "Our queen."

I can't make sense of my friends kneeling before me, so the crunch of gravel under boots is a welcome distraction, and I turn toward the sound to see Juliana running toward us, breathless.

"We didn't know," she says. Tears streak down her blood-smudged face. "I swear to you, we didn't know. We just wanted Finn on the throne. We thought Mab's line was gone." She gasps for air, then blinks at the others, kneeling in the gravel. "My qu-queen," she blurts, and drops to one knee. "Allow me the honor of serving you."

"No." I shake my head. "Get up. This is a mistake. I can't be . . ."

Finn's gaze lifts to mine, and I see the conviction in his silver eyes as his hand squeezes mine. That's when I feel it—power weaving up my legs and down my arms, coming from the earth, from this sacred land of Mab's.

My breath leaves me in a rush. There's no room for air when my entire body is buzzing. My entire *being* lights with energy and potential.

I close my eyes and feel my feet lift off the ground, and over the hush in the clearing, the trees seem to whisper *Queen.*

CHAPTER TWENTY-THREE

THE SUN STRETCHES LOW ACROSS the horizon, casting oranges and reds across the sky. Boots crunch on the gravel behind me, but I don't budge from the rock I'm perched on or turn to see who's checking on me. I know who stands behind me, and now I have an explanation for why his presence has always been so clear to me.

Tethered. The word echoes through me like a hawk's cry in a canyon.

This is supposed to be a quick stop to stretch and take care of our needs, but I'm in no rush to get back on my horse. We've been riding for hours, trying to get back to the Midnight Palace before nightfall, and I've had plenty of time to think. Too much time.

Finn's boots scuff on the rocks as he approaches my side and lowers himself to sit beside me. "How are you holding up?"

My eyes burn. Every time I think I have my footing, my entire world changes, but I have no right to the tinge of self-pity I'm feeling now. "How do you not hate me?"

He gently takes my chin in one big hand and turns me to face him. "Why on earth would I hate you?"

I swallow hard. "Finn, you were raised to lead your kingdom. You've spent your whole life preparing to take the throne, and suddenly you're told I'm supposed to take it instead. How are you so accepting of this?"

His expression softening, he strokes my cheek, his eyes and his touch full of tenderness. "I was raised to *serve* my kingdom. To do whatever I needed to protect my people and provide for them. I once thought I could do that best from the throne, but then everything happened and . . ." He shrugs, his gaze dropping to my mouth. "You need to remember that I'd already come to terms with Sebastian's taking the throne. Suddenly that's not the plan anymore because we have you, and you are exactly what this court needs. I knew it when I knelt before you on that mountain and signaled to the people of Staraelia that you would be their queen. I know it with every breath I take."

"Because I'm supposedly some lost descendant of Mab?"

"That's merely the technicality that will allow you to take the seat. But this court doesn't need you because of what's in your blood." His hand drops from my face and rests on my chest. "It needs you because of what's in your heart."

"Finn . . ." I bite my bottom lip, not wanting to say too much. Some ancient magic has tied our lives and power together, but I don't understand what role this tethering plays in what I feel for him. For now I need to keep these feelings to myself. "I'm scared. I don't know anything about being queen."

"I'm sorry if you feel trapped. If you feel—"

"No." I shake my head, wanting to erase the words that feel

like profanity in the face of the gift I've been given. Because when they knelt before me and called me their queen, my only thought had been *finally. Finally* I can make a difference. *Finally* I have the power to help.

Queen was the answer to the question that's been haunting me all my life.

"Not trapped. I'm scared because I want to do it right. I'm scared because all I've ever wanted was to be able to help those who were powerless to help themselves, and now . . ." I squeeze my eyes shut. "I don't want to fail."

"I'll be right by your side," he says, his lips brushing my ear with each word. "And doing so will be the greatest honor of my life."

"There has to be a way that doesn't require her to go to the Underworld," Sebastian snaps, his sea-green eyes blazing with frustration.

"Mab wants to see her heir, and we need to know how to fix the mess we're in," Finn explains again, rubbing his head. "We need to go."

After our short stop in the woods, we rode directly to the Midnight Palace. We've been here for less than an hour, and the news of my supposed bloodline and my plans to go to the Underworld have sparked pure chaos among our friends. Sebastian's struggling the most. Tynan, Kane, Misha, Pretha, Finn, Juliana, Riaan, Sebastian, and I are all gathered around the long table in the briefing room. The map of the Court of the Moon is spread out between us. We're trying to plan the best way to get Finn and me to the portal, but Sebastian keeps circling back, hoping he can talk us out of our plans.

"I'll go with her, then," Sebastian says. "We're bonded, and the bond will allow me to protect her."

"The problem with that plan," Misha says, "is that you're descended from Deaglan, Mab's greatest enemy, the one who killed her son. If we're worried about Mab deeming anyone unworthy, sending you seems a little risky."

"And I was instructed to take Finn," I say gently.

He's struggling, Misha says in my mind. *The only thing Sebastian hates more than this plan to send you to the Underworld is the idea that Finn is your tethered match.*

Why? I ask, flicking my gaze to the other side of the table, where my friend sits.

Tethering is a lifelong connection. Unlike the bond, the only way it can be undone is through death. The boy is jealous, though you and I both know the tethering is an easy place to direct his frustration. It's harder for him to face the other truth.

And what's that?

That your feelings for Finn have nothing to do with this predestined, divinely granted connection you have.

Kane leans over the table and smooths out the map. "This is where we're going," he says, circling the northern Goblin Mountains with one big finger. "The Mother Willow is here." He taps the map at a spot he's marked with a star, then circles that spot. "And this entire area around that sacred tree is called the Silent Ridge."

"What's the Silent Ridge?" I ask.

"No magic," Finn says. "The bond will be rendered useless in that area, and so will your powers."

"But if magic *is* life—" I say.

Finn shakes his head. "We won't be there long enough for it to hurt us—assuming we're not gravely injured. It's the closest thing to the queen's curse that exists in the natural world, but it affects *all* magical creatures. That's why this part of our territory is uninhabited. People go there to hunt or for a brief reprieve, but no one wants to live there."

"I've never heard of there being a portal there," Sebastian says.

"And you're familiar with the location of the Underworld portals?" Kane snaps.

Finn shoots his friend a look, his expression seeming to command Kane to ease up. "Perhaps it's new, created just for Abriella." He shrugs. "Or maybe it's been there all along and is the reason the Silent Ridge exists."

Sebastian scowls. "This could be a trap."

Finn nods. "I've considered that, but if Abriella is Mab's blood and the Great Queen truly wants us to visit, the portal will call to her once we're close. If she doesn't feel that tug, we'll come back here. You have my word."

"Come back here and what?" I ask. I hate the idea of relying on some mystical *tug* to know if this is the right course of action. "What if I feel nothing at all? What exactly will we do when we get back here?"

"We'll wait for the next priestess to take the oath of the High

Priestess at the temple," Finn says. "And in the meantime, we'll fight his mother's powerful kingdom with our broken one."

"We will lose that battle," Kane says.

Finn nods. "But we'll go down with honor."

I close my eyes for a beat and draw in a deep breath. When I open them, I level my gaze on Sebastian. "It's our best chance to find a solution," I say to him. "We've broken the kingdom, you and I. Something has to be done."

"We'll have goblins get us as deep into the mountains as we can," Kane says, pointing to a spot on the map south of our destination. "Then we'll go on foot. This far north, at these altitudes, it gets cold, so we'll need to pack accordingly, especially for the part of the trip where we can't rely on magic to warm us."

"Then what about in the Underworld?" Sebastian asks. "How does she stay safe there?"

"By the mercy of the gods," Jalek mutters.

I bite my lip. I should be terrified of this trip, but I'm still reeling from everything else. "What is it even like?"

"Juliana?" Finn says. "Would you care to answer that one? Your mother traveled there to be crowned High Priestess. What did she tell you about it?"

"I can't tell you what to expect," Juliana says. "The Underworld is inconstant. It changes for each person who visits. But all those who have ventured there and returned speak of a tremendous distance they must travel between the portal and the Great Queen. The terrain will be rough and the trek exhausting. The purpose is to judge your heart and your persistence. The queen won't show herself to those who give up. You need to carry in water and food and be prepared for the most mentally arduous journey of your life."

"Be on your guard for the monsters that lurk there," Misha says. "Creatures so savage and bloodthirsty they've been cast from our world. They'd like nothing more than to have your souls to toy with for eternity."

Sebastian's chair creaks as he shoves it back, and everyone watches mutely as he storms out of the room.

"I'll go," I say softly.

"With all due respect, My Queen," Kane says, "you don't need his permission."

I give him a tight smile and nod before leaving the room. I find Sebastian on the terrace outside the library, staring out into the night.

"Did they explain to you how dangerous this is?" he asks, sensing me without turning around. "Did they tell you how many people try to speak with Mab and never come back? Because those mythical monsters aren't your only concern. If she decides that someone unworthy has dared to take her time, she makes sure they never find their way back to the portal. Or if they do, they return without their full mind. Did they tell you any of that?"

"Sebastian . . ." I step forward, reaching to touch his back just as he spins around, and I find myself looking at his chest. He's closer than I thought, and my breath catches. I don't know if I've ever been this close to him feeling the way I do now. I don't think I've ever been so close to Sebastian while wishing he would let me go. "I don't have a choice," I say, craning my neck so I can see his face. "I won't allow one more innocent to die at your mother's hands. Not if I can prevent it."

"I don't want you to go to the Underworld," he whispers, leaning his forehead against mine. "I can accept your anger and your mistrust of me — I earned it. I can accept any confusion you feel about us right now. I can even forgive you for letting him touch you, but I won't accept you sacrificing yourself for this. You have no idea how bad that place is."

"And you do?" I ask.

Something flickers across his face before he sets his jaw in a stubborn line. "If you don't come back, if Mab doesn't deem you worthy to return, I cannot accept that."

I step back. I need space. Even with my shields, when we're this close, his emotions muddle with mine and make me question everything. "Sebastian, I'm going."

He squeezes his eyes shut.

I swallow, knowing that was the easy part of this conversation. "Listen, if there's a way to dissolve this bond between us before I leave, we should do it."

His eyes fly open. "No."

"Bash," I whisper. "You and I aren't going to be together. No matter what happens on this journey. We aren't going to get the happily-ever-after. It was never in the cards for us."

"You haven't even tried. You've been with *him* the whole time."

Yes. Right where I belong. "It wouldn't have mattered," I say.

He shakes his head. "I won't do it. Not just because it's an excruciating process and I can't cause you that kind of pain again.

And not just because we don't have the materials we need. I won't do it because I can't. I love you, and I need to know without a doubt that we tried."

"All those things you want to protect me from — capture, torture, painful death? I want to protect you too. I don't want you to suffer through the things I might experience in the next few days."

"Is that it?" he asks, eyes hard, head cocked to the side. "Or do you want to be free to be with him without my knowing? Do you want to be free to have him kiss you and touch you without having to feel how that tears me apart inside?"

I can't hear the pain in his voice without vividly remembering being beneath the waterfall with Finn, that feeling of Sebastian through the bond. His heartache. The betrayal he felt.

"Bash," I whisper. "You need to let me go. Please."

"Don't you remember our night at Serenity Palace? You begged me not to let you go, begged me to hold on because you had secrets. You were *so sure* my love wasn't strong enough to withstand your deceptions, and I promised you it was. I'm making good on that promise."

I squeeze my eyes shut, remembering.

I'm the one who doesn't deserve you, but I'm too selfish to let you go.

Don't let me go. I need you to hold on.

"That was before. So much has changed."

A muscle in his jaw ticks. "You have no idea how much I've sacrificed for you. How much *more* I was willing to sacrifice for you." He steps forward, opens that fist, and presses his palm to my chest so firmly that I'm sure he can feel the steady beat of my heart. "I *feel* you. Despite your efforts to shut me out, I feel you. And I feel you falling in love with him."

"Then dissolve the bond." I can't stand hurting him, no matter what mistakes he's made and how he's hurt me. "Let me *go*—for both our sakes."

He shakes his head. "You ask too much."

"You'll stay bonded to me, even knowing I want to be free of it? Knowing I'm falling for someone else? Knowing the way I feel about Finn?"

He flinches. "Yes." He cups my face. "You're mine, Abriella. I found you first."

CHAPTER TWENTY-FOUR

"WHEN DID YOU FIRST SUSPECT?" I ask as we trek on foot through the frigid northern ridge of the Goblin Mountains.

Kane leads the way ahead of us, watching the trail for threats. Tynan brings up the rear while Dara and Luna weave in and out of the trees along our path, scouting for trouble. We've been hiking since sunrise, when Finn's goblin brought us all here.

Finn arches a brow in question.

"That we were tethered," I say. "That I had some connection to Mab?"

Finn shakes his head, then seems to think better of that response, and he shrugs. "There were signs, but I dismissed them."

"Like what?"

He blows out a breath. "When being around me made your power flare, it was easy enough to blame that on my connection to the crown. Then, after you were turned fae, when you kept the power of the throne, I blamed your surges in power on the fact that anyone on the throne is strengthened by the people and the land." He scratches the back of his neck. "And then there were the other hints, the depths of your power and your connection to mine. This connection you've felt with me from the beginning . . ." He looks down at his boots and smiles. "I should've known."

I shake my head. "It doesn't even make sense. How can a human be the descendant of a great faerie queen? Wouldn't I have been born fae?"

"I don't have those answers," he says softly. "But this answers more questions than it raises. We never understood how my father had done it to begin with — how he'd been able to give his crown to you when you weren't Unseelie. The magic wasn't supposed to work that way."

I flinch. "You suspected from the beginning then."

He shakes his head. "No. Not at all."

"But you said —"

"I never get too caught up in what magic is supposed to do or supposed to be. Magic is rooted in many things — life, first and foremost, but also tradition and love and *change*. To assume that something magical cannot happen because it's never happened before goes against all that magic is and stands for. Magic *is* the possibility of breaking rules. It paves the way for change. I think that's why we all accepted that for some reason the magic allowed him to pass his crown on to a human. But he didn't pass it to just any human." He cups my face and sweeps his thumb across my cheek. "He passed it to Mab's heir."

The swamp looms ahead. The guys spent the first hour of our journey this morning debating the best way to deal with Blight Swamp, arguing whether it was better to waste hours traveling around it or to go through and risk encountering the creatures who make a home in the muck.

Urgency won out, and we ultimately decided we'd go through. We'll scout for the shallowest part to cross, and Tynan will cast a spell to create a temporary bridge over the water while Kane emits a high-pitch sound that should deter any creature from approaching us.

It seemed like a good plan to me, but judging by the way Kane's surveying the swamp ahead, I wonder if he's reconsidering.

"Finn," Kane says, his voice a low warning. "Stay back for now."

Finn stops and steps to my side, wrapping an arm around me.

Kane pulls his sword and scoops something up from the muddy bank. He jogs toward us, holding out the blade to show Finn what he's gathered.

Balanced on the metal is a pile of red stones—no. They're gray and black. The red is a coating. Paint or . . . blood.

Finn stiffens behind me, and that arm around my waist tightens. His wolves rush toward Kane to sniff what he's brought us and then they back away, whining.

Perhaps it's just the remnants of an animal. Some unlucky forest creature captured by a wolf or a coyote, but judging by the serious faces around me, it's more than that.

Tynan jogs to a spot farther down the bank and crouches to examine the water. Even from this distance I can hear him muttering a creative string of curses. "We have to go," he says, straightening.

"You're sure?" Finn asks.

"I wish I weren't," he says, running back toward us. I think it might be the first time I've ever seen him move with any sort of urgency.

He jogs down the path, back the way we came, taking the lead this time as Kane brings up the rear.

"What's everyone so scared of?" I ask.

"The Crimson Fog," Kane says behind us.

Finn holds my hand and leads me quickly down the path. The leaves stir on the trees, and the wind shifts in the telltale sign of a storm rolling in.

Tynan cuts into the woods at our right, and Finn follows him, tugging me along quicker than my tired feet want to carry me.

"The crimson what?" I ask, but either he can't hear me over the wind rushing around us or he's too focused on escape to bother answering right now.

"Here!" Tynan shouts, waving at us before disappearing into the side of the mountain.

The wind howls. I turn to look and see a sheen of red coating the leaves behind us. Finn sweeps me off my feet and tugs me toward Tynan — into a small cave tucked into the side of the mountain — then Kane follows.

"Get down!" Finn shouts over the howling wind. Dara and Luna wiggle their way inside and whine softly as we all crouch to the floor.

Outside, creatures scream and skitter as they run for cover.

"What is it?" I ask. I can feel something looming. Something deadly and far too close.

"The Crimson Fog is a magical, amorphous creature," Finn says in my ear. "A deadly mist that can rise out of nowhere."

"But made of blood, not water," Kane says, peering out into the forest. "It can appear as suddenly as a storm cloud."

“The creature can pull the blood from the bodies of any animal it passes through,” Tynan says, “and each bit of blood makes it stronger and more powerful.”

I shiver. If I hadn’t seen so many awful things in my time here, I might not even believe it. “How do we know it won’t come after us?”

“They’re rare,” Finn says. “But they need the moisture of the swamp to survive. Once it passes over, we’ll be able to return to the trail, but we’ll have to go around. It was a risk, going that way. I should’ve considered the possibility.”

“I didn’t think of it either, Finn,” Kane says. “There haven’t been reports of a Crimson Fog in five hundred years. How could you have guessed?”

“What happened five hundred years ago?” I ask.

“The Unseelie king and queen were assassinated during the first Seelie strike in the Great Fae War,” Kane says. “Our court was in such chaos that the throne remained vacant for weeks.”

“Crimson Fog thrives in a dying land.” Finn presses a kiss to my shoulder. “We’re running out of time.”

“We need to make camp for the night,” Kane says, watching the skies. “And this is as good a place as any.”

Thanks to our detour around the swamp, we hiked hours longer than we planned today. My legs ache from the ascent and my back’s tired from carrying my pack—though I don’t dare admit it when mine is a third of the size of everyone else’s. Once this is all resolved and my days have room for more than trying to keep Arya from destroying the Court of the Moon, my first priority will be to get strong. Whether I'm a queen or a peasant or something in between. I want the strength and stamina Finn and his friends have shown day after day.

In the meantime, I can't argue against stopping. Even as skilled as this group is at traveling in the dark, I've picked up enough comments throughout the day to know that there are real dangers in these mountains.

Finn scans the area and nods. "Let's do it."

"I'll make a fire," Kane says. "That should help deter whatever creatures lurk in the trees."

I shoot him a look, and he grins, saying, "What?"

I don't want to think about what might be in those trees, but I know Kane will only tease me if I admit that, so I keep my mouth shut. "I'll help you gather wood," I say, turning toward the forest.

Finn grabs my arm. "Sit. We'll do it."

I hate that my weakness is so obvious. "I can help."

"You're exhausted, and if you don't rest, you'll slow us down tomorrow."

He has a point. Besides, I don't have the energy for an argument, let alone to effectively scavenge the forest for supplies.

"Drop your packs," Tynan says. "I'll keep her company and get our beds ready."

We all obey, everyone appearing as grateful as I feel to have less weight to carry. Kane and Finn head into the forest as Tynan sets about making camp, his braids falling into his face as he works.

"Ever sleep under the stars?" he asks me, grinning as he unrolls a thin pad that will act as someone's bed.

"Many times." I smile at the memories. "My mother loved a clear night sky more than anything." My smile falls away as I recall why she might have felt that way. I know she loved my father, but it's clear in retrospect that she never got over Oberon. Why else would she have been so enamored with the night? Unless she knew somehow that I have this tie to the Court of the Moon. Unless she was tied to it too.

Tynan watches me curiously for a beat before returning his attention to the bedroll. "As did mine," he says softly. "Sleeping outside isn't uncommon among the Wild Fae, of course, but the nobility tends toward more refined accommodations." He shakes his head. "Not my mother, though. She'd take us from the palace and into the woods at least twice a month. She wanted us to be comfortable sleeping with nothing but a bed of pine needles beneath us and a blanket of stars overhead."

"You were raised at Castle Craige?" I ask, realizing I don't know much about Tynan's background. He's always so quiet.

Tynan nods. "Pretha's my cousin. Our mothers are sisters."

"Will you both go back to the Wild Fae Lands after everything's settled here, or will you stay with Finn?"

Tynan's eyes go wide, as if I've said something unexpected, but he shakes his head and returns his attention to unpacking another bedroll. "You'd have to ask Finn about his plans, but I know Misha would like me back, and I miss my home."

Finn appears from among the trees, carrying an armful of thick branches, Kane by his side. I never thought about Finn's plans. I think I've always assumed he'd end up on the Throne of Shadows. Now they all assume that I will—and as much as I want to be horrified by the prospect, it feels right on some level, like an unexpected puzzle piece clicking into place. But I can't imagine doing it without my friends by my side. I wouldn't want to.

"What about Pretha? Will she return home with you?" I ask Tynan.

"I'm not sure she considers the Wild Fae territory her home anymore. Pretha fell in love with Vexius at the Midnight Palace," Tynan says. "Birthed Lark in the freshwater pools of Staraelia. She changed in these lands."

"Changed how?" I ask.

Finn drops the pile of branches and laughs. "From a defiant young bride to a loving wife and doting mother," he says, and Tynan nods. "When you take the throne, you'll be able to choose your advisors," Finn adds. "You should consider Pretha. She'd be honored, and I don't think she'd be disappointed to have an excuse to stay in the Court of the Moon."

"And what about you?" I ask Finn. "What are your plans?"

Tynan clears his throat, and he and Kane excuse themselves and retreat to the woods.

Finn meets my eyes for a beat, then is quiet for a long time as he builds a fire. "That will be up to my queen," he finally answers, his eyes on his task. "But as your tethered, I can serve and protect you best if I'm by your side."

"And if I'm not queen?" I ask. "If the solution Mab offers doesn't involve my taking the throne?"

"I don't think that's likely. You're Mab's heir. You're the promised child."

"I think we need to consider that it's still possible — possible that after all this, Sebastian will be the one to end up on the throne."

Finn points two fingers at the pile of sticks and branches, and it catches a flame. The fire hisses and crackles as he walks around it to stand before me. "I will be by your side," he says, cupping my face in one big hand, "as long as you'll let me. Wherever you are."

Finn takes the first watch, and despite sleeping through it, I'm completely aware of him when he wakes Kane for his turn and readies himself for bed. I hear Finn's soft steps and the sounds of boots being shucked off, the swoosh of clothing being removed.

We never discussed how we'd sleep, but somehow I'm not surprised when he lowers himself onto the ground beside me, as if the moment his role as my tethered match was confirmed at the temple, he stopped trying to resist the impulse to stay as close as possible. Slipping under the blankets, he curls his body behind mine. His heat seeps through my sleep clothes, wrapping all around me. When he snakes an arm around my waist, I melt into him with a sigh.

I feel so good. So *safe* here, despite what might lurk in those woods.

"Sorry," he whispers. That arm at my waist squeezes for a beat, and he presses a kiss to the side of my neck, just beneath my ear. "Go back to sleep. We have a long day tomorrow."

"I know. My mind is spinning."

He slips his hand beneath my shirt and gently strokes my stomach. I close my eyes and focus on those warm fingertips and the soft figure eight they trace on my belly. The infinity symbol.

We may not be bonded, but we're tied together forever thanks to this tethering. Even as complicated and overwhelming as everything is, I find some comfort in that.

"Tell me about this connection we have," I say. "What does it mean to be tethered to someone?"

"It's another thing we lost when we thought Mab's line was killed off. In its previous incarnation, it described a connection between the Unseelie ruler and another faerie, usually someone in the queen's inner circle. Each ruler in Mab's line had a magical tether to someone else, usually someone quite powerful. The tether is a link that allowed the ruler to pull strength from her tethered partner."

"Only Mab's line?"

He shifts against me, as if trying to pull me even closer. "Yes. We all suspect it somehow goes back to the original forming of the courts, something Mab did to protect her daughter before she passed the crown to her. But we don't know why we've never seen it elsewhere. My line of rulers never had any such thing. Or if they did, none of them ever found their tethered match."

"What is the connection? Is it like the bond?"

He shakes his head. "There's no empathic connection or awareness of location. It's simply a one-way link between one person's magic and another's."

"This is what's been making you sick," I say softly. I roll in his arms to face him. "*I've* been making you sick."

"Only the times you used so much power, and even those times would've required a fraction of what you'd used if you had the proper training. You're getting better, and you'll continue to improve. I'll be fine."

"I don't want to hurt you."

"You aren't. You're improving every day. I'll teach you how to use your power so efficiently you'll rarely ever tap into mine."

"And when I do?" I ask.

"I'll be okay. This is what I was made for."

Those words make me flinch.

"It is a great honor to be tethered to a shadow queen. My ancestor King Kairyn was the last known tethered—before his match, Queen Reé, was assassinated."

"So you're not a descendant of Mab?"

His lips twitch, as if he knows I'm asking if we're distantly related somehow. "No. Kairyn got the crown from Queen Reé when it was thought her line was killed off."

"They were tethered, but were they married?"

"No, but legend has it that she loved him more than any of her husbands."

My eyes widen. "Then why didn't she marry *him?*"

He chuckles softly. "It simply wasn't done. Queens didn't marry their tethered. It was considered too dangerous. The tethered's purpose is to protect the queen. To lend her his strength and magic. If they were married, she might not want to compromise him."

"Were all the queens romantically involved with their tethered match?"

He swallows. "The tethering draws the pair closer together, so chemistry and deeper feelings were easily discovered, but there are as many tales of platonic love between matches as romantic love."

"Is it forbidden for a queen to bond with her tethered match?"

Finn is quiet for so long, I wish I hadn't asked. Maybe I'm wrong about his feelings for me. Maybe he doesn't want more than we can have right now. When he finally speaks, his voice is as soft as the wind. "The power moves in only one direction between a tethered and his queen. If they were bonded, they would be linked and the power would move both ways. For that reason alone, it was never done—or at least never spoken of. Queens couldn't have their tethered matches pulling from their strength."

"But what if that was what the queen wanted?" I ask.

"That, like all things, would be up to the queen herself." His hand drifts down to my hip, squeezing. "But if you are the queen in question, I can say with confidence that your tethered servant would be honored to share the bond with you."

His careful words make my heart ache. I never considered how much my decision to bond with Sebastian hurt Finn. I was too busy feeling betrayed by both of them to give it a second thought. "I told Sebastian that he needs to let me go." I draw in a deep breath. "He's holding on, but I can't have him believing I'm going to give us a chance. Not when I have these feelings for you." I close my eyes. "I know it might seem like I'm being influenced by the tether, but it's more than that. It's been more than that for a long time, and I just want . . . I want a chance for us to explore that. Without the bond in our way."

Finn's lips brush my neck again and he breathes in deeply. His hand drifts from my hip and up my side, his thumb skimming the underside of my breasts. "If I tell you something, will you promise me not to decide tonight or even tomorrow?"

"What is it?" I ask, studying his face in the starlight.

He strokes his thumb across my bottom lip. "On the other side of the portal, deep in the Underworld, the Waters of New Life flow. Water so clear it can strip away your mistakes, your regrets. Water that can, if you ask it, undo the bonds you've taken with others. Only there can severing the bond be your choice alone."

Which would mean I could be with Finn without feeling Sebastian between us. I wouldn't have to shield myself from Sebastian so diligently. It would mean a fresh start. "I could ask the waters to strip me of my bond with Sebastian?"

He swallows. "Only if you wish."

"Then you and I . . ."

Finn shakes his head slowly. "Only if you wish," he repeats.

I *do* wish, but I take a moment anyway, considering what I'd do if I didn't have feelings for Finn. "It's a wonder how I can loathe this bond so much when loneliness dogged me most of my life. It should be a relief, the constant awareness of another. But I was never allowed time to settle into this new body as myself alone. I need that."

"I want that for you." He slides his hand into my hair and cradles the back of my head, kissing me firmly before pulling me against his chest. "Sleep, Princess. These decisions don't need to be made tonight."

Lark visits my dreams again, and the sight of her silver eyes and flowing dark hair makes me smile.

"It's been a while," I tell her, squinting when she fades in and out of being like a weak illusion.

"You can't take the throne from the Underworld." Her little voice sounds different tonight. Tired.

"Why are you telling me that?" I ask. I've learned, after all, that when Lark visits me in a dream, I need to listen.

"When the water rises, you need the white-eyed monster. Don't hide from him. And don't give up."

The image fades again, and I frown, trying to understand. "Can you show me?" I ask. "Explain why I need this monster?"

She fades away, and suddenly I'm floating above a room of sleeping children, like the infirmary in the capital but somewhere different. What does some monster have to do with the sleeping children?

"Lark?" I call.

"I'm so tired," she says, but I can see only her eyes this time, nothing more. "It's almost time for me to sleep."

"You don't mean— No." My throat feels too thick, and I cough on surging tears. "But you're half Wild Fae. How is this getting to you?"

"Don't give up until the monster takes you deeper, Princess."

She fades away, and I bolt awake, alert and panting.

The camp is quiet, and morning is close. Finn sleeps beside me, his breathing even, his arm looped around my waist.

White-eyed monster. What does that even mean? Is it some

sort of metaphor? But my confusion is overshadowed by my fear. We can't lose Lark to the Long Sleep. It would destroy Pretha.

I could wake Finn and tell him what I dreamed, but he needs the rest. We all do. If Lark is becoming one of the sleeping children, we need to fight harder than ever to get someone on that throne.

CHAPTER TWENTY-FIVE

AFTER ANOTHER HOUR OF FITFUL sleep, I wake to the first rays of dawn peeking through the trees. Kane and Tynan are sleeping on their bedrolls on the other side of our barely glowing fire. Finn's left our bed early this morning, and I imagine him sneaking through the woods with his wolves, already out scouting for breakfast.

I grab my cloak and shrug it on, moving quietly so I don't wake the others. I pull on my boots, not bothering to lace them, and make my way toward the trees, where I take care of business quickly before heading to the stream I spotted last night.

I'm in desperate need of a shower, but I'll settle for washing my face and hands. I stumble forward, groggy after sleeping on the hard ground. Jas used to joke that I could sleep anywhere, but my weeks in Faerie have made me soft. Or maybe my sleeplessness had less to do with needing a mattress and more to do with trying to resist the deliciously warm and perfectly solid body holding me.

The stream is smaller than I hoped, but running water is still a gift, so when I drop to my knees beside it, I let it run over my hands for a moment before splashing my face.

Leaves crunch behind me, and I smile. I knew it wouldn't take Finn long to find me.

"Good morning," I call, turning without rising, but it's not Finn.

A white-haired female in a blue cloak throws her hand out, and a burst of light barrels toward me. I reach for my power, throwing up a shield and blocking her before I'm even sure what's coming.

I jump to my feet and reach for the dagger at my hip, flinging it through the air toward her chest. She grabs the blade before it hits its mark and throws it to the side. Opening her palm, she sneers at the blood there.

"You human filth," she says, launching herself at me.

I fall back to my heels, blocking her first swing with my forearm. She lunges, and I sweep my leg out and around, bringing her to the ground. She reaches for her hip, but I pin her arm to the side with my booted foot before she can touch the knife strapped there.

I reach for my power, planning to trap her before she can overpower me. I could do it so easily, but I hesitate. *Finn. I can't risk Finn.* I put my weight on her arm instead.

"Who sent you?" I ask, meeting her icy blue gaze. She spits at me, and I grind my heel into her wrist. "What do you want?"

Her gaze catches on something over my shoulder, and her sneer turns to a smile. I turn my head to see what she's looking at, but I'm too slow, and the needle is plunged into my neck before I see it coming.

I scream as I go down, clawing at my neck and howling as the burn races like fire through my blood.

The male holding the needle has foggy white eyes, and he grabs my wrists roughly, yanking my arms behind me so tightly my shoulders scream in protest. Consumed by the agony snaking through my veins, I can't bring myself to fight him.

The female in the blue cloak hops to her feet, glaring at me. "You're lucky she wants you alive," she hisses. She wipes leaves and dirt off her cloak with her good hand and clutches her bloodied hand to her chest. "Where are the others?" she asks the male holding me.

"They're being handled. Let's go." A whistle comes from the trees, and the male holding me frowns up at them. "Hurry. There are—"

He doesn't get to finish his sentence before a snarl tears through the morning air and two massive wolves charge toward us through the trees. Dara and Luna. One grabs the arms of the male holding me, yanking him back, the other pounces at the female, returning her to the forest floor before sinking her teeth into the female's neck. She screams, but the wolf snarls in her face.

I right myself, reaching for my sword as more black-clad males pour from the trees, heading toward me. Dara and Luna howl and take off after them, not letting them get close to me.

Out of nowhere, arrows fly through the air one after another, taking out two men in black.

A third charges for me, and I hesitate with my hand on the

hilt of my dagger, waiting until he's within reach before I pull my blade from its sheath beneath my cloak and plunge it into his chest. He collapses, and I look up in time to see another arrow take out the male behind him.

Bodies are scattered on either side of the stream, and the wolves prowl over and around them, teeth bared as they scan the perimeter for more threats.

A crack echoes from the trees, and there's another flash of black. Finn is in front of me, breathing hard as he looks me over. "Are you okay?"

I nod then grimace. "They injected me."

His eyes flash and his nostrils flare as he scans the half dozen dead bodies around us. "Arya."

"No doubt," I whisper. "They said she wants me alive."

He's half feral, as twitchy and agitated as his wolves. "I'll kill her myself."

"Are Tynan and Kane okay?"

He nods. "They were ambushed, but they managed to get the upper hand."

I count three of my assailants with arrows through their heads.

"I heard you fighting her. Did you even try to use your magic before they could inject you?"

I swallow and drop my gaze to the ground. He already knows the answer to that question.

"Princess," he growls. "Please tell me you didn't choose a physical assault over a magical one because you were worried about *me*."

"Of course I was worried about you," I snap. "Why should I risk your life just to save my own?"

"I would've been fine. And anyway, they got me too. Tynan and Kane as well, if I had to guess. This group wouldn't have stood a chance against your power."

Shit, shit, shit. He's right.

"I'm stronger than you think, Abriella, and the more you practice using your power with precision, the less you have to worry about pulling from me at all, let alone pulling too much."

Swallowing, I nod. "I know."

"Do you?" His eyes narrow as he studies me. "Promise me you won't hesitate next time. If your life is danger — if a single hair on your pretty little head is in danger — you use your power and pull whatever you need from me. Got it?"

I stare at him, at those fierce silver eyes. "It's not that easy."

He arches a brow. "Do you want my pity, Princess?"

"Don't be an ass." I scowl, and Finn smirks.

He wraps his arms around me and pulls me into his chest. "Gods, you scared me."

I melt into him and start shaking. "I shouldn't have come out here alone. I'm sorry."

He kisses the top of my head. "I've got you." He strokes my back before pulling away. He's as shaken by this as I am, but he holds out a hand, palm up, and I take it. We walk hand in hand back to the campsite, where we're greeted by a handful of dead black-clad males, guts spilled, necks sliced open. The carnage would horrify me if the alternative weren't so unthinkable. I don't want to imagine what the queen would do if she successfully captured me, but worse is the idea that these bodies could've just as easily belonged to our friends.

The only survivors in the camp are a pissed-off Kane and a quietly brooding Tynan.

"I'm sorry," Finn says. "I stepped away for a minute because Dara was acting funny. They must've lured her away from the camp to distract me."

"I don't understand where they came from," Kane says. "No sound of their approach, no sign of horses."

"Goblins?" I ask.

He shakes his head. "No goblin is willing to transport anyone to these parts. And it would've taken several goblins to get them all here at once."

"They were likely masked by the queen," Finn says. "She's too powerful now—and that's not even accounting for the fire gems she's mined from beneath these mountains."

Kane turns to Finn. "They were prepared to kill us all."

Everyone but me, I think, but I don't say it aloud. It feels shameful—a reminder that my life continues to be a liability for my friends.

"Good thing we're better than they are," Finn says.

Tynan meets Finn's gaze, clenching his fists. "I think we need to reconsider our plans for the day."

I follow his gaze and realize that Kane's clutching his side. Blood seeps between his fingers.

I rush toward him, and he glares at Tynan. "I'm fine."

Finn frowns. "Why aren't you healing?"

"Because they shot us up with that shit," Tynan says.

"We need to get you home," Finn says. "We can't heal you, and the injection is keeping you from healing yourself. It's not safe for you out here."

"You saw the Crimson Fog yesterday," Kane says. "Time is of the essence. I am not so special that I can't be sacrificed for our court."

Finn closes his eyes and draws in a deep breath.

"You're right," I say. "And I agree — with the part about time. But I'm rather fond of your grumpy ass and would prefer to avoid an unnecessary sacrifice."

The corner of Kane's mouth hitches into a lopsided smile. "I'm not so easy to kill."

"Tynan and Kane should go back," I say, meeting Finn's eyes to make sure we're on the same page. He gives a subtle nod. "Finn and I can keep a lower profile if it's just the two of us, and you two can get to safety and give yourself some time to get the toxin out of your system."

"Don't be ridiculous," Kane grumbles.

"I agree with Abriella," Finn says. "That doesn't look good, Kane, and we don't need you slowing us down. At least not more than you typically do."

Kane flips him off, and Finn winks.

I turn to Tynan. "You'll help him?"

"I don't need help," Kane says.

"Sure you don't, buddy," Tynan says, patting Kane's arm and nodding to me. "You two should get out of here. Take the alternative route we discussed last night. I don't know where they came from or how they knew where to find us, but I don't like it."

"Agreed." Finn tilts his face to the sky and a hawk circling overhead. "Misha knows where to meet you, but Storm will follow you in case there's any trouble."

"His hawk?" I ask.

Finn nods, smirking grimly. "There are sometimes advantages to his compulsive spying."

"Be safe," I tell my friends. "I'm counting on seeing you again when I get back. Don't disappoint me."

Finn's already busy pulling things into his pack. "Hurry up, Princess. We have a long way to go today."

Thick snowflakes pelt the right side of my face, making me squint to see the path ahead. "Are we close?" I ask. The tug is stronger and stronger with every passing mile, but I have no idea what it should feel like when we're almost there, only that we're getting closer with each step.

Finn scans our surroundings and nods. "I think so. Maybe a couple more hours of hiking, and we should arrive at the Mother Willow. If I'm right, we should be deep enough in the mountains that we're on the Silent Ridge now." He passes me a canteen of water.

All I see is rocky path behind and more rocky path ahead. The only thing that's changed since we parted ways with Tynan and Kane is that it's gotten so cold I can no longer feel my toes in my boots or the right side of my face where the wind is pummeling me. "How can you tell?" I ask. Thanks to those injections, it's not like we can test our powers to see if we're in this magic-free zone.

He takes the canteen back and clips it onto his pack. "Can you feel Sebastian?" Finn asks. "The toxin doesn't interfere with the bond, but the Silent Ridge does."

"Oh." I hadn't thought of that. I mentally search for that ever-present connection. "It's gone." I close my eyes and draw in a long breath. All my feelings are my own, and it's a relief.

"You can't feel him at all?" Finn asks, stepping closer. "Even when you reach out and try?"

I mentally reach out to the other side of that wall I keep between us and shake my head. "Nothing."

He scans my face. "Good." He doesn't miss a beat before lowering his mouth to mine, hot and hungry and impatient.

Everything inside me thaws and sprouts to life like flowers pushing up through the dirt and meeting the sun after a long winter. In my belly, a thousand tiny butterflies stretch their wings under the warmth of his touch.

Angling his mouth over mine, Finn threads his fingers into my hair and tips my head back. I moan, taking a handful of his shirt in my fist, trying to get closer.

When Finn pulls back, his silver eyes are at half-mast and smoky with lust. "I've been waiting this whole trip to do that."

I bite back a smile. "Ah, so that's the real reason you came with me."

He flicks my nose. "Kane's complained so much about the tension between us, if I didn't know better, I'd think he got himself sliced open on purpose just so we could be alone tonight."

He continues up the path, and I stare dumbly at his back for a few beats as his words echo in my head. *Alone tonight.*

Alone.

"The sun will set soon," he says without turning back to me. "We should find somewhere warm to sleep."

"Right," I murmur, forcing my feet to start moving again. Two minutes ago I would've rejoiced over finding a spot to camp and cheered loudly for anything resembling *warmth,* but now nervous energy dances in my core.

We slept together last night and at Juliana's. It's not like this is so different.

Except it is.

We're alone, and my connection to Sebastian is nonexistent here. It's completely different.

Finn stops walking and whistles for his wolves. They return to their master and follow when he pushes through some underbrush at the side of the trail. "This way," he says, nodding for me to follow.

We tromp through the brush for several minutes before reaching the opening of a cave mouth. The wolves head in first, then return to the opening and sit, panting happily as they look up at Finn.

"There we go," he says, ducking his head to look inside while he scratches both wolves behind the ears. "This will be good."

"You want to *sleep* in there?" I cringe. "We don't know what lives in there."

He chuckles. "Abriella, child of Mab, killer of the false king, and future queen of the shadow court, scared of a little cave."

"I'm not scared. I'm . . . cautious." I roll back my shoulders.

"Do you truly think no creature has made this place their home? Just because nothing is in there now doesn't mean it won't return later."

His gaze slides over me. "I promise to keep you safe," he says softly.

Something shimmies low in my belly. His gaze seems to be promising something else entirely. Something much more exciting than simple protection. "Right after you," I say.

He laughs again and ducks inside. I follow, thanking the gods for my ability to see in the dark.

Though the opening is low to the ground, the cave is tall enough that I barely have to stoop as I make my way toward the back. I scan for signs that we're stealing a creature's home for the night, but find none.

Finn stays crouched as he drops his pack and unfolds his bedroll on the ground. He grabs mine and puts it in the only spot it will fit—right next to his.

"Would it be safe to build a fire?" I ask, shivering.

Finn scans the rocks above us and shakes his head. "Not in here. That much direct heat can cause the limestone to expand, and then the rock can crack and fall." He nods toward the entrance. "If I build it right out front, the cave should trap some of the heat."

"The snow will likely snuff it out before morning," I say, watching the heavy sheets fall.

"I'll keep you warm," he says.

My stomach flips, but before I can think of a response, he leaves the cave and begins gathering wood for a fire.

I peel off my soggy clothing and replace it with dry, clean layers. By the time I'm done, I can feel my toes again and there's a fire crackling just beyond the cave entrance.

Finn stands at the edge of the cave mouth, staring out at the fire and the blowing wind beyond.

"I'm surprised the wood wasn't too wet," I say, already feeling the warmth trickle into the cave.

"Lantern oil," he says. "Next best thing to magic for starting fires." A little smile tugs at the corner of his mouth.

"What's that smile about?" I ask, moving to join him. I pause for a beat, wondering what it would be like to wrap my arms around him from behind, to press my cheek to the middle of his back and feel his strength. Instead, I step up beside him and keep my hands to myself.

But Finn doesn't seem to share my trepidation about touching. He immediately turns and pulls me into his arms. On a sigh, my whole body goes loose. I fit here. We fit. In so many ways we haven't let ourselves explore.

He tucks my head under his chin and strokes my back. "This feels like a gift," he says roughly.

I pull back and look up at him. "What's that?"

"A night here." He searches my face, then traces the line of my jaw with his thumb. "A night with you. Where I don't have to share."

He dips his head and brushes his mouth against mine. It's not much as far as kisses go. Could even be deemed as innocent. Friendly. But I recognize it as the prelude it is, and it sends my heart racing. "A gift," he repeats.

I shiver. The sun is going down, and my fingers are numb from standing here only a minute.

"Come on." He takes my cold hand in his warm one and leads me back inside.

I sit on our bed, my arms wrapped around my knees, and he shucks his damp outermost layers before settling down onto the bedroll. "May I?" he asks, extending one arm as if he's about to wrap it around me.

I shiver harder this time, my teeth chattering. "It would be suicide to refuse," I say, but I'm not kidding either of us. We both know I want his arms around me for reasons that have nothing to do with the cold.

We lie down beside each other, and he pulls the blankets over us before wrapping his arm over my stomach and pulling my back against his chest. My muscles relax against his heat, loosening.

"I never thought I'd be *glad* to be visiting the Underworld," he says, his voice gruff as he strokes his thumb across my stomach. "But I'm grateful . . . to be alone. Without him. Where I can pretend you're mine."

My heart stutters. I roll so I can see his face. "And pretend *you're* mine?" I ask.

He shakes his head. "I'm always yours. That doesn't change."

My stomach flips at the words and how easily he gives them to me. "Maybe it's not so much pretend in either direction."

He sighs. "Out there, he's always between us," he says. "No matter how well you block, no matter how well you shield, he'll always feel you on some level. You'll always feel him. But here . . ." He closes his eyes. "In here it's just us. Even if it's just for tonight."

"It's not," I whisper, lifting a hand. His cheek feels like velvet beneath my fingertips. "I want to go to the Waters of New Life. I know you want me to think about it, but there's not much to consider. I made a mistake when I bonded with Sebastian, and since he's not willing to free me from the bond, I want to do it myself while I can." I brush my fingers through his curls. "I want to do it for myself, but I want you, and when the time is right, I want to be able to be free, not just for myself but for *us*."

He studies every inch of my face, his eyes glowing in the firelight that reflects off the cavern walls. Brushing the pad of his thumb over my bottom lip, he draws in a ragged breath. "How can you be here with me when I've done nothing to deserve you?"

"I don't think love is about what we deserve. It's an opening of our hearts, not a judgment we make. But Finnian, if I were judging you, I would find you completely deserving of this . . . and more. Your people don't follow you because of who your father was. They follow you because of who *you* are. And they're your friends, not because of what you can offer them. They're your friends because they know being around you makes them better and makes their life worthwhile."

"I've made terrible mistakes, Abriella."

"We all have," I whisper. "But your mistakes are part of who you are, and I don't mind them so much. I happen to be in love with *exactly* who you are. And that has nothing to do with this tethering." I drag my bottom lip between my teeth and search for my courage. "Whatever magical connection we have was what drew me to you that first night we met, but it is who you are and the choices you make that made me fall in love with you."

He closes his eyes and presses his forehead to mine, drawing in a deep, shuddering breath. "I love you too. I desperately want to show you how much."

"Then why aren't you kissing me?" I ask. I barely finish the words before his mouth crushes mine and he rolls me to my back, shifting until his thighs bracket one of my legs.

His kiss is like a brand, marking me more permanently than the rune inked on my skin from my bond with Sebastian. Every sweep of his tongue makes the worry knotting my muscles unfurl, guides me to let go for just a minute.

When he breaks the kiss, he doesn't go far. His mouth is so close to mine I can feel his smile. "Have I told you that you taste just like you smell?"

I laugh. "After the day we've had, I'm not sure that's a good thing."

"Like cherries and moonlight."

"You didn't kiss me that night," I say, rubbing my hands up and down his back. "In the shower."

"No. I didn't."

"Why not? I asked you to."

"Because I wanted your kiss more than anything." His voice is rough. "I knew you were attracted to me from that first night we met. Between the drugs and that attraction, it would've been easy to take what you were offering and work it to my advantage, but I wanted you to ask me when your mind was clear. And I didn't want the first time I kissed you to be about the crown. Even if it should've been. So I didn't kiss you. Even though I wanted to."

"You did kiss my neck."

His smile is slow and devious. "I'm not a saint, Princess. I had to taste you."

Need coils hot and low in my belly, and I grab the hem of his shirt and pull, tugging it off over his head. Once it's gone, my hands explore every inch of his powerful chest, his strong back, the softer skin at the waistband of his pants. "I think I mentioned wanting to taste you too," I say, stroking the spot over his pelvic bone where I know a bisected five-pointed star is forever tattooed on his skin.

Chuckling, he rests his weight on his forearms while looking down at me. "Trust me, that's not something I'd be able to forget." He pulls a lock of hair between two fingers and smiles as he twirls it around his fingers. "This haircut . . ."

"It's ridiculous," I say.

"It's cute."

"Yes, that's what every lustful female wants to be. *Cute.*"

He laughs. "You're certainly other things too," he murmurs. "Shall I compose a list?"

"Hardened, bitter, *boring,*" I say. I try to sound light—joking—but my tone reveals far too much of what I really feel.

"Stunning, powerful, persistent, *breathtaking,*" he says.

I bite my bottom lip and shift beneath him before reaching up and toying with one of his curls in return.

His eyes are hooded as he gazes down at me. "The night in the shower . . . do you remember what you said to me when I carried you to bed?"

I shake my head. I have no memory of that night beyond the shower. "You said I asked you to stay."

He nods. "You did. And then you told me that I made you feel as safe as a starry night sky."

My cheeks heat. "Sounds like I was pretty pathetic."

He shakes his head. "No. You don't understand. You were saying everything I wanted to hear. I was pathetic because of how much I wanted to believe the drugs had nothing to do with your confessions."

"It's true, though," I whisper. "I have always drawn strength from you."

"That's the tether."

I shake my head. "Not just magically. I find strength in the way you believe in me. In our friendship. It's a strength that has nothing to do with my power."

His silver eyes blaze into mine. "It's the same for me. I never thought I could feel this again." He swallows. "I didn't think I wanted to."

I shiver beneath him.

"Are you cold?"

I shake my head. "Not anymore."

"Me neither." He traces my lips with his thumb, and I can't get over the awe in his eyes, the adoration. How could this beautiful, powerful, kind male be so grateful to be here with me?

Pushing up onto one hand, he slowly unlaces the front of my shirt, letting it fall open and exposing my breasts before dipping his head. The air is cool, but his mouth is hot as he flicks his tongue over my peaked nipple. I arch my back up off the hard ground and moan as heat and pleasure zip through my blood.

"Do you have any idea what it was like to know you were

sleeping in my bed at the Unseelie palace? To see you there when I'd imagined it so many times? I can't wait until I can have you there again. I've dreamed so many times of holding you there, having you in my arms as we sleep under the stars together." He nuzzles my neck, and I arch into him, loving the feel of my breasts against his bare chest, needing more pressure between my legs.

"Finn," I breathe, dragging my hands up and down his back. "I love you." I just want to say it over and over again. Until he feels it in his heart, until he believes it and believes he's worthy of that love.

"I love you too."

"Do we have . . ." I bite my lip. "Is there a tonic we can take once we return to the capital—to prevent pregnancy?"

"Yes." His mouth sweeps over mine so sweetly. "But we don't have to do anything tonight. We have our whole lives ahead of us, we can—"

"Please?" I shift under him, pulling my knees up on either side of his hips and urging him to settle between my legs. I groan at the feel of him through the layers between us. "I don't want to wait."

He grins down at me in the darkness. "I don't either," he says, "but I would. If you really plan to swim in the Waters of New Life, we'll have all the time we need, and every opportunity to—"

I thread my fingers into his hair and pull him down to me. He smiles into the kiss, and his hands begin a leisurely exploration of my stomach, my sides, my breasts. His thumb skims across my pebbled nipples.

I lift my hips, rocking into him and showing him with the

rhythm of my body just where I need this to go. But Finn won't be rushed. He trails kisses down my neck, across my collarbone, nipping at my shoulders and the curve of my breasts and down over my stomach. He trails his tongue down my stomach to just below, where he sucks lightly at the sensitive skin beneath my navel. I gasp.

He nudges my thighs wider and nuzzles his nose between my legs. "Let me kiss you here." He opens his mouth, pressing his tongue against me through the fabric.

I can't breathe. His big hands trail down my sides, and his fingers hook into my pants and peel them off me. I barely have time to catch my breath before his mouth is on me again, big hands on my inner thighs, holding me open for him as his tongue dances along my most sensitive skin, his mouth alternately teasing and demanding until I'm whimpering and incoherent.

Every inch of me is hot and alive and needy, and I tug on his hair, needing him closer but also needing more—more of this, more of him, more of this night. He stays put, worshipping me and murmuring his love and his desire until I'm finally flying over an edge like I never have before.

Flying and falling and not even a little afraid because I know he'll catch me. I know we'll catch each other.

When he kisses his way back up my body, I slowly settle back into myself. I'm breathless and sated as his mouth finds mine again, but I slide my hands down his sides and shove his pants down his hips.

He grunts approvingly into my mouth and helps me peel away the last of his clothes. When he finally settles back over me, I shift my hips, urging him to slide into me. Instead, he props himself on his elbows and studies my face. "I didn't think I'd ever feel this again." Dipping his head, he sweeps a kiss across my lips. "I didn't think I could." He pushes up and looks down at me. "I was fighting for my people but barely living. Until you entered the portal. Until you looked me in the eye and asked me to dance with you. Nothing's been the same since. I hope it's never the same again."

I hook my legs behind his back and pull him down. "I love you, Finn." I tuck my hips and find him between my legs, slowly leading him into me.

His breath leaves him in a rush and his eyes close for a beat. I revel in the feel of our connection. There's no room here for doubt or fear of what's to come. No room for anything but hope. Anything but love — and I feel so much of it I close my eyes to revel as we move together.

"Abriella," he breathes. "Abriella, open your eyes."

I obey, and find starlight shining all around us, bright and luminous, as if the cave has become the night sky itself. As if there weren't a storm raging outside. "Beautiful," I murmur, but my gaze leaves the stars to lock on his eyes.

He slides a hand down my body, to my hip, squeezes, before he drives into me again, deeper than before. "Stunning," he says, but he isn't looking at the stars either. We're locked onto each other in the middle of the mountains before the most dangerous day of our lives. We have only each other, and it's more than enough.

"The stars are gone," I whisper later. We're tangled up together under the blankets, both on our sides, staring at each other. We've been in this position for so long, I'm not sure when the stars disappeared from around us.

Finn rolls to his back, and I watch him in the flickering light as he studies the rock formations that seem to drip from the cave ceiling. "I think they may have only been there while we were making love." He smirks. "Which might just be the cockiest thing I've ever said."

My laugh comes out in a snort. "But there's no magic here," I say. "Where did it come from?"

He gathers me against his side and smiles. I've never seen him look so happy. "I think we were wrong about this place. Magic isn't gone here. It's just different — detached from us."

"Sometimes different is good," I whisper.

"I'd have to agree." He presses his lips to the top of my head and breathes me in. "We should sleep."

My breath catches as I remember my dream of Lark. I'd planned to tell Finn about it this morning, but with the attack on the camp and Kane's injuries, I'd completely forgotten. "Lark visited my dream last night."

"She did?"

"She said something about a white-eyed monster saving me?" I shake my head, not remembering clearly. "Maybe it was metaphorical. What would a white-eyed monster symbolize to her?"

He hums. "I'm not sure. I'm not sure she thinks like that."

"Maybe not. But that wasn't the part of the dream that has me worried. She said she was tired, and she faded away from my dream before we were done talking. I think . . ."

"You think she's going to fall into the Long Sleep?" he asks.

I hug him tightly. "I hope not."

"Pretha hasn't let herself think of it. That's part of why she left Lark at Castle Craige. Being an Unseelie child is so dangerous right now, she wanted to focus on Lark's Wild Fae blood."

"Tomorrow we see Mab," I say. "That's the best we can do for her right now."

He tenses for a beat, then relaxes again. "I think so. I know it won't be easy, but I believe she'll have the answers we need. I haven't felt this hopeful in a long time."

"So why now?" I ask. "What's changed to make brooding Finn feel hopeful?"

He presses another kiss to the top of my head. "We have *you* now, Princess."

"Still with that nickname?" I smile. "I thought you would've figured it out by now. I'm not a princess. I never was."

"I know," he whispers into my hair. His lips brush my temple, just a ghost of a kiss, but the warmth laps over me like a summer tide rolling to shore. "I know that's not who you really are. I think I knew it the first time I saw you. You're no princess. You're my queen."

CHAPTER TWENTY-SIX

The portal is exactly where we were told it would be: in the cave beneath the roots of the Mother Willow at the northernmost peak of the Goblin Mountains.

It took us less than an hour to hike here this morning and find it, and less than thirty seconds to slice our palms open, mix our blood together, and open it. Shivering, I stare into the murky darkness awaiting us on the other side of this ring of light.

I woke up so content and hopeful, with Finn's arms wrapped around me, that until this moment I forgot to be afraid. Forgot that we would be stepping into an unknown world where we will face dangerous creatures, where we will be judged, and where we'll be locked forever if we're found lacking.

I can't let myself look at Finn. He's a reminder of what I could lose if this all goes to hell. Instead, I focus on the memories of those sleeping children and walk through the glowing ring and into the gloom.

Finn follows, coming to stand at my side. The Underworld is full of mist and shadow. Typically, I would feel right at home in a place like this, with plenty of opportunities to hide and sneak around, but every inch of me screams that I don't belong here. The portal is a beacon of light behind us, and every inch of my being wants to turn around — to reassure myself that it's there, that we can get back out — but I recall Juliana's words. If Mab needs me to prove that I will persevere, then I will. I force myself to face forward.

Finn offers his hand, palm up, and I consider refusing for a moment. I'm not ready to reveal my weaknesses to anyone or anything that might be watching. But we're stronger together — down here and everywhere else — so I take it, and he gives it a single, firm squeeze and we begin walking.

The ground creaks, and the sky moans. The earth shifts on either side of us, surging up to form mountains — and a path between them.

"I guess we're going this way," Finn says softly.

This time I squeeze *his* hand, and we walk silently down the newly formed corridor. With every step, the light from the portal behind us dims, but we don't dare look back. We don't even speak of it. The only sound is the wind in this unnatural tunnel and the rocks shifting beneath our boots as we walk.

"I've been here before," I whisper. The wind carries my words in circles around our heads, and they repeat three times, softer and softer before falling away. "The time my mother took me to the beach. We came here."

He squeezes my hand tighter. "You recognize it? It looks familiar?"

"It didn't look a thing like this, but it *feels* familiar. I know I've been here before." And Mab—was she the woman I remember my mother talking to? The one who scared me?

Time feels like it moves in slow motion, but I focus on putting one foot in front of the other. Sometimes we climb. Sometimes we descend. Sometimes the terrain is so flat and repetitive that I think the monotony itself might break me.

There's no sign of the monsters the others warned us about. Just endless, bleak desolation.

When it feels like we've been walking too long in an endless loop and my instincts beg me to run back to the portal, I think of those children, of Lark, of all the innocents who will be imprisoned and enslaved if we don't continue.

When I'm sure that we've walked miles and miles to nowhere, the towering rock on either side of us falls away into the mist and reveals a dark and gloomy forest.

Mist winds around the trees and crawls among the roots. My heart races.

"You okay?" Finn asks.

I nod and continue on. "If I'm Mab's descendant, does that mean Jas is too?" I ask, if only to give me something to talk about that will take my mind off this unnatural place.

"I don't really know," he says. "If Mab's blood came from one of your parents, I suppose so."

My lips twitch. "Before Mordeus imprisoned her and made her so afraid of this world, Jas would've really gotten a kick out of this—the idea that we're descendants of some great faerie queen."

"*The* Great Faerie Queen," Finn says. "And I'm sorry—sorry that Mordeus hurt her, made her afraid of us."

I swallow hard. "So am I. But I hope . . . I hope one day I get to see her again. Somehow."

"I'll make sure of it. We can teach you to glamour yourself—or have a priestess do it for you." He squeezes my hand. "I know what she means to you."

"She's all I had for so long." I watch my feet and take step after step. I feel like every sacrifice I've ever made for my sister has brought me to this moment. That I was preparing for this—whatever is next for me, whatever I can do to save this kingdom.

"Tell me about Jas," Finn says, stepping ahead of me, pulling his blade from the sheath at his side to cut through a web of vines in our path. "What's she like?"

I smile. "She's wonderful. Jas makes everyone around her happier. She's loved stories as long as I remember. Even when she was a toddler and we didn't think she could understand, she'd sit curled in my arms as my mother told me about the magical land of Faerie. I think Jas liked the sound of Mother's voice and the cadence of the tales she'd weave."

His gaze, always so busy searching for threats, stalls on my face for a moment. "Do you think your mother knew that you had a role to play in our world?"

"I don't know." I shrug. If I'm right and I've been here before—if my mother brought me to the Underworld—then surely she knew something.

A hawk made of mist swoops down in front of our faces. I jerk my head back but don't dare slow my feet. Finn squeezes my hand.

"Is any of this real?" I ask.

"That depends on your definition of real," he says. "Just don't look down."

Because he said it, I do, and there, on either side of the mist at our feet, the ground has fallen away, revealing a massive drop into nothingness. My steps falter.

"Eyes up, Princess," he says, gently tugging me along.

We walk and walk, until my legs burn, until I doubt that we should have come at all.

I have hardened my resolve for the hundredth time when the mist and the shadows fall away and the mountains re-form around us. Until suddenly we're standing in the center of a— "This is a throne room," I whisper, eyeing the stone dais before us and the gnarled throne of tree roots that sits atop it.

"Queen Mab," Finn says, tilting his face up to the skies that are neither skies nor ceiling. "I am Prince Finnian, son of Oberon, and this is Abriella, child of Mab. It is she who holds the power of the Unseelie crown, and I am her tethered match. We come seeking your guidance so that we may save your kingdom."

The throne is empty, and in the next moment black flames surround it, flickering to reveal the hazel-eyed female. Her hair is the color of a blazing fire, and it flows down to her waist, weaving in and out of the black flames like some strange dance.

I've been here before. Seen those black flames before.

On her eighteenth birthday, Mab said, and the words hurt my ears. *She will become her true self. Do not try to prevent it.*

Beside me, Finn drops to one knee, and I am so shocked I don't think to follow until he tugs on my hand.

"You may rise," Mab says without moving her lips. Her voice isn't something I hear with my ears, but an echo in my head. "I so rarely get visitors. Come closer and let me see your faces."

Finn and I slowly stand and take two steps closer.

The black flames around Mab retract. Only now do I see how pale her skin is — almost gray — and her lips bloodred. She cocks her head at Finn and smiles ruefully. "You have your father's eyes, but that skin, like the desert sands, that comes from your mother. She wasn't the one your grandparents picked to rule beside your father."

Finn swallows, but I feel tension rolling off him. "She was a good queen nonetheless," he says.

"Too bad she had to die so young." Mab's smile steals any sincerity from her statement, and one thing is clear: she might want the best for her people, might be the only one who can help us save her court, but she is not the benevolent ancestor I imagined. Child-me was right to be afraid.

I squeeze Finn's hand, willing him to take a breath, urging him not to let her bait him.

"You look just like my granddaughter," Mab says, those glossy red lips curving into a siren's smile as she turns to me.

"I was told that I'm a child of Mab. Is this so? Am I a descendant of your granddaughter?"

"Yes. The beloved Queen Reé. She watched all her children and her children's children be slaughtered by the Seelie Court, and she knew she couldn't pass the crown to her own without risking the end of our line altogether. So she transformed her last child into a human and sent her to the human realm, where she would be safe, so that generations later, when the court needed it the most, you could return to us and save my people and our land from being completely annihilated."

"We thought your line was gone," Finn says. "We were never told."

"The prophecies were there," she says. "Didn't you hear them? Whispers of a queen who appears as an outsider, one who will balance the sun and shadow and end the war?"

I draw in a breath. "A *queen?*" That was the prophecy Sebastian talked about when he justified his plans to take the throne. But he believed it would be a *king.*

Mab flashes that beautifully creepy smile. "It is the females in my line who have the true power. Of course a *queen.* Your mother was to tell you everything when you turned sixteen, and then when you turned eighteen, the suppressed magic in your blood would've been freed and turned you." She barks out a sound I think might be a laugh. "If you'd never bonded with Arya's son, you never would've needed that Potion of Life. Your blood would've done it for you without the painful death."

I shake my head. "I don't understand. My mother was human. If she was your blood as well, why didn't she turn fae at eighteen?"

"Because it wasn't time," Mab says. "Not for her or for any before her. They weren't the promised ones. They were not *you.* So that which made her fae was suppressed, just as it's been in you and your sister."

Her words slowly settle into my bones, as if they were always there. "My mother knew this."

"And Oberon too, the night he saved you," Mab says. "Her

blood was part of what drew him to her to begin with, though he didn't know it then. When he was able to return home after the long night in the human realm, he wanted her to come with him. She denied him because she knew her role. She knew she'd be the mother of the next great shadow queen. She knew Oberon's realm would need you more than she needed him. Only when you were dying did he finally understand the truth."

Finn studies the earth at his feet and shakes his head. "He was protecting the court after all," he says, and I can hear the relief in his voice, can tell that he needed to know this about his father.

"He would've had more time if Queen Arya hadn't interfered."

"Arya—she knew I was your descendent?" I ask.

"Gods no. The power that masked you was far too strong to be detected by a descendent of *Deaglan.* Her seer prophesized that the eldest daughter of King Oberon's lover would end her, cut into her heart with her own blade. So Arya sent her nasty sprites through the portal to start that fire. They set a trap so the house would collapse just as you ran for the door. But you chose to save your sister first, and because you put her before yourself, you weren't where they planned the worst of the collapse. Because you saved your sister, Oberon was able to save you by passing you his crown, though years earlier than planned."

My heart races, and I backtrack in my mind and reconstruct a puzzle I already thought I understood.

"I thought you would figure it out when you were able to sit upon the Throne of Shadows," Mab says. Her hazel eyes, so much like mine, burn into me. I feel that she can see right through me and into my past. "The throne was yours. You could've kept it. Though ruling as a mortal might've been . . . tricky."

I shake my head. "I didn't know. Why didn't you tell me?"

"Those of us in the Twilight are unable to speak directly with the living unless they make the journey here. You're here now only because the priestesses united their power to send you the message, despite the traitor High Priestess's efforts to keep you away."

"The Unseelie Court is dying," I say. "You say I have a role to play, but I cannot sit on the throne without the crown, and Sebastian cannot sit on the throne without the power. Tell us how to get someone on the throne."

Her smile is wide this time, showing a mouth of black teeth and, between them, endless darkness. "If he forfeits his life, he could surrender that crown to you, my child."

Snakes slither through those flickering flames around the base of her throne. Their hissing sounds like a warning, a ticking clock.

"That can't be the only way," I say.

"It depends what question you want answered," she says. "Do you want to know how to get a ruler on the Throne of Shadows, or do you want to know how to save the kingdom?"

I meet Finn's gaze and see frustration brimming in his eyes.

"Help us save your court," he snaps. "That is why we're here."

The snakes lunge toward us, fangs exposed, hissing louder now. "You need more than just crown, power, and throne to save the shadow court," she says. "Queen Arya has gotten too powerful. You need to bring balance between the courts. The solution demands sacrifice."

Finn goes pale. "You can't mean for Abriella to—"

"Sacrifice herself? No." She cocks her head to the side. "She would, though. Do you realize that? Her love for you would not be enough to keep her. If she believed Arya's son could be the ruler the Unseelie need, she would already be down here with me." She tsks. "Foolish girl."

"Please help us," I whisper. My voice feels hoarse, as if I've been screaming. "Children are dying. The *court* is dying."

"Yes, because Queen Arya's power is too great. Even if Prince Ronan were willing to make the sacrifice, his mother would still grow more and more powerful, and my precious court would still die. She must be dealt with."

"Your solution is to kill Arya?" Finn growls. "How are we supposed to do that? She's too well guarded, too well hidden, and too powerful."

"More powerful every day," Mab agrees. "The Court of the Sun has grown too strong, and continued imbalance will only make her stronger."

"You want me to ask Sebastian to sacrifice himself just so *I* can sit on the throne, but you're telling me even that won't be enough if we don't kill Arya."

"Yes, girl. You must also kill the queen. Only *you* can."

"What if I can't?" I stare at this ancestor of mine. "I'm nothing special. I'm just a girl who—"

"Who loved so deeply she braved an unknown realm to save her sister," Mab says. She takes a long, slow breath and looks me over. "*I* was just a mother who would've given anything to save her son. It is our *love*, my child, that makes us fit to rule, but it also makes us wicked. It was my love that drove me to curse a kingdom and yours that led you to deceive your lover by stealing from the Seelie Court. Don't lose sight of that darkness in you. Let it serve the light."

I want to *scream.* We came all this way for her to tell us what we already knew? For her to suggest that we convince Sebastian to do something I couldn't live with, even if he *were* willing?

"But . . ." she says after a long pause. "If you cannot bring yourself to sacrifice your bonded partner's immortality and find a way to kill Queen Arya, there is another way."

My heart races, as if it's trying to get a head start back toward the portal. "How?"

"When I created the Throne of Shadows, I already wore the crown, so I tied the throne to my soul-bonded partner."

Finn steps forward, in front of me. "Your partner?"

"The throne recognizes a bonded pair as one — as long as the bond has been solidified by the magic within the River of Ice."

"No," Finn breathes. His beautiful face has gone pale.

I look back and forth between Finn and Mab, not understanding.

"The River of Ice doesn't just solidify the bond. It ties your lives together. So if anything ever happened to Sebastian . . . if he were to die . . ."

"Then I would too," I whisper.

"Yes. And if you trek to those holy waters together and solidify your bond so that it may never be undone, so that your lives are inextricably bound together, both you and the male wearing the crown may take the throne — together but never apart. In this way, the crown and its power are worn by two but never truly divided. Having Prince Ronan's Seelie blood on the throne along with mine would bring the courts back into balance."

I don't move, but I feel like I've been knocked back three steps.

Mab turns her gaze on Finn. "As her tethered, I trust you'll support whatever path she chooses. I trust you'll grant her the power she needs to follow through with her choices."

Finn's shoulders straighten and his jaw hardens. "Of course. It will be my honor." When he turns, there's a hollowness in his eyes that I haven't seen since he told me about Isabel dying in his arms. He's spent his entire life preparing to take that throne, and now he has to give it up to Sebastian. And he has to give me up too.

I graze my fingers across his wrist. "Finn."

"We should go."

"*You* go," Mab says, nodding at him. "But I need to speak with my child for a moment."

Before Finn can do anything, she waves a hand and he disappears.

I gasp.

"He'll be there when I'm done with you."

"What do you need?" I ask. I'm still trying to process everything she's told me—trying to wrap my mind around what my future might look like. It's not as if I can turn my back on this kingdom.

"You crave mortality." She cocks her head and narrows her eyes. "Or . . . you *did*. You're changing quickly. Perhaps you no longer care that you already carry the answer you hoped for."

"Don't speak in riddles. Tell me how to save the court."

"Save the court. Is *that* what you want most? More than a short human life in your cruel mortal world?"

The question feels important. Heavy and fragile at the same time. "Saving the court is what I want most."

She nods once, with a finality that makes me feel as if some major part of my fate has been decided. "You are not ready to rule."

I nearly cry out in frustration but bite my lip. "I will do what I must to save the court."

"But you will fail if you don't accept the darkness in you. Why do you refuse it?"

"Refuse what?"

"Your shadow self."

My breath catches. *My shadow self.* Images flash through my mind. The mutilated corpses of the orc guards around the fire. The bloody knife glistening in the flames. The locks of Juliana's hair on my nightstand.

"It's a weapon that lies in wait, and you refuse to wield it. Loving Abriella. Devoted Abriella. Caring, dutiful Abriella. There's another side of you too. Your shadow side. And she has *power.* All you have to do is be willing to accept the parts of you that you pretend aren't there. Accept the darkness, and she will wake, and she will *serve you.*"

"I don't need her."

"Yes, you do." Mab smiles. "She holds the parts of you that are wicked. That are jealous and angry. The selfish parts that will take what you *want* for once." She cocks her head and narrows her eyes as if she can see right through me. Her lips twist, and I can't tell whether she's amused or disgusted. "Just remember, if you think to sacrifice Prince Ronan so that you may be bonded with your tethered match, you'll need to find another way to balance the power between the courts. Kill the queen, or watch her destroy the shadow court."

"I won't sacrifice him." I shake my head. "I'm not that selfish."

"I know," she says, her voice turning melodious. "And so does the queen. That's why you need your shadow self. Because *she* isn't so tenderhearted. *She* isn't afraid to use the tools at her disposal."

"What tools?"

"Finnian, son of Oberon, is more powerful than his father and his father before him. You can use that power. With access to his magic, you'll never be powerless."

"And risk his life?"

"Loving Abriella. Devoted Abriella. Caring, dutiful Abriella," she repeats, and there's no missing the mocking lilt to the words. "Your court needs wicked Abriella, maleficent Abriella."

"You have me confused with my sister. I am *not* goodness personified."

"Of course not," she says.

Just as suddenly as he disappeared, Finn reappears by my side. Gone from his expression is the reverence for this ancient ruler, and in its place is a barely restrained glare that says he has no tolerance for being separated from me.

"Go now," she says. "The monsters have come out to play, and they would like nothing more than to destroy your portal before you can reach it."

Horror snakes through me at the thought of being trapped here. "Can't you protect it?"

"The portal straddles the planes, and I cannot touch anything beyond the Underworld. Go!" She disappears, and the walls of the otherworldly throne room fall away. Finn takes my hand, and we turn back the way we came. I don't know how fast we need to move, but it took us what felt like hours to reach this spot.

Finn nudges me forward. "Run," he says.

I obey, turning my feet under me as fast as I can, feeling him just behind me with every step. The Underworld plays its games with us as we tear our way back to the portal. Mountains rise and fall on either side of us and shift beneath our feet. Oceans form from the depths, and waves surge up our legs, threatening to pull us back with them.

We keep going. I don't dare slow down until I can see the portal in the distance, the ring of light calling us home. I can't catch my breath, and I can't stop.

The mist around us turns to rain, relentless, pounding rain that cuts into my cheeks and seeps its cold into my bones. The mountains quake. My boots are soaked through, and when I look down, rising water has reached my ankles.

Finn swallows and scans the mist. "My father's here," he whispers. "I feel him."

I look all around us, but all I see is lashing rain, rising water, and dreary skies in all directions.

"I understand now," he says, slowing to a stop. He's not talking to me. He's speaking to someone I can't see.

The glow from the portal flickers, then dims.

"Finn," I say, tugging on his hand. If I had a chance to speak with my mother again, I would take it a heartbeat, but we need to get out of here.

"Shit," Finn shouts, his eyes on the water that's now knee-deep. "Run!"

I don't need to be told twice. I race toward the dimming light of the portal. My legs can't move fast enough through water that's surging up toward my thighs. Then I'm swimming.

I glance back to make sure Finn's behind me, but he's stopped again. His face is tilted up and his eyes shut. "Go!" His voice is strong, but his body . . . he's fading away. Like a cloud that's dissipating in the light of the sun.

"Not without you. Hurry!"

"I'm stuck. The rocks shifted. Go!"

I swim toward him, and he shouts at me. "Damn it, Abriella! You don't have much time."

The portal glows behind me, beckoning to me, but I can't turn my back on Finn. I won't. Mab's taunting words echo in my head, but I ignore them. The girl who came to a new world to save her sister is the same one who won't turn her back on the one she loves.

I take a deep breath and dive, swimming down to the rocks around Finn's feet. The icy water rushes around me in a powerful current, and I have to swim hard to stay in place. One second of weakness, and it will tear me away from him.

I loop one arm around his thigh, then use my other hand to tug the rocks trapping his other leg. They're too big. Too heavy. I have to use both hands, kicking against the current the whole time. My fingers are numb and won't work properly, but I keep pulling away the rocks that keep magically reappearing.

A keening cry rips through the water, and when I open my eyes to look, I see eerie white eyes coming straight for me. I pull and pull until this strange place recognizes my persistence, and the rubble trapping his legs falls away.

Hands slide under my arms and Finn's yanking me to the surface. "Go!" he shouts, shoving me forward, toward the portal—toward the monster.

I gasp for breath, shaking my head. "Something's coming from that way. We need to go around."

"We don't have time." He wraps one arm around me and pulls through the water with one arm.

"I'm fine." I wiggle free and swim beside him. My legs and arms are numb, and every instinct says we should be swimming away from those eyes, not toward them, but I force myself to keep moving toward that ever-dimming portal light.

"We're almost there," Finn says.

Pain slices through my thigh and I'm dragged under.

Deeper, deeper. Until the pressure's building in my ears and my lungs burn.

Deeper.

I can't see the creature that has me, but judging by the mouth around my leg, it's massive. It weaves around rocks and into the current until we're entering an underwater cavern. I search with my hands until I find a rock with sharp edges and I slam it right into one of those creepy white eyes.

The creature releases me, and I waste no time following our

path back out of the cavern. Finn meets me halfway, wrapping an arm around me and dragging me toward the surface.

The air burns when I pull it into my lungs—burns like poison, burns badly enough that I can't force myself to take another breath.

"I've got you!" Finn pulls me onto a rocky ledge above the churning water. He lays me down and stares into my eyes.

"Breathe, damn it!" he shouts, those silver eyes too full of anguish.

And I do. I breathe. And it's utter agony. I want to sink back into the water and go to sleep. It hurts so much.

"Again!" Finn commands.

I obey, once, twice, three more times. Each breath hurts a little less.

Only then does he tear his gaze off me and look around.

The world spins, but I try to follow his lead, to see what he's seeing. The sky above us isn't dark. I can see in the dark. This black is nothingness. It's a void.

Water laps onto the rocky ledge, and the glowing portal in the distance—

"Where is it?" My voice is raw, my words more choking sounds than words, but he doesn't need me to explain.

"It's gone," he whispers. "The portal is closed." His gaze drops to my thigh, and his expression turns grim.

Only when I see the deep, bloody gash in my leg do I feel the pain of it. Numbness and adrenaline had masked it, but now it aches and burns and throbs, and there's *so much blood.*

I'm going to die here.

CHAPTER TWENTY-SEVEN

WHEN THE WATER RISES, YOU need the white-eyed monster. Don't hide from him.

That creature that almost drowned me—was that the one Lark foresaw?

Don't give up until the monster takes you deeper, Princess.

"I think there's another way," I whisper, blindly reaching for Finn's hand. "The white-eyed monster has the path out—there must be another portal deep beneath the surface, another way."

Finn's eyes glow in the darkness. "Did Mab tell you that?"

"Lark," I say softly. "In my dream."

He takes a breath and looks at my leg again. "Can you swim with that?"

I shake my head. "Go without me."

"The hell I will," he growls.

"I will only slow you down. I don't know how deep the cavern goes or how far you'll have to swim. You can't make it if you drag me along."

He yanks off his jacket and tears it apart, making one long strip. "You have a choice: you can swim or I can drag you," he says, wrapping my thigh. The binding is tight, painfully so, but the blood stops flowing.

The rocks around us tremble and crack, as if the world itself is falling apart.

"Go!" I shout. "And keep swimming, even if you lose me." I nudge him toward the water.

His eyes blaze as they connect with mine. He cups my face in both hands. "Don't you *dare* die on me, Princess. We are going to find that portal together, and we're going to come out the other side. You understand?"

The rocks beneath us quake again, and more water gushes from the cracks. "Finn . . ."

"Do you *understand?*"

He's not going anywhere until I agree, so I nod.

"Good. Let's go."

Standing, he leads me to my feet. Then he takes a deep breath and dives in. I follow, and it feels like diving into a sheet of ice. Every sense is assaulted by the sharp cold, every inch of my skin feels like it's being stabbed with tiny frozen needles, and every instinct tells me to resurface.

Before I can consider it, Finn drags me forward, and we're swimming back toward the dark mouth of the cave. Back toward those deathly white eyes and that massive maw. I wrap my numb fingers around my blade and swim harder, digging for energy I don't have.

Finn leads the way into the murky water, knife in hand, and I follow, looking for those eyes. There's nothing but black ahead—not darkness, but a void, like the sky above us. Finn grabs my hand and points, and I follow as he turns to the left. Then I see it—another ridge and the surface of water—air within the cave. When we break the surface, we gasp in unison.

Finn wipes the water out of his eyes before scanning our surroundings. "I can barely tell which way is up," he mutters.

"Deeper. Lark said we have to go deeper." My teeth chatter. It's all I can do to tread water. Nausea surges, and my pulse feels erratic. "If I don't make it, promise me you'll keep trying."

Finn glares at me, the broody shadow prince back in full effect. "I'm going to pretend you didn't just say that *right after* promising me you wouldn't die."

I try to laugh, but it comes out more like a whimper.

"You ready?" he asks. His voice is rough too. The water swishes around us.

"Something's coming," I say.

"Swim and swim hard." It's a command I dare not ignore.

We dive under together and swim. I let Finn lead the way by whatever intuition he has. Because he's right. This place is disorienting.

My legs feel like blocks of ice, my arms like dead weight, my lungs so tight they could burst. If I doubt his confidence for a single moment, if I think there's any chance we might be swimming in the wrong direction, I'll give up.

When we surface again, the water is so close to the top of the cavern that there's only room for our mouths and noses to grab air. It's torture. I can feel the rocks converging, closing in on us, stealing our air. Little shivers crawl up my spine, up my legs and my arms.

Then I'm dragged under again. This time there's no sharp pain, no monster latched onto my thigh, just tiny invisible hands pulling me down down down *down.*

Just when I'm ready to pull water into my lungs, Finn's face appears before me in the murky water and he grabs me under the arms and hauls me to the surface again, but only long enough to get a breath before he urges me beneath the surface again.

Again and again, we dive and swim, surface and breathe. Dive and swim, surface and breathe.

When I think I can't swim anymore, I do anyway. When I think the cave can't get any darker, when I'm sure I can't possibly swim any farther, I see it: a faint, pulsing white ring of light.

My body screams to stop, to let go and sink to the bottom, to the promise of the warm arms that would cradle me there.

Finn grabs my hand and tugs hard. *Do not stop. Don't you dare give up.*

His will seeps into me, and I kick hard, heading into that tunnel of light. It's blinding and everywhere, all around us, but that hand in mine is dragging me up up *up,* and suddenly we break the surface and there's sun and fresh air and the sound of birds singing in the trees.

"Almost there, Princess." He doesn't let go of my hand as he drags me through the water and toward dry land. When the water goes shallow, we crawl on hands and knees onto the sandy shore.

I cough, my chest heaving, as if my lungs were trying to make up for all those minutes underwater, all those minutes without air. Then I collapse and roll to my back, letting the sunlight pour down on me, soaking it up.

Finn turns toward me. "Is your leg okay? Can you walk?"

I adjust my torn pants to examine my thigh and gape at the unmarked skin. "It's gone."

He studies my leg with wide eyes. "No pain?"

"I'm . . . fine."

"When I got stuck, you should've gone through the portal without me." His jaw is hard, eyes glittering with anger.

"Never."

So quickly I almost don't see him move, he's over me and his mouth is on mine. These aren't the gentle kisses from last night. There's no room for tenderness in a kiss that is already so full of too many other things. He pours everything into the cruel slant of his mouth over mine — anger and frustration and profound relief.

I take all of it. All of *him.* I slide my fingers into his hair and kiss him back with everything I have. Everything I am.

I should be dead right now. I should be dead three times over. That I'm not is a glorious gift. That Finn's here with me, that he can kiss me is a gift.

He tears his mouth from mine and pulls away, but I grab a fistful of his shirt and bring him back, guiding his mouth down to mine. I don't want to argue about my choices, not now. All I want to do is focus on the feel of his lips and the delicious weight of his body. I need to be as close as possible.

He groans into my mouth and surrenders, giving me what I want.

Finn trails his hand up my side, over my wet shirt, until his big hand is cupping my breast, his thumb grazing the taut peak through the wet fabric.

I gasp into his mouth, into the kiss, and arch under him.

"Brie," he murmurs against my lips.

"Please."

The strangled sound he makes in response breaks my heart and intensifies my frenzy to keep him close. Instinct has me drawing a knee up so he can settle fully between my legs. I slide my hands down his back and tug at his shirt, stripping it off. Mine follows in a flurry of hands and mouths.

I don't even know who or what I am right now. I'm desire. I am need. I kiss him with all the desperation I felt as we fought our way toward the portal. I'm kicking toward the surface all over again, but instead of needing air, I need *him*.

He drags his open mouth down the side of my neck, his hands skimming roughly up my sides and back down. He tugs my pants from my hips and down, tossing them to the side before settling over me again. He scrapes his teeth across the swell of my breast and he flicks his tongue against the aching peak.

I fumble with his clothes and mine, needing my hands on his skin, needing the reassurance of his heat.

"Brie." Suddenly he grabs my wrists and pins my hands above my head. But when he lifts his head to look into my eyes, the tenderness I saw last night is gone. He looks down at me through pools of raw *need*. Lust lined with agony.

"I need you." I shift my hips beneath him.

Holding my gaze, he thrusts into me, and my breath leaves me in a rush of pleasure and relief as we find a rhythm that gives and takes in equal measure.

His hands slide up from my wrists until his palms

flatten against mine, our fingers intertwining. Pleasure builds and stretches, spreading through and filling me until it invades every last inch and there's no room for more. His mouth claims mine, our release hits at the same moment. The intensity of it shocks me, and I bite his lip and taste blood.

When he lifts his head, he's panting. His eyes are unfocused, his lip swollen and cracked where I bit him. He releases my hands and strokes his thumb along my jaw, scanning my face over and over.

Too quickly, the heat in his eyes cools. I can see him shut the door on this connection between us, can sense him withdrawing even as he tenderly touches his forehead to mine. "I'm sorry. I shouldn't have let that happen."

Is he serious right now? Apologizing for something we both wanted? I would laugh if I weren't still a little dizzy from our frenzy.

He rolls off me and hands me my clothes — my shirt, pants, and boots I don't remember ever removing. I accept them and dress as he grabs his own shirt and pants.

I feel like a wall of ice has been dropped between us.

"Why is my leg healed?" I ask. I just want him to look at me again.

"They say when people die on visits to the Underworld, it's their mind that gets them. I didn't realize that meant the injuries weren't real." He focuses on the buttons on his tunic instead of glancing my way. Some of the hurt we sustained on that visit, it seems, was plenty real. "We should go."

My body, hot everywhere only seconds ago, is too cold. I feel confused and rejected. I force myself to follow. "Finn, wait." He stops, his back to me. "What's happening right now?"

Without turning, he shakes his head. "We need to get back to the palace."

I bite my lip. "I'm sorry that I ruined your chance to take the throne. I'm sorry that I ruined everything—that the only way you can save your people is to give the kingdom to me and the brother you hate. I'm sorry that—"

He spins on me, eyes flashing, jaw tight. "You think *that's* why I'm upset?" He tilts his face up to the sky and shakes his head. "We should go," he repeats.

I swallow, feeling hurt and rejected and like I have no right to either emotion. I shove it all down and look around. "Where are we?"

He cocks his head to the side. "You tell me, Princess."

"I don't know. How would I—" But then I feel it. It's in the way my power hums, in the way energy sparks in my blood. "We're still in the Unseelie Lands, but my magic isn't back. We're still on the Silent Ridge."

He nods.

"But where?"

He huffs out a laugh. "I have no idea. I don't exactly visit the Underworld very often."

He starts walking. Away from the coast, with the afternoon sun on our right. *South.* All we can do is go south.

We hike for hours in silence before my magic returns, and only then do we take a break.

There you are, Misha says in my mind as I take drink from a cool mountain stream. *We thought we lost you, Princess.*

We made it, but I'm not sure where we are. Can you ask Sebastian to find us and bring a goblin if they'll travel to wherever we are? We need to get home quickly.

Already on it.

When I stand, Finn's staring at me, his brow arched. "Making plans with Misha?"

I nod. "Sebastian will meet us with a goblin."

"Lovely. Just the male I want to see," Finn mutters, stepping around me.

"You're in a mood."

He grunts. "My apologies."

"What are you thinking about?"

He shrugs. "Duty, honor, sacrifice. The usual." I think it's supposed to be a joke, but his voice is far too hard for it to come out that way.

"Such a noble prince," I whisper. I mean it, though. The difference between Sebastian and Finn is that Sebastian wanted the crown, but Finn just wanted to help his people. There's no question in my mind which would make the better king, but I don't get to choose.

He huffs. "Not so much, and therein lies the problem."

"What does that mean?"

He stoops to his haunches by the stream. "It means I'm a selfish bastard, Abriella. But I think we've already covered that."

"You're angry with me." I frown. "You understand that this

isn't my choice. I wasn't *looking* for an excuse to stay bonded to Sebastian, so it's not fair that you're—"

Standing, he spins on me. "You still don't get it, do you? The only reason I'm angry with you is because you risked your own damn life to save mine. You should've gone through that original portal and left me behind, just like you should've used your powers when you were ambushed in the forest. You could've been captured by the queen or stuck in the Underworld because you're busy protecting *me*."

"How can you say that when you did the exact the same thing for me? When my leg was injured, you refused to leave me behind."

"*You* have something to offer this world. You have a purpose, and this court needs you. I'm just—"

"Just the one I love. *I* need you, Finn. And so does this court. That's true even if you never sit on the throne." I drop my arms to my sides. "I won't let you give up just because we don't like the solution she gave us."

"I more than don't *like* it, Abriella. I didn't *like* that he kissed you in the dining room. I don't *like* the way he touches you any chance he gets. But watching you spend your life at his side is different. It will destroy me, and that has nothing to do with the fucking throne."

"I wouldn't really be with him. We'd be bonded and ruling side by side, but it wouldn't change how I feel about *you*."

"And where do I fit into this picture? Am I your lover? Your *consort?* Does Sebastian learn to deal with having intimate knowledge of exactly how I make you feel when you come to my bed?

And what about when it's time to make an heir? Would you like me to be your stud for that — or will Sebastian get the honor?"

My stomach contracts, as if he just punched me there. "You're not being fair."

He curses. "I know I'm not. And I know none of this is your fault." He tips his face up to the towering trees overhead, and dappled shade darkens his beautiful face. "After Vexius passed, I never understood why Pretha didn't return to Castle Craige — why she'd choose to be miserable and alone rather than becoming a mistress to the woman she loves." His throat bobs as he swallows. "I get it now."

He's breaking my heart. "Tell me how I can make it better."

He closes his eyes. "Abriella, I am your tethered, and you are my queen. I will do whatever I need to do to protect you. To serve you. But I can't be your lover while you go on to make a life with him. I can't take these pieces of you when I know he will have your bond until the day you die."

I reach out and touch his arm. I hate this. When Lark told me I could be queen, I told her I didn't want to have so much when other people went without.

I guess this is perfect then. Because you'll lose everything.

After I woke up from my transformation and found that Sebastian had betrayed me, I thought I'd already lost everything. I was so wrong.

"I'm sorry," I whisper. "I don't know what else to say."

He lifts his head, and the unshed tears in his silver eyes cut through me. "There's nothing more to say."

When Sebastian appears with a goblin, Finn and I are staring at each other.

Sebastian sniffs, and his eyes narrow, jaw ticking. *He knows we were together.*

I can't begin to worry about that right now. For the first time since I met Finn, I'm grateful to step away from the shadow prince and give Sebastian my hand.

Moments later, we're back at the Unseelie palace. Pretha and Kane rush to our sides, and questions come at us from every direction.

"Are you okay?" "What did she say?" "Is there a solution?" "What happened to the portal?"

"You're well," I say, managing a smile as I look Kane over.

"Yes. Good as new." He looks me over and then his prince.

I desperately cling to this little piece of good news. I need it after all we learned today. But then I see Pretha's face, and any positivity leaks out of me. "Lark?" I ask softly.

"She hasn't woken in two days," she whispers, though she didn't need to say anything at all. I see the truth in her tired eyes, in her haggard face.

"I'm so sorry," I whisper.

"Tell me you learned something," she says, pulling back her shoulders and lifting her chin in a way I imagine she's done hundreds of times. "Tell me we have a plan."

"We do." I gently squeeze her hand.

"What happened?" Kane asks. "What did you learn? Can we fix the throne?"

Finn gives a curt nod and avoids my gaze. "There's a way. Abriella needs a hot bath and some food, and then she'll need to talk to Sebastian before we reconvene."

Kane huffs. "That's it? That's all I get?"

Pretha looks back and forth between us, her face tight with worry.

"I'll be in my room if you need me," Finn says, and then he disappears.

I don't let myself stare at the space he just vacated. I don't let myself think about the loneliness that fills my chest in his absence.

I did, in fact, need a hot bath and good meal, but as I walk the halls of the Midnight Palace after indulging in both, I know I've only been putting off the inevitable. When Finn disappeared earlier, part of me wanted to rip off the bandage and blurt what we learned to the group. But he's right. I need to talk to Sebastian first. What happens next depends entirely on Arya's son.

I find Sebastian in his chambers. He sits in front of the crackling fireplace, staring at the flames, a glass of amber liquid hanging loosely from his fingertips.

I watch him a long time, not knowing if he senses my presence and not caring. When I study his profile, I see the mage's apprentice I loved so dearly back in Elora, and I see the conniving prince who betrayed the girl he loved to secure his father's crown.

He was both, I realize. Never one or the other, but both at once. I was wrong to ever think he couldn't be.

"Hello, Abriella," he says without turning to me. "I trust you had a nice journey."

I hate that he senses the change between me and Finn. Even if Sebastian wasn't able to feel us the night we made love, he's aware of it now. Maybe that's why he hasn't looked me in the eye since retrieving us from the mountains, why he doesn't look at me now, even as I step farther into the room.

"It's good to be . . . home," I say awkwardly.

He closes his eyes and pinches the bridge of his nose. "Home. What a strange word. Is this place really anyone's home? Finn didn't grow up here, and gods know my father didn't exactly invite me to visit. And you . . ." Now his eyes flick to me. "Once you wanted *me* to make you a home. This was supposed to be it. But I guess you don't want that anymore."

I swallow hard. I can't tackle another conversation about *us* until he knows what we need to do. "We made it to see Mab."

He tilts his head to the side, stretching his neck. "Let me guess. She suggested that I die? That I sacrifice myself to give you the crown? I'm sure she'd enjoy seeing Arya's son forfeit his life so young so that her descendant can take the throne."

"That wasn't on the table."

When he lifts his gaze to mine, his eyes are wary. And part of me—the part that is still that lonely girl who was just trying to climb out of debt, who wanted nothing but to keep her sister safe—*that* part of me wants to say whatever I must to take the hurt away. But I can't. It wouldn't be fair to either of us.

"We were right," I say, going on when it seems clear he's not going to comment. "The Long Sleep is a symptom of the dying court, and as long as no one sits on the throne, there will be more and more affected. Sickness will spread, and Ar—your mother—will grow more powerful, until this court dies completely."

"So Mab told you exactly what you already know," he says dully.

"She also told us that the queen has grown so powerful that if we can't end her life, we *need* Seelie power on the Throne of Shadows. Only that will pull the imbalance back to center. Mab said that her blood and Gloriana's power can take the throne together to save the realm."

He swallows hard. "I never meant for any of this to happen." Standing, he drains his glass and crosses to the small bar in the corner to refill it.

"There is a solution. One that doesn't require us to sacrifice ourselves."

"Killing my mother?" he asks. "I'm guessing you want me to do that. Sorry to remind you, she's not responding to my messages or my letters. I have no better idea where she is than you do."

The boy I knew is gone. This one has had the hope beaten out of him, and I can't stand it. "We're operating under the assumption that your mother can't be killed—at least not so long as she holds such a disproportionate amount of power."

"So what do we do?" he asks, rubbing the back of his neck.

I take a breath. "You and I can take the throne together. The crown and its power ruling together. Because we're bonded. Because, in that way, we are one. All it would require is a trip to the River of Ice. If we go together, the waters will make our bond permanent and tie our lives to one another." I swallow. "And then we can rule side by side."

Leaving his glass where it is, he turns toward me. "And what do you think about that plan?"

The glimmer of hope in his eyes is a knife to my chest. "Sebastian, I can't be with you romantically. We're past that, and it wouldn't be fair to either of us to try."

He scoffs. "Right. Because you're worried about being fair to *me*."

"This is bigger than you and me." As I struggle to find the words, he keeps those beautiful eyes on my face, scanning again and again for answers. "We'd be doing this to save thousands of innocents from death and slavery under Arya's rule."

"You have to believe I never knew her plans. I never wanted the Unseelie Court to suffer like this."

"I know," I whisper.

He steps closer. "So you'll stay bound to me? You'll rule by my side?" He takes my hand. "You're willing to do this for people you once loathed?"

I draw in a breath for patience in light of this evidence that Sebastian still doesn't understand me. "Of course I will. These people . . ." Images flash through my mind—Finn and his crew and all they did during the years of the curse, the people at the Unseelie settlement in Misha's territory, the sleeping children, and the friendly faces in Staraelia. "I was bigoted and wrong. These people have suffered too much. A leader who will protect them is the least they deserve."

"I would've done anything to prove myself," he says. "Anything to get you back. And now that I finally get you, now that our future is sealed, you're in love with another male."

"I didn't mean to fall in love with him." I swallow hard. This hurts too much. My heart's being pummeled from every direction. "But this is bigger than you or me."

"What you feel for him — it's because you're tethered. Generations of Mab's line felt an undeniable draw to their tethered match. It's not your fault you have these feelings."

My connection with Finn may have started that way, but the love I feel for him is more than that. But does it matter anymore? Would the truth do anything but hurt Sebastian?

"If I agree, does that mean you're going to give me a chance?" he asks. "Give *us* a chance? Or do you intend to keep sleeping with my brother?"

I flinch at the accusation in his voice. He didn't say the words *cheater, adulteress,* but he might as well have.

"You think I didn't know what he planned to do once he got you to the Silent Ridge?" He huffs out a dry laugh and shakes his head. "You think I couldn't smell you all over each other when I arrived in the mountains to bring you home?"

I open my mouth to apologize and snap it shut again. I got one beautiful, perfect night. I'm giving up so much. I won't regret that night on top of everything else. "I don't know what will happen between me and Finn," I finally say. "But this plan isn't one where you and I marry and fall in love again."

He takes a step back, and his expression goes blank.

"I don't want him here," he says. "I can't rule by your side if he's around — if I have to feel you . . . *longing* for him."

"He is my tethered match and can provide me power when I need it. He can protect me in that way."

"You can funnel his power from afar. *I* will protect you from your side," he barks. "I am your bonded partner. If we are to spend our lives together, ruling side by side, you can give me this at least. I don't want him in the palace, and I don't want him in your life as anything more than your faithful servant."

"So you'll exile him? Like Mordeus did?"

"I'm not banishing him from these lands, I just . . ."

I hang my head and focus on my breathing as his pain tears through me. I let it. For once, I don't block him out. I need to feel this. I need to understand just what this solution will cost him. Otherwise, my own pain—my own anger and selfish desires—will break me.

Given Finn's initial reaction this afternoon, I don't think he'll remain in the palace, regardless of what Sebastian demands. He likely won't even want to stay in the capital. I can't blame him. I can't blame either of them. And I don't blame myself for the anger I feel toward everyone who brought us to this point.

If Oberon had never seduced Arya as a way to weaken the Seelie Court.

If the queen had never sent those sprites to burn down my childhood home.

If my aunt had never tricked Jas and me into that exploitative contract.

If Sebastian had never tricked me into bonding with him.

My resentment is a prowling shadow of destruction itching to be released on the world, and I shove it down. Down, down, down and away, where its darkness can't sway me.

When I lift my head, Sebastian's watching me, and the longing is so stark on his face that I don't need this bond to know how much losing me is killing him. "Okay," I say softly. "Finn won't stay in the palace. I won't have a relationship with him. He's not thrilled about this either, Bash. It's not like he was hoping to be my lover while you and I ruled together."

His face crumbles, and he presses his hand to my chest. "You never loved me like this. Not with this much of your heart. How did he do it? What made you choose him?"

My eyes burn, and I step back, letting his hand fall between us. "I'm not choosing anyone. I don't get that luxury. I'm choosing the future of the court."

Sebastian's jaw ticks. "Fine. Let's get this done."

I hold his gaze for a long time before I realize that I'm hoping for a fight, hoping he'll refuse altogether.

Hoping he gives me an excuse to get out of this.

I close my eyes and focus on the little tunnel of connection between myself and the Wild Fae king.

Where is everyone? I ask Misha in my mind.

We're in the briefing room, trying to determine if Juliana is a traitor. Find us when you're ready.

CHAPTER TWENTY-EIGHT

MAGIC HUMS IN THE AIR when I enter the briefing room. Juliana is in the corner, but judging from the way her feet are just off the ground and her arms are glued to her sides, she's not there of her own volition.

Finn spares me a brief glance as I enter alongside Sebastian. He quickly returns his focus to Juliana as we take our seats at the head of the table.

"It's clear we have a security problem," Finn says, addressing the room without taking his eyes off the female who was once supposed to rule by his side as his queen. "Someone is reporting to Queen Arya. She knew when the children were moved to the capital and when Abriella was there with them. Juliana knew that too, because I was in communication with her that day."

Juliana shakes her head. "You think I would murder innocent Unseelie children, Finn? That I would lay siege to my own capital?"

Finn ignores her and continues. "Then there was the attack on us from camp on our way to the portal. *Someone* had to clue the queen in as to where we'd be."

"Why would I want to help that bitch?" Juliana growls. Tears roll down her pretty porcelain cheeks. "I am on your side."

"*You* knew we were there."

She shakes her head. "Why would I want to hurt you when I'm in love with you?" she whispers. "I've always been in love with you, and even when I accepted that you wouldn't ever return those feelings, everything I did, I did to help you take your rightful place on that throne."

Finn's jaw goes hard, but his eyes are harder—silver chips of ice. "If you want to prove your innocence, drop your shields for Misha. Let him see into your mind."

"There's no way to know that she's dropped them completely," Misha warns. "With Juliana's training, she could easily show me bits and pieces. It's not proof of her innocence if I see no thoughts tying her to Queen Arya."

"Finn, I swear to you," Juliana pleads. "We didn't know who Abriella really was. Mab hid every sign that she had an heir. We had no way of knowing. And if Mother had known, she would've opened the portal for you."

Finn folds his arms and leans back in his chair. "Drop your shields. Let my friend into your mind."

More tears stream down her cheeks, and she whispers, "I'm sorry, but it's not what you think."

Misha draws in a long, shuddering breath. "She was responsible for the Barghest," he says coolly. "She and the High Priestess used their magic together to send the death dog after Abriella. They believed the crown would shift to Finn if Brie died."

Finn's expression is schooled, but I still see the hurt that flashes through his eyes. I hate this for him. I might not like Juliana, but she has been his friend his entire life. He cares for her, and losing her now, when he's losing so much, has to hurt.

"You," he growls in her face. "*You* sent that beast after her?"

Her eyes glisten with tears. "Mother felt it the moment Abriella arrived in our realm. The High Priestess was serving you, Finn, just as she swore to do. She served you from the beginning, and when her oath to Mab took her life, she *still* thought she was serving you."

Finn's eyes blaze with anger, his hands clenching and releasing over and over again, as if he's desperately trying to get a grip on his temper. "And the Sluagh? The fire?" he asks, his jaw hard.

"Mother was able to tap into the power of the mirror," Juliana whispers. "She lured Brie there and the Sluagh did the rest. We wanted to do it for you so you wouldn't have to. You've always put love above duty, and it's cost you. It's cost *all* of us."

"You don't get to speak to me about *loss,*" he snarls.

"I had nothing to do with the attack on the capital and nothing to do with the people who tried to stop you on your way to the portal. I would never have disabled the portal when I knew you were on the other side."

We all turn to Misha, waiting to see if this is true.

He stares at Juliana for a long time before shaking his head. "As far as I can tell, she speaks the truth, but I can't guarantee anything."

"See?" she whispers. "Just let me go. I love my court. I want to *help.*"

Finn stares at her. His inner turmoil simmers through the room.

I lift my chin and muster up my best queenlike authority. "No," I say, saving Finn from having to do it. "Keep her locked up until the throne has been recovered. We can't risk having the queen find us when we're so close."

Misha's wide russet eyes turn on me. "So it's settled then? You'll go to the River of Ice so you can take the throne together?"

"We will," Sebastian says. He turns his gaze from Misha to Finn. "But I have no intention of sharing my bonded partner with another male, so you'll need to leave the palace and find another place to live."

Finn's smile is so icy it chills my veins. "Consider it done."

Pretha's worried gaze moves about the room from Misha to Kane to Finn before finally settling on me. "Please hurry," she says.

Finn's expression softens as he turns to his sister-in-law, but Pretha shoves back her chair and runs from the room.

"We'll head out at first light," Sebastian says. "If you think you can handle it."

I nod. There's no reason to wait.

Kane clears his throat. "Finn, you should go as well, in case they encounter any trouble."

Finn flinches. "You can go in my stead, Kane. It will be easier for everyone that way." He stands, and his eyes flick to me for just a beat before settling back on the floor.

The fist around my aching heart blocks the air from my lungs, and I feel light-headed.

"Riaan will accompany us as well," Sebastian says. "He knows the Golden Military better than anyone else here and has helped the Unseelie forces defend the Goblin Mountains against them. He'll be able to help us avoid their units on the trek to the river."

"Good," Finn says. He takes a step toward the door before stopping suddenly and turning to me. Our eyes meet, and my aching heart stumbles as I remember what it was like to lie in his arms in the cave, how happy I felt, how hopeful as we discussed the future. "Be safe, My Queen," he says softly. "And be well. I'll be gone before you return."

He walks away before I can reply, taking that fist around my heart with him. I thought it would be a relief, but no matter how many greedy breaths I gulp down, I'm still hollow.

I can't sleep. Can't settle my mind enough to try.

I wander the dark hallways aimlessly and find myself at Finn's door. I can't leave without seeing him one more time, so I step inside, even knowing he might demand that I leave.

He's lying on the bed, staring up at the starry night sky.

I don't ask permission. I just crawl into the bed beside him, letting myself be close one last time.

"Are you okay?" he asks without looking at me. His voice is gravelly.

"Not really," I whisper. "But I wanted to say I'm sorry. For all of this. I hate that I'm hurting you." I feel his long exhale before he rolls away in one sudden movement, swinging his legs over the side of the bed to sit.

He cradles his head in his hands. "I'm not sorry," he says, peeking back at me. "Not for loving you, even when I know seeing you with him is going to tear me apart. You are the queen my people deserve, the blessing Mab promised us. I just want . . ."

"What?" I reach for him and skim my fingers along his spine. It feels so good to touch him, and he shivers beneath my caress. "Anything."

"I think you should consider having a priestess wipe me from your memories."

I yank my hand back as if he's burned me. "Why? Why would you ask me that?"

He presses his palms against his eyes. "Because I want you be happy. I don't want to be the reason that you don't have a good life. You loved him once."

"But I didn't. Not in any way that counts."

He braces his hands on his knees and swallows hard. "Part of you still cares for him. If you could love him, if he could make you happy, I don't want a single thought about me to keep you from it."

"Finn, I can't," I breathe, shaking my head. "Do you regret it that much?"

"No." He turns his body toward me and smiles, even as tears run down his cheeks. "Loving you, feeling the gift of your love—it's the best thing that ever happened to me. Regretting that just because you won't be mine anymore would be . . . That would be like regretting a glimpse of the stars before being plunged into eternal darkness."

My heart squeezes hard around the knife he's plunged into its center. "Then don't ask me to love someone else the way I love you. And don't you dare ask me to forget you." I scoot toward him on the bed and wipe away his tears. "I'd choose to love you even if I'd known what was coming. I'd choose to love you through the pain of knowing I can't have you. I will choose to love you still tomorrow. I could sooner choose to stop breathing than stop loving you."

He turns his head and presses his lips into my palm. "Thank you," he whispers. "I don't deserve that."

"You do. But that's where my choices end, isn't it?"

He shakes his head, and a tear rolls down his cheek. "That's why Mab chose you," he murmurs. "Because she knew you would carry pain of your own before letting innocents suffer. I would hate her for it if it wasn't exactly what my people needed."

I swing my legs around and off the side of the bed to sit next to him. He wraps one arm around me and we lean our heads together. "In a different world, in a different life, we'd be together," I whisper. "No kingdoms to rule, no people to save, just you and me and a simple life loving each other."

"But we're in this world. In this life." He presses a kiss to the top of my head, and it feels like goodbye. "So I'll have to save that for my dreams."

The numbness I feel as Sebastian and I hike through the mountains has nothing to do with the cool air or the setting sun. This is how it feels to sacrifice your heart for something bigger. It feels like abandoning it, locking it away in an attic, where you hope it might be safe but where it's disconnected from your life.

I keep catching Sebastian's inquisitive gaze on me as we walk, but I don't have the energy to ask him why. I can only focus on the task at hand—putting one foot in front of the other and knowing that each step is a step closer to a future without Finn. A future with my heart locked away and my duty taking charge.

A goblin brought us as far into the Goblin Mountains as he could and left us to travel the rest of the way on foot to the River of Ice. We should arrive before nightfall; then we'll swim in the water to solidify the bond and make camp. Tomorrow we'll return to the palace and take the throne together.

Kane leads the way. Apparently he grew up in this section of the mountains—west of Staraelia and farther south than the range we traveled to reach the portal. He hasn't said more than a few words to me. I know he's worried about Finn too. Likely worried and torn between his duty to the prince he swore to protect and the court he's trying to save. I'm glad he's not talking about it. I know exactly how he feels, and finding the words might break me.

Behind us, Riaan keeps watch, looking for signs of Queen Arya's Golden Military.

"I want you to promise you'll give us a chance," Sebastian says, breaking a long silence.

I flick my gaze to him. I can't do this right now.

Kane skids to a halt and spins around. "Are you kidding me right now, boy?"

Sebastian glares at him. "Stay out of this."

I shake my head. "Bash, please don't."

"I just need you to give me—" Sebastian stops, gripping his arm, where an arrow has lodged.

"In the trees!" Riaan shouts, stepping closer as Kane rushes toward our attackers.

Magic zips through the air as Riaan gathers us close to him, blocking us with his body.

"Poison," Sebastian croaks. "Abriella, get down."

But it's too late. An arrow strikes me before his words register.

CHAPTER TWENTY-NINE

WE'RE TAKEN SOMEWHERE DEEP IN the Goblin Mountains to a fortress built into a mountainside, but the moment we enter, we're thrown into a dark cell without instruction or explanation. I weave in and out of consciousness, my body weak from whatever poison they pumped into me.

This toxin is different from the one they've used on me before. This one blocks everything — not just my magic, but even my ability to reliably control my muscles. I can breathe, but not well, and every bit of air my lungs manage to accept leaves me desperate for the next. This is death without dying. This is a nightmare.

Sebastian is next to me in this cramped, dark cell. He must've been drugged with the same poison. Every time he tries to shout, his words sound as slurred as I'm sure mine would be if I tried to talk.

I don't waste my energy on screaming. Not when I can barely muster the strength to breathe.

I think of Lark sleeping. Of Pretha grieving.

I think of Finn's good heart, his endless sacrifices, and how much he wanted to save his kingdom.

Riaan stands in the corner of the cell, his head tipped back against the stone, but I see no sign of Kane. I hope he got away. I hope he and Finn are on their way to get us now.

But where are we?

What do they have planned for us?

And why did they take Riaan? What do they want with him?

Unconsciousness tugs at me, and I welcome it, slipping down, down and away from this useless body.

"Wake them up." A sharp feminine voice yanks away the comforting oblivion of sleep. Riaan's boot nudges my side, and when I peel my eyes open, he kicks Sebastian.

"Brie," Sebastian rasps.

I lift my head and see Queen Arya standing at the door to our tiny prison, her beautiful blond hair flowing down her shoulders in stark contrast to the bitter, twisted scowl on her face. She is too young to be so old, but the bitterness that has aged her soul shows through her eyes.

"Mother," Sebastian chokes out as he stumbles to stand. I wonder how he can manage it. I can't even get my feet under me.

Light blasts from Arya's hand, throwing Sebastian against the back wall of the cell. "It's my son," she says, "who tried to be king and failed. Only a fool would try to take the Throne of Shadows without the power it demands."

"I din know," he slurs.

"But what was lost, really?" she asks, cocking her head to the side. "Is there any real victory in being king of a dying court?

Ruler over Unseelie filth?"

Sebastian presses a hand to his chest. "*I* mmm Uh-seelie, Mother."

"Exactly." The queen's nostrils flare in disgust, and she lifts her chin. "And your inconstant loyalty has proved to me that you're no better than they are." Hurt flashes in Sebastian's eyes, but his mother doesn't see it or doesn't care. "You might be young, but you're not that stupid. You forfeited your claim to that throne when you let that *girl* keep your father's power."

"I din—"

"You gave her the Potion of Life. Magic is life, my son. You know this."

Half his face contorts in anger; the other half falls slack. "What woo you had me do? Le'er die?"

"Yes. That was the plan from the start. That girl literally stood between you and your father's throne." She shakes her head. "You think I didn't know that you tracked her down? Two years you tried to pretend you were still searching. You thought I didn't *know?*" She stares at her son, her eyes as hard as sapphires. "My magic may have been weak, but my people are loyal. I knew you'd found her, and when you lied to me, I chose to test you."

"This was . . . a *test?*"

"Yes. And you failed."

The hatred on her face is so cruel, I ache for Sebastian. He knew that his mother made bad choices, that she was wicked and deceitful, but he loved her nevertheless. And this is what he gets in return.

"But I should thank you," she says. "You made a difficult decision much easier to make and a difficult war easier to win."

"What happened to uniting the courts?" he asks. His words are clearer now, as if the poison is weakening in his blood. "What happened to the promised child? What happened to everything you told me about my birthright and my future as king of both courts?"

Her eyes blaze, and golden light blooms around her. "You thought I was going to hand my crown over to you? To lie down and die after all I've done, all I've sacrificed *for you?*" She shakes her head. "That stopped being the plan the moment you first lied to me. You're no better than your lying, scheming father."

"I am still your son."

"Do you think I can look at your face without hating you for the part of him you carry? Why do you think I spent so much time traveling without you? Why do you think I sent you away so often?"

I want to stand. I want to take his hand. But the drugs must be affecting me more than Sebastian, because I can't. I can't even whisper his name.

"What will you do with us?" Sebastian sags against the wall as if he's used up the last of his strength.

"Soon, we'll dose you again. This is more powerful than the anti-magic toxin we used in the past. As long as you have a steady dose slipping into your system, you will be trapped without your magic until I say otherwise." Her hands glow with a pulsing light, as if she's pulled in so much power it can't be contained. "Don't worry. I won't kill you. I need you both to live. Otherwise, I risk one of you dying before the other and the crown and its power being reunited. I'm still stronger than either of you, even if that happened, but I see no reason to draw out this ugly affair."

"You plan to leave us in this cell?" Sebastian asks.

I watch Riaan, who's strangely quiet in the corner.

"Of course not!" Her eyes widen, and she presses her delicate hand to her chest in mock horror. "We'll move you to these cozy little chambers."

Rusty wheels squeak and rumble as they roll across the stone floor and an upright iron sarcophagus comes into view. It reminds me of the kind used to hold the bodies of rulers in Elora.

"These have been equipped with a system that will keep you on a steady dose of this brilliant new formula." She smiles. "Once the Court of the Moon has fallen, I'll decide what to do with you. Or maybe I'll just leave you there. I do enjoy collecting relics."

"What's the point?" Sebastian asks. "Why destroy half the realm when you can't even rule over it?"

"Can't I?" Her smile is slow and wicked. "The gods gave us a promise when they split this continent down the middle. They promised that as it was done, so can it be undone. It was Mab's blood spilled in the mountains that created the River of Ice. The last drop that left her body was the catalyst that divided the land into two courts. Mab's blood divided the land, and it will be Mab's blood that brings them back together."

"No," Sebastian breathes, turning to me.

"No, no," Arya says. "Not *her* blood. You see, if I use Abriella's blood to reunite the courts, the moment she dies is the moment the power shifts — the power of the land, but also the power she carries. I need her *alive.* I need Oberon's throne dismantled — power, crown, and throne in pieces — so as not to risk control of the new kingdom shifting to the wrong person. But I also need to bleed out someone with Mab's blood. As it is done, so can it be undone."

No. Please no.

The queen smiles. She snaps her fingers, and I'm so horrified by what I see that I manage to cry out.

"Abriella," my sister cries, reaching toward the cell.

The queen yanks Jasalyn back by her hair. "No, no," she says. "You're not here for a reunion."

"If you want to destroy the shadow fae, why do you want their land?" Sebastian asks. "What's the point?"

"The fire gems," I wheeze.

The queen smiles, as if I'm a particularly adept pupil. "The girl understands." She shifts her gaze to Sebastian and her face goes slack. For a beat, I think real remorse might flash in her eyes. "Goodbye, son."

She disappears in a flash of light, my sister with her.

For a long, pain-filled moment, Sebastian stares at the spot where she just stood, and Riaan watches him from his corner of this too small cell.

"Riaan?" Sebastian's voice is deadly quiet as he turns to his friend. "You told her about Abriella. She knew all this time."

Riaan disappears and then reappears outside the cell. I had no idea he had that power, but now I realize that's how he got us away from Kane. How they got us here. "I had no choice. She's my queen, and soon she will be queen of *all.* At this very moment we're sitting in a fortress built above the River of Ice. We're positioned exactly between the courts. That way, when the Unseelie Court dies completely, when the last bit of its power has trickled to Queen Arya's side, she will be prepared with Mab's blood, prepared to reunite both halves to create a whole."

"There's nothing whole about a kingdom when half of it was destroyed for greed and power," Sebastian says.

Riaan's back in the cell in a flash, right in Sebastian's face. He plunges a needle into his arm, and Sebastian sags. "That's better," Riaan murmurs. "She wanted you more lucid for your little talk, but you can rest now."

"You were supposed to be my friend," Sebastian says, each word weaker than the last.

Riaan's mouth is a flat, angry line. "And *you* were supposed to be *king. You* were supposed to put that first—above all else. Instead, you saved her." He points a shaking finger at me. "You should've known this would happen. You should never have risked it. You were a fool. And now you're a fool with a useless crown." He sneers at his friend one last time before he disappears.

Sebastian collapses against the wall and closes his eyes.

I reach for him, hoping to offer him the little comfort I can, but I barely manage to move a single finger.

I'm in a tomb.

For the first time in my life, the darkness is not my friend.

I can't move.

I can barely breathe.

My dreams are my only refuge.

Time has no meaning. I'm a child in the womb. I'm an old woman on her deathbed. I'm a shell holding nothing but decay.

Have days passed? Years?

I try to measure time through the mechanical whir of each new injection, each new dose of toxin. Until I don't wake. Until I can't. I'm trapped in unconsciousness. Trapped in a body locked in an iron tomb.

I can't even call this limbo sleep. There is nothingness. There is fear. But that hidden part of me, my shadow self, she stretches like a cat in the corner of my mind, slinks along the perimeter of this cage, cries to be set free.

Mab used her shadow self without her power, but mine refuses.

I reach for her and miss. I beg her to save me, and she laughs in my face.

CHAPTER THIRTY

Use it, Abriella. Wake her up. Set her free.

The voice is one I recognize. One I traveled to the Underworld to hear.

She has power, the voice tells me. *Don't be afraid.*

"Can't," I rasp into the darkness, but even as I say it, I'm reaching for my power, *begging* the shadows to play.

Accept the darkness, and she will wake, and she will serve you.

I've spent most of my life needing to be the very best version of myself. First for my sister and then for this realm I didn't even understand. Nine years ago, after my father died and I was spared, after my mother left Jas and me to fend for ourselves in the mortal realm, I didn't have time for grief or resentment, so I forced it down. Every selfish want and need was shoved to the side as I tried to protect my sister.

I was never good like Jas. I'm bitter and blackened, like the charred remnants of my childhood home. But Jas's goodness—her sweetness and her joy—it was something worth fighting for. And I fought for *years,* giving my sleep, my health, even my life to protect that goodness.

Loving Abriella. Devoted Abriella. Caring, dutiful Abriella.

Mab wasn't saying that I'm goodness personified. She was saying my power comes from being more than that. From my anger and my hurt. From my bitterness and charred edges.

My mother was trying to protect us by trading her life for seven years of our protection, but she *still walked away.*

Sebastian was trying to do what he thought was right for the Unseelie Court when he tricked me into the bond, but he *still stole my human life.*

And Finn . . . Finn, who deserves happiness and love unfettered by this mess we've found ourselves in. Even Finn planned to abandon me to protect his own heart, and I love him so much that I didn't argue that I need him close, that I've lost too much already to give up the happiness I feel when he's near me.

I am not just the girl who understands. I am the one who wants *better.*

The anger and pain unfurls inside me until it hurts worse than the toxin, until it's bigger than my body and darker than the shadows. My shadow self brushes her fingertips over the charred edges of my heart and smiles. Too many years of silence. Too many years of pushing aside my own pain to take care of someone else.

This part of me is just as valid as the rest.

"Go," I whisper, but my shadow self is immobile.

The legends of Mab accessing her shadow self from inside the iron room are false. At least, the way they're understood is incorrect. Just like any other magic, the shadow needs power to escape this tomb. Needs power to move and do and be my servant.

Thanks to this toxin, my magic is gone. Muted almost completely. Almost.

Magic is life. And the queen can't risk killing me.

There's one thread left—enough to keep me breathing, enough to keep my heart beating. I use that thread to tap into my connection to Finn. I have to trust that he can handle this, that I can draw from him without taking too much.

My shadow self expands as his power fills her.

I become her.

Slowly, I step forward, moving through the iron of the coffin as if it were a summer breeze. I stretch and smile. Rooted in my shadow self, the darkened, bitter parts of me too long ignored.

I find the tubes pumping toxins into both sarcophagi and yank them free, cutting off the endless supply of poison to my body, to Sebastian's. Then I head off to find the queen.

The halls of this fortress are quiet at night, but not empty. Arya has guards standing every few feet along the corridor leading to her bedroom. Light shines so brightly from every direction that her sentries have to wear face shields to protect their eyes.

Chuckling silently, my shadow self slithers along the bottom edge of the wall, undetectable to even the guards' keen fae eyes. I creep toward her door, past the males who stand on either side and past the guards who stand just inside.

Anger pumps through me, feeding this unfamiliar form. I itch to take their knives from their scabbards and plunge them into their chests.

I whisper soothing promises to that angry, vengeful part of myself. I promise that if she'll be patient, she can have the queen's heart—and the queen is who she wants.

Deeper and deeper into her chambers, where I pass under another door and find myself in the room where Arya sleeps on a bed of light. She's lying atop piles of fluffy white blankets, her beautiful blond hair fanned out around her. And there, right by her side, an iron and adamant dagger gripped in her palm.

I smile at the sight of it and slowly peel her fingers from the scabbard one by one. *One. Two. Three.*

Her eyes fly open, and she yanks the blade back, driving it toward my heart. I laugh, disintegrate, and reappear on the other side of the bed, where I take advantage of her shock to snatch the blade from her hand. I plunge it into her chest, right into her blackened, bitter heart.

Her scream is so loud, my ears hurt, and I hear it all the way from in my tomb. My shadow self skitters, almost retreating, but I take a calming breath and tighten my leash on her. *We're not done here.*

Alerted by her terrible scream, guards rush into the room. I stop one with a single hand to his neck, and his eyes go wide as he takes me in. I love to imagine what he sees—a female formed of shadow in this room full of light. I smile and saunter slowly toward another, swinging my hips to the silent beat of my vengeance.

He draws a sword from his waist, but I snatch it from him before he can strike. I drag it across his throat, all while smiling at the guard behind him.

I use my blade quickly. My shadow self wants to play in their blood, torment them for all the pain they've brought to the Unseelie Court. I rein her in and slaughter them one by one.

Maybe it's because I'm already so weak, but for once I can almost pinpoint the tether between myself and Finn. I feel his power flowing through me — not in sips or gulps, but in this steady stream. I focus on that flow as my shadow self works her way back to our tombs.

She releases Sebastian first, using her knife to break the lock holding him inside, before turning to mine.

Like a whip cracking, my shadow's gone, and I'm back in my own body. Light floods my prison as my tomb opens.

I stumble forward and fall to the ground. Next to me, Sebastian is weaving on his feet, squinting into the light that's painfully bright after so many days of being locked inside that darkness.

My body is heavy with the queen's poison, so I close my eyes and focus on that tether for two more breaths, letting Finn's power rush through me.

Please be okay, Finn. Please don't let me take too much.

When I open my eyes, Sebastian's next to me. His eyes are wide as he turns to me. "You killed her. The queen . . ." He blinks, and a thousand emotions cross his face in that moment, but relief and devastation are the last two standing. "She's dead?"

"How do you — the power passed to you?" I ask.

"Yes. I feel it." He grimaces and swallows. "Wearing both crowns is . . . they weren't meant to be together."

"Are you okay?"

"We need to go," he says.

I shake my head. "Jasalyn."

He closes his eyes. "Get her," Sebastian says. "I need to find Riaan."

I obey, leaving him because I have no choice. I will not leave this place without Jasalyn. I run and stumble toward the stairs, weak and groggy, but determined, crawling on hands and knees up to the battlement.

I see my sister in the darkness, tied to a pole at the end of a plank, her blood slowly dripping from the gashes on her legs and arms into the icy river far, far below.

"Jas," I gasp.

She doesn't turn to me. She's too tired, too weak. But I see the shallow rise and fall of her chest and know she's still breathing.

I scramble toward her, going for the rope that's tying her to the post. I fumble with the knots with blurry vision and clumsy fingers.

"Abriella," she rasps. "You need to go. You need to run."

I shake my head. "Not without you."

When I get the last rope off, she collapses into my arms and I sway on the plank.

I'm still too weak from the toxins. Even with Finn's power flowing into me, my muscles are useless from the time inside the tomb. Months? Weeks?

Or has it only been days?

I can barely stand on my own, and the weight of her slight form threatens to topple me. I waver under her weight toward the river below.

Jas straightens before I lose my balance, and together we scramble off the plank.

I reach out a hand to help her take the final step onto the safety of the roof, but I'm stopped by a sharp, burning pain through the back of my leg. I look down in time to see Riaan's blade sticking out through my thigh before it's yanked out of me, leaving a white lance of pain in its wake.

I fall to the ground.

"Where do you think you're going?" Riaan asks.

Jas cries out, and he grabs her by the waist, pulling her off the wobbling beam and close to him. Before I can feel any relief that she's safe from a deadly fall, he wraps his big hand around her neck.

"Let her go," I plead, words hard to find around the pain and hard to speak through this weakness.

"I have worked too hard to let you destroy everything we've fought for."

"For what?" I ask. "For your queen? For your intolerance for the Unseelie? For your self-righteous belief that you are *better?*" The words spill from my lips and take the last of my energy. "The queen is dead. You've lost."

"Have Sebastian surrender the Seelie crown to me, and I'll spare your sister. He'd do it. For *you,* he'd do it."

"Abriella," my sister gasps, and Riaan's hand tightens around her throat.

Hold on, Finn, I think, taking another draw from his power. I stagger to my feet, clutching my hand to the gushing wound in my leg.

"Get me that golden crown, Abriella," Riaan says softly. "We can both get what we want. I'd be on the golden throne and you can have the Throne of Shadows. I promise to heal your sister and let you live after Sebastian passes on those crowns."

Let me live, but not free me. He'd lock me back in that tomb. He'd find a way to keep me from escaping this time. He'd take the golden crown and let me take the Unseelie crown, but he'd keep me from taking the throne. He'd hold me prisoner so this power didn't pass to someone else, so the Unseelie Court would continue to weaken. Until it died.

"Please. I only care about Jas." It was true once, I realize as the lie slips from my lips. Once I cared only about her. I didn't believe I had the power to save more than one innocent. But by the time I plunged that knife into Mordeus's heart, the human girl I'd once been was already gone. Long before I bonded with Sebastian, I'd become something more. Long before I drank the Potion of Life.

Fat tears stream down Jas's cheeks as she shakes her head. "Don't do it." Her voice is weak. So damn weak it chills me to my bones. "Don't trust him."

Riaan's hand tightens around her neck. "Enough out of you."

Still gripping my sister, he lunges for me, and his hand wraps around the fire gem at my neck, but he doesn't get a chance to pull it off, because Sebastian plunges his blade into Riaan's back.

Gasping, Riaan releases my necklace, then my sister. His eyes are wide, his lips moving as he looks down at the blade protruding from his chest.

Sebastian steps close behind him, catching him under his arms before he falls. "You were like a brother to me," he says into his ear. "My only friend through so many lonely and difficult years."

Jas stumbles to my side, pressing her hand to the wound on my thigh, her fingers turning red with my blood. "Brie," she whispers, and we sink to the ground together, neither of us strong enough to stay on our own feet.

"Arya's . . . kingdom . . ." Riaan sputters, blood trailing down his chin.

Sebastian sneers. "Her kingdom — the whole damn realm — is better off without you both." With that, he brings his blade to Riaan's neck and slices though, ending his pain and his life.

The last thing I see is Riaan's head falling from his body. The last thing I feel is Sebastian scooping me and Jas into his arms.

CHAPTER THIRTY-ONE

It's dark when I wake, and I'm immediately aware of Finn next to me. His even breathing as he sleeps, warmth radiating from him.

I roll over to see the stars twinkling in the sky above me. We're on the rooftop terrace of the cottage in Staraelia — the mountain home Finn gave me back before he knew I was Mab's descendant. Someone brought a bed up here so I could heal while sleeping under the stars. Heal while sleeping next to my beloved, my tethered match, the one I draw strength from.

I need to get up and find Jas, or someone who can tell me where she is. I need to make plans with Sebastian. But I don't want to leave this bed. I want to hold on to this moment for as long as I can. I never thought I'd be here again — under the stars, in Finn's arms. Even in my strongest, most optimistic moments inside that tomb, the best I'd hoped for was to see his face again.

Finn stirs beside me, and when I turn my head, he's awake and watching me. "How are you?" he asks.

"I'm okay," I say. "Thanks to you."

"And thanks to Sebastian. He brought you to me."

"But you . . ." I swallow hard, but it does little to keep the emotions bubbling inside me at bay. "I had to pull power from you."

He finds my hand between our bodies and brings it to his chest, pressing it there against his heart. "We looked everywhere. Ten days you were missing, and we couldn't find any sign of you or Sebastian. Arya was using her power to shield her mountain stronghold. It could've been right before our eyes and we would've missed it. I've never been so scared."

"I'm sorry," I whisper. I can't imagine how I would've felt if our roles had been reversed. I'm not sure I want to.

"When I suddenly felt you drawing from me, I could've wept."

"Did I hurt you?"

He shakes his head. "No. You drew a lot of power from me, but less than I had to give. I only cared that it meant you were alive. Shortly after that, the shield was down — it fell once you'd killed her — and my people were able to find you and Sebastian and bring you home."

Home. Yes, here with Finn certainly feels like home to me, but I wonder if anywhere feels like home to Sebastian after being sacrificed by his own mother and forced to kill his best friend.

"You wielded your shadow self." Finn strokes my cheek. "I didn't know you could control her."

"I couldn't," I admit. "Not so long as she scared me."

"You're not afraid of her anymore?"

I shake my head. "After days in that tomb, it was easier to face the darkest corners of myself. I've been hurt and betrayed. I've been angry for so many years. And I've hated those parts of me — the bitter, hardened, brittle pieces. But that is who I am. I'll never be sunshine and smiles like Jas. Once I accepted that, accepted that there is this darker, crueler part of me, only then could I control her."

"It's so good to see these eyes looking at me again." He drags in a ragged breath. "I shouldn't have let you go without me. I should've been there to protect you."

"Arya's dead," I say, though I don't quite believe it myself. "She's gone. We'll be okay."

He nods, his eyes never moving from my face.

"I know we need to get these courts sorted out — need to figure out what the future looks like."

He huffs out a breath. "All that matters is that you're safe. The rest can wait." He hooks one arm over me and the other under me before burying his face in my chest. His whole body trembles. "I cannot lose you."

I brush my fingers through his hair. "I'm right here. Don't give up on me."

"Never." Finn presses a firm kiss to my sternum, right over my heart. He swallows. "We owe a great deal to Sebastian. When you killed the queen, the power of the golden court passed to him. When I realized what I was feeling in his presence, I half expected him to head to the Court of the Sun and claim the throne. I underestimated him."

"What will he do?"

"Rule both courts just like he always planned," Finn says softly. "With you by his side, of course."

"How will that even work?"

Finn shakes his head. "We don't really know, but Juliana's

gathered the priestesses, and they're working on it. We all agree that the first step is getting you both safely to the River of Ice so you can solidify your bond and officially take the Throne of Shadows together. This time, we'll send an entire battalion with you."

"But the queen's dead. Do you think someone else is after us?"

"I don't know." He tucks a curl behind my ear and studies me. "I can't risk losing you again. Just let me keep you safe until you're on that throne. And all the days after. Let me do that."

"I still wish there were another way," I say, and he squeezes his eyes shut.

"I was wrong before," he says. "If I've learned anything in over a century of life, it's that you have to make room for hope. Always. I don't have any answers right now, but I promise you I'll never stop trying to find a way we can be together."

I close my eyes. *I'll never stop trying.* I had to be trapped in that dark tomb to realize how much I needed to hear those words. "You still want that?"

"With everything I am. Even if it's just our last breaths."

"Finn," I whisper. "What if . . ."

"If it never happens?" He kisses my jaw, my cheek, the corner of my mouth. "Abriella, if it never happens, I still get to live in a world that has you in it. And I will relish every moment of that. Even if you're never mine, I will always be entirely yours. Love like this is worth hoping for."

"Good," I say, tears streaming down my face, "because I don't want to do this without you."

"Of course." His hand grips my hip tightly. "It is my greatest honor."

"I still don't quite believe I'm the key to all this, that I'm somehow worthy to be queen."

"You are. There's not a doubt in my mind. You've already saved so many. The children are beginning to wake. The balance of power is slowly being restored."

"Lark?" I whisper.

He smiles. "She's been asking about you. You've been here, in and out of consciousness for a week. Healing's been slow, but these last couple of days have been less about your body and more about restoring your magic."

"What about Jas?"

He strokes his thumb across my cheek and releases a long breath. "She's recovering, but slowly. All we can do is let her sleep. Her mortal body can only take so much magical healing at once."

"Where is she?"

"At the Midnight Palace. I can take you to her if you'd like."

"Please?"

An aching tug in my chest has me lifting my gaze to the doorway. I find Sebastian there, his eyes melancholy as he takes in the scene before him.

"I just wanted to check on you," he says roughly. "We can talk later."

Finn shakes his head. "You two need to make plans. I'll meet up with Kane and finalize the details of the trip into the mountains. Will you be ready by morning?"

Sebastian and I nod together, but I can feel his reluctance. Who can blame him? He'll be permanently bonded to a female who loves someone else. Finn and I aren't the only ones making a sacrifice here.

"I'll return with a goblin after a bit so we can visit your sister," Finn says. He kisses the top of my head, then climbs out of our rooftop bed.

I watch Finn go before turning my attention to Sebastian. His white-blond hair is tied back at the base of his neck and he's dressed in a fine black tunic, as if he's been attending meetings all day. "Thank you," I say. "Thank you for bringing me to Finn so I could heal."

His eyes go wide. "I'm the one who needs to be thanking you. You saved me from that tomb. I thought I'd die there."

"Don't diminish what you did. We both know this isn't how you wanted things to turn out."

Silence stretches between us for a long time, but it's heavy with everything we're feeling. I don't block our bond. Instead, I open to him and welcome it when he opens to me. His grief, heartache, and loneliness are all tinged with something brighter. Relief and . . .

"You're grateful," I whisper.

"I promised I'd protect you," he says, tucking his hands into his pockets. "I meant it."

"Your mother's power transferred to you. You hold the power of the Seelie throne. But you're not there. Why?"

Sebastian hangs his head. "I never just wanted to be king, Brie. I wanted to be a *great* king. One who could end wars and save innocents. One who made a difference. *You* made me want that—way back when we were in the human realm. You'd talk about how broken the systems there were, how everything was stacked against the weak and the poor. If I went to the golden court now and took my mother's throne, I would be king, but the shadow court would be right back where it was when we started all this—weakening without a leader on the throne. I want better than that for these people. Whether you believe it or not, I truly do."

"I do believe it, Bash," I whisper. "None of that surprises me."

I feel it through our bond the moment before he throws up a shield. My words, my belief in him—it hurts him worse than my anger ever did.

"We'll go to the River of Ice and try again," I whisper. "And then we'll figure out the rest from there."

"Are you sure that's what you want?"

I tear my gaze away. "I told you once that personal sacrifice is what makes great kings. They're willing to give up what they want for themselves in exchange for what's best for their people. The same is true for queens."

"So if you could undo all this—if you could trade your power for a mortal life back in Elora with your sister, if you could undo what I did when I got you to bond with me and cornered you into taking the potion?"

"I don't see the point in dwelling on the past. What's done is done."

His gaze shifts to the sky, as if he's searching the stars for the right path. "I need to know the answer."

I shake my head, marveling at how different my answer would've been only weeks ago. "I want my life to matter, and I can make a difference here. Serving these people isn't just a duty for me. It's the greatest honor of my life."

Sebastian meets my eyes again and nods. "I understand."

Jas sleeps in lush guest room at the Midnight Palace, her breathing even but shallow, her face pale. She looks less like she's recovering and more like she's inching toward death.

Finn's on one side of me and Sebastian's on the other as I look down at her and swallow my tears.

"We have to save her," I whisper. I meet Finn's eyes, and he nods.

On the other side of me, Sebastian clears his throat. There are tears in his eyes as he takes my sister's hand and strokes it with his thumb. "We will," Sebastian murmurs, and somehow I believe him.

Finn wasn't exaggerating when he said he'd send an entire battalion through the mountains with us. Gone are the attempts to be stealthy about our presence. Instead, we're announcing to the world that we're here. *Come after us if you dare.*

No one does, and we make it to the river with relative ease. Kane suggested a place where the river runs beneath the earth through a massive cave, and the others agreed that this would be the least vulnerable spot for us.

As we head to the cave mouth, Sebastian stops and looks at the others. "Could we do this alone, please?"

Finn's face falls, and he looks back and forth between us before nodding. "Kane and Jalek will go in first to make sure it's safe. Once it's secure, we'll send you in. Just shout if you need us."

"Thank you," Sebastian says softly.

My heart aches. I can't look at Finn for more than a few seconds. This is the right thing to do. An entire court rests on our shoulders, and considering all that's been lost thus far, what is this sacrifice of ours? It's not much. And . . . I have hope. We might not have a way around this today, but there's a chance the magic will make room for it—room for us—in the future. Magic is about change, Finn said. About possibility.

When Kane and Jalek return and give the all clear, Sebastian takes my hand and leads me into the cave.

"Are you having second thoughts?" I ask.

"No," he says. "I know my duty." Finally, he smiles at me. "I just wanted to be alone with you for a minute."

"Okay."

He turns to me and holds my hand in both of his. The position reminds me of the night we said the vows to create this bond. How appropriate, since today we make it permanent. "You are better," he says, "and more deserving of this crown than I will ever be."

"Don't." I flinch. "Don't say that."

"This is all my fault. I'm the one who got us into this position. I should've found a way. I should've—" He swallows. "I owe you so much. You . . . you taught me about love and friendship. The real kind. I never had that before you. Thank you for—" He looks up at the ceiling of the cave, studying the many stalactites that hang there. Or maybe he doesn't see them. Maybe instead he's seeing our history play out in his mind. The good moments and the bad, the joyful and the painful. "You're going to make an amazing queen. I am honored to play a part in that. And I'm sorry." He swallows hard and squeezes his eyes shut. "I'm sorry for the all the secrets I kept and all the pain I caused you. You deserved better."

My heart clenches. Because I feel him. I feel sincerity and how much he wants me to understand what he's saying, how desperately he wants me to believe his love. "Sebastian, it's okay. I want to do this." I take a step toward the river, and he comes with me.

"They'll see her when they look at me," he says. "The Unseelie will see Queen Arya when they look at me. They deserve better too."

"We'll prove that you're worthy," I promise. My stomach twists with the grief I feel through our bond.

He holds my hand tight, so tight in his grip it would hurt if I weren't so distracted by the waves of emotion flowing from him. He reaches out and brushes his fingertips across my neck before pulling the green fire gem from beneath my dress. "I almost expected you to destroy this."

I'm struggling to follow his volatile mood, but I shake my head in response. I'm surprised I didn't destroy it in those early days, when my anger felt like it might eat me alive. "Somehow I knew I needed it. It amplifies my power, right?"

He huffs out a breath. "It would if it were a fire gem, but it's not. You're just that strong." His smile is tender. "Mab's bloodline was always stronger than Gloriana's. It made my mother crazy. That's why she was so obsessed with collecting fire gems and stealing Unseelie power."

"If it's not a fire gem, then what is it?"

"It's something else." In one sudden movement he yanks it off my neck, snapping the chain. He studies the gem in his palm. "My mother dedicated her life to finding fire gems, but in her quest to collect as many as she could, her servants found another element beneath these mountains. An element even more scarce than the fire gems . . . When Mab died in the Goblin Mountains, the gods saw the injustice and mourned the loss of a loving mother in a cruel world. They brought her back to life and gave her the choice between magic and immortality, or a mortal life with a court of her own."

"And she tricked them into giving her both," I say. "Finn and Kane told me the story. What does any of this have to do with the fire gem?"

Sebastian lifts his gaze from the substance in his hand. "This isn't a fire gem. It's a bloodstone."

I shake my head. "Mab destroyed the bloodstones."

"Mab was tricky, but the gods were trickier. They hid the remaining bloodstones deep beneath the mountains where they'd be shielded from her powers. My mother never believed that the gods would allow Mab to destroy them all, and for years she's had her Unseelie captives search for the sacred stones. I claimed and hid this one before she knew they'd been successful."

"What are you trying to say?"

He closes both hands around the gem and repeats an incantation under his breath three times before opening them again. Now, instead of a gem, he holds a pool of liquid in his palm. It rolls around like mercury and is the gray-blue of a stormy sea.

"I'm trying to tell you that all this time you were wearing the very thing that could've given you back your mortality and allowed you to pass on the crown. I'm saying that even now, you could take this sacred water of the bloodstone into your body and become human again. But if you do, there's no turning back. You could never become fae again."

All I wanted a few short weeks ago was to be human again. To be free of this power and have the choice to live in Elora with Jas. But now . . . "Why didn't you tell me about this before?" I ask. "That first night I came to you and asked you to dismantle your mother's camps?"

"Because I'm a selfish bastard, and I wanted you more than I wanted your power." He swallows hard. "Do you wish I had?"

I might have taken advantage of it if I'd known. "I'm glad you didn't tell me. I have work to do here. This court needs me, and I . . ." I need more than a mortal existence to love Finn, and I need this power to truly help this court.

"I know," Sebastian whispers, taking my hand. Before I realize what he means to do, he uses my hand to shove his cupped palm to his lips. All at once, there's a flash of light. Nothing but power surging in front of and through me. And then I feel it—a rush of power, of magic, of *life* in my veins. My back arches as the power of the court thrums in my blood.

Sebastian collapses, and I fall to my knees. "Bash? What did you do?"

Finn rushes into the cavern and drops to kneel beside me. "What's wrong, what's happened?"

Sebastian's still for far too long as we stare down at him in horror and my tears spill onto him. "Come on, Bash. It's not supposed to end like this."

Fear ripples through me, but I close my eyes and exhale, releasing it, making room for *hope.* In this world of magic, I won't believe this will be the end for him.

Finn gasps and stares at me in awe. "The crown," he whispers.

I turn to the water and see my reflection, see the Crown of Starlight glittering atop my head. And my scar—the symbol of the crown, my sun and moon—has returned to my wrist.

What did you do, Sebastian?

"Sacrifice," Sebastian whispers, cringing as he rolls to his side. "You said sacrifice is what makes a good king. And I always wanted to be a great king."

Relief is so sudden that I feel weightless. Laughter slips from my lips. "You're okay."

"He's . . . mortal," Finn says, shaking his head at his brother. "How . . ."

"The bloodstones," I whisper. "Arya searched for them, but when her prisoners found one, Sebastian stole it before she could get her hands on it."

"We believed they were gone." Finn draws in a long, ragged breath. "Where's Arya's crown?"

"I still have it," Sebastian says. He coughs and groans. "That hurt like a bitch."

Did it? I didn't feel . . .

I tug down my dress to expose the tattoo that symbolizes my bond with Sebastian, but it's gone. "The bond."

"It survived the end of your mortal life through the magic you gained becoming immortal, but it couldn't survive the end of my immortal life," Sebastian says, pushing back to sit on his heels.

Mortal. "How will you rule a faerie court?" I ask him, shaking my head. "You'll be so vulnerable."

"We tell no one," Finn says. "Juliana can glamour him to appear fae until he can find a priestess he trusts. The rest we can figure out as we go." Finn wraps one arm around me, pulling me tight into his side, his gaze still on Sebastian. "Thank you, brother. I will not forget this."

A laughing sob tears through me—relief and grief overwhelming me in equal measure. Mab never said that Sebastian had to die. She said he had to give up his life, and he did—he surrendered his immortal life. For the good of the realm. But I know in my heart he did it for me.

"I forgive you for your deceptions, Ronan Sebastian. You have indeed become the kind of leader this realm needs."

CHAPTER THIRTY-TWO

I DON'T REMEMBER THE JOURNEY back to the Midnight Palace. Everyone stayed close, keeping me safe, keeping this crown safe. But it all passed in a blur until suddenly I found myself in the throne room surrounded by my dearest friends, the Throne of Shadows waiting before me. Standing in the center of the throne room is my sister.

It's true that even when I was human, I dreamed of having the power to save the weak and unfortunate from the powerful and exploitive. But that dream was always a distant second to keeping my sister safe.

The moment I set eyes on Jas, I'm reminded why it was so easy to risk everything for her. She represents everything good in the world. Everything worth fighting for.

"Abriella," she says, rushing into my arms.

"You're okay." I wrap her up in my grasp, holding her as if she might disappear.

She hugs me tightly and I hug her back.

"I have so much I need to tell you," I say softly. "So much to explain."

"It's okay," she says, but she smiles as she tugs on one of my short curls. "You know how much I love a good story."

"Soon," I promise.

"The Throne of Shadows waits for you, Abriella," Pretha says. "It's where you belong."

I draw in a ragged breath and step toward the throne, putting one foot in front of the other. This is how I've always done hard things — taking the next step, doing the next right thing.

Lark rushes out in front of me, her dark, silky hair bouncing as she spins to face me. "Wait!"

The whole room seems to hold its breath as we wait to hear what the little seer has to say.

"What is it?" I ask.

"I *told* you," she says. "Didn't I tell you?"

I laugh, and tears spill down my cheeks as I nod. "You did. You told me." I take another step and find myself at the dais. The spot where I killed Mordeus.

I hesitate, and then Finn's there, offering me his hand to help me onto the dais. Always helping me, always lending me his strength.

"Come on, Princess," he whispers in my ear. "Make me call you something else."

I turn and sit on the Throne of Shadows for the second time. The moment my back hits the stone, my power purrs in approval. This is a throne of the night, of the misfits and the lost. This is the throne for all those who had to endure the darkness to find the stars. This is my throne, and it's been waiting for me.

Finn stands by my side — the king I choose, the partner I was given and whom I fought for. The match my heart needs. We've been given a second chance, thanks to Sebastian's sacrifice. And as I take Finn's hand, more power flows through me than I can even describe. Power of the night, power of the shadows, power of every shining star. It's too intense to label, but it feels a lot like *hope.*

Celebration erupts in the palace, and in the capital, and then in the court. Everyone feels it — the energy in the air, the electric click of power restored to a court that hasn't had someone on the throne in more than two decades.

The golden court probably has no idea that their queen is dead and surely has no idea that their future king is a mortal with an alliance with the Unseelie Court. We can't make centuries of hatred and prejudice go away overnight. I probably can't even make them go away in my very long lifetime. But that will be tomorrow's problem. Tonight, Sebastian gathers his allies in the Court of the Sun, and in the Court of the Moon we celebrate saving this kingdom and a future of peace.

Finn presses a kiss to my shoulder. "How's my queen?" he asks.

I reach back and find his hand, squeezing it in mine. "Still reeling," I say, not bothering to sugarcoat the truth. Not for him. "But I'm okay. We're *going to be* okay."

He wraps his arms around me, pulling my back flush against the front of him. "I'm so proud of you. And I'm so proud to serve you."

I spin in his arms and look up into his eyes. "Serve me?"

"Of course. I'm your tethered servant. That is literally what I was born to do."

"Because the power only moves one way, right?" I ask, brow arched. "But if we were bonded . . ."

He strokes my cheek. "I'm not asking anything of you. You were just freed from a bond you didn't want. I don't need anything more than I have right this minute."

"Finn, you have given me strength from the moment I met you. As my friend, as my mentor, and as my tethered match. Someday soon, I'll want this to go both ways. I want you to pull strength from me too. Just like I pull strength from you."

He leans his forehead against mine. "If that is what my queen wants," he says, a little breathless, "then it would be my absolute honor, but there's no need to rush anything."

We hold each other like that and eventually begin dancing. One song blends into another, and my grief and gratitude for what Sebastian did swell in my chest.

I look up at Finn through my lashes, and he's grinning. "What are you thinking about?" I ask.

"I'm thinking about how you're the most amazing creature I have ever met." He buries his face in my neck, and I can feel his smile. "And I'm thinking how good it feels to be right."

"Right about what?" I ask.

"About you being the queen this realm needs."

EPILOGUE

"ABRIELLA, YOU LOOK AMAZING," JAS says, scanning me with bright eyes.

But to me, *she's* the one who looks amazing. Her last six months in Faerie have been good for her. Her face has filled out and her eyes shine bright with good health, and though she still jumps at shadows and doesn't trust the fae easily, she's improving.

In the months that have passed, I've learned a lot about being queen of a strife-filled land. I've learned about how people — even the kindest, wisest among them — buck against change, and I've learned that those same people will happily take credit for the same innovations they fought you on.

But most of all, I've learned that I'm my happiest, best self when my sister's around.

"You're sure it's not too much?" I ask, looking down at the black leather dress Jas made for me. It's a bit . . . *wicked.* But I like it. It's long-sleeved but off-the-shoulder, and the skirt is slit high on each of my hips so that I can still run if need be — something I unapologetically demand in anything I wear. Not that there's a lot of running these days. Mostly, there's a lot of sitting. Meeting after meeting. Listening to heartbreaking stories from distant parts of our lands and sometimes listening to ridiculous whining from the overprivileged. This job has it all, but most of it is done from the safety of my throne room, with Finn standing by my side.

"So sure," Jas says.

Pretha nods in agreement. "Finn will *definitely* appreciate the way it shows you off."

I grin and look over my shoulder to see the back of the dress in the mirror. I haven't let all the meetings and throne sitting get in the way of my training. I'm faster and stronger than ever and enjoying every minute of it. I don't mind these results either, though I know Finn can't keep his hands off me either way.

"Are you nervous?" Pretha asks.

I shake my head. "Not even a little."

Tonight, Finn and I will complete the bonding ceremony. We'll get married too someday, but for now the bond will allow us to share power both ways, which, as I've told him repeatedly, is important to me. But the truth is, I simply crave this additional connection to the male I love.

"The last time I did this, I was looking for the wrong things," I tell Jas. "The Banshee had scared the pants off me, and I wanted the bond with Sebastian so he could protect me. I thought it would be fine, because I loved him, but it was a mistake, and I think we both knew that."

"It's not too late to change your mind," Misha says, pushing into my chambers as if he owns the place.

He'd gone home to the Wild Fae Lands after we celebrated my taking the throne, but he visits often. Sometimes I think he's afraid that Pretha will take his spot as my best friend if he doesn't see me frequently.

"Why are you here?" I ask. "We're not doing a public ceremony."

He clutches my hand to his chest. "I'm here just in case you decided you'd rather have me."

I snort. "Maybe next time, Misha."

"Can't blame me for trying." Dropping my hand, he kisses each cheek. "You look stunning. He's a very lucky male."

"*I'm* the lucky one," I say, grinning.

Kane is next to stick his head in the door. "Is the party in here?" he asks before pushing in. He spots me and stops in his tracks. "Gods above and below, look at that dress."

I blush. "Thank you."

Kane looks at Jas and gives her an uncharacteristically charming smile. "You're still gonna make something for me next, right?"

Pretha grunts. "You realize she's not your seamstress, right?"

"I don't mind," Jas says, and my heart swells a little. It feels so good to see my sister finding her place in this world. "It gives me something to do."

Finally, when Jas and Pretha are done fussing over me, Finn appears, and his eyes are all over me — hungry, lustful, loving, and grateful all at once.

"How did you know black leather was my favorite color?" he asks, sliding his arms around me and pulling me close.

"Well, I . . ." I realize that everyone's staring, so I wrap us in our own little cocoon of shadow where they can't see or hear what we say. "If I recall," I say once we have privacy, "you said anything I wear is your favorite."

His mouth quirks into a lopsided grin. "Right. I forgot." He presses a kiss to my lips. "Are you sure you want to have a front seat to my nonstop lustful thoughts about my tethered match?"

"What part of *I don't want to wait another day* makes you doubt me?"

His face softens. "Give a male a break, Abriella. This is hard for me."

"How so?" I ask.

"I'm afraid I'm going to wake up."

I melt. "Don't make me look soft; it'll ruin my badass queen look."

"Never." He winks at me. "You love me?" he asks.

"I love you," I say without hesitation or reservation. "You love me?"

"I love you," he says. "But I would love you even if you never wanted to bond with me."

"Same," I whisper. "Always."

He squeezes me tight. Our little cocoon falls away, and we appear on the rooftop terrace of our mountain cottage. The stars shine so brightly overhead that they bring tears to my eyes.

"Pick a star," he whispers in my ear. "Make a wish."

I thread my fingers through his and make the same wishes I've made every night since taking the throne. The only wishes a queen should hold so dear.

I wish for peace. I wish for every faerie in my court — in the entire realm — to know and have a love like this.

ACKNOWLEDGMENTS

First, I need to thank everyone who read *These Hollow Vows,* the first book in this duology, and contacted me with giddy excitement for more of this world. I needed your enthusiasm more than you know, and I am so grateful for every kind word, review, rant, and rave. Thanks to my longtime romance readers who don't necessarily read YA or fantasy but read *These Hollow Vows* and cheered me on through this new career plot twist. I'm so grateful for your support!

I have so much gratitude for everyone who got me through 2020. Drafting this book (and two others) while also trying to get through a pandemic and all that entailed was challenging in so many ways. Thank you to my kids, who would've rather had their mom's full attention while they navigated eLearning but thrived anyway, and to my husband, who listened to more than his fair share of meltdowns when I truly didn't think I could play the role of super mom for one more day. Thanks also to my sisters and friends for your understanding, support, and encouragement when I felt like I was failing at everything. I can give sugar coatings and talk silver linings with the best of them, but 2020 was rough, and the people I love most got me through it.

Thank you to my friends, who encouraged me through the hardest phases of this project and many others. Mira Lyn Kelly, my bestie, my brainstorming buddy, I still owe you that Toyota Corolla. (Okay, we both know you deserve something way nicer.) Thank you to the writers in my Write All the Words Slack group—for listening when I was struggling and for keeping me company while I work. Thanks also to those who try to get my thoughts away from work—whether it be with talk of CrossFit, our kids, or cheesecake for breakfast. You always make me smile. To Emily Miller, my own personal elf-advisor and fellow lover of all things fae, thank you for being a sounding board again. I hope someday you write a book and show the world the magic in that beautiful mind of yours.

A special thanks to Lisa Kuhne and Tina Allen, who are both my friends as well as my assistants. Tina, I'm so glad we've gotten closer over the years. You're truly a gem. Lisa, thank you for always reaching out when I need you.

Thanks to my family. I was blessed with a big one and I love them more than they know. Special thanks to my brother Aaron, to whom this book is dedicated—your map truly helped me see this sequel in a new light. My mom always listens and knows what to say to make me feel better, and my brothers and sisters are so supportive. I wish a family this wonderful for everyone.

To my agent, Dan Mandel, who was enthusiastic about this book from the beginning and who helped me through some rough patches over this past year. I love having you on my team!

I am grateful for the team at Clarion Books, who's helped me make this book what it is today. Special thanks to Lily Kessinger and Gabriella Abbate for your editorial notes and help through the several drafts. Thanks also to Emilia Rhodes, Helen Seachrist, Emily Andrukaitis, Catherine San Juan, Tara Shanahan, Taylor McBroom, Kimberly Sorrell, Colby Lawrence, Tommy Harron, Jill Lazer, Melissa Cicchitelli, Emma Grant, Erika West, Maxine Bartow, and Samantha Hoback. I appreciate all you do!